BLACKBIRD SECRET

A Novel

G.A. Chamberlin

Titles by

G.A. Chamberlin

The Handmaiden Legacy
Cultural Attache
Rare Earth Element
Outbound
Somma
Unintended Consequence
The Particle
The Kneeling Woman
BLACKBIRD SECRET

~

Kathleen The War Years

BLACKBIRD
SECRET
Printed in the United States
ISBN 978-0-578-79696-3

Crown Eagle Publishing

Distribution by Ingram

Cover Image: BLACKBIRD
National Air and Space Museum
Steven F. Udvar-Hazy Center

This is a work of fiction. Names, characters places, and incidents either are the product of the author's imagination or are used fictitiously, and any resemblance to actual persons, living or dead, business establishments events or locales is entirely coincidental. The publisher does not have any control over and does not assume any responsibility for author or third party websites or their content. Nor does the author assume any responsibility for activities that might have been published as source material for fiction. Cultural courtesy is the professional standard.

BLACKBIRD SECRET

A Novel

by

G.A.Chamberlin

"…When a empire art portrait donated for charity raises $250 Million at auction, the darker side of its socialist revolution emerges to reveal an ongoing battle for dominance.

"He may be entertaining a bidding war for space defense systems" said Admiral Arguetta

If that was the prize, Amanda knew, their emerging propulsion for space aviation technology could be used for experimenting with a new human order.

Unfortunately, the enemy had already found a possible *Achilles' heel*… "

…"the latest international suspense thriller in the Amanda Wells series written by G. A. Chamberlin, opens with a bang. Literally."

International Thriller Writer, Feature2018, NY

The Kneeling Woman

by

G.A.Chamberlin

"Amanda Wells, in examining the provenance of a statue brought from Spain and donated to a city Museum as a fundraiser event, finds her husband's Firm suddenly under investigation as she discovers its story during WWII. ...Where it went, what it meant…And the traitor who underwrote an investment bank with his stolen assets…and a *murder –*

October 31, 2018 By ITW

"And suddenly, we're off and running, as THE KNEELING WOMAN seesaws back and forth between present time and the early days of World War II…"

Charles Salzberg, *International Thriller Writer*

November 25, 2018 by ITW

G.A. Chamberlin. ROUNDTABLE participant at International Thriller Writers Association

"Her latest, *The Kneeling Woman*, is her ninth in the series."

BLACKBIRD SECRET

A Novel

G.A. Chamberlin

Chapter 1

In a wide-brimmed Hermes hat, white wool suit strewn loosely by a silk floral scarf, and standing in Italian stilettos, Amanda Wells stood almost as tall as the men around her.

A woman approached them.

"Elyse!" said Amanda

"Oh! Mrs. MacDonnell..." gasped the woman.

"You have worked very hard," said Amanda "and we appreciate all that you've done here!"

The woman beamed, her brown eyes matching a brown dress with a single string of pearls. The tag she wore held "Director of Museum Collections, London UK"

"Ah... *Bien sur!*" agreed one man.

"Thank you Amanda. Your support was wonderful..." she said.

They spoke of new arrangements in the Auction Gallery, but it was Jacques de Toulaine who set them all laughing about earning a living in Antiquities.

The Exhibit room of the Auction House filled with people.

Patrons wandered about viewing displays before finding their seat in the bidding auditorium.

Most had been prequalified to bid, the rest were still with pen in hand completing Entry Registration, each holding a copy of the catalogue. Chatter was laced with nervous excitement. The moment for bidding was about to begin.

Anticipated for almost a year, this Auction had taken the directors of the Auction House six months to coordinate. Much secrecy shrouded the event, even a promise by the Auctioneer in his blog suggested 'something big' on the day of the Auction.

The Lots advertised in the catalog were of some significance, bringing in collectors and Museums from across the world. Marketing was less about money since this was posted as a fundraising event. But there was something erratic about the temperature of investment markets, much of it turning to commodities like rare items of interest in portfolio securities. And there had been complications. Appraisals, which came armed with provenance or certified documentation, were given little credibility. Underwriting was still shy. The issue was with the sponsor of the event.

Energy investors loved Art. But in recent events, a downturn on valuation followed an incident in the United States where a coal mine was damaged and mining operations ceased. Worse, global volatility in the stock markets had been triggered, it was rumored, by the Insurance sector needing to pay deeply for future fossil fuel claim losses...

Trevor's bank had come to the rescue. Several items needed insuring. When asked, it was to his wife he would turn for advice on Appraisals, and then he simply left with a big smile. That was his gentle way, Amanda knew, of showing his confidence in her abilities.

A crystal bell rang for Order.
"Thank God for Trevor..." whispered Jacques in Amanda's ear as the room came to order. She gave him an assuring look.

The painting he referred to had caused him some distress. Not only had it been recovered after 70 years, but in the discovery process its authentication had been hard to establish and the insurance even harder to get.

As some people had pointed out, Jacques stood to make money from it. And Amanda had agreed to make a bid for it at the Auction herself. That was assurance.

"How much will you bid?..." asked Sean, Auditor from the Appraisal Company.

Amanda opened her mouth to speak.

"Ah, now that's a question you *never* ask!" interrupted Peter Barring, the Auctioneer. "It ruins the suspense" he grinned.

"Especially if she's a beautiful woman..." added Jacques, his words protective of his client and slewed with French lilt.

He turned aside for a word to Amanda. "If the painting goes for one penny more than two million.... than you must stop..." he admonished. "You've already done enough!"

"I'll be fine" she told him. "It's worth four times as much. You'll see. But at least it gets the ball rolling."

"Yes. Your interest has generated some excitement already. But please be careful. These are shark-infested waters!"

Jacques smiled at the gathering crowd. Then for theater, he raised her hand to his lips in grand gesture of courtesy to give his compliments. "Trevor is such a lucky man!" he said.

Trevor was already seated in the audience. He had Sandra at his side, a third seat waiting for his wife Amanda Wells.

Trevor looked back and saw them. He waved.

The Auditorium settled down.

Amanda took her place and tucked her hand into Trevor's fingers. She smiled at her daughter.

This was Sandra's last night of staying with them. She was in London because Jack her husband was attending a conference in the city as the representative for the Energy company he worked for in Switzerland. Tonight, Sandra would be flying back to Europe with Jack.

Sandra and Amanda had enjoyed three wonderful days together. They had toured the city, strolled the parks and sampled Artisan specialty bakers; chocolate makers and everything in between. They bought boots, coats and fur hats for Sandra's next trek up north, again with Jack going on an exploratory expedition.

Sandra had not long been married. She and Jack had met, remarkably, while on a polar expedition!

Jack was Canadian-born and trained as a scientist, but he was also credentialed as an international lawyer. His job was to broker new trade deals for energy concessions around the Arctic Circle.

He'd been a Park Ranger when they met, and always an avid naturalist. But since embracing new technologies servicing energy industries, he focused on clean extraction practices. A natural evolution, he had told Sandra – the Adventurist who delighted in new frontiers, as she put it. Better for the West to find legitimate sources of fuel for integrated energy than to hijack the environment for competing economies...

Trevor understood. He and Jack would spend hours discussing the matter long after the ladies retired, and they had become good friends.

But as Amanda had to remind Trevor, Sandra and Jack were in love. "Arranged by the stars," as Jack put it, having proposed to Sandra while viewing a spectacular display of the Northern *Aurorae Borealis*.

Today was Amanda's event, and they were excited and nervous. The gavel was tapping for a quiet room, and everyone turned to the business at hand.

Amanda was worried. The Auction about to begin suddenly filled her with apprehension.

It was one thing to help the Museum by agreeing to serve on its board of Directors, but it was quite another to contribute to their Frundraiser with a painting from their private family collection. Hanging on a wall in Scotland, the thing had become part of the brickwork, unnoticed and uneventful. But now it was set on a pedestal behind a curtain. It would be revealed under gallery custom-lighting focusing on every brushstroke.... airing on the open market for valuation of its true worth and value.

"What if nobody likes it?" she whispered to Trevor.

Her thoughts ran to the ground with questions. What if the expenses couldn't even be covered?

Who would be asked to cover the insurance bill? Certainly not the Museum! Of course she knew the answer. They would. Always the generous husband able to support her community commitments, Trevor never complained. How generous he'd been, she thought with a measure of guilt...

"Ladies and Gentlemen..."

But yes, she had expressed her reservations. And no, Trevor had insisted that she not withdraw her offer. Besides, there was Jacques to consider. Trevor was also doing this for Jacques, one of their oldest and dearest family friends...

Trevor had uploaded its provenance onto her laptop. She'd even had a small photograph printed up for the Museum shop and for publicity, charming enough. The Museum loved it. She was left to make all the arrangements for the Auction.

So. This was it. Trevor squeezed her hand. Amanda looked up nervously.

Today her painting would come up for public Auction. She wondered if she had made a big mistake to have Trevor update its insurance value. Would it even recover the two million valuation, she wondered. It's only an Insurance policy, he had assured her.

Sandra nodded at her mother. The gavel came down for the bidding to commence.

Two telephone banks along the perimeter of the Auction house were arrayed behind glass. Attended by certified agents, each phone booth was protected to ensure conversational privacy and anonymity of the bidder, and each telephone bidder had been registered to bid. He too had been pre-qualified to place a bid on any item at auction, if by simultaneous telecast.

 Those seated in the auditorium could bid to compete instantly. In-house participants were also informed of those bids coming in from remote devices. Thus, if the Auctioneer was precise, and his signaling was clear, this process ensured a forum of global bidders to participate in the Auction simultaneously.

* * *

The curtain opened on the painting and the room fell silent. There it posed, set upon an easel and about to make its debut.

The audience gasped.

Finally, the voice of the Auctioneer broke the spell. "Ladies and Gentleman, I give you the *Officer with Children*"

Immediately recognizable was an officer of the Queen's Royal Hussars in full armor regimental dress of the White Horse of Hannover. But he was at ease, behind him on a chair was thrown his cap bearing the Crest of the Angel Harp, and the Garter Belt of the Queen's Crown.

His head was bowed, and the subject of his attention came into focus.

A child, with two others watching, was inspecting a parting gift. Together, with his hand gently on the child's shoulder, they were observing a jeweled egg, a gilded sphere encasing a team of racing horse and carriage. The racing team, held fast by time and space, was as captive as he, the officer to his military command. And the child understood.

The room filled with murmuring as the house lights came up. Bidders turned to the catalogue, flipping pages impatiently.

Where was this Lot listed...?

"...Believed to be painted in 1902 by Valentin Serov" the Auctioneer said "this was part of a private collection donated for its proceeds to go to a Museum Charity."

"Previously, the painting was on loan to the Royal Scots Dragoon Guards Regiment Trust. Believed to be a portrait of His Imperial Majesty Tsar Nicholai II Alexandrvitch, Tsar of All the Russias, this painting was made during one of their family reunions" he said, pausing "of which there were many, especially as the socialist revolution erupted..."

He waited, but the room was captivated.

"Queen Victoria ...was grandmother to his bride, the young Empress Alexandra, and the Queen proffered upon the Tsar the title of Honorary Admiral of the Fleet. Just two years before their overthrow in 1916, Queen Victoria made him a British Field Marshal..."

"So, this painting, while its authenticity is verified, remains without prior appraisal value and is by default untested: Neither is there any official portrait confirmation, nor is it known who stood in. The regimental dress does exhibit the Queen's proffered insignia. The likeness of the subject suggests a relative." The auctioneer paused.

"So, Ladies and Gentlemen, the surprise I promised you is this: We shall let *you* be the judge of this painting's value! Yes, you represent the open market, and it is here to test its full worth and price. So. May the bidding begin!"

A left- bank telephone rang and broke the silence. A second call came in, and the Auctioneer took the opening bid from callers through their respective agents.

Sandra, seated to the left of her father, leaned forward across him to audibly whisper a few words to her mother. "Wow... Mom! That figure in the portrait is so handsome!" She giggled, adding "for a moment, I thought it might be Dad in that portrait!"

Trevor frowned sternly at his daughter. "Who's the artist?"

"That's not entirely clear yet..." began Amanda "We're still searching..."

"Ladies and Gentlemen, we have an offer of $100,000... Thank you! A most generous opening offer for a painting undiscovered until recently..."

Amanda raised her card.

"$150,000?" asked the Auctioneer. "our opening offer is increased to $150,000!"

Amanda squeezed Trevor's hand and could feel her heart pounding as the pressure mounted. But Trevor was adamant. He encouraged her to bid again for the prize on the stand.

She was about to open her mouth.

"One million!" proclaimed a jubilant Auctioneer. "Do we have any further interest Ladies and Gentlemen?"

She never got the chance.

The room remained silent, and the charged atmosphere seemed to have run its course.

Then the phone rang again.

"Two Million!" announced the Auctioneer, and Amanda's eyes opened wide with surprise.

Trevor nudged his wife, but Amanda's gaze remained fixed on the painting.

What had she unleashed?

Enough money had been expensed for her efforts to advance the portrait as a charity donation. She had promised herself ...and Jacques too for that matter, not to raise funds for charity over two million! This, Trevor had agreed to. But now as she looked around the room, the flush on the faces of bidders was visible, their eyes wide and focused as the bidding pushed higher.

Stay calm, she decided. Life is full of surprises.

"Two million and five hundred thousand?" asked the Auctioneer.

The room coasted for a moment, until a bank of phones set off another round of fierce bidding.

"Four. Four million...Wait... Five!" squealed the auctioneer "Five Million in the back row. Anyone else?"

A card went up. Amanda's head spun around. She could not discern who bid that amount. But it didn't matter. A telephone agent nodded.

"Six? Six million now Ladies and Gentlemen..."

"A raise to ten million on the telephone, I am told. Ten million..."

Amanda looked at Trevor, incredulous.

"Fifteen. Fifteen million..."

Trevor was generous, and in his business, he was accustomed to large sums of money. He sat motionless, his nerves in check and under control. But he was troubled, she could tell.

The auctioneer paused to consult with an attendant, and Amanda looked about.

The room was brimming with excitement, and patrons chatted.

Minutes passed, the room still buzzing. Then suddenly one offer broke out, and the auctioneer looked up. He resumed his position at the podium, took a sip from his glass of water, glanced at his House manager, then returned to the business at hand.

He cleared his throat.

"Twenty Million Ladies and Gentlemen, what a sum, eh?" he said.

Amanda took a big breath. Surely this would bring the matter to a close.

There was murmuring, the room afire with impulse, and she called softly for hush...

The Auctioneer returned. He spoke.

Amanda's throat felt constricted. "My God..." she said, and looked at Trevor.

"Thirty five million..." announced the auctioneer.

Trevor turned to look at her, his eyes full of warning, but his demeanor calm.

She controlled her nerves.

"Fifty. Fifty Million and counting!" wailed the Auctioneer. Then he paused, adding "I understand we have three bids waiting. How extraordinary! I can't tell you how pleased we are at our Auction House to have such interest from the market. Evidently, we have a prize!" He glanced nervously at his House manager and sipped from his glass. "However, I propose we take a recess for half and hour. Then we resume our bidding!"

Down came the gavel. "Ladies and Gentlemen, again, recess for 30 minutes, please!"

"I'm astonished..." muttered Amanda. "I can't believe this... this...frenzy!"

From the rear of the Auditorium, where security personnel stood, a subdued rustle of spectators in the lobby called them away. Evidently, growing interest came from the Media, now entering the building. News of the event has spread. They were barred from entering the Bidding Gallery.

It seemed endless, this relentless grasping for acquisition of the painting.

Clearly, the auctioneer was now entertaining not individuals but institutions such as museums, insurance companies and equity fund groups from around the world.

"Sixty. Sixty-five million from the telephones, Ladies and Gentlemen, we have a sixty million bid for the portrait of the *Officer and Children.*"

Amanda noticed that the room was falling silent, their capacity to bid was now topped by outside bidding.

"Clearly..." said the Auctioneer "we're in unchartered territory with all this interest. May we consider this a settlement final offer then?"

A woman shot up her hand. She surprised everyone. A woman in her fifties, she was slim, but darkly dressed and unexceptional.

Amanda wondered about her ability to proffer such a bid. Big spenders rarely liked to go unnoticed in the world.

"A dark horse..." muttered Trevor, sharing her sentiments.

The woman triggered another bout of bidding.

"Seventy. Seventy Million, Ma'am? Is that correct?"

The room was heating up, and several cell phones were buzzing.

"Ladies and Gentlemen" said the Auctioneer, his voice betraying some surprise. "We have a bid for seventy million for the portrait."

He took a moment and for a moment, the phones remained quiet. But for just a moment.

The soft humming came in. A phone.

The auctioneer stared in utter surprise. He waited, then announced. "Eighty. Eighty Million is being bid from the West Bank of phones..."

"Trevor..." whispered Amanda. "Is this possible?"

"It is remarkable. But not without precedent." He looked over his shoulder. "Derek is looking at me and he has not stopping the proceedings...So, its legitimate. Over there...See?"

"Ninety. Ninety million... "

Amanda knew who Derek was. Derek Parker was senior vice president for legal affairs at Trevor's bank. Even if the painting had been sold for a modest sum, Trevor knew better than not to have him present for any kind of financial exchange that held bank interests.

Amanda noticed that even he was standing along the rear perimeter of the room, clearly having gone outside to take calls from his office colleagues and advisors. He eyes were now fixed on Trevor.

For his part, Trevor was holding his cell phone in his hand, checking for text messages.

"Oh my goodness!" said the auctioneer. "Ladies and Gentlemen. I am pleased to announce that we have reached the threshold of one hundred million, from err...overseas..."

From outside the Bidding Gallery the Media were ranting for admission into the room.

Two police officers went outside to intercede, clearly calling in reinforcements.

News had hit the public arena outside.

The room was hot. Amanda looked about her and saw pale faces everywhere caught up in a frenzied bidding war. They seemed surreal.

This was not thoughtful valuation. This was something terrifying, like a dopamine attraction. *Who thought like this?*

"One hundred twenty million!"

Trevor's cell phone vibrated. He looked down, and Amanda saw the message from Derek.

Time to Leave!

"Stay calm..." said Trevor, squeezing her hand.

The crowd grew restive, as if the walls were closing in.

In the front row, a woman called for assistance, her face flushed and agitated and her breathing rasping. They gathered around.

Behind her, others cast about nervously, bewildered. A few reached for their cell phones.

"Now Ladies and Gentlemen, we are having fun aren't we now?" grinned the Auctioneer gamely. "Let's all take a big breath, and relax. We shall continue shortly. Hush now. Order! Order in the House now, please!"

The Auctioneer nodded his approval to the House manager, quietly escorting two additional police officers into the Gallery. They took their position at the rear of the Auditorium.

Outside, a siren could be heard and fresh security entered the building.

At the entrance, a crowd had gathered. This added to the hailing in the lobby by Media crews.

"One hundred fifty million!" declared the Auctioneer suavely.

"Oh my God" Amanda muttered, looking back to see how Jacques was withstanding the onslaught. He saw her and nodded his head, his eyes wide. He caught the signal from Trevor who stood up to leave. Amanda and Sandra followed.

The room started to spin, and as the sounds faded into the background the audience in the gallery was getting flustered.

One woman stood. Behind her two others began to growl about a rigged Auction.

"Shall we recess, Ladies and Gentlemen?"

"Hell No!" yelled one voice from the rear.

Laughter.

They recessed. Two hours later, they proceeded.

"Right then. We continue..." said the Auctioneer, two police officers at his side.

A hand rose with a card number from a bidder on the phone.

By now, Television crews pulled up outside the building. City papers and broadcasting services were assembled.

"One hundred...and...and ...um... *seventy five* million ...May we close on that number?"

Amanda and Trevor heard the podcast from their car, having emerged from the underground parking garage and turned the corner.

A lull ensued, then another sound.

"Understood!" said the Auctioneer calmly. "Ladies and Gentlemen. We have a final bid for...for...two hundred million dollars for the *Officer and Children*"

No sound followed. The feed had been cut off.

Trevor turned the radio dial in the car and heard the news.

"Two hundred and twenty five million... "The bidding closed at two hundred and twenty five million."

They drove in silence, if not in shock. The Auction was over.

The portrait had fetched two hundred and fifty million dollars.

Derek called.

Trevor and his family could not be open to public spectacle. Of that Derek would make certain.

Inside the vehicle the engine ran silent and the world slipped quietly passed them.

"What just happened?" asked Amanda, her eyes wide. "I don't understand..."

Trevor's cell phone buzzed. It wasDerek.

"Yes" he said. "We're both safe. We're driving home!"

"Unbelievable...I know" nodded Trevor "We're totally shocked by those prices!"

Amanda could hear Derek's voice, if not entirely his words. "Oh really? You think so? But surely..." Trevor said, turning to Amanda and adding "Let me talk it over with Amanda...

"Yes. It's absolutely astonishing. Let me assure you that neither Amanda nor I had no idea that the painting would raise so much money. We thought a couple million, if we were lucky! And of course, the proceeds were for charity, as you know... "

Amanda put her hand to her mouth, her face full of apprehension.

"Look. I'll call you back" said Trevor, ending.

"What have I done, Trevor?" Amanda asked. "I didn't mean to cause you any difficulty like this! It's..It's..I don't understand what happened. I'm so sorry!" she gasped.

"You did nothing wrong Amanda.We thought only to raise money for a charity. It was not for financial gain. And you can't blame yourself!"

"Oh...but..."

Derek called. He spoke rapidly into Trevor's ear.

"Well, if you think it advisable, we can make some adjustments. I'll ask Amanda... Can I call you back?"

"What is it?" she asked.

"He wants us to stay away from the house for a few days. He says the media will be all over us and we need to keep a low profile. Would you mind if we stayed out for a night or two? The Hilton, for example? He'll make the arrangements...And, if he insists, we can even go north for a few days?"

Amanda stared at him, about to object. But she quickly realized what a spectacle they had just caused.

Trevor's position at the bank should not be compromised by surprises. Nor could he be thrust upon the media unprepared. They needed a chance to collect their thoughts...

She nodded.

Trevor dialed Derek with a text: The Hilton. Two nights.

Trevor changed direction and arrived at a ramp onto the main motorway. He turned to head across the city.

Derek called back. Trevor put the phone on speaker.

"We have you on speaker, Derek"

Derek answered. "The painting. Best to make no comment at the moment... At least until we have more information about the bidder..."

"Oh?"

"Yes. The Auction House called us. They want to meet. They have some suspicion that the bidding was orchestrated somehow..."

"Orchestrated?"

There was a pause, the car was quiet despite a noisy world outside.

"What does that mean exactly?" asked Trevor.

"They want to check it out. That's what they said."

"I see..."

"And err...Well, we're liable for its safety" he added, his voice tense. "Having insured it, we're exposed to its value as the underwriter..."

"Yes. I'm aware. These prices change all expectations!" said Trevor. He turned to look at Amanda, reluctant to proceed. But he had no choice. "We've put ourselves at risk..." he said.

"Yes. I'm afraid we have. We should consult with the board before we go further..."

"Yes. Of course"

"I'm... very worried Trevor" said Derek

"How do you mean?"

"We've over-extended the bank's insurance exposure" he said simply.

Trevor and Amanda looked at each other. "What are you saying, Derek?"

"Someone wants to break us!"

* * *

Pennsylvania was dark by five P.M. at this time of the year.

The mining company north of Pittsburg was quiet for the night, all quadrants of its mile-wide operations protected with boundary fencing.

With all gates secured and barriers down, the property, muddy from rain and melting snow slush, had multiple access roads for heavy hauling equipment. Even maintenance yards and storage facilities were closed by chained-linked barrier walls.

It was easy to forget the force of Pennsylvania coal production legacy. The extraction of coal from surface or underground mines had fueled the industrial revolution and changed the world. Coal, extracted from its rich anthracite rock deposits from deep within the mountains, was processed to produce energy.

Power grids of modern cities were much advanced from the hard history of coal mining, yet it was evidenced everywhere. Since early days of modernization, coal had been used as fuel. It burned longer than wood, and could sustain higher temperatures.

Easier to consolidate, it served growing populations and changing demographics, and it had fed the industrial wealth of the Western civilized world.

Coal was a hardened carbon mineral, created through the ages of time and compacted deep within mountains. It solidified as veins that ran for miles between strata of rock, like a solid river. When extracted and exposed to air, it was pure black, and its crystalline surface shone and glistened in the sun. Heavy as it was, tons of it could be transported by wheeled vehicles.

It burned easily when ignited. From coal burning fireplaces in a home to industrial furnaces that smelted iron, it produced finished steel and ironworks used for propulsion of engines in trains and ships.

It had long lasting qualities, it could sustain fuel to light cities with electricity.

Coal could be harnessed to heat buildings in boilers, it could allow winter uses for men to work in factories for manufacturing, or large office structures for the use of communications, warehouses for transportation and food distribution.

As a result, markets created jobs, needing no more a subsistence agrarian economy. Men could work in cities and earn a living wage for a day of laboring. With wages, men could be independent, using their disposable income to purchase items and live in a democratic society with economic vibrancy and commercial trade.

But it had come at a price. The rock that contained veins of coal was hard and deep within the mountain.

Coal miners chiseled coal from deep tunnels inside the mountain. Men, digging coal from beneath the surface filled trolleys with black rock that came up to be crushed and carried away for the owners of the coal mine. They sold it for profit and paid their coal miners from it, even as it revolutionized the world.

But it was hard work, and dangerous. Those that worked in the mines, it was said, carried the wealth of nations on their shoulders.

From the ranks of coal miners, unions had organized to claw for more than their wages. They challenged corporate management with collective bargaining, socialist manifestos and labor reform.

In Europe, the wealth of empires rested in owning the resources, and managing that wealth distributed amongst land holders and those who governed. But the growing demand for coal gave rise to an entire middle class of wage earners, able to purchase and engage in trade as a market, such that Europe saw its share of organized labor union protestations, revolutions and uprisings.

When politically organized, labor unions infiltrated governance and with their demands for fair trade practices shaped democratic governments, such that only with them as partners could conservative owners operate. It was often a delicate balance that frequently led to bloodshed and remorse.

But here in Pennsylvania, an advanced technological mining venture owned by corporate entities was in full operation. Legitimately licensed to excavate using synchronized management, updated industry standards and registered compliance requirements per state regulation, this operation used safety standards, environmental concern and efficient excavation methods, such that coal mining was now a modern enterprise for Wall Street investors.

Everywhere, large hauling trucks shifted slopes of mine tailings, moving material like slow giants across vast landscapes.

Geologic excavating showed a main basin, a pit as large as a lake comprising of rock drilling and blasting operations, protected by slopes that rose in circular steps for road access to the core-sensitive working area.

Designed for eventual restoration, the mountain would be returned to its natural surface, complete with habitat and reforestation. Until then, it ran like a blockchain of operations using technologically advanced hydraulic mining methods. And for its corporate owners, it was profitable.

Here, it was carefully protected on premises secured.

Nobody unauthorized was allowed near the site. Even those who worked there were restricted to particular sectors to meet safety and regulatory standards. It had multiple systems for security, including private security.

It was patrolled by government police. It was guarded by remote electronic surveillance and sensors at various gates. It was computer controlled and monitored in every respect.

It was vast. Without particular knowledge, and especially at night, only a Foreman would know where the gates and entrances were located.

The man standing at a roadside outcrop was wearing heavy gear of rubber and dark over clothes. The mountain chill of the night brought vapor to his lips when he breathed, but he was not feeling cold. He held up his binoculars and waited. He was actually a trained engineer, a man who had begun as a draftsman years ago. And he knew the premises like a mining manager.

Finally, he re-entered his pick up, and drove to the designated area of the mine shaft, passing through a gate that not locked.

From under tarps, he unloaded several drums of TNT explosives and fuses. Over the last two weeks, he had managed to accumulated enough explosives to set off a fair volume explosion down a shaft half a mile beneath the surface.

But he loaded the elevator platform, and with a remarkably simple hoist, lowered the cargo down into the shaft. A small panel told him how deep he had gone, and he raised the platform by twenty five feet just to be sure. Then he waited.

With no sound above, he proceeded to lodge his cargo into place, finally climbing to the surface on trellis ladder footholds affixed to the walls.

It was long before dawn when he tossed into the shaft an open fuse, knowing that it would take almost two minutes to ignite.

He moved with stealth through the darkness to his Ford pick-up, then drove quietly through the gates without headlights.

He veered off-road and up a ridge through a woodland trail before emerging at a parkway curb for scenic viewing. Switching on his headlights for the hour before a winter dawn, he merged with morning rush-hour traffic on the highways, and was gone.

The mine ignited and began to burn underground.

There would be no significant surface signs. But he knew what would happen.

First the fireball would explode and on impact might dislodge rock and debris from the shaft tunnel as it thundered along channels like a rush of wind. But it was fire and gas.

Then a trail of smoke might rise to the surface, but being dark, nobody would particularly notice.

The sound or ground movement was too insignificant to elicit alarms, and with the operation closed for the night, nobody who felt tremor would feel any threat to life. No more than a thunderbolt in the distant night of the mountain, perhaps. Or a train that plied these rails laden with rock. No. This explosion would go unnoticed.

Besides, by tomorrow there'd be no evidence. This remote area hadn't been worked for years.

It would burn. That much he knew. It would disable the operation and damage value made by the energy company.

And it would take a long time to rebuild its name brand.

****

Trevor's legs were smooth. Amanda ran her toes up the calf of his leg then snuggled into silk sheets to lie against him.

"Hmm" he murmured from his sleep, his hand reaching behind him and pressing her thigh closer.

With her breasts nestled softly against his back, she planted a small kiss on his spine, her breath warm.

"Hmm"

Trevor McDonnel was not a young man. Yet he could command the attention of women when he walked into a room, his tall demeanor and grey hair arresting. But it was his gate of distinction, his cornflower-blue eyes that could settle upon a face with an attention that made people feel important. It affected those around him and infused them with devotion. He could be demanding, yet kind; high-minded yet understanding. And for Amanda Wells, never ...in their many years of marriage... did he turn away from her caress.

Nuzzling her nose gently against his back, she drifted into a dreamy slumber.

The cell phone vibrating nearly tumbled off the bedside table at four o'clock in the morning, the night sky at the window dark like charcoal.

"Jacques?" said Amanda thinly "What...um, couldn't wait... a couple hours?"

"Is Trevor there....*Please!*"

Amanda reached up for a bed-light and tapped Trevor on the shoulder with the cell phone, her silky hair falling freely off his shoulder.

He sat up. "Yes?"

Even Amanda could hear the rasping words through the electronic device.

"Trevor...The painting. It's been vandalized..."

* * *

The room was dark on the fifth floor of the Pentagon. Lit by electronic devices and two large-screen LED monitors transmitting by SatLink from a ship in the Baltic sea, the ambient air was dry.

Admiral Arguetta reached for the crystal pitcher at the center of a pool of light, an illuminated conference table. He filled his cup of water and resumed his seat in the shadows. But for an occasional medal-glimmer, he was a specter in a room of senior command personnel. And they'd been in attendance since before daybreak.

He sipped.

It was a situation. He would have to make his assessments before reporting to the Secretary of the Navy. In turn, the White House would be advised.

The screen showed a vast grey heaving sea, In the distance, a ship of the line was visible. Sharp raspy gusts of wind could be heard through the live-feed.

The LED monitor filled with the form of Captain Bar, transmitting from the US Naval Vessel USS Arkansas.

"There's been no movement in just under six hours."

Commander Roberts, standing within the window of conferencing, was in view to the Captain aboard ship. At his flank in the shadows was a bank of electronic stations maintaining the link of communications as support systems.

The weather was changing.

"There's a shifting current and wind dispersion pattern developing from a weather system...We'll transmit the data..."

"Standing by" said Roberts.

Arguetta stepped out of the shadows and tapped Roberts at the elbow. "How many contractors do we have with this kind of technical knowledge?"

"No more than a handful...It's pretty specialized and requires little less than a nuclear physicist to manage."

Bill Robert was head of the technical code on nuclear propulsions systems at the US Department of Navy. Everyone knew what he meant. Due to lack of support from the last White House, most of the technical talent had been released.

One technician looked up and indicated a thumbs up "Got It" with download feeds from the ship.

Roberts reopened the transmission.

"So Captain, what've you got for crew on your ship?"

The image momentarily pixilated, and it was uncertain if the link was viable. Roberts was about to restate his question when a delayed relay came back. Roberts spoke again.

"..If there's any shifting of the ship's position, given the changing weather, we'd like to be kept on feed..?"

"Acknowledged" said the Captain, adding with a slight grin at the corner of his mouth "There is one officer, Lt.Cmdr Monmouth Sir. Navy Reserve Corps. He just graduated and he's doing a tour with us."

They waited for the Captain's assessment. It came. "He knows his stuff Sir."

The room was quiet.

The captain had added little to assuage apprehension. The situation was serious. Any show of bravura in the line of duty was demonstrably insufficient as two nuclear vessels at sea drifted two miles apart.

"Thank you Captain. Stand-by."

Roberts turned.

Colonel Sims came out of the shadows. She too had been in the room most of the day. As a US Marine political officer with a technical background she'd been helpful to Arguetta at the Pentagon.

He nodded, and she stepped into the viewing window of transmission.

"Captain" she said, "If we're at the molecular level here, what's to say that their technology and know-how is reliably *contained?* Is a solution within their capabilities, or are they relying on intel from outside sources?"

A small lag followed.

"It's hard to say Colonel" responded the Captain.

"A breach of containment is possible."

"Thank you Captain" said Sims, signing off.

Sims turned to Arguetta. "We need the NSA in here."

Roberts addressed those in the room behind him. "There are only a handful of core groups able to ascertain such an event. But we're not fully updated on fresh global developments elsewhere at this time. So lets get on that..."

"Well" said Arguetta, "We do have pretty accurate intelligence on where the research is with this development. What we *don't* have is a real grasp of how well apprised *they* are of what's happened to them! It's an assessment question: Is this a thinly veiled distress call with and agenda?..."

"to discover how far we've advanced with our solutions in technical capabilities" interrupted Sims.

"Or is it a ruse?" asked Roberts.

"I don't think so" said Arguetta. "What if it's an Emergency and they're appealing for help? I recommend we contact the Russian embassy. Find out how informed they are of their ship...?"

He turned to the ship's transmission "Captain. How would you assess their onboard technical status. Is their appeal genuine, in your opinion?"

"Sir" said Captain Roberts "The Russian vessel knew we were here! They opened communication and revealed their position to us. But that said, we can't be sure it's *not* a ploy to expose ourselves. It's been done before..."

"Stand by" said Roberts, closing the transmission.

Arguetta suppressed a smug grin but said nothing.

Then Jim Barksdale, a middle-aged man with a legal mind stepped out of the shadows and stood besides Arguetta.

"We'll need a full understanding of what this is before NAVSEC takes it the White House. Have him make a detailed presentation for our benefit will you?"

Arguetta nodded.

He turned to Sims, they chatted quietly.

"Yes Sir" she said.

"And...err. Argutta, can you add any scenario assessment in terms of strategic significance? Short clock I know. But needful, please?"

Barksdale turned and stood still to address the room in full.

"I need to anticipate if they're after something we've got. Have we overlooked something? There's clearly a disparity between our technical developments and what they need. So, think critically...Thank you, all."

The house lights came up.

Arguetta turned away, appalled at the idea of adding crisis to a White House already putting out fires from the previous Administrations.

But what intelligence was all about.

'Two hours then..." he said aloud, consulting his watch. "Let's take a break. Then back to work here at 1300."

Arguetta moved across the room, his crisp whites now damp with perspiration. Secure rooms didn't allow for the best ventilation, he decided. He drank more water.

It occurred to him that today was registered as scheduled Maintenance and Upgrade to Facilities Day. Yet here they all were in the throes of a naval crisis!

A voice rang out.

"Oh! Wait... Excuse me...Err...I just got off the phone from SECNAV's office" said Barksdale. "He wants to be here in person for that briefing. Just a forewarning folks!"

"Gee thanks..." said Arguetta and they walked out the room together towards the elevator.

"Well why not? The Secretary of the Navy needs to know and he will be taking it to the White House. So, what's your take on this?" asked Barksdale.

"Not sure" answered Arguetta.

The elevator doors opened. Two women joined them, one in military uniform, the other a young civilian Intern.

"Ladies" acknowledge the gentlemen.

They smiled, then exited.

"Nor sure *what?..*" pursued Jim "For the Admiral of a nuclear cruiser you're remarkably obtuse!"

Arguetta half chuckled. "I've been called a few names... *Obtuse?* That's a good one!"

"You know what I mean. Is there something you're not telling me?"

The elevator door opened. A Lt. Commander entered, and with a quick nod proffered rank-acknowledgement.

They all walked out towards the Cafeteria at ground level.

"No. It's just that this kind of technology is somewhere in the realm of sustainable energy systems for space applications."

"Oh, you're kidding right? Since when did we hold out for space travel?"

"Not in the last two Administrations, that's for sure!" responded Arguetta. "But we might need it and NASA's done some great R&D..."

"I'll remember to remark on that" said Jim

"No don't..." said Arguetta "You know it's a hot button for political opposition..."

"Damn straight! We're NOT spending on space-goddamn-travel, with so much to do down here!"

"Precisely my point. So, what do you want?"

"I want to know what's happening with our R&D that makes this issue so damned sensitive?"

"It's a potential threat..."

"A *threat?*" glowered Jim.

"Yes. So, pizza or salad?"

"Soup..." came the response.

"One Soup. One salad. Two Pizzas to go..." chuckled Arguetta to the wait staff of the dinning hall.

London, 1881

The assassination of Tsar Alexander II shocked the world. Returning from a ceremonial parade with his wife and son, a bomb was tossed into his carriage. He died at his winter Palace in St. Petersburg within hours. He was 62.

In London, where society was enjoying the fruits of an Industrial Revolution, such news could not have been more alarming.

The streets, as thy they said, were just filling with pretty petticoats and carriages! Now that electrified cities saw people coming in by rail, and that fuel was attainable for heating homes, social gatherings for entertainment and meetings were popular events...

It was an attack against the empire, some said. Particularly to men of the hierarchy engaging these days in challenges of sport and mixing freely with the community: Social class was sub-vented to symbols of charity. And public sentiment could now take liberties with opinions offered from the heart - even published in pamphlets, daily newspapers or works of literature.

Yet in England the event was acutely felt. Here, tolerance for free speech was encouraged, and the monarchy was neither without the adoration of its people, nor was it devoid of love and charity for the needy. In fact, such posturing was the hallmark of good society - to remain on the sidelines of controversy.

But if such success was due in part to the adroit statesmanship of her prime ministers Palmerstone; Benjamin Disraeli and Gladstone who had marshaled for the British empire vast territories under Queen Victoria, it only helped blunt the stark realities of what had just happened.

From Amsterdam to New York, street-corner newsboys filled the air yelling *Extra! Extra!* Newspapers could not print enough copies about the assassination of March 13, 1881.

Russia, one of the great empires of the world, was dealt a blow to its leadership of autocratic rule.

The Russian domain occupied the northern latitudes of the Northern Hemisphere and comprised one-eighth of the Earth's inhabited land area. Boundaries encompass all northern Europe and Asia. With its industrial activity centered between the Dnieper River and the Ural Mountains, it contained natural resources in great abundance - raw materials, fuel and minerals for the advancement of civilization.

The question was, who would fill this vacuum of leadership?

The wife and son of Nicholas Alexander II had survived the attack and remained uninjured following the assassination. But little information emerged. Only years later was there a full account discovered in the diary of his wife Empress Marie. Even as the event would change the course of history.

Within weeks of the Tsar's assassination, his son Nicholas Alexander III was announced to be heir to the throne. He would be crowned as the reigning monarch of the Russian empire.

But before his coronation, the matter of his marriage had to be resolved. He and his wife together were to reign as Emperor and Empress of Russia, a royal family.

Further, the bride he was to marry was the granddaughter of Queen Victoria of England.

Whereas royal displays of imperial splendor attained front pages in newspapers, what was noticeably absent were the darker implications of what had happened in Russia.

In Russia social unrest filled the streets. Rebellion, restive populations and a nasty sentiment towards Jews fanned the flames of turmoil, and it was in this conflict that Tsar Alexander II had been assassinated.

Remarkably, the private life of his surviving widow, Marie, was less known. Yet her role in subsequent years would take unexpected turns, even as the empire collapsed.

Daughter to King Frederick VII, she was known only as the Grand Duchess Maria Feodorovna.

Denmark, it was told, was an odd country from which to find a wife for a Russian Tsar. Traditionally, royal marriages of Europe issued from the greater families of Germany. But Frederick VII King of Denmark had two beautiful daughters: Marie and Alexandra.

Both daughters became the wives of leaders of two great empires. Marie married the Russia Tsar; and Alexandra married into the throne of England. For the rest of their lives, as history would unfold around them, these two sisters would remain close...even binding their two nations through most tempestuous times.

In England, Alexandra of Denmark, unlike her sister Marie, was the focus of the British press. They adored her. Alexandra had been selected by Queen Victoria of Great Britain as a suitable bride for her son Prince Albert.

When first married, they were known as the Prince and Princess of Wales, and they would hold that title for as long Queen Victoria lived.

Eventually, when Albert ascended the throne of England in 1901 as Edward VII, he and his wife Alexandra ruled England for ten years as King and Queen of England. Their son was heir to the throne of England, and he later became King George V.

Thus, at the time the Russian Empress Maria Feodorovna was bereft of her husband at the hand of an assassin, she received the love and support of her sister Alexandra, Princess of Wales, as well as the sympathy of the English people.

Especially now that her son was to be crowned Tsar to ensure the transition of power.

Above all, the affairs of state must deliver public assurance that stability would continue in an orderly fashion. Many from the English court were sent to assist in that transition:

Firstly, in grand ceremonial style, the wedding of Nicholas II occurred in St Petersburg.

Shortly thereafter, young Nicholas II and his new bride were crowned and installed as reigning monarchs of Russia.

Maria Federovna, her son now on the throne, had become the mother-in-law to the new young bride Alix of Prussia, a granddaughter of Queen Victoria. Her own title was now officially *Dowager Duchess to Tzar Nicholas II of Russia.*

As history would show in the years that followed, Marie Federovna and her sister Princess Alexandra of England would share confidences. Such that by the time Queen Alexandra of England became embroiled in the politics of WWI, she harbored a deep and abiding dislike for their nephew, Wilhelm II of Germany.

The painting that was put up at Auction in London had a history. Masterfully executed with exquisite artistic coloring and attention to detail, it was painted on Russia soil during a period of turbulence when socialist upheavals, bloody revolutions and war swept through Europe.

The story behind the painting was a tale that involved Trevor's grandfather. And it had remained in the family collections of Scotland for over a century, quietly ignored.

When it came up at Auction, the painting had reignited passions of hatred so deep as to burn like the fires of dark mountain coal..

* * *

Chapter 2

"What we have here is a deterioration of the containment system..." spoke the voice of a young man clearly uncomfortable with the situation. He paused. As an analytical physicist, this was his job, if on a nuclear warship for a tour. He would rather be at his desk in Langley. But he looked deep into the lens of the Comsat system, knowing that what he had to say would be of interest to Washington.

"As you know, in our ships the nuclear marine propulsion system is produced by a nuclear power plant which heats water to produce steam. The turbine fuels the ships' propeller through a gearbox or electric   generator. Naval nuclear population is common to our supercarriers, although a few experimental civilian nuclear ships have been built with that installation - like the super icebreakers for North Sea Atlantic conditions..."

He waiting for a feedback loop in case the audience had questions. There would be a lag.

Arguetta took the opportunity in Washington to brief the group watching the screen. "Russian, American and British ships rely on direct steam turbine propulsion, whereas French and Chinese ships use the turbine to generate electricity for propulsion..."

The SECNAV nodded, as did Jim Barksdale, head of technical support for the Atlantic Fleet. He appreciated the simple terms in which Captain Jennings explained things.

"Our reactors use pressurized water, the Russians warships are powered with liquid metal cooled reactors..."

The image fuzzed for just a second, then reinstated itself. Captain Jennings proceeded. "What we have is nuclear ship with radiation-decay..." He jerked his head to indicate the other ship, clearly frustrated with what he had to say. "It should be contained. At the core of a power reactor, the probability of a neutron intersection with a fissionable nuclear element before it escapes into the shielding is much lower: *Their* reactor runs on a highly enriched uranium..."

He paused, then proceeded. "There are technical difficulties in designing fuel elements which will withstand a large amount of radiation damage. Fuel elements may crack over time, and gas bubbles may form. This, they claim, is their problem..."

Arguetta asked the next question "Is their ship contaminated and compromised?"

"Yes Sir. They are" answered the Captain. "They plan to stay adrift until they resolve their issues. But they have communicated to us to hold our distance." Arguetta saw the puzzlement on the Secretary's face. He returned to the screen and asked.

"So, what's the problem?"

The Captain accommodated his shipboard specialist who answered.

"Yes Sir. Marine reactors are designed for long core life: Enabled by the relatively highly enrichment of uranium, and incorporating a "burnable poison" in the fuel, the process serves as a throttle. The throttle slows depletion of the elements with age to become less "reactive." It acts like a mechanism to increase/decrease consumption of the burnable poison, and it regulates the speed with which they can lessen reactivity..."

"Go on" said Jim Barksdale.

"Right. Life of the compact reactor pressure-vessel is extended by an internal neurtron "shield." This shield reduces the damage to the steel from constant bombardment of neutrons. In this case, the disabled ship has its shield damaged...So, essentially, they are at sea awaiting the gradual degradation of their reactivity."

"Will they survive?" asked Jim

"They should, judging from what they've communicated. However, they have identified unfriendly passes by aircraft on their radar."

"How long do they have?" asked the Secretary. It was Jim who answered him, quietly.

"Some of the fission products generated during nuclear reactions have a high neutron absorption capacity. The iodine -135- decay has a 6 to 8 hour half life. After that, it's a 40 to 50 hour decay period."

The captain has resumed his position at the Comsat. He waited.

Finally the Navsec looked up and said "Thank you Captain. We'll be back to you..."

Arguetta instructed the technicians present to kill the link. He turned to those in the room.

"Any thoughts?"

"If we go to their rescue. There are rules of engagement. But they're a toxic liability. It's too dangerous..." said the Secretary. "They'll just have to wait it out..." adding, "I'll brief the President"

"...I don't like the enemy aircraft circulating?" said Arguetta. Turning to his Lt Cmdr he said "Find out from NavAir who they are..."

"We can offer deterrent support. We have a carrier close by" said Captain Woodward, observing from the shadows. He was on the staff of strategic defense at the Pentagon.

"We can't shoot down their enemies... That's a joke right?" said the Secretary. "Congress would have a field day laughing...let alone demanding for explanation." He paused. "There's something more here, isn't there?"

"Bill?"

Arguetta looked down thoughtfully, then nodded to Jim Barksdale to come forward.

Jim spoke softly "They'll realize that we've reached a new level technology for our propulsion systems. In fact, the whole drama could be a ploy to bring us out into the open with our findings and research..."

"What research?" insisted Woodward. "Propulsion technology? For what...?"

This time it was the Secretary of Navy who spoke up. "It's a matter of fuel and space energy. A nuclear propulsion system!"

"Correct" said Arguetta. "There is a race for space dominance going on. NASA has looked at new propulsions systems for distance flight, fueling and colonization..."

"Gee that's nice to know. Where did all this come from?" he asked.

"Private enterprise, new R&D developed in the private sector..."

"Oh really?"

Rear Admiral Woodward could have acted with more discretion. His position at the Pentagon certainly engaged with strategic warfare. But his scope was limited to those resources already available. Not to technical innovation and new possibilities or concept planning. That he felt outranked was just a show of professional authority.

The Secretary of the Navy said "I'll bring you up to speed Jeff once we're on firmer ground..."

Jim continued with his explanation.

"A nuclear propulsion system is far reaching in possibilities. We're getting away from conventional rockets that burn fuel to create thrust. The atomic system uses that reaction to make propellants like liquid hydrogen. But it's heavy and cumbersome. What we're exploring is huge. Especially for very difficult missions that necessitate a lot of propellant such as a Mars Flight..."

"And the crews, excuse me, the *humans* on board?" asked Woodward. "Or is it robotic?"

"Not robotic" said Jim. "Live personnel would need to be shielded from the reactor's radiation, just like this ship..."

"So, all this ploy to expose our hand in science and research? Why not just sign up at any American University with open access to our intellectual intelligence and take out the technology?"

"Good point!" agreed Arguetta.

Jim continued. "It's more. NASA has an eye on atomic technology to power human colonies once they get to Mars. The Department of Energy is developing space-ready nuclear fission reactors, known as kilopower. It could be deployed on other planets and moons for colonization. We could dominate the space of our universe, even alter the natural environment once on the surface... NASA has employed radioisotope thermos-electric generators – batteries that run off the heat from radioactive materials..." said Jim

Arguetta consulted his watch. "I'd love to chat guys. But we're on a time element here."

"So, are we they just playing cat and mouse here with this situation?" asked the Secretary.

"It's possible" said Arguetta. He turned to Sims, a figure who had sat in the shadows with Woodward. She was an environmental and social scientist.

"It's a legitimate concern. It's not a matter of if, it's a matter of when we find the earth compromised for habitability or stable tranquility. Unimaginable as it is, we are cultivating ideas about colonization. Mostly, we try not to alarm populations. Some call it climate change. And perhaps it is...But we're watching out now for any byproduct of terrorism..."

Jim jumped in. "Or maybe just fierce industrial competition...It revolutionary stuff, cutting edge technology and on the cusp of new financial frontiers for some. So, we'd be well advised to show caution."

"I get it..." said the Secretary, stepping away.

"A Black Swan event...."

Arguetta switched back to the live feed on the monitor.

 "Captain. We render assistance as Standby, with Vigilance ...to ward off any mal-intentioned buzzards. No boarding. No sharing. Await further instructions."

"Aye, Sir!"

He killed the link.

* * *

The beaches along the Eastern continental United States had taken a beating this year. One storm after the other sent surges of ocean surf across Especially along the coastlines of South Carolina.

Normally a sandy haven for winter-weary northern visitors or those now retired from lifelong careers and daily commuting, Amanda and Trevor kept a house in there, in Charleston.

Years ago, they had come with their children to scuba-dive off sandy beach-dunes where once pirates, shipwrecks and historical tales filled abounded. But that was a different world.

Today, with all children grown, Amanda and Trevor strolled along the frothy line of gentle surf, and they were alone together.

The beaches were largely abandoned. Even for a winter resort area. Up north they knew, most roads and cities were under a foot of snow.

And they had sold their beach house in Delaware on the advice of their Accountant, and taken instead a house for wintering further south. Better suited to a climate for retired people, he advised. They did so with remorse, since Delaware weekends at the beach were years preoccupied with toddlers when they lived in Washington DC.

There was no lack of things to do here in the south. The Carolinas held large business concerns for Trevor. He had contacts and meetings everywhere, it seemed. Tomorrow he was going to the Boeing Manufacturing plant where his bank was heavily invested...

But for now, walking the beach with Amanda in balmy weather was for Trevor a moment to breath.

A soft ocean breeze picked up. Both of them remained quiet, contemplating the turn of events of the last few weeks.

Following the turmoil of the Auction, the vandalism of their Artwork, and the media publicly that stormed their life, they had managed to get away. Amanda paused, closed her eyes and filled her lungs with sea air, the sun soothing upon her face, erasing weeks of anxiety.

What had happened to so turn their lives upside down? And why...? The questions remained.

London was home. From that they would never retreat.

This was that time of the year when they wondered if they had achieved all that was expected by family, friends, philanthropic giving. It was Christmas.

Where had the year gone so quickly?

Now, they were relieved to be away from the city.

Of course they had conferred with lawyers, insurers, accountants and all those involved. Of course there was Jacques, the Museum, the Auction House, all of them sharing in their assurances.

But now it was quiet and they were alone.

All alone, isolated.

"What happened?" said Amanda, finally.

Trevor did not respond. He laced his fingers into Amanda's hand and took a deep breath, looking out to a blue sea and its distant horizon. He understood her question.

This was no longer about the sudden surge of interest in a work of Art which she had put up for Auction as a Museum donation. Neither was it about the astronomical sum of money it fetched at final bidding; nor even about the vandalism that followed, leaving them feeling exploited by an third party laying bare their most private world to open broadcast and public view...

No. This question was about meaning.

What was the significance behind such public scrutiny?

The figure in the painting... Why was the painting of such interest? The internet..?

The purpose was to damage his reputation.

The motive, or 'criminal intent' as the Chief Inspector of Police from New Scotland Yard put it, was social contempt.

"He was my grandfather..." Trevor said. "When the Tzar of Russia was assassinated in 1894 and succeeded by his son Nicholas II, Marie his widow called for her sister Alexandra, the Princess of Wales.

Alexandra her sister was married to the Prince of Wales, son of Queen Victoria and next in line to the throne of England. He became King George V. They travelled to Lavidia, Russia for the funeral...

It was a huge risk for the royalty. Labor uprisings everywhere, the overturning of the monarchies in Europe by socialist revolutionaries was a threat to democracy itself, let alone a free world of industrial economies.

By then, monarchies ruled in name only for pomp and circumstance as a cultural emblem. Mostly run by Parliamentary rule of law, those nations looked like modern governments of today in governance.

Further, it was the age of an industrial revolution, creating great wealth for some, and opportunity for populations that the monarchy fostered as a hierarchy. It was progress. It was mass production and factory work for a burgeoning bourgeoisie able to earn a living wage for themselves...

The socialist abhorred that emerging wealth. Instead, they focused on overturning the monarchy for redistribution of wealth, disrupting traditions of infrastructure, transport, agriculture... adding greatly to the burden and suffering of populations still dependent on agrarian subsistence, not yet fully emerged.

Chiefly, it was a money-power grab.

The socialist movements of Marxism under Lennin seized control of a burgeoning bourgeoisie rooted in tradition and centuries of cultural flowering. They appropriated power by force and stole national resources. By killing off celebrated hierarchy of monarchy, they cut down the hopes of individuals to excel…They reduced society to state-run totalitarianism."

Trevor paused.

"My great grandfather served in the Scottish Highland Regiment at the time. It was the pleasure of Queen Victoria's to send her Highland Guards to accompany her son and his wife Alexandra to Russia.

Subsequently, England made several attempts to rescue the Russian royal family from the ferocity of social revolution…

On one such a mission, it was my great grandfather's portrait that was painted…"

Amanda was stunned. She looked up at Trevor in utter disbelief. "That was *your* grandfather's father in the painting?"

Trevor nodded apologetically.

"No wonder the resemblance to you is so striking of the figure of the painting!"

"You *knew*…?"

"From the first moment I saw the painting. I knew… Yes."

They walked, the seagulls screeching above them. Neither spoke.

"Why didn't you say something…?"

Trevor looked away, far away into the horizons of history. "It was a sad time for the aristocracy…the monarchy. Nothing but desecration and death. And not only for them. For patricians. For artisans. For tradesmen. For Jews…Also for peasants with trusted bourgeoisie networks and emerging markets across Europe, slowly flourishing and modernizing. And for their freedom of religion…"

They walked in silence.

"I knew it was him because I have a photograph of his uniform from my grandmother's collections. He was in Russia with the Royal family …"

The surf came and dissipated in quiet rhythmic misting.

"Your grandfather?" asked Amanda "What happened?"

Trevor looked down as if measuring the steps of time. "Everybody knew who painted the portrait..."

The words hung in the breeze, unnoticed, uneventful. But they were said.

Beneath them the sand gave way to a natural cadence of quietness. Warm and moist with familiarity, but harsh with reality. That which had not been said was missing.

It was Amanda who had to speak. " You... knew who the *Artist* was?"

Her face jerked slightly. "And you claimed no knowledge of the painting's provenance?"

"I had to..."

"Is that why you so willingly agreed to insure it for two million pounds?"

Trevor looked ahead, unable to seek her eyes "Not exactly..."

"You kept us all in the dark about the painting and *you knew what it was?* who... the figure was. Who... the artist was?" she managed. The surf rolled in with a warning thrash as they passed by. She watched it recede, raising her hand to her brow to block the glare.

Then she returned to his side, her thoughts uncertain. They walked.

"Was that to throw off Jacques and everyone else who searched....Or was it to preserve a family portrait as being your legacy...?" she asked.

"No!"

"Then why weren't you... *honest?* Why couldn't you tell us all that you knew about the painting? And what about the price valuation? For your *banking* interests...? "

"Amanda, please!"

She walked on, her thoughts a jumble of doubts. She turned to him, hair flailing across her face in the wind. "You know, now? I *don't want to know*... To hell with you!"

"Wait! Amanda..."

"No. *You* wait... Withholding critical information about a valuable asset is misrepresentation: Being in a fiduciary position...*You knew!* Worse. You misled us all..."

Amanda didn't wait for an answer. She left him standing on the beach, her mind puzzled beyond measure, and she felt angry.

She returned to their place, and she nearly left. But she didn't.

The events of the past few weeks in London were stressful. She felt she was owed an explanation, if not an apology, and she waited. She considered the facts.

Auctions offering high-priced works of art didn't just happen by accident. Details revealed with honest authenticity would be expected to be disclosed, described, advertised, promoted as fully transparent, and real.

Art works, articles of rarity, were a commercial commodity listed as valuable assets. Investors had to believe that. Collectors and Antiquity dealers had to know that. But it was more: Those who loved fine things saw not just the value of the item, but drew from such rarified work inspiration as something that touched the human spirit in timeless ways...

Nor was the documentation any less rigorous for certification or insurance purposes.

Provenance reports were mandatory. To fail to disclose the truth behind any item of value was tantamount to fraud. Or worse, counterfeit. It damaged the reputation of all affiliated. Amanda's own professional integrity was now suspect...

She felt resentful of such willful neglect.

It was not acceptable neither in the world of antiquities nor collectors to be less than honest about the history and the value of any item. Period.

This revelation by Trevor had stunned her. It was a an error that she didn't expect. Especially coming from her husband. She felt her trust betrayed, and by the man she most trusted. How was that possible?

So damned if she was going to leave without an explanation!

Trevor opened the door and walked in.

* * *

The Annual Economic Summit, Trevor MacDonnell was a guest speaker. His role was distinctly carved as an innovative thinker. More importantly, as a banker his perspectives were highly valued in forecasting.

His was the platform of capitalism and independent investment assets. His speech at Davos was redolent with those who sacrificed greatly to protect it. He spoke of things that venerated individual enterprise as a traditional doctrine of value. Steeped in conservative protestant commercial mercantilism, such values secured for the West stability and freedom of rights. It represented the rule of law and honored the legacies of rights and freedoms offered by military protections and defense. He spoke of advancement and development as freedoms of any constitutional democracy. Banking, Trevor told them, for all its cyber security and regulation for compliance, should be protected by democracies and government that truly valued it's workers, their families and their communities as citizens.

He took questions.

Chief amongst those issues discussed was the stability of central banks.

He answered sagaciously. In a world of conflicted politics and terrorism, the threat of disruptions was a concern. Alarming was the rise of socialism in South America. Today, Venezuela was considered a country teetering from poverty and hyper-inflation under a vocal socialist dictator. But there was more to consider, those more subtle and without the will of people. Those nations with years of protective stability were at threat. Socialism and liberal governments were now of concern. Those governments run by progressive leadership seeking to tear down protective barriers and sovereign rights were alarming. Reform and redistribution of wealth threatened free market economies. Capitalism was under assault by global interests for control of markets.

Under the guise of popular demand, policy was being rewritten by bureaucrats. Politicians were pandering to revolutionaries. Electorates were now subjected to unfettered electronic technologies, upheavals of cultural stability by tactical disruption from social media.

The West had become complacent, public treasuries undisciplined, pressure of growing populations unplanned.

Most alarming was the flow of financial liquidity to large accounts only.

For Trevor, it was an achievement. Switzerland was beautiful at this time of the year.

He had arrived for the conference together with his family. His daughter and son-in-law Jack were living in Switzerland. Jack held a job as an Analyst at an energy company whose corporate headquarters were located in Zurich.

Given the difficulties of the last few weeks, Trevor was at least happy that they had gathered here, all of them.

The rift between he and Amanda had deepened. The affair of the Auction still rankled. And the matter of the art work itself, now valued as worth millions, continued to rage on amongst litigants: There were issues of provenance, criminal charges of vandalism, insurance valuations, security questions that incited public outcry and political reaction in the media.

In deciding to invite everyone to the Swiss Alps for a family reunion and ski trip, Trevor managed to frame a family truce. It promised a respite from the stressful subject altogether, and for a wonderful week, it brought them all to the Alps for a family reunion and vacation.

It worked.

Amanda agreed to attend. So did their son Tray. There was Sandra and Jack; Tray and his girlfriend, Jacques and his wife and two others in their group.

They all came together, and they relaxed. There was much to do, sites and tours, hiking, sledding, skiing and gatherings at nighttime parties for meals in the chalets of the Swiss Alps.

Amanda found pleasure surrounded by friends and family. Together they laughed, more than once toasting a victory over a sumptuous meal where the glow of an evening fireplace reflected off happy faces. They each had their challenges, she knew. And the years, if passing too quickly, would bring to memory the moments of this gatherings.

Her legacy, she prayed, implied unity and harmony to be found in family. Even if for her it seemed elusive.

Once, she caught Trevor looking at her from far across the table, as if pleading for reconciliation. She looked away.

Of their rift, the family knew nothing.

Only once did Trevor excused himself from the Forum. He met quietly in a luncheon café with someone who spoke of the painting. The meeting lasted less than one hour, and as agent to a party of interest, he spoke discretely about his concerns. Trevor alone knew of whom he spoke. He represented the buyer.

He was informed that in London, nobody affiliated with the Auction had prior knowledge of the identity of the winning bidder of Art. It was the wish of the bidder to remain anonymous. Payment received came from independently transferred funds and into a bank account for its purchase. The money was certified by the appropriate authorities, its source verified as legitimate and without illegal ties.

Finally the Auction House was satisfied with the transaction and entitled to accepted the bidder's money.

The matter was closed under the rules of Trade. The transaction was concluded once the painting was restored.

After that exchange, the man blended into the assembly of suits that had come to Davos.

Trevor told no one.

Sandra and Amanda went shopping, buying clothes from a boutique for Sandra, and boots for Amanda to take back with her. Italian made, pretty, they said, ideal for her "long walks with Dad..."

Sandra smiled. The day before, she and Jack had talked about his conference in Zurich. He had detached from the group for two days to deliver his research work at a Conference on Nuclear Energy. Then he took a flight back to join them in Switzerland.

For Amanda and Trevor, the subject of deep space travel made for a lively conversation that evening over dinner.

"Last year.." Jack told them " NASA partnered with BWXT Nuclear Energy for an $18.8 million contract to design a reactor, and develop fuel, for use in a nuclear-thermal propulsion engine!" He paused, waiting for their questions."What? ...you don't believe me?" They stared at him.

"...powered by atomic energy?" asked Trevor.

"And why not?" Jack leaned forward over his salad. "You know how efficient that is, when properly managed. You were a submariner in the Royal Navy, yes?"

"Well...I...err"

"So, unlike conventional rockets that burn fuel to create thrust, the atomic system uses the reactor to heat a propellant like liquid hydrogen, which then expands through a nozzle to power the craft..."

Sandra looked at her husband with a grin of admiration.

Amanda asked "How does that help in a program of long duration flight?"

Sandra nudged at her mother, impressed with her question.

Jack's eyes lit up. With a fork in the air he explained "It *doubles* the efficiency at which the rocket uses fuel, allowing for a "drastically smaller" craft and shorter transit time. It's huge!" he munched. "Especially for very difficult missions that need a lot of propellant, such as a Mars flight"

"Umm" said Trevor, interested.

"See..." continued Jack, now putting down his food "While the system would provide a niche market in the global nuclear industry, it could be highly lucrative for the company that cracks the technology!.."

"Especially for nations like the U.S., where the atomic energy sector has been waylaid by environmental regulation and activism" said Trevor.

"Exactly! Space applications is a modest but extremely important area of technical development.."

The waiter came around and refilled their glasses with wine.

"But we have been running on nuclear energy in France for decades..." interjected Jacques, lifting his glass.

"Umm" said Trevor, also lifting his glass.

Jack was animated "Elon Musk, as you know, has vowed to get people to the red planet. *Space Exploration Technologies Corp.*, founded by Musk, is developing a liquid oxygen and methane fueled engine..."

"What about Jeff Bezos..." added Trevor, sipping. "Doesn't he have a company called *Blue Origin* testing an engine that uses liquid oxygen and liquefied natural gas...""

"He does!" said Jack "In NASA's human exploration plan for Mars, a policy developed in 2009 stated that nuclear thermal propulsion is the preferred option. The only other technologies being considered are solar-electric and chemical propulsion..."

In jest they all booed the notion of opposition and Sandra had to giggle at them all, a loyal family rooting for Jack.

Finally they settled down, and Jacques spoke "Nuclear propulsion may be the favored option for deep space travel, but the intricacies of the technology - the testing means only that development costs would be a major barrier...*n'est ce pas*?"

"Well yes. And no..." said Jack, leaning back. "Sure. Getting to Mars is no small task — it requires a 55 million-kilometer space flight, more than 100 times the distance from Earth to the Moon. NASA probably won't send humans to orbit the planet until at least the early 2030s."

"Is that your area of concern then Jack" asked Amanda

"It is. But more. We are dealing with a race for *new* energy sources. A way to monetize energy for a world population – even colonization, and its potential importance to survival, sustainability free of fossil fuels. It is the stuff of self determination and environmental management!"

"It is the key to world peace and good governance" added Trevor, raising his glass, and they paused to reflect on those words.

Then Jack looked at Trevor. "It's important work. Your company is developing something along those lines, is it not?"

Trevor looked down, hesitant. "It is" he said, taking a deep breath. Adding soberly "Jack is right. We do need new options. See..its the issue of the *decay* of nuclear fuel. It's toxic, but can be absorbed by poisons, as we call them. In a propulsion system, that's essential. Some of the fission products generated during nuclear reactions do have a high neutron absorption capacity... such as xenon-up to 3 million bars in reactor conditions."

Jack was nodding as Trevor explained "Because these two fissions produce "poisons" – that's the dissolvers – to *remove* neutrons from the reactor...they do affect the "thermal utilization" factor, and thus the reactivity."

"So… err…the poisons are good to slow down the reactivity?"

"Yes. The 'poisoning' of a reactor core by these fission products may become so serious, or slow it down so much, that the chain reaction can come to a standstill…"

"Not good for propulsion!" said Jacques.

"Time for coffee and dessert!" announced Sandra.

* * *

It was almost the end of their stay in Switzerland when Trevor and Amanda first had a moment to themselves. They'd been busy, cordial, but not close. She agreed to walk with him to the open air café and they ordered a night drink each.

They had not spoken much since their discussion on the beaches of Charleston. Amanda had been on a different itinerary from Trevor. She had flown to Zurich and stayed with Sandra for a few days before leaving for Davos.

Arriving in Davos at roughly the same time, Trevor's business kept him busy both in Switzerland and in London.

Certainly, the no mention was made of the painting, let alone the mistrust and hurt that had erupted between them in Charleston.

It was cold that night, starry and the resort town was well lit for tourists and guests.

Walking at night was not unusual as space-heaters accommodated customers with units and blowers at every corner in the busy little town after dark.

He was bundled up in his winter parka gear, and she in her black fur coat bought in Russia years ago, but they strolled without saying much.

The town twinkled with lights and sounds, a crisp wintery place located high in the Swiss Alps for venturesome visitors here for skiing. Or, for the business banking conference where Trevor was invited as a keynote speaker, a man representing banking integrity at its highest level of trust and veracity.

Periodically a distant crowd of laughter filtered through the night air, and as they passed by alcoves and bars that made the town square, a rousing cheer was added to their walk, crunching on pavements of ice crystals, but silent.

Suddenly Trevor stopped. He reached out and put his hand on Amanda's. She paused.

"I'm sorry" he said softly, warm breath lifting from his mouth. "I didn't mean to cause you any distress over this painting..." his voice trailed.

Amanda looked at him, her face pale in a corona of fur trim.

His eyes searching for words, what could he say next? Here he was, this celebrated banker representing the essence of integrity and honesty in the finance world of risk, disclosure and investment...a man who had said nothing to his wife about a painting they had that brought almost $200 million at Auction?

Where was the trust between them, her eyes seemed to say...

"My knowing...or recognizing the figure in the painting hardly seemed to matter...I honestly didn't think the painting was going anywhere at that Auction...Truly!"

Amanda looked around, then down at her leather gloves. "I'm not a prideful snob Trevor, it's not the money...It's that I felt so damned stupid standing there uninformed and unprepared..." she searched for words "without a clue about its true provenance. Especially when you could have told me more..."

"I'm sorry. Believe me, I didn't realize it would go that far..."

"I fell in love with the image. The tender soldier's face sheltering his children from war with a gift, their hair shiny, their hearts trusting...That's all I ever saw in that painting...That's what I thought a museum should exhibit..."

"I know. It's your heart. And that's what I love you for. Always have! Amanda. I'm truly sorry!"

"Come on" she gestured. They should get out of the cold. He followed.

They sipped their brandy, and slowly the thoughts of that day came back to them as understandable. They processed the sequence of events one incident at a time. But mainly they sat together, thinking it through with the benefit of hindsight.

Finally she turned to him and looked into those eyes of his, so full of concern, always trying to make the world right for everyone...

"You're right Trevor. I was perhaps...harsh!"

There. She said it, and somehow the words just hung there in the air. But Trevor squeezed her fingers.

"It's never easy, you know. I've seen this too many times in my business. Money changes things. It affects people...I know it does. You felt responsible for the provenance, especially when the bidding took off?"

Amanda nodded. She closed her eyes, thoughtful.

After a moment he added "What I want to know Amanda, is who is behind this. Has it occurred to you that there might be more at play than free market value, here?"

"How do you mean?"

"Maybe, someone was playing us..."

"Oh...that's a lot of play-money, for sure!" muttered Amanda.

Suddenly Trevor leaned over and planted a kiss on her lips. "Can you at least give me a chance to explain the story of the figure...?"

She narrowed her eyes. Trevor had been heroic, especially in his gestures to bring the family together for the week. At least he deserved a chance to explain himself.

"Yes" she said. "I would like to know."

"I promise!" he said. "Come on..." he added, looking up "It's getting late. Let's call it a night."

"Yeah" she sighed. "Tomorrow is our last day. Let's make the most of it."

Cold blue ice crystals glimmered in the moonlight of the resort town where they walked, her hand tucked inside his arm for warmth.

* * *

The last day went well. They'd all enjoyed themselves, buying a few gifts to take home, mementoes. But they were clearly preparing to return home.

Tray, Sandra, Amanda and Juliette had spent the day skiing, mostly. Jacques, Jack and Trevor had gone shooting skeet. Later, they watched an Archery contest - even spectated the second half of a soccer game on a clearing, they said.

At their last dinner together, they toasted to success, vowing to reunite here next year for an anniversary, and thanking Trevor for making this treat possible.

After that, the call of the band lured most of them to the dance floor, leaving Trevor and Amanda to sip coffee and nibble dessert at their end of the white damask table littered with crystal glass, silverware and long-stemmed roses.

Amanda watched Trevor and realized how heavily the events of the last few months had been on him. Why?

Because a painting that depicted a figure who resembled his grandfather's father came to life in a painting.

This figure, seemingly, had unleashed a force of revenge. It carried all the hallmarks of the past, the pain and the disasters of WWI, conflict from a world turned upside down.

Had Trevor become the target of that resentment? Or was she imaging things?

He looked tired. This man who had dedicated is life to her... who had achieved so much, and loved them with full devotion had been made to relive through something awful.

What?

Something had wedged itself between them...

What in the world was happening to them? Why had it becomes such a divisive issue? Then a thought crossed her mind. Unless... *by design?*

Surely not!

She squeezed his hand and, looking up, drew a deep breath, about to speak. Then from somewhere in the background she caught a glimpse of recognition...*Who?*

Trevor was looking at her.

She narrowed her eyes and saw nothing but a mob, people enjoying their last night of the Conference in the Alps. She returned Trevor's gaze. "Come on let's dance!"

He looked puzzled, then smiled gamely.

Of course!

They should dance and shake free of this topic, was the tease. It was their last night here...

Trevor led her to the dance floor, his hand down her back, and he smiled at her.

That's all she needed to see. The music carrying them slowly into a soft healing process. She tucked soft scented hair under his chin, and he nudged gently into her hair.

"Excuse me interrupting..." said a voice behind them.

It was Jack, still holding Sandra's hand.

Behind him was a man hidden from view, yet in full military-dress uniform.

"I have someone who wants to talk with you Amanda! He found me at the Conference hall this evening" he said, then stepped aside.

Admiral Arguetta came forward.

"Bill" they both exclaimed.

"What a wonderful surprise to see you here!" said Trevor.

Arguetta was grinning widely in greeting. Trevor led the way back to the table where they laughed and chatted. Trevor ordering a round of beers, and Jack pulled up a seat next to his father in law.

"Wow!" said Amanda, still excited from the surprise.

"How long have you been in Europe?" asked Trevor.

"Oh, just a couple weeks. I've been in Brussels recently and had to hope over to Naples. NATO keeps us busy in Washington! Thought I'd stop in Zurich for a couple, and had to make an appearance at the Conference on Nuclear Energy. I liked Jack's presentation, and of course we chatted...He told me you were here!"

"And how's Meredith doing?" asked Amanda, noticing a cloud cross Arguetta's face

"Here health is improving, we all are optimistic. Thank you!"

"Well. We spend a few days in Charleston, and honestly, we'd have rather been sailing on your boat off Annapolis!" laughed Trevor.

"Me too... Cheers!" said Arguetta. But by the time Jacques showed up at the table with introductions all round, it was clear that matters of the high seas was not good for Jacque's health. And they laughed.

The evening passed all too quickly, and Jack and Sandra said goodnight. His Conference on Nuclear Energy concluded and his paper delivered, he and Sandra were scheduled for an early flight in the morning.

Trevor and Amanda invited Bill Arguetta back to their cabin for a night drink where all phones were put in the fridge, and the radio switched on.

It was clear he wanted to talk with them quietly.

As it was, they drank coffee. Arguetta shared confidential information with them. Given that Amanda had in the past provided research services for his department as a subcontractor in Washington DC, he felt it was within his discretion to include her. But he did ask about her security clearance and asked her to upgrade her status.

Trevor, on the other hand, already had clearance. Trevor had served both as minister for his government on US soil, and even engaged in inter-government Joint military ventures, needing no special access at the present time.

More importantly, Trevor MacDonnell, if presently recused voluntarily, was the proprietor of an engineering firm in Washington holding a support contract for the US government.

Arguetta told them that this conversation was well within his authority to divulge, given its urgency. And he proceeded to disclosed the incident of the Frigate.

"As you know, nuclear energy is a growing and dynamic part of our strategic defense planning. We're in development for a number of breakthroughs...Its highly competitive. But we're not quite sure what to make of this event. It might be a ploy. They claim they're dead in the water waiting on nuclear decay on their reactor. It might be genuine. But it has its risks, and I'm afraid I'm not convinced that it isn't concealing some later act of sabotage...I'm uncertain as to how to read it..."

"Are their fission products active?" said Trevor, knowing full well the capabilities of the US assessment analytics.

"Oh yes. Very much so!"

"Rate of poisoning to their reactor core?"

"Slow..."

"What's the window of opportunity?"

Arguetta spun his wedding ring and looked away at the wall. Trevor answered for him.

"Not long enough to prevent a full chain reaction meltdown?" Adding "..and they're warning you of that possibility...?"

Arguetta looked at him. "Yes. And we're standing by...But the threat is so existential that we may have to plunge in and rescue with all the tech know-how that we have. Even if we have to sacrifice our ship and crew doing so.. "

"Hmm"

"The Chinese doubtless know."

"You think this is a man-made threat to get you to show your hand in rescue?"

"Yes"

"Hmm"

"Hell, I'm not even convinced if it's a home-grown screw-up, or something manipulated by a third party..."

Amanda looked at Trevor, recognizing something familiar in that sentiment.

Trevor spoke "I'll call my firm in Washington. We have some savvy R&D experts up there. They can drop what they're doing and give you all the support you need."

Arguetta nodded.

Trevor quickly grasped the gravity that any such incident at sea involving two super powers might have global impact.

"Also, I'll check in with my government's intelligence on fleet observations, see just who's aboard that ship..."We'll look closely at their political affiliations of personnel, technology, policy etc. I'll let you know if they find any anomalies."

"Thank you"

Amanda spoke. "And I'll keep my eyes open for any foreign national interest that might have a broader social scope. There are a lot of factions stressed by Open Immigration policies. It's put a strain on national resources. There are outbreaks of activism. Resistance movements...I'll take a look?"

"Thank you both. I may call you into Washington for a briefing if it comes to that. But I realize you're both retired, and don't deserve that kind of punishment... So, unless it's necessary, I'll just leave it at that for now and wait for your feedback..." said Arguetta. He drained off his coffee, and accepted a cognac.

"You know..."said Trevor "Jack may be the one to know more about this by the way. He's in the thick of their R&D here in Switzerland. He'd know of the players; the parties behind the technology, the funding sponsors, the financing interests etc. It's a hot industry with plenty of attention just now..."

"Oh! That's for sure. But I'd rather keep Jack sheltered, for now. The less he knows, the better. And his work is terrific, we know..." said Arguetta, if perhaps hiding a small frown.

"Thanks!" grinned Amanda, taking full credit for her daughter's choice of a spouse. "He's terrific!"

"Hey, you guys. You're the ones that are *terrific*! I'm so glad I caught you..." said Arguetta, standing to leave, then pausing "I don't have to remind you how dangerous this could be." He reached for his coat.

"Here. I'll call a cab to your hotel..." said Trevor, picking up his cell.

They said farewell. "Call us in Washington when you're in town my darling" said Arguetta giving Amanda a family hug.

Amanda knew her boss. That was his way of saying that he expected answers. And full answers. This was no casual encounter, she knew. Switzerland be damned. And he was hiding something, something to do with Jack...

He meant business.

Something was terribly wrong.

* * *

Under night skies, the Eurostar train snaked along the contours of the terrain flanked by forests or field, then down deep mountain valleys and into rock tunneling carved out by man. Day or night, it negotiated steep Alpine curves and meandered German Black Forest hillsides, emerging only for brief claims to open air before submitting to thick landscapes and rugged timberland.

Inside the train, passengers travelled in seamless luxury.

For Trevor and Amanda, it was a sensational trip. The service, as they later told it, was a journey of excitement and adventure. Not that this surprised anyone who knew them. Enjoying trips was the trait that branded them as a couple of explorers. More than that, it encouraged their friends and family.

Still, it was Trevor's many interests and professional liaisons that placed him in demand wherever he went, especially when they travelled by rail. With no lack of meetings and appointments, he was tracked by colleagues. On this voyage, the Eurotrain would stop at Cologne, then Brussels, before travelling to London, UK.

Amanda learned to adjust.

This trip however, held a somber tone. With black hills racing past them, and the distance shortening to their destination, they had talked, if relaxed.

Between coffee breaks and meals, they spent the time in review. And it soon became clear to Amanda that it was therapeutic for Trevor to talk about his family.

Long interlinked with royals and leaders of his country, his family had legacy ties that had placed them in the forefront of Britain's modern history. The Industrial revolution. Wars. Depression.

Nor had their history of tradition and affiliation been easy. Sometimes not even honorable. Many of his family had been thrust in the vanguard of social upheavals and turmoil, leaving them damaged or blemished.

Price of loyalty, as he always said. Generational loyalty.

Yes, thought Amanda, Trevor talking about the past was helping him wipe away some scars long ago inflicted.

"It was a bad time in history..." continued Trevor to sharpen the account that was in the ledgers of ministerial reports. The world was teetering between an agrarian subsistence economy and an industrial revolution. Domestic unrest pushed Europe into chaos and disruption, usually at the cost of many lives and treasure. But who was to know the real danger that would come?"

"Russia was in need of reform. How well had the Imperial families handled the problem?" Trevor looked out the window but saw little as darkness all but obscured the mountains they contoured.

His mind was many, many worlds away. "It ran well behind Europe in development, by end of century, it still failed to manage the problem of equality and aggrieved populations. That left socialism and peasant revolts..."

"My grandfather, Equerry to the British Royal family on the occasion of the Tzar Alexander's funeral, was asked to inform on the Russians. There had been trade competition in Europe amongst the empires. Ship building. Precious metals. Oil discoveries. Mining. Manufacture. Railways, cars, electricity and their sources of treasure." He paused, then added "People bought stock in new inventions and worthy causes. Women bought mass produced products. Men earned a living wage..."

"Just as the industrial revolution had modernized Europe and generated larger domestic consumer economies in the 1880s, it was now the dawn of the 20th century"

Amanda sat across from him, listening.

"Not peasants and serfs, but individuals engaged in commerce and communications..." his voice trailed.

"Add a bitter cold and difficult winter of war, and disaffection by those left behind sowed threats to authority, overthrows and spreading anarchy...."

"Go on" said Amanda.

"Little did they know that they were about to plunge Europe into darkness ... and America with it!" Trevor gazed out the window. "It...err. It was about this time... that...that the events in the Russian royal family would fall apart and leave a vacuum in authority ...to be overtaken by the spread of communism and socialist revolutions."

"You see, there was something very off about the new young Tzar of Russia, Nicholas II. Following the death of his father he married Alexandra and ignored the council of his mother, the former Empress. And although the royals of Europe were related by marriage, especially with ties to Queen Victoria of England, they was division between them, often along the lines of national interest and sovereign borders..."

Previously, in Russia, there had been incidents. "When Tzar Alexander III and his Empress Maria reigned, opposition had gone underground. However, when students aspired to assassinate him six years later by hiding dynamite in their books, the Russian secret police uncovered a real plot. Five of the students were hanged. One was the older brother of a man called Vladimir Lenin..."

"Really?"

"As the potential for opportunity for Russia became clear, Lennin seized the emerging power by force. The great Russian revolution would overturn monarchies in Europe and sweep across the world as Communism."

In the royal family of Russia, the Grand Duchess Maria Federovna's – as she was known after her husband was assassinated, was the mother of Nicholas II, heir to the

Russian throne. He married an English princess, Alexandra, granddaughter of Queen Victoria. Later, as the Russian Revolution raged, Nicholas II and his English princess and children were murdered at Ektrograd in 1918, ending all dynasties of the Russian Tzars."

The train thundered through a dark tunnel then emerged briefly to an open night sky before re-entering another rock-walled tunnel carved through a mountain. The lights flickered slightly, but they remained on.

"And err..." continued Trevor "my great grandfather, and the English royals, were concerned when he discovered that within the Russian Royal family there was division about the way the new young Tzar Nicholas managed his government in those critical years before WWI."

"Britain was vulnerable...?"

"Very much so. My grandfather was sent over. He became the confidant of the Tzar's brother and his wife, the Grand Duke and Grand Duchess.

The Grand duke was a self-styled artist, and insisted on painting a portrait of my grandfather...

"But his reported information was untenable. Especially about the Tzar's family affairs. The Tzar's wife, the English Princess who was neice to the Queen of England, was now an Empress of Russia and still without a male heir...

Oh sure, she had daughters. But what Europe needed as it was plunging towards war, was strong leadership full of hope and progress with a future for reform and enduring government."

"thank God for strong women!" interjected Amanda.

"Yes!" Trevor smiled back. "But that was an era of male patronage. Today, it would be like a company without a CEO!"

Amanda chuckled.

"Finally…" continued Trevor "the Russian Empress did produce a male heir. He was a hemophiliac who absorbed all attention by the royal family and distracted them from their duties.

"Nicholas was weak. *She* was obsessed with her son and relied on help from an itinerant monk called Rasputin whose influence threatened the stability of the throne.

A clandestine *coup d'etat* was plotted by the Tzar's brother, the Grand duke.

"But he did not succeed, right?" said Amanda, knowing her history.

"Well. Yes and No. It's hard to say. They were overtaken by events, really." Trevor's gaze fell on a passing landscape too dark to delineate, but his mind fertile with fragmented accounts and information.

"The communists toppled the monarchy after Nicholas abdicated, and they executed the royal family. But something occurred, if unverified, that was possibly the reason for their final demise, and for the revolution that followed."

The train rocked gently, and the minutes passed in quietness and reflection.

"Revolution came to Russia in 1917, first with the February Revolution; later with the forced abdication of Nicholas II on March 15th …"

"Who were the English Royals at this point?"

"Queen Victoria had died in 1901. So now it was her son the King as George VI, and his wife Alexandra - sister of the widowed Empress Dowager of Russia, mother of Nicholas II."

"Did they have any influence?"

"They did. My grandfather was sent over for a rescue mission, for one thing. That's when the painting was made, I believe. But during that decade, a deep rivalry had developed between the Tzar and his brother the Grand Duke and his wife the Grand Duchess."

"Did they survive the revolution?"

"They did"

"What of their *coup d'etat* efforts?"

"It's hard to say. The matter is moot. Once WWI took root and Russia became an Ally to Britain, France and United States against Germany, the fate of the royals was rendered of less consequence..."

"Did you know of the painting, previously?"

"No. I did not" said Trevor. "Well, it may have once been catalogued in the family collection in Scotland years and years ago. Like memorabilia. But nobody knew. And I certainly didn't recognize it when you brought it home!"

"So. What are you saying?"

"I'm wondering, myself! In the first place, how did it get out of that dusty collection, even if it preserved? And secondly, why now? What is its relevance *today*?"

"Well. On the first question. That was me. Your mother pointed it out to me before she died. She said it meant a lot to your grandfather and that I should take care of it. It would mean a lot to you, she told me. So I did. It's been in the safekeeping our storage facility for a long time. By the time I asked you about it...for an gift to the museum that is, you approved!"

"Right"

"But as for the rest...I have no idea of its meaning and significance" said Amanda.

"You mean, for its value and interest at Auction?" said Trevor.

"Yes."

The train hummed as it bore through a mountain tunnel. They sat in silence, each in thought.

Finally Amanda spoke.

"You know. Jacques did allude to something when we spoke to him..."

"Hmm?"

"He implied that there might be a message behind this Auction, considering the vandalism?"

"I can't imagine what it could be...there's so much to extrapolate from any kind of a message, don't you think?"

Amanda shrugged. "Well, one thing is certain. It is redolent with memories of a turbulent era, socialism and revolution..."

"What are you saying? That it signals the hand of socialism and activism?"

"I have no idea..." said Amanda. "But it clearly means a lot to someone with money. That's for sure!"

"Umm"

"I do remember *one* thing though" said Trevor. "It was something my grandfather told me as a boy. He said he had taken a great train ride. A memorable voyage, as he told me. I did not know the facts behind the event. But my mother told me about it fter I returned from University."

"Do you suppose that was when your grandfather travelled to Russia as a spy for the British?"

"I'm certain of it" nodded Trevor. "It was in the summer of 1914. The Tzar's mother, the Empress Maria Feodorovna was in London when WWI broke out. She was visiting her sister Queen Alexandra, wife of King George. The news of the war reached them. Europe was in foment."

Amanda watched him. He looked up briefly, unclear. "The great empires of Europe were threatened by angry anarchists. Monarchs of Europe were toppled after centuries of sovereign rule and societal stability. Governments fell. The Church were losing influence over restive communities. God lived no more! It was terrifying, the prospect or war and blight and starvation in cold regions. How would it all end, they must have wondered..."said Trevor, his voice trailing.

"It was then decided in London that the Empress Maria would actually travel back to Russia with the idea of sending back intelligence about the disposition of the Russian empire. The man to accompany her was my grandfather..." Trevor said. "What happened would reshape the world" he whispered. He had to take a long train ride in Russia before reaching the sea at the Crimea."

* * *

Philadelphia, Pennsylvania

The Court for the United States Attorney's Office for the Eastern District of Pennsylvania was one of the nation's largest districts. Covering 4,700 square miles and a population of 5 million people residing within its jurisdiction, the courts heard matters from the largest metropolitan city to farm valleys and mountain towns. Within its District Court presided 37 sitting judges, 5 bankruptcy court judges, 11 magistrate judges, a Court of Appeals and a Third Circuit Court holding 19 judges and commissioners for commercial and financial oversight over industry sectors.

Coal mining in Pennsylvania was one of the oldest, having fueled the industrial revolution of America. Today it was at the center of new energy production technology.

The attorneys presenting their case for insurance claims, having just satisfied all compliance issues, now turned to the matter of the incendiary – a word which had to be defined at the outset.

Incendiary was the technical term. Or, as the Fire Chief Marshal Mr. Hatch explained.

 "A fire that is deliberately ignited under circumstances in which the person knows that the fire should not be ignited."

The Commissioner had her recording secretary take careful notes. The Hearing was not without its challenges:

Was it a criminal act, she wanted to know. Or how did it constitute a claim?

"As defined by the National Wildfire Coordinating Group, an incendiary fire doesn't necessarily meet the definition of arson."

The Commissioner asked if that was even relevant since multiple fire investigators said that was not typically how the term was used...

"Incendiary suggests somebody set the fire with the intention of watching it burn or causing economic damage. There's an intention there" said Mr. Harm, an expert on fire forensics as a metallurgical and materials engineer familiar with law enforcement on wildland fire investigations.

"If they've categorized the fire as incendiary it means they've got a suspect or suspects and motivation, and generally some evidence at the scene that somebody did something intentionally to start the fire as opposed to being careless..."

"Gentlemen" interrupted the Commissioner consulting her watch. "I've heard enough! This fire was no accident. And it's time for a lunch break!" She peered at them over her red-spotted spectacles, styled to match her red ruby colored high heeled shoes. She paused.

If anyone wondered about her flamboyance they were quickly disabused. "It's now become a homicide potentially. Regardless. Especially if it was set deliberately. We'll consult the Oregon law when we come back. Does arson that causes a fatality qualify a felony murder charge? So, we are adjourned. See you all at three."

It was a welcome break for everybody in the courtroom.

The legal factors qualifying an "Incendiary" were endless: Was the "Origin area" clearly defined and searched? Was there no reasonable 'accidental' ignition source found after a thorough search? Was there a lack of accidental ignition sources, or a history of known and documented incendiary fires in the area? What of geospatial clustering of incendiary fires? Was there a modified fuel bed? Or ignitable liquids present..?

Was the roadside area with low detection risk, or access? What about Fire Suppression Equipment - committed or disabled...? Any witness statements.

Finally, the procession of witness testimony was in earnest.

Australia uses satellite imagery to investigate crime scenes, the Chief Fire Marshall was told. This however, was an altogether different ball game. Finding the perpetrator of an incendiary was a long shot on a mine within acres - if not miles of terrain was close to impossible. Even if to investigate for clues.

The Chief Fire Marshall looked at the Forensic pictures once again.

"This is not Australia" said the cross examining Prosecutor. "Illegal logging is one thing. Setting a mountain afire is another" he said, his voice dry and angry.

"Yes Sir. But technology advances are now enabling far more accurate and reliable imagery that could revolutionize 21st-century policing. It could transform law-enforcement through highly detailed surveillance."

"Is this admissible as evidence in a court of law?" asked the prosecutor to the Bench.

"It is" said the judge facetiously. "But only if there is cause to resort to such innovative technology. It's expensive, having an eye in the sky. So you'd better impress the court with your stuff, and show that there was every effort made by truer means?"

An expert technician was sworn in, and the prosecutor posed his question again.

"How much truer will we be when we monitor this thing two years from now...?" His implication that policy could change was not lost on the judge.

"Most pixel resolution used to show only one meter at best, with most sensors in the two to five-meter range" said the technician. "But we have Earth observation specialists at Satellite Observatories that supply technology to solve crime. Now we have 30cm resolution, which dramatically changes the potential for detecting things, or monitoring a site of interest."

"My God!" said the Chief from his seat in the court room, his face set in a distasteful expression - less from the frustration of solving a crime than from the prospect of satellites spying on human activity on earth. Twenty minutes later, he was called up as witness and asked the same question.

"Since 9-11, the reality is that the United States is vulnerable to attacks from within its borders."

"So, can imagery that collects evidence and increases police surveillance power become a new technology embraced by law enforcement? That is, thermal imagers, night vision, GPS tracking devices and other tools?"

"Absolutely!"

"I rest..."

Kevin McConough was an avid environmentalist. He sat across from the two corporate representatives of the coal company that filed the claim.

Here was opportunity.

He was a short man with dark tangled hair, and he had intended to make a scene in the court room that would play well to social media...

On one occasion the judge read his mind. "Approach!" she bellowed, her hair coiffed and pinned stylishly.

"Gentlemen, while I am filled with wonder at innovation, we should also not be deluded by its potential as a tool, a tool also used by competitors and dangerous adversaries..."

"Yes Ma'am. Err... Your Honor!" said the senior advocate for the defense. "A growing commercial spy satellite industry today profits widely from selling slightly less detailed imagery to markets in both the public and private sectors.."

"I'm aware of that Mr. Bellows" answered the judge. "...Even as government develops its own next-generation of spy satellites. But we now have a new Space Command added to the Armed Services of the United States for our defense."

Both advocates knew better than to argue.

The judge turned to McConough and looked him directly in the eye. "Domestically, activists crying *Infringements* serve no national interest! What is before me is the importance of preserving that delicate balance of trust between a government and its people: It is the right of the sovereign authority to weigh national interests against those limits on government-surveillance powers – as the mandate dictates by the Supreme Court's Fourth Amendment jurisprudence. Do you get this Mr. McConough?"

"Yes Ma'am."

The judge cleared her throat, her disclaimer fully discharged. Then she added "Look, any democratic government must take risks. It has to balance the will of the people by election, and the responsibility to discharge its duties for safety and civil order..."

The judge turned to both attorneys, the proceedings still in abeyance. "This is a court room for justice, not a platform for politics against fossil fuel energy, understand? Gone are the by-gone eras of anti-charter sentiment by Pennsylvania locals set against the mining of coal and other minerals in these parts. I am a conservationist myself. I don't know where your Law Firm resides, but this is Pennsylvania. Coal has been our heritage and our economy beginning with the earliest mention made in 1698 when Gabriel Thomas wrote an account of it dedicated to William Penn, followed by George Washington himself who led an expedition across the Allegheny Mountains in 1754 where coal was cited as being in abundance. Neither do I have to remind you of coal being used in the war of 1812; the building of American canal systems including our own Lehigh canal, Schuylkill or the Delaware and Hudson canal, nor the Railway, Iron or ship-building and industries let alone the energy production for electric power...Yes?"

"Yes, Your Honor!" smiled McConough, acknowledging the array of corporate suits behind him "But if I may... I'd like to point out how it is that this shaft ran so deep into the ground. That is, if you find it relevant to the case?"

The Judge got the hint. "Carry on!"

"Coal is not only your heritage, but it is indeed your treasure!" said McConough now pacing before the Jury in his statement.

The judge rolled her eyes, but added nothing.

The proceedings carried on for two days before the full impact of the fire was entirely understood. Cross examinations, exemptions, objections and evidence was adding up.

"You point, Mr. McConough? You stray..." interrupted the judge.

"If I may remind you, it was the railroad companies who dominated the industry as they bought coalfields to control both production markets, shipping markets and other monopolies..."

"Objection!"

"Careful!"...added the judge in her ruby red lipstick.

The chief prosecuting attorney rose from his chair. "The defense seems to be making a case against the coal industry itself rather than the event of one perpetrator.."

"Sustained!"

"I digress..." conceded McConough. "Still, with such financial capital they were able to create deeper and deeper mining shafts to reach new levels of coal, were they not?"

"Objection! Is the defense suggesting that the perpetrator *chose* this shaft for his explosion on purpose?"

"Your point?" asked the judge.

"Let me put it this way...By the end of the 19th century the Pennsylvania anthracite industry was controlled by a handful of industrial railroad corporations. Would it not be possible to say that this act was not one of vandalism, industrial sabotage or arson even, but an act of non-aggressive *protest*...?"

"against *what*?" asked an exasperated judge as the room erupted with guffaws.

The defense rose to answer the argument.

"The mine is operational, but neither used for making crude iron any longer, nor even for generating steam power. It's just another source of fossil fuel...hauled off in heavy trucks and lumbering rail cars to export overseas, I'm told."

"Capitalism!" said McConough.

"How about energy terrorism?" called out one of the corporate legal aids.

"Order!"

"It's an Act of Protest..." insisted McCullough, happy to deliver his coup de grace. "And it deserves the protection of our constitutional provision for free speech..."

The room erupted with laughter.

Give me a break ...

McConough turned about and smiled for the cameras and iphones.

At the table of corporate councilors, only one man was not chuckling at the drama of events unfolding. As the case adjourned he got up and smiled deferentially to his colleagues, then carrying his briefcase he walked out of the building.

Karen MuCullock caught up with him outside o the main granite steps.

"What's up Bill?" she asked.

He paused. "Call Jeff Ballentine at BP will you?"

"Border Protection?" echoed Karen

"Yeah. They know people up at DHS... I don't like this case. Its theater. What worries me is that it's a targeted act against a critical-list industry. Have him call the Anti-Terrorism Units at Homeland for possible alerts against other energy industries sources like Dams, or God help us, a nuclear power plant...Something like that?"

"You think...?"

"Let's just say I'm wondering. I have no idea... But I'm getting concerned. We should say something. Better to alert the authorities than say nothing..."

"Memo as an observation by a responsible party in a fiduciary position, like that..?"

"Exactly."

"Sure. Consider it done!"

"Oh, and Karen...err. Be discrete! Everything is an open mike these days!"

"Got it!" said Karen.

* * *

Admiral Arguetta led a team of men out of the Viewing room and proceeded down the hallway.

On the upper levels of the Pentagon, few offices were fully occupied by staff. Some doors were open, most were closed. Judging from the titled Commands posted at the overhead of each entrance, it was clear that many of the leadership and their staff were deployed or engaged in directorate oversight of operations.

One door was wide open. Arguetta's quarters.

Three young navy commanders materialized as they turned the corner. They approached Arguetta and his team with the severity of authority on their shoulders.

They acknowledged Arguetta, one of them recognizing a buddy walking behind him. He said nothing.

They entered his office, all of them.

At this level of the Pentagon building, only matters of classified or grave sensitivity prevailed.

Such was the task of the military on these floors, to defend the nation from severe and dangerous threats. Today was such a day.

Normally, personnel of these hallways include cyber-threat specialists, strategic weaponry technicians or scientific experts -privy to matters far from the public eye. And then only as analysts, problem solvers, systems developers or software technicians able to describe the phenomenon of situations for strategic decisions. The leadership had to be informed by intelligent experts to make strategic decision and appropriate responses.

Arguetta knew the signs of shock. He began by closing the door to his office and encouraging the team to have coffee and take a seat. There was little discussion. Today, he needed thinkers.

The house lights dimmed and he played the video feed on his wall plasma screen. Then he switched on the lights again.

"So, gentlemen..."

The video film they had just witnessed was a fearsome thing to behold. Trained as they were, and sufficiently informed to understand what just happened, actually witnessing such an phenomenon shook them to their core.

"The work ahead was clear. We all know what to do. We must analyze what just happened and explain it..." He paused, knowing that they needed to absorb the issue.

It was his job to put together a working team. That was their reason for being up here.. Still, as inured to theory as they all were trained to be, they couldn't believe what they just saw.

Two stood up and refilled their cups of coffee, mainly to open discussion. But it was slow moving. They talked, asked questions. But they were puzzled.

Arguetta showed them the footage again and allowed them to download it to their secure laptop screens.

They footage they watched was recorded from their own Frigate with orders to Stand-by and observe the foreign nuclear-powered vessel. Perhaps to render assistance, if needed. Or perhaps to engage in other ways, the Frigate was under orders to observe and to hold their distance. It was a clear assignment.

Posted on both radar and satellite tracking, the Skipper had the vessel under continuous observation and video feeds: Topside two-man posts had Watch duty, and one in communications. Below decks, one officer was posted at observations on a tracking station, another at appointed electronic data feeds with continuous surveillance updates as uplinks. That, plus electronic cameras recording from two points of the deck. This was real time, and live feed.

It began very gradually as a sea state. The sea churned around the ship with agitation, as if summoned by some extraordinary force to induce conflicted direction, neither settling with a following sea motion, nor mounting for wave build-up. Just a sea state of increased fluid motion that collided and created surf at every angle with increasing intensity.

The foreign owned grey hull remained unchanged, as it had for two days. Then it started to pitch and roll in the agitated sea now reaching storm-like conditions.

As the US Frigate began to feel the fall out of the heaving seas, the Captain was called on deck.

The rest of the surface remained relatively calm. No wind velocity. Not barometer pressure change. No temperature change. Only a rise and fall emanating from the ship under observation as it appeared to be pounded by weather.

Then one by one the lights of the foreign vessel went dark. Neither was there any attempt to signal for help, nor further communications with the US Frigate.

The Captain on deck recognized danger and immediately sounded the alert to ships crew to Quarters. He called for full engines and barked at his commander to signal Code Red and alert Navsec. This was a possible electromagnetic pulse, and he attempted to gain for distance...

The video footage continued to transmit for several minutes longer.

The foreign vessel took a thunderbolt pulse that exploded the ship and sent up a mushroom cloud, its shock wave hitting the cameras on deck the US Frigate with such force as to jump and waver into a drizzle, damaging the digital signal still transmitting...

The US Frigate, now dark, remained without further transmission.

The evidence was compelling.

Absent all trace of presence from satellite tracking at precisely that timing, the same pulse, it was presumed, hit their own ship and vaporized it.

They stared, all thinking along the same lines.

The assault they had just witnessed was induced by what weapon? What electronic armament was at hand? Where...

Only one comment was uttered by the team watching the video feed. It came from the youngest, a new graduate from Eastern University with a degree in fluid dynamics. "What caused the sea to agitate like that?" he blurted, his words lost to a silent room.

* * *

The next day was not much easier. Now at the Navy Yard on Capitol Hill, they were preparing to brief Homeland, NASA, Langley and NSA with first possible thoughts and explanations. They were seated at a conference table in an electronic situation room.

"Still, I can't believe that such a weapon would be deployed, let alone that it should even exist" nodded Lt Cdr Harry Boling, his head tilted.

Cdr Benning beside him nudged his elbow.

Shut up!

"Right then..." continue Arguetta at the plasma screen.

"So what we need to find out is, what is the composition of this pulse, or beam technology? That is, if we are reading it correctly. Where did it come from? What source generated it?" He looked at them, waiting for questions.

"*Who* deployed it, and, if we're still asking, *why?*..." he added, looking at the two men representing the NSA counter espionage team.

They said nothing.

Arguetta managed, for the most part, to contain his anger, let alone his surprise at what just happened to a US navy vessel.

That he must report to his superior officers was what he had to do at 9.30 in the morning. And with good intelligence.

But the white anger that surged within him masked a thousand doubts. It happened on his watch! He had advised the Captain.

Regardless, it was his job to supply answers. Above all, the intelligence was to remain contained.

This could not be leaked. They all knew this. The Pentagon knew this. Navy and Air technology R&D knew this. Weapons strategic development knew this.

Why?

Precisely because the perpetrator was to be denied recognition.

On the matter of technology R&D, their own development was the latest. Or so they thought. Until now.

Silence would frustrate the enemy no end! The world would not know because the media would not know...

For Arguetta, one of the hardest elements to his job was to look evil in the eye and not flinch. That was the discipline. That was the command of the strategic counter intelligence at Weapons Development codes.

Further, any political fall-out would be bad enough, let alone the analysis that would need to be substantiated.

For the moment, a Press Office had released information that the ship had experienced malfunctioning in heavy seas. Mostly, they would be ignored, he knew.

But Fake Media existed, chiefly to supply revenue for their financial investors targeting American consumer markets, and most of them global. But neither was it helpful by liberal administrations to stir up controversy for political propaganda.

"Let's take a break!" said Arguetta, finally.

For the moment, Arguetta was looking at was a series of god-awful images created by dysfunctional digital feeds. His face hardened, his eyes bulging and his brow moist.

They waited.

"We're dealing with the...*Not* knowing what this is...." he said, adding "Somehow, it managed to agitate the sea state. Then vaporize two military nuclear-powered vessels of the Line from two different navies! My God..."

The room remained silent.

Bill looked about, hoping for some engineering support from his analysts, at the very least.

None came.

"Any questions?" he said irritably "Then you have work to do! Same time. Same place. Tomorrow gentlemen!" he finished.

He left the building, knowing they would work all night and come up with some answers by morning. He should get some sleep. It had been a long two days. He could stall not much longer for the senior leadership. There had to be answers!

***

Trevor had never read it.

Somewhere in the archives of the King's reports was a dossier full of details, pictures, notes, postcards, addresses and names. It comprised of a complete account of what happened on that momentous time of upheaval as the war began to unfold in Europe. It would remain a private collection of papers. Certainly, history would tell the story of the war.

It was his grandmother told him, years ago, of the events that happened. Some of it in letters handwritten by her father, an Equerry pro tempore.

The train came to an abrupt halt. Seated in her cabin suite with her attendants was the Empress Dowager Marie Feodorovna, mother of the Russian Tzar of Russia.

She asked anxiously why the train had stopped in Berlin. They needed to reach the Russian border...

An hour passed. Then another and still the train did not move...

Maria Feordorovna was returning from London where she had been visiting her sister Alexandra, wife of King George V of England. It was July 1914, and news had just been delivered that World War I broke out.

Maria wanted to return to her home immediately. She knew it was dangerous. Russia was implicated in this war. Her son was the Tzar...

The Royals in London insisted that she be accompanied by one of their own, Sir Roger Alexander "Sandy" McDonnell, the King's Equerry. He was to escort the Russian Empress

Dowager back to Russia, then to report on any intelligence that he could dispatch back to London.

The station master returned with a message. The German authorities refused to let the train proceed to Russia.

Maria was furious. It seemed that the Germans were delaying her mission to get back immediately in July...

Another route had to be found...

She and her retinue must travel to a neutral country Denmark, then Finland. Finally she would proceed into Russia. But by the time she and her Escort arrived in Russia, it was August.

"I'm so sorry Sandy" she said "I am truly sorry to put you through this. I shall take up residency at Yelagin Papace, because it is closer to St. Petersburg – Oh! Excuse me... it's called *Petrograd* now...But we'll be safe there. I can be close to Nicky and the children until this infernal war ends!"

"Yes Your Highness" said Sandy. "I shall explain it to his Majesty upon my return to England Ma'am!"

There was much that troubled Maria. Although a docile and popular Empress when her husband ruled Russia as the Tzar, she was now to engage in the politics of her son's reign. She was, after all, the Dowager Empress, a member of his royal household. But these were difficult times.

For one thing, the Tzar picked ruinous political advisors. Maria had to intervene several times as he faced political unrest; peasant revolts and rabid revolutionaries since he succeeded his father.

Demonstrators, clamoring for bread, had taken to the streets of Petrograd. Supported by huge crowds of striking industrial workers, the protesters clashed with police. And now Russian radical elements were calling for an overthrow of the monarchy. Specifically, her son Nicholas II and his English Empress, Alexandra.

Until recently, there was only one alternative contender for the throne. Grand Duke Vladimir, a cousin, was largely viewed as the next successor to the monarchy - if not the free sovereign state of Russia.

As the Czar's cousin, Grand Duke Vladimir and his wife were descendants in line to the throne from Frederick William III of Prussia, and Vladimir's palace was lively. And they had several children.

The Grand Duke Vladimir and his wife were both witty and ambitious. They enjoy entertaining at their residence in St. Petersburg. It became the heart of the Imperial capital social life. Lavish, new, aspiring...

Sandy MacDonnell had visited before in the company of the royals, and he and Vladimir had enjoyed many escapades together. Unfortunately, the Grand Duke had died.

Thus, after years of new construction using artisans and architects, the Vladimir palace stood like the Winter Palace of the Czar, as a Marble Palace on the Neva at Dvorstsovaya Embankment. And it was well known that the Grand Duke Vladimir decorated his apartments with his collection of Russian painting by the best artists of his times Ilya Repin, Ivan Aivazovsky, Feodor Bruni, Vasili Vereshchagin, Ivan Kramskoy, Mikhail Vrubel, Nikolai Sverchkov and Rudoplh Frenz.

He at times declared himself to be a self-styled painter...

Presently, it was only Maria Feodorovna arriving to offer assistance.

Her fingers covered in lace, rings and fur-trimmed leather gloves drummed irritably.

Of course she knew why this happened...

He was weak, she decided. Her son.

For another thing, his wife was obsessed with a peasant monk called Grigori Rasputin leveraging his influence over her as she coped with her boy, a hemophiliac.

The train could not travel fast enough.

Maria turned to her Escort. "I fear that the matter provokes the public and endangers the safety of the imperial throne and the survival of the monarchy!"

"These are difficult times My Lady" said Sandy in full Scottish brogue. As chief of the Highland Royal Guards, he had been sent to assist her. Sandy was no fool, he knew of the growing disaffection with monarchical rule, and it was spreading across Europe. Things did not look good. It was a very precarious time, and he was keenly aware of every shadow and doubt that followed them. But he was to remain calm.

After the bloodshed of 1905, Maria's son Czar Nicholas II promised the formation of a series of representative assemblies, the Dumas, to work toward Reform. That was the plan.

Instead, Russia entered into World War I in support of the Serbs and their French/Anglo allies.

Their involvement in the war, they all feared, might prove disastrous for the Russian Empire. Militarily, imperial Russia was no match for industrialized Germany. Russian casualties would be great. Already, food and fuel shortages plagued Russia, the Bolshevik revolution had disrupted markets, inflation was rampant.

More importantly, Sandy understood why Maria was rushing to Petrograd. Her son Czar Nicholas II wanted to take command of the Russian Army front - the worst possible position to take!

It spread little risk management across the political landscape. Strategically it was a blunder. For the Czar to lead an Army was a gross tactical miscalculation.

Clearly, the British advised against it.

That's what Maria was sent back to do. That, and to save the monarchy!

Before leaving, King George V of England took his Equerry aside and spoke in confidence: The situation was critical. He and Nicholas II were cousins. But England could not afford war...

Sandy was to advise the Empress Dowager, sister to the Queen of England that she should not be rash or divisive. Above all, she should avoid conflict.

And if she was in need of extraction, then she should flee to the Crimea over the Black Sea and back to London. The warship *HMS Marlborough* would be there to retrieve her and take her to the British base in Malta.

Sandy understood his mission and watched with horror as the situation worsened.

To begin with, the journey had been delayed, especially with the detour. It was now August and they just reached Petrograd.

War had already broken out in July.

Sandy was worried. He discovered that not only were the lines of war solidifying across Europe and revolution overthrowing monarchies, but the Russian royal family itself, under misguided advisors, had indeed been plunged into disarray.

Within the royal palace household, Sandy knew, spies and revolutionaries lurked every where. The leadership of Russia as an imperial monarchy was dissipating and Britain was in this war as an ally to Russia.

The crisis deepened. Tcar Nicholas II and his stubborn wife Empress Alix refused to take council, including advice from his mother the Empress Dowager Maria Feodorovna.

Instead, she was banished from the capital for running interference, and so she left Petrograd and moved into the Mariyinsky Palace in Kiev.

Rumors circulated that a *coup d'etat* was imminent, including one planned by Maria herself to replace her son.

Still, as World War I unfolded, Maria Feodorovna turned to her role as president of the Red Cross, offering her train for medical support and transportation. And she was refusing to leave Russia.

But by the winter of 1916, the royal family were in fear of their lives. The February Revolution of 1917 was followed, on March 15, by the abdication of the Tzar.

Only once did Maria leave Kiev to meet with her deposed son.

After that, he and his family were taken prisoner and executed.

* * *

Chapter 3

Victor had been in a prison for 30 years. When he was released, his family had become so accustomed to visiting him in jail that they found it hard to adjust having him at home. He was a stranger.

A judge had shortened his sentence and Victor was now operating in a different field -- not with prison mates as his cohorts, but with family and friends as colleagues and partners, all of whom had become agents for his business in drug trafficking. And it was big business.

Croatia had changed. Situated along the cusp of a Mediterranean sea where young tourists and sports fans took to the streets and highways of progressive Europe, it was a new world.

News travelled fast.

For Victor, all messaging was divided into two camps of people. The *have's* and the *have-nots*. Or, as politicians put it, the wealth of Europe under assault by socialists needing to redistribute wealth for their global agendas. And it was succeeding. Chiefly by environmental regulation; open immigration social budgets, and taxation by the leadership, nothing could have pleased him more. The world was now ready for Victor. The life of the individualist was over.

Victor had George now, his nephew aged 27; and Alicia his sister's daughter, aged 22. Both had lives and mostly, it was a vigorous market for their product. They came and went to their homes, not far from his villa, just up the coast.

Plus, there was his wife's brother, Leo and his family.

Leo's wife Lucinda was attractive at age 45, all her ladies and cohorts with whom she engaged in an upwardly mobile social society were affluent and well connected and enjoyed a steady supply of high grade product for their sophisticated parties, gatherings and events. In this world, drugs were served as party favors.

He liked them.

With Leo her husband in the Construction business, Lucinda was highly recognized. Leo had Polish workers, and his accomplishments had earned him a certain respectability in the community whereby local government officials frequently awarded his company with government works and projects. His cement factory had supplied seven housing projects, and his sand and gravel business had surfaced for two interstate highways.

Victor's phone was rarely silent. One caller he never ignored. This caller lived in the United States. And he worked for the Federal Government.

Victor was spotted in Switzerland having lunch with a colleague. Ostensibly, a road contractor whom Leo used occasionally, but there was another man sitting at the table.

They talked freely. That is, until the third man produced a brown envelope. The envelope, when opened, appeared to show large photographs.

The third man, clearly in focus through high-powered telescopic binoculars, then handed Victor a computer electronic device. He pushed it across the glass top table towards Victor. They sat, the data device before them.

Victor not only had a market in waiting, but two competitors in the wings, it seemed.

There in the open sunlight, where *au-giardin* dining of white table-napkins occupied a terrace meticulously manicured with ornamental lights and a mountain view of fir and snow peaks, it was beautiful. Such remoteness required no precaution. The exchange was made without need of concealment.

Here, nobody would see them.

Later that night, Victor downloaded the contents of the digital file. It contained a video feed of a meeting held in Berne just one week ago. He recognized the speaker.

* * *

"We're close!" said Jack Lucas, peering at the sidebar of his laptop which told him the time. He stretched, his eyes then needing a rub behind reading glasses.

"Let's pick this up again in the morning..." he advised.

Downstairs, his wife Sandra would be arriving in exactly half an hour.

"Our survey of the Artic was good, and we're on solid ground as long as we stick to the guidelines of leaving no footprint. This, we can accomplish with our latest technology..." he added, evidently pleased with himself.

"But Jack, you're at the Research Lab in Berne, your job as an Analyst for an energy company has commercial aspiration, does it not?"

"Yes. And there's no harm in that. There is no conflict. Not yet, anyway..."

"So...No apology needed for being a capitalist!" said the woman seated across from him, reviewing her nail polish. "I like my Ralph Lauren shoes. Besides, we do great things for society..."

"That we do!" chuckled Jack, turning to his colleague.

She was olive-skinned with dark shiny hair, her face free of blemish or anxiety. On her lab coat was a badge. Dr. Sophia Adji.

"So, tell me. How we are progressing on this acquisition investment?"

"Well. It's promising, I can tell you that. Our capabilities for manufacturing systems for space applications is viable. Ha!"

Jack was putting on his coat. "I don't know what you plan to sell our technology for, but I'm paid to develop in-space nuclear power systems for electrical or propulsive power as an alternative source!"

Sophia slid off her lab stool. "Isn't this going to be tough political battle?"

"Well yes and no" said Jack. "It depends on who gains, I suppose. NASA faces competition from private industry. It...err...pins its hopes on atomic technology to power human colonies for habitation."

"How about other adaptations?" asked Sophia, putting away her stuff.

"Ok. The US Department of Energy is hoping to developing a space-ready nuclear fission reactor, known as Kilopower, that could provide up to 10 kilowatts of power..."

"For...?" said Sophia, playing the progressive advocate.

"Ok. To be deployed on other planets and moons. NASA has employed radioisotope thermoelectric generators — batteries that run off the heat from radioactive materials — But I agree, it's a tough sell. Especially with the activist socialist movement determined to bring industry to its knees. Regulation. Environment. Climate. Progressive regimes..."

"It's overpopulation!' sighed Sophia in her matter of fact Indian accent. "Too much sex going on!"

Jack chuckled, almost out the door.

"Actually, it is a concern for populations to generate energy efficient systems. But try to explaining that... "

"Well, in any case" she interrupted "send me your data on all your recent findings. It's volatile. Like everything else, some technologies carry underlying threats... "

"Will do!" said Jack.

The phone rang in Jack's pocket.

Jack smiled, and he listened.

"I'll see what I can do!" said the caller, "I'm a banker Jack. It's what I do for a living. But this is huge and frankly, its scary. Tell your boss that we'll look at this closely. OK?"

Sandra was waiting. It was raining outside the lobby. Jack had his raincoat with him, even though he also wore a heavy coat.

"How did the Proposal Presentation go?" asked Sandra.

"Good. It went well, I think. They should continue to finance us! The project is solid. We can schedule more research... "

Sandra gave his arm a soft squeeze and smiled.

They walked out together, arm in arm and paused beneath the sheltered entrance canopy, just about to dash across the street in the rain. They waited a few minutes.

"Jack!" called out a voice from behind them. "Jack!"

Jack Lucas turned and saw Sophia Adji approaching. Her face was horrified at the downpour.

"Hi" he said

Sophia came up to them. "Sophia this is my wife Sandra..."

"Pleased to meet you!" she said, nodding cheerfully.

Jack turned to his wife "Sandra, meet one of my colleagues at the Lab, Sophia Adji"

"Hello!"

"I'm so sorry to trouble you Jack. It's just that I'm alone up here and without transportation to the hotel. Would you mind giving me a lift back?"

"No problem" said Jack. "In fact, why not take my car?" he added, producing the keys. "It's Valet-parked here, and I was planning to pick it up in the morning. Sandra is here with her Jeep..."

"We're going out for a quick dinner" said Sandra, glancing at Jack "You're welcome to join us!"

"Thank you. That's very kind of you to offer. But I need to get back to my computer at the hotel. Email the family etc.." said Sophia. "I'll take your offer on the car though, if you're sure its alright... Thanks!"

Later that night, Jack and Sandra returned to the hotel and were informed by the Concierge at the Front Desk that two detectives were waiting for them in the foyer of the Hotel.

They had bad news, they said. A car registered to Jack was traced to their travel itinerary programmed at the Hotel. They wanted to ask him some questions, they told him.

"Yes. We loaned it to a colleague, Ms Adji...It's not stolen!" explained Jack.

They paused.

"Ms Adji is dead" they said. "The car is badly wrecked. We need you to answer some questions, please."

"An accident...?" began Sandra.

The detectives looked at them both. "An explosion. The car was rigged with a bomb."

"No. Wait. You must be mistaken or something...?" began Jack.

"Ms Adji was holding the detonator' declared the detective.

"*What...?*"

It was almost two in the morning before Jack was released from the police station. He answered all questions. He had called the Consulate of his Embassy and a representative Bill Sullivan from the US government stood with him.

After some questioning, Sandy was relieved and she retired to their hotel suite upstairs. Jack was ready to join her. He was asked one final question.

"Mr Lucas. "Do you know a Victor Kerensky?"

"Why?"

The room was quiet. "Because he will now make it his business to know you!" came the answer.

Sullivan made some calls.

Outside, Jack waited for an explanation. "They traced Ms Adji's last call out. She called him just minutes before she blew up the car. Victor Kerensky is a fugitive. Russian-born. International terrorism is the new name for socialist activism. "

"How...how does that concern us?" asked Jack, his voice fatigued.

"Evidently, Kerensky has turned to the Energy industry as the focus of his endeavors."

"So. If you think Sophie Adji had anything to do with betraying her work and divulging sensitive data as espionage, then you'd better tell us Jack..." warned Bill Sullivan.

"No. You're wrong! She was Indian-born, British trained. Efficient as hell, if with a light-hearted sense of humor about building a perfect world...She would never betray anyone!"

Sullivan was shaking his head in disagreement.

"What then?"

"He's after you!"

"Who? Why?"

"You're at the vanguard of space technology power fuel..."

"Was he trying to kill *me?*" Jack husked, his face worn and his brow hot with perspiration. "It was your car she was driving, wasn't it?" Sullivan said. "Its entirely possible you were the target?"

"What are you saying? What does he want from me?"

"Your research and technological developments!"

Jack paused, and they stopped walking. He leaned against the wall. "This is bullshit. Bullshit! Sophie would never..."

Sullivan waited. "This was...a warning!"

"Com'on" he added. "Let's get out of here before they find another reason to detain you!"

Sullivan consulted his watch, and now it was almost dawn. "I'd like to take you to the Consulate for a full statement. That way we can defend you..."

Jack called Sandra.

It was still raining as first light appeared, if threatening to retreat into dense clouds.

"Let's get some breakfast and clean you up. Later we'll return you to your wife at the Hotel" said Sullivan."It's good she's returning Stateside."

Jack nodded.

"You have other family here, yes?"

Jack nodded. The thought of the family – Amanda and Trevor and Sandra – all of them enjoying fun just recently was a wretched contrast to what just happened tonight.."

"I supposed you want me to pack up and return to the US....and I just secured some funding!"

Sullivan did not rush to respond.

"The funding you were promised was sourced to Victor Kerensky..."

"He's *funding* this research?" blurted Jack, appalled.

Sullivan raised his hand. "Let him! We've got your back."

"Wait...you want me to continue?"

Sullivan waited.

"Please."

"A decoy! *I'm the decoy*?"

"No. You're the real McCoy..."

Sullivan did not move his head. With his fingers he offered forward a card. "You call us whenever you want. We're watching."

"Gee thanks!" said Jack. "And thanks for asking. But if you're recruiting an operative for the CIA then the answer is ..."

"You've already been recruited by Kenesky!"

Sullivan added, leaning forward. "Sophie was the price!"

Jack stared at him, thoughts of remorse and anger coursing through his head.

"Look. You and your family are safe. It's your technology he wants…We'll be monitoring"

Jack looked at him, his face grim.

Hours later, Jack said "It's been a long week. I've worked on a deadline, presented a proposal, and slept barely with my wife…"

"Of course…"

They were in a government vehicle.

Finally Sullivan just looked at Jack Lucas, the card emblazoned with the crest of the US government again offered. Clearly, it held interest in Jack's work.

Jack took it and disembarked.

At the hotel, Sandra was already packing.

"I guest this is it" she said simply.

He nodded, his face somber. He turned to the shower.

"Jack?…"

He emerged 20 minutes later with a towel at his waist and another rubbing his wet hair. "I guess it's best if you return home. Perhaps stop in the UK…?" Hearing no response, he paused and looked about.

Sandra had left.

* * *

Jack walked in the great central park where gentlemen sat on benches, and mothers pushed strollers with small children. He had a few days off now, and he needed to relax and think.

The Lab was dark now, their work ended. He had returned to clean up Sophie's work and send it all to her University sponsor.

His own papers and research were also boxed. He sent them back to his office in Zurich.

Bad enough that Sandra had walked out, but the reality of what happened just struck him.

Sophie was killed. Why? So that an assassin could get... *what?* Technology that they were working on? Surely not? *What for?...*

And now also the government. What was their motive to get involved?

He walked. It was his second today.

The park was almost dark - the sun long gone and the commuting crowds thinning to expose urbanites living downtown in Berne. Some wore masks. Some did not.

Mostly the city belonged to the business world. But at night the locals emerged with little distinction, other than casual scarves or sneakers tucked beneath formal overcoats. They hung in the shadows, lumens from a quiet cigarette, or a sniffing animal on his dog-walk.

Jack noticed an open coffee shop across the square from his hotel. It rang out through the night air in bright neon lighting. He entered, finding it strange that he had never even noticed it. Not that he'd been here long. But clearly every corner of this city had its function of...of....*what, exactly?*

He was in shock. How to explain what happened? Everything was so altered now.

The reality of what he did for a living was woven so seamlessly into the fabric of his daily routine that he never saw the danger. He sipped his coffee.

No...Not just danger, a nightmare of the worst kind, if the truth be told.

Now that he thought about it, that's what research could do if left to its own devices! In the academic, pure research could neutralize itself with immunized platitudes. But when applied, then the world was in on it.

Yet the reality was incontrovertible truth. He was conducting some of the most threatening technological developments known to mankind...the creation of dark energy and the production of anti-matter.

He stirred his coffee aimlessly. If he thought about it, the work he did was horrifying to contemplate.

A waitress came. He looked up.

Hell, just yesterday they'd laughed at an article in *Physical Review Letter*, a scientific journal. An astrophysicist explained that space was not empty but filled with an enigmatic 'substance' — *dark energy* — pushing matter away, like outward. String theory, the article asserted, was that all matter consisted of tiny, vibrating 'string-like' entities, creating a bubble dimension of another kind...

So what did he do for a living? Oh yes. *Positron Dynamics*. And his funder was conceivably the richest man on earth...?

Now he got it.

Last year, NASA partnered with his Nuclear Energy company in an $18.8 million contract to design a reactor and develop fuel for use in a nuclear-thermal propulsion engine for deep-space travel...

And what did he tell his investors just earlier in the day? That *unlike* conventional rockets that burn fuel to create thrust, the atomic system used reactors to heat a propellant like liquid hydrogen, which then expands through a nozzle to power the craft.

That's what he did for a living!

So what did that mean, exactly? It meant double the efficiency for something half the size for longer flights. *Such as a Mars flight."*

Christ! No wonder the government was concerned.

He was toying with antimatter...*Anti-matter!* He hadn't even fully explained it to Sandra, come to think about it.

His team was working on Positron dynamics. Tampering with the basic elements of nature...to see the beginning of the age of commercial antimatter within five years?

He sipped his coffee.

Already he could scale to a gram of antimatter per year using about 11 GWe of power. That's 2000 times the production of what Positron Dynamics produced from one linear accelerator! Yes? Sophie knew this, of course...

The death of one researcher like Sophie Adji was one thing. But if today's new thinking of planning for human colonization of another planet was a dynamic in the hands of one man...the wrong man - and for the wrong reasons...?

That could seriously threaten earth's stability. An earth where governments tried to find stability. An earth where he and Sandra lived.

He paid his bill and left.

Academics could be the dumbest people on earth, he decided.

* * *

Trevor was outside his office building when he received a call from Jacques.

"How's London?" he began in his punctilious French accent.

"Refreshing!" chuckled Trevor.

"Oh. You mean it's raining?"

"Are you still in Swizerland?"

"Yes. I go back to Paris Tomorrow…"

"Hmm"

"Lizette loves to ski, and once were got back to our chalet, it's hard to pull her away!"

"I don't blame her. Thank you again for your kind hospitality by the way. We all have a wonderful time up there!"

"You're presence at the DAVOS Conference is *sans pareilles*. As always!   And I'm proud to be your host…Anyway, I have some news. I want to talk with you personally. I'm on my way back, and without drawing attention to our rendezvous, do you think we could meet somewhere discrete and talk?"

Trevor knew that when people like Jacques moved about, or met with anyone, it was noteworthy for news if not politics. They carried influence. They carried money. They shaped culture.

Jack was a celebrated Antiquities dealer with high-stakes investment money at his fingertips. To say nothing of Trevor's presence. Put the two of them together in a photograph and it would make newspaper copy in less than 24 hours.

"Mmm" said Trevor reflectively. "I'll take the train and meet you at Calais?"

"Perfect…" said Jacques. "As you now I have a car collection with a mechanic who lives. He is the best for restoration and conservation of valuable automobiles. I'm showing a beauty next month in America, and I want it to be the finest specimen I can produce...So I shall go there to talk with him."

"Up for Auction?" asked Trevor.

"But of course. Always!"

"So, you know the place. I'll stay at the Inn by the Normandy coast.

"Any particular subject that I can guess about?"

"Let's just say ...I found some information!"

Trevor said nothing. He knew what Jacques was talking about the vandal who damaged the painting after the Auction. Jacques had evidentially discovered his identity."

Thank God, thought Trevor. It helped with his insurance claim.

More dangerous however, was the motive of a suspect whose aspirations had to be understood. This was no common criminal. There was a bigger picture in play. Trevor understood Jacque's insinuation.

"I see. Perhaps then we can have coffee and croissants at that bakery...Yes?"

"*Absolument...*" finished Jacques.

"Oh yes. Several croissants!"

There was clearly more to talk about here. Forensic analysis was huge in this business, considering the amount of money that passed hands. Photographs alone could speak.

Jacques said   "We could have spoken actually in Switzerland. The cards were already on the table..."

Trevor understood. Jacques was not referring to *Chemin de Fer* at the Casino tables in Switzerland. The subject was about the suspect. He was in Switzerland.

For a vandal to be spotted at Davos - tracking Trevor's every movement meant this was a man with an agenda. He was well financed. Trevor understood the danger of illicit networks in Europe of which there were several.

Trevor was more than a retired silver-haired individual with some credentials in commerce.

He was an authority with some fiduciary responsibility, and he was still a public official as a minister.

"Be careful, see you soon!" said Jacques.

Trevor hung up.

For those who believed in socialist progressive doctrine, Trevor was anathema. Tear down the rule of law, and you could tear down the free world of its hierarchy. Undermine capitalism and you shook the authority of venerated values. Devolve civil liberties, and you could redistribute wealth citing entitlement by those who had no appetite for hard work, industry or ethics.

The danger was ever present. Level such values with new leadership and you could replace conventions of ancient scriptural morality. Introducing man-made liberal agendas was an old enemy.

Trevor had no delusions. He was indispensable. As was anyone else in a system built on trust and affection.

 Activism was one way to destroy it. Political bias and financial ruin was another.

Destruction was another, beginning with figures of influence and centers of authority. Yes indeed.

It was no stretch to concede that there were new and more advanced pathways to destroy Western civilization.

Trevor was a target. This he knew. And recently, each time he looked into the attractive face of his wife Amanda - her features ever lovelier and sweeter as they matured with age and grace, he knew it was a threat drawing closer to home.

Yes. He was a target.

This, Jacques also understood.

* * *

Chapter 4

"HELL NO! We won't go!"

Marching protestors circled the university with enough voice to fill the campus.

"I am so sorry Ms Wells..." said Professor Yardley, his hands about his mouth to be heard. "We... we try to be as tolerant as we can, but you know, sometimes it's impossible to think! These protestors have laid siege to our Quad since last week. They just won't move on..."

Amanda chuckled. "It's that stage of their life I suppose..." she said, waving at the protestors. "University is when you're full of aspiration to explore new ideas and revolutionary thoughts in open ways..."

"Quite so Amanda" grinned Yardley, pleased at least to find a compatriot sympathetic to his walk of life as an academic professor.

"But not this open! I regret that we've got an entrenched group of angry strangers who have picked our campus to muddy the waters for our students...They're not on our college rolls!"

"Perhaps they 're marching from another university?"

He shook his head. "We work so hard to be open and inclusive, it's disconcerting when they scare off people..." The noise surged. "Free speech is a right. It's especially encouraged at this age..." Adding, "It's our job to safeguard their safety to do so without fear of reprisal"

"Are they disruptive or violent?"

"No!" said Yardley, his eyes full of uncertainty. "But they are not resident students. And I am responsible for the safety of our university student body. "

"Can you talk with their organizer?"

"I've tried. They just won't budge. Neither will they tone down their rhetoric, nor will they engage with any opposition. They silence critics who approach them, and they shun any debate with our students...It's impossible to negotiate!"

"I wish I could sympathize Professor Yardley. But unless they are a threat, I'm afraid I'm a free-spirit myself. And I can't help you..."

"What?"

"I said..."

"No" interrupted Yardley. "They aren't exploring. They are intimidating...In fact, I find this coercion a form of abuse!"

Amanda raised her eyes to the clock tower. She had come with a purpose and she had a schedule to keep.

She was beginning to doubt her decision to take the day for research. She was scheduled to fly to the United States tomorrow. One day of research up here was what she thought she could accomplish on short order. Had she miscalculated her planning, she wondered.

"Ah yes! Ms Wells..." A pause. "Amanda, please?"

"Can we talk you into a year's teaching as an associate professor?"

"I'm afraid I don't have the stamina Professor!" said Amanda "I'm flattered that you should ask, though" she smiled. "Besides, my specialty is not social science but cultural anthropology. But thank you!"

"Well. We're very impressed with your publications. We so encourage new approaches to conventional thinking..."

"In that case, it's my daughter you want...She completes her dissertation this summer. Only, what can I say. She's too busy being in love with her new husband just now..."

"Hmm!" grumped the professor.

The crowd advanced. "HELL NO! We won't go!"

Then again walking forward. "Hell No. We won't go!"

"Do they ever come up for air?" asked Amanda, covering her ears from the yelling.

The Professor was conflicted, his eyes darting. "We do have to encourage their rights to peaceably assemble. But I'm afraid they are becoming threatening. We're getting concerned."

Amanda stepped into a side brick pathway. Yardley followed.

"They've made camp and they sleep down by the cloisters at night" he muttered, his breathing uneasy.

"Anyway..." he said, turning to Amanda. "I'm keeping you from your task. Please do enjoy the lecture! We'll have lunch after the session, and I'll be here to pick you up?"

"Thank you!" she said, entering the darkened auditorium where university students filled the seats.

She'd been asked to attend the lecture as a special invitation. Professor Yardley knew Amanda from her own academic engagements over the years, especially her research on early literary works.

As University Dean, he was proud of his curriculum and suggested she attend today's talk on the subject of societal reflections of distress seen in ancient writings, including the demise of the Mayans.

"Sorry. I'm one of the few who believes in diffusionism. I'm a sailor, remember. Trade winds travel from east to west.." she chuckled.

"Not so alone as you might think these days. As it turns out, you're right!"

The topic was something she had written to him about at great peril to her reputation.

Today however, Amanda was on a quest. She came to research on evaluating a painting made at a time of severe dislocation and disruption in statehood. And she explained it, somewhere between the two wars. Especially if it shed light on the world where the painting was created.

"Who painted it?"

"That I don't know! Or why. Bad enough that the author is a mystery, but my husband's bank is having to insure the thing. It went on Auction, and the bidding went through the roof..."

"Hmm" he said. "Come with me."

She talked all the way to the university library..,

She followed him and talked compulsively as if she were once again a student. She had to help, she told him. They were analyzing the painting and...

Yardley turned the corner and she followed.

Besides underwriters, auditors and research specialists, she needed to find out for herself, she told him.

Yardley took a flight of steps to the next floor and finally put up his hand to stop her nervous chattering.

She stopped. "I'm sorry..." she said.

"No. That's what made you such an intense researcher where you were a student Amanda...No need to apologize" he said, adding "And the world is a richer place for it, I know!"

"Thank you" she smiled.

"This is where you want to begin your research" he said. "I'll see you later. Although, perhaps I should warn you. Those lectures can get a little err...lively!"

Amanda settled into down at quiet alcove of the great library and collected her thoughts. With limited time on hands, she focused on ways to best utilize the resource.

Trevor had made banking and insurance enquiries in London. Sandra was searching for information too, especially she attended the Auction.

That electrifying event put the whole family on edge, media plagued them wherever they were located.

But more importantly, Sandra wanted to find out more about the figure in the painting because it resembled her father. That question by itself had touched off an analysis of a figure association with her father. Or grandfather. Or someone...

Here today, Amanda sought something else. She wanted the background of circumstances that might induce such a painting. Was it pure artistic license? A mere creation? A whim?

Or was it a record, a last image of something in the face of adversity? Was it telling a tale of inevitability?

She knew the approximate date. Therefore what gave it meaning?

Every university had its brand and reputation. All were legitimate centers for learning. Yet each had their specialty and legacy and concentration of study.

This university library was the place to find out more. Here, some of the greatest thinkers had brought their early ideas about philosophy and mercantilism. Here were records and archives of enormous social upheaval and change.

Could she find some background relevance to the painting? What insights might she discover here in these collections of papers?

Centered in the heart of England, this region had seen its share of disruption and change to early society and demographics, politics, community trade, overseas expansion, textile manufacture, food markets, and new frontiers.

Later, it was the center of scientific development in agriculture, forestry and manufacture of metals, including the factories for war-time armaments.

Today, this university was at the frontier of medicine as a medical training school.

"We have amongst the best faculty in disciplines of international policy, business management, current affairs, history and modern social studies" Yardley had told her.

Amanda was only too happy to be back on a campus. She would have liked to linger...But she was scheduling much for her two day visit.

She worked fast.

Finally, she was pleased with her findings. She had asked permission to take images and photographs using her digital camera, careful to make notations of her sources for later citations and reference.

She looked at her watch, closed up her materials, and thanked the Librarian for her assistance.

She dashed over to the Lecture hall. As promised, Yardley sotted her and waved above the crowd across the auditorium.

She took her seat.

The house light dimmed, and the lecture began with a slide show on the plasma overhead screen.

Professor Myer was well known for his thoughtful analysis of various economies.

"Throughout human history" he began "people of all cultures have sought freedom."

His topic was interesting, students settled to listen. "In the political arena, there are a variety of liberation theologies. Gustavo Gutiérrez wrote his *Theology of Liberation* with a focus on the political and economic situation in Latin America. James Cone wrote *A Black Theology of Liberation* to develop a black theology that identified with the oppressed. Others have developed feminist liberation theology that focuses on cultural problems that have limited women's freedom." He paused.

"Dr Art Lindsley at the Institute of Faith, Work and Economics writes that most perspectives involve a freedom from constraints, but are not clear about what the liberated situation would look like. He says that this "freedom from" is at the heart of our secular culture."

* * *

Amanda had been seated for just twenty minutes. She had drained her bottle of water. She looked about the auditorium for an Exit.

Her head was throbbing, and more than anything, she wanted a drink. A snack machine might offer some beverage or something.

Her throat was really dry as she inched her way down a row of students and out into the halls, and she repressed a cough. Perhaps she had a fever.

The discussion of the lecture shifted.

"The business of Freedom is big money! Disruptive elements topple conventions, make new markets…And usually ends up being political activism. So, let's unwrap this concept of "Freedom." For us, freedom is money to live and survive happily, right?"

The room filled with a chuckle.

"Mainly, its freedom from slavery of one kind or another. Religion marks it as a sort of spiritual liberation, starting from within the soul, then extending to outward realities. Hindus seek an experience of oneness with the universe that frees them from the illusion of this world of distinction. Buddhists seek enlightenment that involves a detachment from desiring anything in this world. Atheists want to be free from the constraints of any objective moral rules…." The room was still.

"Many people in our culture believe freedom is meant to be a lack of norms, rules, or laws restraining us from doing what we want…So, If God exists then this freedom is limited."

"Right!" yelled a student from the rear of the auditorium. They all turned.

Amanda had lost attention to the lecture. For some reason she was feeling unwell.

She looked about for a space to retreat. One recessed alcove at the end of the hallway looked promising. A snack machine would be there, she felt certain. Her throat was so parched, and added to a throbbing head, she felt as if she were really aching...

There was a line, or rather, a gathering at the vending machine. She waited politely for another fifteen minutes. Then she angled herself forward to insert money into the slot.

The door to the lecture hall opened and she overheard the speaker at the podium.

"Perhaps we might agree that twentieth century warfare was organized by minorities with unscrupulous leaders who could seize power and use it to do terrible things..."

She reached down for her drink.

Suddenly a student burst out of the auditorium. It took everyone by surprise.

"Why does it not matter...?"

"We do have a history of collective bargaining, normally...." answered the professor.

A protestor pushed up his poster. "Here!" he said with a fierce gesture.

More protestors from outside poured into the auditorium and stood at the rear of the auditorium, shouting.

Others standing at the vending machine fled. Amanda hesitated.

They saw her. One pointed and indicated that she sit down. She was two steps away from ducking into a side recess.

She froze.

They returned inside the auditorium and pointed to the speaker.

The lecturer stiffened, recognizing that he was being challenged. But he was responsible for the safety of the audience. He took a step back. Then he spoke, saying

"Freedom, for Plato and Aristotle, is essential to a state. In other words, freedom was within the structure of the law. In Stoic philosophy, freedom was inwardly directed. Freedom was inner freedom for the Stoics and primarily outer freedom for Plato and Aristotle. In Old Testament scripture, freedom was primarily a freedom from slavery....God was the liberator."

A hand shot up. "You mean like communist manifestos?"

"Well politically, the analogy is not inconsistent" answered Myers. "The Assyrian conquest of the kingdom and the Babylonian captivity of the southern kingdom are illustrations of this pattern. In later Judaism, freedom movements arose to gain political freedom in order to allow religious freedom. The Maccabeans and the Zealots are only a couple illustrations of such movements..."

He looked up. "In ancient scripture, the inner rebirth of the scripture implies outer flourishing and safety. With the Greeks, the problem was with the mind, but in the New Testament, the problem was the bondage of the will. That freedom is the essence of the messiah message!"

"Can systems be blamed for atrocities?" he asked again, the same hand.

"Yes!"

"Your beliefs Sir?" asked the protestor. Myers did not respond.

"Are you a professor for the lecture?"

"Yes"

"Very well" said the protestor, walking down the aisle. "Liberal capitalism at least allows the separation of economic power from politics and decentralizes decisions to firms and households in markets. This is because, in the words of North, Wallis, and Weingast in 2011, it is an "open-access order.""

"Yes" replied Myers. "He also said communism is a "closed-access" order that restricts who may exercise political power. It concentrates control of the economy in the hands of that privileged elite…"

"Bullshit!" yelled the protester, enraged. Amanda spotted movement towards the rear of the hallway. More protestors were filing in.

"Further…' continued the professor, now showing some steel in his voice "If you're asking which of these systems is more likely to permit the abuse of power and allow abuses to be hidden from the public gaze…"

Amanda slipped to the side hallway in one quick side step.

Once out of sight, she pulled her cell phone and called Professor Yeardley. "Please help!" she said" the lecture hall has been occupied by protestors!"

"I'll call Security" he told her.

Amanda slipped back into the shadows and walked briskly down the hall towards the Ladies Room.

The Ladies Room was a newly decorated utility area of modern architecture, granite counters, mirrors, lighting and bright faucets of chrome and black.

Behind them were several stalls for privacy and utility, including locks and sanitized toilets.

The temperature was cool and fresh, with soft music filtering from the main lobby of the building.

Amanda walked to the far end of the mirrored counter and dabbed some water on a paper napkin and passed it along her brow and the base of her neck. She looked up. Her face was red.

She took another drink from the fountain and heard a far away train approach, fill the room with noise, and shake the very building. Perhaps it was railroad, close-by. She heard a soft shuffling from one of the stalls and realized she was not alone.

Amanda moved from the water faucets and faced the bank of mirrors.

She decided to take a headache painkiller. She unzipped her purse and began foraging for a bottle of pills. She popped one into her mouth and swallowed more water. Then she searched for her make-up bag.

The main entrance into the Ladies Room burst open and a young woman stood there, her expression tense and distracted.

"Hello!" smiled Amanda with a glance, masquara still in her hand.

The girl standing at the door was a protestor, her wide eyes gave her away.

Behind her a commotion could be heard. Amanda had been mistaken about a train. The noise was outside, people now fleeing and in terror shouting, the uproar sending many to crash into the door of the Ladies Room...

The woman braced against the door, her eyes darting with fear as she shoved back and blocked shut the door, as if sheltering from danger.

"You!" said the girl, recognition coming to her eyes. "I saw you...outside!"

Amanda stood still.

"I suppose you don't like protestors, either?"

Amanda stood still, saying nothing.

"I am talking to you!"

Amanda answered calmly. "I think you are... campus agitators. Not civic protesters. There's a difference..." she shrugged lightly.

"Oh, so now you're making fun of us?" shrieked the woman

"No. Just not liking the way you have to make yourselves heard, that's all..."

"And how would you *suggest* we make ourselves heard?"

"Well, in the first place, you can be invited to speak...."

"So, you don't like our methods?"

Amanda looked at her carefully and shifted her weight. This was no college prank. I was an organized campaign. "I don't like... your angry threats..." said Amanda softly.

The door flung open.

"He's dead!" cried someone behind her. "You killed that professor, Gin!"

The girl shoved at the door then turned, her eyes aflame with fear, flight. She raised her arm and revealed a gun. "You don't believe in socialist doctrines, do you?"

Amanda, drawing suddenly from somewhere deep within her soul, said "Moral accountability. That's what's missing in your socialist system. "

The girl stared at her, a wildness about her eyes as if unseeing, yet seeking a target for her rage.

Precisely at that moment, hesitating as if she would have liked to stay and debate, she was hit in the face by a stall door that slammed open and a student leapt out. "Oh My God!" she screamed, "don't hurt me!"

The protestor spun off balance, moved her arm and a shot discharged from the gun.

Amanda staggered back against the wall. Her head jolted backward and her elbow banged hard against the tile. The sting sent a searing pain up to her shoulder and neck. She next felt a wetness squirting against her neck and face.

They fled.

Alone in the Ladies Room, she sank slowly to the ground. Her skirt wet with blood now, and a blackness blurred her vision.

* * *

Slowly, the details emerged. Amanda had been shot.

Security officers found her concussed and paramedics transported her to the hospital of Warwick. But that was it. The damage was not serious.

"We can't seem to reach your husband Ms Wells..."

"Yes. He thinks I'm in the United States!" answered Amanda, still groggy from the night time medications that she'd been given for rest.

"I'm supposed to be a going to a lecture being given by a colleague of mine in Chicago, I'm booked for a flight tomorrow from Heathrow. I stopped up here for the day of research at the Warwick University Library Archives."

"Well. I'm very glad things turned out to be less serious than it could have been...You were grazed, and there was some bleeding. So we gave you some stitches and monitored your vital signs, just in case. But it was only a flesh wound." said the Doctor.

"Thank goodness!" chuckled Amanda. "Books do have a way of inciting reform. But reactionary violence...in an Archive no less...well I'd say that's a *First!*"

They laughed.

"And yes. You are discharged. Just be careful to get some rest for the next few days. It's been a shock, after all. Trauma has a way of delayed response sometimes. So, here's some medication if the pain persists. But check in you experience headaches, or nausea. O.K.?"

"Yes doctor" said Amanda.

"Anyone you should call to have them come and pick you up?"

"I'll be fine. Thank you doctor!"

"Right then," he said, and signed off from her medical report. "Get in touch with your GP when you get back."

Amanda had submitted a report to the police.

There had been a gunshot discharged, and a wound of any kind as a result would require a report. She did so in the manner of explaining a campus accident that needed monitoring, if not university guidance review. But no charges were filed.

Amanda was sitting on her bed, showered, changed, and ready to leave. A nurse was fetching a wheelchair for her exit.

Psst!" said a whisper from the doorway. "May I come in?"

Amanda looked around behind her. She grinned. "Oh, please do!"

Paul Myers came in with an awkward clutch of daisies from the gift shop downstairs. He was wet, his raincoat stained and his trouser pants splashed and darkened. He'd forgotten to worry about his disheveled appearance, as most professors were prone. He was the one who had made the arrangements for her access to the library.

"I'm off the hook and can go home..."she said brightly.

"Oh my God, Amanda. I am so sorry! You can't imagine how bad I feel that this should have happened...Is there anything I can do?" Like most professors, he felt responsible.

"No. Not at all. And it's NOT your fault. Students get randy. They agitate and demonstrate. I got in the way. That's all. Yes, one girl fired a shot in the Ladies room, and she's in custody. So that's the end of it...No need to make a media event of it."

"Alright. Alright...I get it!" said Paul, an envelope getting sodden and bent with the daisies. "Had you not accepted my invitation you would not have..."

She smiled. "I'm fine. I'm catching a plane in the morning... Sit!"

"Well then" he said, taking a seat across from her "I brought these. It's what you came to research..." He adjusted his position, and he talked.

"Our Modern Records Centre was founded on the principal of adding to the body of knowledge with original documents from the era of post industrial history. Our collection goal was to locate and preserve primary sources for modern British social, political and economic history. In particular, the Labor movements. Especially for industrial relations, industrial politics and labor history. It is the institutional repository of the University of Warwick and holds the records of the activities, decisions and events of the institution, as you know."

"Yes"

Before long, she had him pacing the room like a man delivering his lecture. Periodically he paused to peck at a slice of toast from her breakfast tray, which she offered.

For the rest of the time, she was gleaning more information about the girl who shot the gun.

An unprovoked assault, they told her.

And it was Yardley who needed attention. Evidently, the stress of the day, along with his diabetes condition had induced medical emergency and he had collapsed.

Amanda informed Trevor who was in Brussels. Then Sandra called. Tray called. Jacques called.

She gave them a full account and assured them that she was fine. She would postpone her travel plans, he told them.

Trevor had wanted to return to London, but she insisted he complete his business. She was fine, she stressed. No need.

Truth was, Amanda did feel fatigued and she was only too glad to be returning to her planning.

Tomorrow, she had been scheduled to take a flight to the United States. That could wait, as far as she was concerned. For now, all she wanted was to rest.

It took her several days to recover fully. And she spent most of the time resting or watching the News. Or reading the materials that were given her by Paul Myers. His visit filled in a lot of information. She reviewed it all carefully.

As the days passed, she turned from TV watching to her laptop. Occasionally, she took a pain killer to ease her abrasions and headaches. But she left most of her work unattended and answered few calls. Mostly, she wanted the time to detach herself and stay calm. Even to question herself as to what she was doing these days. Had not Myers not come to see her, she might have found the entire episode at the University a wasted effort. She valued what he had told her, up there in her hospital room, and she had taken notes as she recalled his account, like class notes to review carefully:

"It was a turbulent time, your period of enquiry...In the history of Britain, that was the turn from an Edwardian agrarian subsistence economy to the industrial age of earning a living wage for laborers. It empowered people. It was an exciting time. And we do have a prodigious collection of pamphlets, pamphleteers newspapers written by reformists and suffragettes, it was all about social unrest. We have more collections and documents here than anywhere else recorded..."

Amanda drank her orange juice.

"The British Parliament was worried" he said, "unrest had swept throughout Europe. Reform was ending conventional methods of interacting... The markets were roiled by financial collapse. People took to the streets in protest. Mobs demanded change! Law and order strained to contain civil unrest, rebellion, demonstrations and organized activism..." his voice drifted in thought.

"Before you know it, rank and file within the military were defecting and abandoning the hierarchy of a traditional Europe. One monarchy after another toppled. Then, it was only a matter of time before Britain was bowled over. Parliament was utter turmoil..."

Amanda nudged. "Please, carry on!"

"Britain was dependent on trade with Russia. You have to understand that WWI was a nightmare from which few had really recovered..." his voice trailed.

"In any case we were Russia's ally in the First World War. Great Britain was active in their civil war: The Bolshevik administration formally ended Russia's involvement in the First World War with the signing of a peace agreement with Germany, the Treaty of Brest-Litovsk. But it was a mess."

"It must have been a terrible test of wills in this country..." said Amanda.

"Oh God! Not since the Cromwellian civil war had Britain been so divided."

"Who exactly were the official Allies at that time?" asked Amanda, the period of the painting now becoming close.

"Well. Between 1918 and 1920 allied forces represented Britain, France, the United States, Japan, Greece, Italy and China – all active on Russian territory, and all embraced by the promise of riches from an industrial revolution shifting from an agrarian to an emerging free market economy. Even the White Army was given financial backing."

"But the Russian Revolution of 1917 changed everything. It was a sudden, violent revolution that marked the end of the Romanov dynasty, and centuries of Russian Imperial rule. The Bolsheviks were led by Leftist revolutionary Vladimir Lenin. He seized power and destroyed the tradition of Czarist rule and the hope of any free market economy. The Bolsheviks would later become the Communist Party of the Soviet Union."

"Lasting well beyond WWII, I imagine."

"Oh Yes..." said Myers. "And beyond, well into the cold war. Stalin who inherited Lenin's mess was pissed at the Germans. Those two nations had been playing with each other for decades."

"Umm"

"But the social unrest prevailed?"

"Hell yes! We were supposed to be liberating Russia. In our Library Collections we have quite a cascading sequence of events that occurred. One collection reports on Bolshevism in Russia of 1919. We have reports from His Majesty's official representatives in Russia. They cited Bolshevik atrocities and the state of Soviet Russia.. Including the killing of the British naval attaché, Captain Francis Cromie at the British Embassy in Petrograd, and the arrest of other British officials...in Russia at the time"

"Really!"

"Yes. In Britain the newspapers were full of it. It roused the public and caused an uproar in the local media at the time: In our Library collections we have all that correspondence between Rear-Admiral Kemp, recently the British senior naval officer in North Russia, and Douglas Young, the former British Consul at Archangel, reprinted from *The Times* by the *People's Russian Information Bureau*. They debated the actions and aims of British intervention...It became a national sensation, if not an obsession of controversy in England.."

Myers turned to Amanda. "I don't want to bore you with all this..."

"No. Not at all. This was what I came for, actually. "

"Well then. Here's a copy of an article called 'Hands off Russia' July 1919. It's a public appeal for British workers to stop the transport of munitions to Russia, published in the journal of the United Society of Boilermakers and Iron and Steel Shipbuilders."

"You've armed me with much" said Amanda. "What I want to know if there might be contemporary interests with legacy ties, like a corporate mission, or covert operation of some kind?"

"Hmm...Well of course the Cold war caused enmity between the West for decades." He paused.

"Well my dear. You can look no further than the plight of the Jewish populations during the second world war."

"And today...?"

"Sure! Movements underlying this socialist agenda remain. A benign form of Democratic government, as we know it, is socialist at heart, seeking ways to reinvent itself! "

He paused.. "It's tempting to topple establishments that survive the tests of time. They do get brittle and boring! But populism is a viral strain of activism."

Myers smiled, adding wearily "They say we learn from history. I say, *beware* of history!"

* * *

With the last 48 hours behind her, Amanda was ready to move on. She would call Sandra.

But her thoughts strayed.

Someone had seriously damaged the family! Deep feelings stirred within her. If anything, she felt they were all now exposed to more danger.

The question was why. Or how?

She made fresh coffee, collected her thoughts and put together sketches. She examined her own findings.

Many were digital images of original records captured on her laptop.

She would review, she decided. But her concentration wandered.

Where were the questions?

What nagged at the inquisitive mind?

She felt tired. She thought she saw a path forward..But then again, not really. Nothing seemed to coalesce.

The next day was easier, even as Amanda's arm remained heavily bandaged. She would recover. She would take an early morning walk.. stop for a coffee.

She regained composure, she felt, and strolled through the park.

Suddenly the street seemed hazardous. She veered away from busy venues. She felt detached, overwhelmed. By the time she returned to her place she was exhausted.

She rested for a while, then picked up the phone and dialed the University. She spoke to Yardley's Assistant, Joan.

Yardley was recovering in the hospital apparently. He would be undergoing a few tests before being discharged.

Joan chatted, explaining the outpouring of sentiment by students, all of them hankering for news. She had taken over the management of the department, she told Amanda, assuring everyone that he'd be back in a few more days.

With the seriousness of the matter now submerged, Joan could say that had Yardley not been in the hall when the mob turned violent, well... But yes, she would pass along the message that Amanda had called.

Two hours later Joan called again with an update.

Professor Taylor had been shot.

"What?" said Amanda.

Taylor was shot in the chest. He did not survive his injury. He died in the hospital.

Amanda was appalled, a dizziness drained her of all thought. She listened, docile. Joan had lots to say.

Later that night, with a scotch in her hand, Amanda thought about it.

It was inconceivable that a professor had been killed by student protestors. This was no proletariat. What should have been a fun campus experience for giggling adolescents turned violent.

Something wasn't right.

Who was behind this with such animosity? The more she thought about it, the less she saw any rationale. What had turned so malevolent?

Taylor's attack had apparently occurred that afternoon when Amanda was hedged in the bathroom.

So...there were other guns on the premises?

The protesters had been apprehended by now. But by the time the police had arrived, they'd become an angry mob, evidently incited by chaotic aggression. Or had the guns been pre-positioned before the protest began?

That suggested outsiders.

Officially, the University was in Lock-down. That, to avoid further incident of course, if to protect the students within...

Still, police patrolled the premises and they questioned everyone.

Neither did it go unnoticed in the media, nor was there any restraint shown. An abundance of suggestive commentary, criticism, political harangues and acrimonious accusations were issued out of nowhere it seemed. Why?

Had someone leaked something else?

Were students the menace?

Were un-authorized outsiders the problem?

Who then?

From the office of the Provost, the college administration issued statements and met with the Press. Their primary obligation was to parents, they asserted.

Amanda listened sympathetically, recalling Yardley's observation that most of the protestors were not students!

This demonstration had been orchestrated by unrestricted mobs, agitators.

Many of the protesters, Amanda later discovered, had travelled from London with little money and nowhere else to go. They had camped on the grounds, and without the authority to do so.

After their shooting spree, the situation deteriorated and got out of hand.

The next day was an interview with the police investigators.

By the time Amanda was wounded, apparently, security had been summoned to be on the premises. A squad of anti-threat forces had penetrated the building. They had managed to disarm the assailant and round up the group without further injury.

 "Clearly, your call to Professor Yardley alerted him, and he gave them sufficient warning," one police officer told her.

Late that evening, Amanda got a call from Yardley. They chatted briefly, but it was clear he was cautious. The matter was still under investigation.

"They were vagrants..." he told her. "Aliens, it would appear..." He hesitated, then added wearily "They didn't mean do harm. Otherwise...I can't understand what happened. Many of my students are implicated...They haven't got a clue!"

Amanda agreed. She recalled the girl with the gun. She seemed at a loss. She didn't mean to shoot, Amanda felt certain. It was an accident, the girl seemed conflicted, unsure of what she was supposed to do. In fact, she barely know how to handle the instrument.

It came down to a decision.

Amanda firmly decided against pressing charges. The fact of matter was that many of the students had been apprehended and would be charged with unlawful activity. Some even accused of intent to do harm.

Still, she decided to say little and not encourage further agitation.

"How are you recovering?" she asked when she called Yardley the next morning.

"That's for another agenda" he said.

"Hmm"

"I know one thing. They had all been exploited by angry activists. Activists bent on overturning the establishment and betraying the trust of young students."

Amanda said nothing. She knew the girl was not a killer. The gun went off. But she had not meant to harm. Of that she felt certain.

"Are you sure you won't press charges?" he asked.

"Certain" said Amanda, unwavering.

"Life is too tenuous...The kid needs every chance she can get. This was a trick she walked into, I could see the puzzlement on her face.."

Yardley understood.

"So you're off to the States then?"

"Yes"

They agreed to stay in touch.

It took a day more, and she did feel tired. But what mattered was to get on with her life.

Especially after her chat with Yardley, she most definitely knew she had to move on. This was one battle that was not hers.

Amanda collected her baggage. She had a trip to make.

She assembled her documents, those for which purpose she had come to the University.

She had to repurpose her mission: She had come to research materials about that period of time related to the topic of her painting..

If the painting was now under scrutiny, was there any connection to its past? *Was there a cause – or a movement that had triggered hate for the meaning of the painting?*

Tomorrow was a new start. Amanda needed to refocus.

On her way out, she received a text from Yardley. Her forwarded a statement issued by the investigative police body at the University.

"We have received a communiqué from the organizers of the demonstration that left one man dead, and several injured on this campus. They claim to be a chapter of the Antifa/Communist manifesto of the Red Guards promoting open borders and socialist agendas. They vow to spread their activities to other campus demonstrations, and they invite students everywhere to revolutionary violence.."

Amanda closed her eyes. As if history had not seen this enemy before...

What saddened her most was that young students with talent attending universities would be damaged, hijacked by angry agitators justifying violence on social media. Most of it funded by Leftist anarchists.

Amanda put down her cell phone. She was at a hotel near Heathrow Airport preparing to take her flight to the United States the next morning.

She so very much wanted to chat with Trevor. There was so much to discuss. But she couldn't reach him. There was so much to chat about

She had called Jacques and left a message. She talked with the curator restoring the painting and confirmed that the project was advancing satisfactorily.

Amanda answered a call from the Auction House where the painting had been initially put up for Auction, and she assured them that the painting was under the care of a certified restoration company fully bonded and secured.

She tried Trevor again.

What she heard was a recorded message. An apology, followed by a message that Trevor was unavailable. She dialed to his senior financial officer and found his administrator absent.

She listened to her latest message. Two others lit up her device screen as she listened.

"We are sorry to inform you Mr and Mrs MacDonnell that we have some unsettling news. You Insurance Company is challenging the claim. Apparently, there was a challenge to its authenticity! We do need to meet with you and your attorneys as soon as convenient." She waited a hour.

She'd made three calls into Trevor's office and twice talked to Rosamund, his office manager. Finally, she left a message since it was by now after office hours. Rosamund would understand when she came in the next day and hear the message.

At least she could relay to Trevor that Amanda was calling, even as Amanda would be underway on her flight across the Atlantic.

* * *

Normandy, France

Trevor waited at the *Café de Napoleon* for almost an hour. It was windy, but occasion for the natural grey stone of the coastal town to be penetrated by sun and color.

Jacques failed to appear.

Twice Trevor called him. Once, a secretary answered to say that he was at the Gallery. Trevor left a message.

The next call was met with an efficient recorded recital. By now, it was after-office hours.

With the sun beginning to wane, Trevor was getting cold. He wondered if he was wise to be sitting outdoors. And now he was getting hungry.

He consulted his watch.

Finally he called London. He would be delayed for the night, he said in his message. He would take tomorrow's train back, and report in for work at his office.

He contemplated walking indoors, having chosen is place to be visible to Jacques upon his arrival...well that was the idea.

The landlord came out to supervise the enclosure of outside patio. He and his league of attendants were to lower restaurant awnings for evening clientele. By the time they finished, the place was a twinkling café of night lights, two overhead heaters and a flashing billboard that served the space well for that time of the year.

Customers came, a giggling couple of newlyweds tucking themselves beneath the *au giardin* night awning to sip hot Irish coffee together.

Then out rolled a small trolley buffet, a barman offering drinks and snacks, his red hair of clear Scottish descent, and his languages many.

Trevor ordered salmon, and a small savory dish of sausage and grouse *foie gras* pie; salad and fresh crusted baguettes with locally made butter and cheese.

The Scotsman offered warm cider with rum made from regional orchards. Trevor accepted, adding pastry with crème fraise and fruit, followed by a cup of rich French coffee.

Honfleur was a lovely town, even as it dimmed into the night.

In the region of Calvados in France, it was part of Normandy which, with weather like England, had grown over the centuries to perch resolutely on the estuary where the Seine river met the English Channel and the Vieux-Bassin.

From his seat, Trevor observed several townhouses built originally in the 16th century, and despite the deepening cold, he took in a deep breath of fresh air. Here, Monet had been inspired to paint, as was Eugène Boudin.

Further up, the 15th-century church, St. Catherine's Church, had been constructed with vaulted timbers erected by early shipbuilders.

He would tell Amanda about it, he decided. Old churches were of interest to him. Their works, their artisans, their trades, all articulations of generations before.

He picked up his cell phone and listened to his messages, of which there were two. Twice he heard Amanda's voice. The first was to inform him that she had arrived safely in the United States. The second to inform him that University activism was alive and well on campus! Clearly, she valued her ties to academia.

He left her a message.

> *"Darling, you need to see this beautiful town. And St. Catherine's Church. Perhaps we enjoy a week here together...Love you!"*

Before closing, Trevor noticed two calls registered on his phone from the United States.

Other calls held local numbers. At Davos his number had got out and circulated amongst other speakers. Financial brokers promising higher returns on investments, doubtless offering services...

He was finishing his meal when a slim figure appeared at his table. A woman in a dark tailored pantsuit stood looking down at him and his food.

"Je m'appelle Caterine. Je suis avec Colby International. Jacques m'a envoyé pour te rencontrer?" she said simply, her lips ruby red and sharp. She lay down a card on the table, the hand in black leather.

Finally! Trevor made to stand up, removing his table napkin, a courtesy proffered for woman entering his environment. "C'est mon plaisir!" he said.

"Jacques asked me to apologize for his absence" she said in flawless English.

She sat down, removing her long shoulder strap.

Trevor smiled.

"Jacques has been detained. He asked me to show you these..." she said, placing an envelope on the table.

The waiter appeared.

"Please..." said Trevor, offering the invitation to dine.

"No thank you."

"A drink, perhaps?" added the waiter.

She looked up. "Café au lait. C'est tout." she said brusquely.

"There is a rumor...A portfolio inspired by you up in Switzerland contains precious paintings. I have an investor who wants to meet with you!"

"Umm. That means someone is waiting..?"

"Mais, bien sure!"

"What kind of prize are they hunting for, do you suppose, in their investment strategy?" asked Trevor, his words chosen.

"Big game! The kind that is taken by surprise!" she said. "With predatory ideas that scatter herds from their peaceful grazing...if not their watering holes"

"Do you see much of that in your Underwriting business?" said Trevor, reading her card.

"We do!"

Trevor chuckled. "Ah!...Such behavior for migrating herds is disruptive. It alters the natural habitat and separates them from the source of their survival?"

"Yes. *Precisement!* At any rate. Your prize is suggesting serious exposure for us. We want resolution"

"I'm sure you do!" said Trevor.

"But on the other hand, it is good to discover the original source of disruption?"

"Absolutely" agreed Trevor. "What you mean is, motivation to bar future competition?"

"Yes."

He waited.

"In any case" she continued, contemplating her gloves "we heard the news about the car accident up there. We may be close to something that looks like sabotage."

Trevor eyed her carefully.

"Tragic. Most perilous ..up in those Alps. And that snow storm that we had...Most dangerous for accidents up there," she said.

Trevor waited. He understood what she was saying. She was pinpointing a specific period of time. Only towards the end of their visit did the snow descend, then rain begin. So clearly, they had been spying on him in Switzerland.

"Anyway. I'm sure they'll find out more information."

"Umm" he said.

"And tell me, did you get a chance to go skiing?" she asked.

"Yes! Thank you. It was excellent! We will go every year."

She sipped her coffee.

"Especially under the night lights. On the slopes I mean. It was good to be skiing down those slopes at night, and easy to be watched from the clubhouse?"

"You were the subject of much admiration" she said. "You are a known figure, especially at the Auction."

"Really?"

"Yes. Drunks talking, you know. It was said that your err...your prize...could be a fraud. Imagine what the cost to the Insurer would be once the item was proved to be a fake!" she chuckled.

"What are you implying?"

"Well. That could mean the loss of a lot of money for the insurer, a lot of money for us to pay out in a claim."

"Of course. Enough to perhaps ruin the insurer?" he finished.

"Yes!"

"Oh. And err...the car belonging to your son-in-law?"

"Umm?"

"Well. It was snowing, and anything can happen when it is snowing..." he said.

She looked at him closely.

This was a warning.

There was no snow storm when the accident happened. It had been raining. She was giving him a warning about being followed, but she had been uninformed.

No. This was a veiled threat, telling him the power of an adversary, a vandal, able to inflict severe harm.

Moreover, the claim of insurance for damages inflicted upon a work of art would require a certificate of authenticity. If it could be proved a fake, then there would be public outrage for its value at Auction.

And if there was any doubt as to its authenticity, then its owner might be a fraud too! Trevor's reputation as a leading investor with banking integrity might be in question.

"And what is it you came here to know?" asked Trevor.

"A disputed claim would cost millions..."

"True. But that is not all, is it?" said Trevor. "You want to know what the perpetrator is demanding from me. Is that not right, Ms Caterine?"

She looked down. "May we go somewhere...somewhere more private. For a drink, perhaps?"

Trevor called for the check.

What worried Trevor was the precise timing of the accident. Clearly there was a perpetrator. That was no coincidence.

More importantly, he was not told the truth, and he leaked his intentions...

It was not snowing. It was raining when it happened. If they were involved with the car incident, they would have known... So the two incidents might not connected.

The painting, if that was her concern, was just the beginning. She was here on a fishing expedition. She wanted to know what else the perpetrator had his sights on...

Somehow, there was something more to this visit. Something she could not understand, even if Trevor was the immediate target.

Yes, she was toying with Trevor. But what she wanted was the bigger picture.

Something she did not understand.

Trevor did.

* * *

Chapter 5

Amanda was worried.

Rosamund had received no news about Trevor's whereabouts.

He'd left for France last Friday to meet with Jacques, and he was supposed to be calling in regularly, which he had no done, except for one message: Saturday evening he did call from a café in Normandy to announce that he was delayed by a day. He said he'd check in the minute he set foot in the UK. He was returning by train. Rosamund was at a loss. She told Amanda that Trevor's itinerary was unknown.

Rosamund further informed Amanda that there was some unopened correspondence waiting for Trevor, by Special Delivery. It was from the Bank's Insurance Company. She had signed for its receipt, but the matter needed attention. "It looks like legal matters needing his certification..." said Rosamund.

Amanda suggested she forward it to their attorney. That is, if Trevor didn't show up by the end of the week, which was two days away.

Amanda felt miffed. Or was it anxiety?

She'd have expected some kind of message from Trevor - something he always did in the event of prolonged separation between them, a courtesy of accountability. But he was retired now, as he put it, and less tied to an agenda.

"What kind of retirement is that?" she asked him one day. "Who does that?"

He laughed it off of course, that was his way.

"The kind of retirement that allows me to start work at nine in the morning instead of seven!"

Amanda thought about that and she knew her husband. He was a restless man, inquisitive beyond believe, and always active... He would *never* fully know how to retire, of that she felt certain. And, well.. she loved him for it, even as it frustrated her.

Still, they almost daily in touch. Yet for some reason, he'd neglected to check in...? Perhaps he knew that Amanda was on a travel itinerary herself, and he dispensed with the obligation?

Amanda's cell lit up. Here was another call from Sandra. Sandra had been alarmed to discover that her father was absent. He had diabetes, and...

Amanda sighed.

Sandra and Jack had separated in Berne. They'd been under a lot of stress. Neither could they find closure from the investigation of an accident that occurred, nor unveil the secrecy linked to the research project which their Lab had been working on. Truth is, they hadn't really had a chance to recover from an incident which had taken the life of a colleague.

Trevor had initiated a private investigation into the matter, and Amanda had wanted to consult with him about it. But nothing came to light.

For now, Amanda listened.

Sandra groaned. "It's just that I feel responsible..."

"No, you are not!" admonished her mother. "Nor could you have known the situation. You and Jack had made plans that could not have anticipated what was to happen that night..."

"Well, Jack and I had some disagreements. That's for sure. He seems...I dunno, totally distracted as if called into another universe somehow. It's as if I don't exist any more. Is it possible that I had intruded unexpectedly into his professional world?"

"No. You didn't..."

"Do you suppose there was another woman?.." "Stop!" said Amanda. "He seemed happy. *He adores you!* That's abundantly clear. Look, every family has their moments, especially when under stress. And *every* married couple have their ups and downs through the journey of life! You can count on Jack to come through. He's absorbed in his work at the moment. Give him time..."

Sandra sighed. "Yeah. Maybe you're right. Call me the minute you land, ok?"

Amanda smiled.

Sandra had a sixth sense about people. She must have realized that Trevor's unexplained absence was causing some anxiety.

"Relax! I'm fine. Dad's whereabouts will be solved, I'm sure. You don't have to pursue this...I'm in touch with Rosamund."

"Oh, but I do want to know where he is and how he's doing. After all, he's the center of a lot of attention with his good looks poised on a painting...."she chuckled.

"Umm..."

"How did your research go, by the way?" asked Sandra.

Amanda told her.

No. Well... She actually omitted the incident on campus since no charges were filed.

Sandra was interested in the painting and its provenance.

Amanda gave her an abbreviated overview. Mainly she explained that it was professionally being restored and conserved in France. "The Auction Gallery was fully apprised, in terms of valuations."

Amanda omitted the matter of its Insurance appraisal being challenged.

The last thing Sandra needed, Amanda knew, was more anxiety. Best to keep things simple. For now, anyway.

In a few days, Sandra was delivering a major public presentation, and her mind should remain clearly focused on her work: The scholarship underlying her professional analysis was full of controversy. It was not an easy field to be in at the moment where conventional assumptions were today politically charged, especially in conflicted public sectors.

"Oh, and I have good news!" popped out Sandra. "But...it'll wait till tomorrow. Have a safe trip and keep me informed. I want to know when you land. Call me!" finished Sandra.

"Ok. Will do! But please do not feel that you have to chase this business... It'll be settled soon enough."

Still no word from Trevor.

Amanda finalized her packing, and checked all her luggage. Then settled herself at her laptop to complete some details.

She looked at her watch. It was dinner time, and the hotel did have a restaurant. Amanda went downstairs and ordered a meal.

A glass of rich Bordeaux helped her relax from the anxiety of the day, even as her thoughts flew to the topic of Sandra's upcoming presentation of research. But she found little consolation. How often had the tides of an angry proletariat surface to deny new findings built over time by scholarship: It was the way for the body of wisdom to grow. No, she decided miserably as the last morsels of food reached her mouth, who would have guessed? Big tech, and the money behind it, sought markets for globalist interests, manipulating information for political gain. Today's populist political parties served them well and gave them the power they needed.

This would be little more than a book burning!

Back in her room she switched on the News displayed on a widescreen TV. She was tempted to turn it off. A sudden outrage lit up the screen. Parliament was in turmoil over a foreign affair that would have long term ramifications on its economy.

"Economic growth in Britain has stalled" said one angry member of the House.

"...there is a one in four chance that the country is entering into a recession, according to the National Institute of Economic and Social Research...Market fluctuations combined with a virus epidemic left a "very murky outlook."

Amanda rolled her eyes. She reached for the remote controller and was about to turn it off when the next question gave her pause..

"Excuse me" said a young interviewing reporter "But what are we to make of a report that describes the economy as *very murky*? That's hardly empirical data?"

Amanda chuckled.

"I believe that the institute said that Europe had the potential to "throw concrete" in the wheels of the British economy, knocking 5 per cent off gross domestic product in the long term. That's data!"

"Please explain..."

Spoken like an American, as Trevor would say...

Oh Trevor!

She got up, walked to the window and watched rain splatter the city with shiny surfaces and city night lights.

She tucked herself into bed and decided that she would listen to the rest of the TV show after all.

And why not?

Tired as she was, she felt argumentative. Had she lost touch with the realities of today, she wondered.

Were they all doing the right thing, she wondered...

Trevor was overseas.

Jack was in the energy industry.

Sandra in the field of paleontology and climate change.

And she...she was tossing about with charities and painting to raise money for values that gave meaning and quality to life..?

Suddenly she felt tired.

The TV show was lively. If with more conflicted views.

She thought about it. The Brits never got it, she decided. Perhaps Trevor was right. She was American...

Much as they like to make fun of American republicanism, the British might tire of their own "grey, incompetent managerialists" as one Parliamentarian was saying on the show.

She turned up the volume and listened to the debate on the floor of the House of Parliament:

"The United States of America has always confused British establishment types...."a Tory Member from spoke with the musical intonations of a Welshman.

"A serious country doesn't elect the likes of Jimmy Carter, a peanut farmer; a Ronald Reagan, a B-list Hollywood actor; or Donald Trump, a gold-tapped, orange-tanned hotelier as their political leaders..."

Amanda had to laugh and raised her hand to her mouth.

But the statesman was subtle. "Such amateurs can't compete with the type of PM Britain tends to prefer.

Nearly all of our PMs went to Oxbridge. Most of today's MPs have now spent all their life in politics..."

The House went quiet.

"But what have we done? Are they *Thinkers?* No! *Innovation?* No! *Disrupters who create and achieve new markets and new economic opportunity?* No! Well, Mr. Speaker. I submit to you that it's about time we did!"

"Here! Here!" roared the body of representatives.

Well said! added Amanda.

A member of the Opposition party arose to speak. He was recognized from Ireland.

"Should we turn this august body of politicians over to Dublin for the kind of management that a company like Google could provide?..."

Amanda sat upright in bed.

The notion sent a chill up her spine. Google was in the business of information, data mining and selling...all but the rights of an individual to earn a living. My God!

The House erupted once more.

"Nay, my friend ..." said the Welshman, rising slowly to the bench. "Rather, where is the love of country that instills in our bones the desire to work honestly with our hands? And where are our hearts to produce something good and wonderful...?"

"Here! Here!" went the uproar.

 "Here! Here!" said the House.

Nor was the Welshman done.

"...Not...I say, not...for a socialist state of populists, encouraged by financial elite and globalists whose investment funds do better without sovereign fetter? Give us rather, sovereign leaders! Give us men of boundaries and protection who root for their citizens, and we shall be the capitalists of the century!

Why wait for immigrants to teach us to be Entrepreneurs?

Where are the middle class who must retire early?

Why rely on foreign talent to write Code for our software program when our own young adults sit idle at home?

"F" is not a dirty word. It means Factory. It means Faculty. It means Fearlessness to risk. We test. We invent. We make things. We fix things.."

Amanda was stunned, watching. *Way to go!*

Smiling at the performance, Amanda switched off and rested.

Amanda moved about and set her alarm. She had five hours of sleep before getting up to for her flight out of Heathrow.

Just as she switched off the bedside light just as her cell phone rang

"Hello?"

"Amanda! Its Bill Myers here...Just wanted to check in and see how you were doing?"

"Oh...hello Bill! Yes, thanks. I'm fine..."

Bill spoke at some length about the events on the campus, mostly turning his attention to her good nature and graceful patience... He asked about her recovery. Clearly he would have liked to talk longer, but she kept it short.

"Well then, just wanted to say Good Night! Call me when you get back? Please do!"

In the darkness, Amanda fell into a deep if uneasy slumber.

*　*　*

Chapter 6

Amanda stepped through the portal reserved for passengers arriving at Reagan Airport, Washington DC. They proceeded down the passage and turned the corner of the corridor to the exit gates where guards stood to observe disembarking passengers and baggage.

Amanda's luggage was not a problem. She had carried her bags onboard - a suite of London Fog travel gear fitted for overhead stowage, so she was little encumbered.

Wearing a dark silver shirt over grey tweed pants with a black coat, Amanda blended in. Striding comfortably in leather deck shoes, it was clear she knew how to dress for travel.

She smiled as she approached the gates, happy to be on US soil.

Trevor MacDonnell was a British national, and Amanda's married years at his side did little to mitigate her joy whenever she made landfall on home turf. This was such an occasion. Nor was she disappointed as airport fenestration opened up to show grade level weather outside.

A bright sunlit blue sky that never ended presided over the Nation's capital, even as icy temperatures gave winter barks their crispness bearing dark little buds, and Amanda couldn't wait to feel the chill of air against her face. The air smelled freer, she often teased Trevor whenever they travelled to the United States as they often did. Especially on the Chesapeake Bay where they had kept a boat.

Amanda took a deep breath. Yes. She was home!

The passageway took a last curve through a final gate and she emerged on the main concourse of the airport.

Immediately she saw a face that she recognized. He stood with his shoulders square and his stance assertive.

"Bill..." she exclaimed.

The Admiral in uniform approached.

"Hello Amanda!" said Arguetta.

"I wasn't expecting to be met at the Airport..." she said, grinning. They greeted with a family-style hug.

Behind him stood a young naval officer. He took a step back. "Lt Gerald Afflix. My duty officer for the day..."

"Ma'am" the young officer said curtly.

At his rank in the military establishment, Amanda knew that no Admiral would roam around Washington on business in uniform without an escort. But neither was Arguetta here as her reception party, she realized.

This was official business.

Arguetta looked beyond Amanda, as if expecting someone else. "Trevor?"

"Trevor's in France" she explained, omitting the particulars. "I'm here to attend a conference where my daughter Sandra is presenting her doctoral theory on Paleontology, something hosted by the Philosophical Society of Philadelphia..."

"...Jeffersonian! If I'm not mistaken, Thomas Jefferson founded that organization following the Lewis and Clerk expedition, right?" he smiled.

The Lt Cmdr took her luggage.

"Any down below?" asked Arguetta, asking for the Lieutenant to extract it at the baggage carousel for arriving passengers.

"No" she said. "I travel light. I sent it in advance. What I need, I can buy locally..."

Amanda got the hint. She wasn't expected to arrive without Trevor. They needed a moment to talk, unofficially.

She kept it casual.

"Bill, if you don't mind. I'm parched, and I wonder if we could pick up a quick coffee?"

"Sure! There's a coffee shop beyond the book shop."

"Perfect! Thanks..."

She ordered and they moved to perch quietly at two seats just inside the rail perimeter of the public concourse.

"How's the family?" Amanda asked, looking at him.

"We're all good!" he said, tipping up his cup. The recent loss of his wife Beth had taken them all by surprise. She had been the noise in his life, if not the center of his boating life and sailing. No more. "We miss her. The house is empty. Family-time rings hollow.." he added.

"You had a good life together" said Amanda, touching his arm.

"Oh yes. We did!" he said, his face resolved. He glanced at the Lieutenant waiting a few paces away.

He had a task to accomplish, Amanda could tell. She had worked for him for years, and she knew her former boss. He stood up.

"It's Trevor we need to talk to" he said, reaching for his head-cover and preparing to leave.

"We've some high stakes matters to discuss. They require immediate attention" he said, "they involve sensitive material related to privileged technology. We need to confront our Prime contractor for the project..."

Amanda was surprised at the sudden change in stance. But she understood that she'd been given a few moments to the side.

"I get it. Trevor's Firm has a contract for work for the department of defense that needs immediate attention?"

"Yes. And since I know you both as personal friends, I volunteered to pick you up at the Airport and deliver him directly to the Navy Yard for questioning..."

"Questioning?.."

He looked at Amanda gravely. "It's alarming that we don't have him here...I was expecting him! Where is he Amanda?"

Amanda's face gave her away, and a chill went up her spine at his tone. *Where is he Amanda?*

Bad enough that she felt like a fool for being so clueless. Or that here was Arguetta had come to officially escort him from the plane...But that Trevor was absent from an obligation in Washington was seeding a fearful thought.

Oh God...

Was Trevor detained against his will?

Her mind tumbled through the possibilities...The phone messages. Rosamund, his secretary?

His itinerary...France?

Amanda looked straight at Bill Arguetta. There was little she could keep from his scan.

"What's wrong?" he said, his voice controlled.

Her face must have reflected her apprehension, and she felt her lips quiver. Before she could speak again he said

"I'm afraid he's in serious breach of a contract to the United States Government. I must report him absent immediately."

She knew what that meant. Trevor was the head of the company. Something happened.

"Do you understand...?"

She nodded.

"I'm sorry Amanda. But this is serious. As the lead principle of the entity that holds the contract...I must hold him directly responsible and accountable"

Amanda's head swirled, and the words she was hearing had the tone of a threat, not questions.

"Where are you staying?" she heard him asking

"I was...err, I was going back to our house in Chevy Chase" she answered. "I've made arrangements to have it opened up... and provisioned for the week!"

"Sir" said the Lieutenant, approaching.

"Excuse me" said Arguetta.

The Lieutenant whispered in his ear.

Amanda pulled herself together and looked down at her cell phone. It was buzzing. She was about to switch it off when she saw the image sent to her by text mail.

Headline of a Tabloid newspaper in London

 "Couple accused of fraud in sale of fake painting at Auction!"

There was no question as to who the couple were. She and Trevor were being indicted for fraudulent activity in the UK.

Sandra sent the text message.

They climbed into the waiting car at the airport and Arguetta turned to face her. "Amanda. Trevor is not in compliance with his obligations, and we have a crisis. That's unacceptable" he said, his eyes dark. Adding "And since you are listed as a Member of the Board at his company, I have no choice but to keep you under Protective Custody until you tomorrow morning and give us a the deposition of all that you know. Is that clear? I'll have a security detail posted outside your house tonight..."

"*Deposition...?*" Amanda nodded.

"I understand"

"I'll expect you at 10.30 a.m. sharp, at my office please!"

She sat, feeling numb.

Not only was Trevor in default of oversight of contract for work by his firm for the United States government, but somehow something of some danger had occurred!"

The thoughts swirled.

If now compromised, or if was found that any criminal charges lodged against him in the UK, such as fraud... were pending, there would be serious consequences for him. This, she must avoid at all costs.

For now at least, her thoughts were in turmoil. She felt exhausted. Her shoulder still ached...

Only later, just before arriving at Chevy Chase did Amanda listen to her messages.

Still no word from Trevor.

Sandra had called her three times and was now leaving a message.

"I wanted you to be the first to know Mum. I'm having a baby!"

* * *

The room was warm, if softly glowing in red filtered black light.

Arguetta was in short sleeved fatigues and he tossed down the chalk from a sketch board, frustrated.

He turned to face the specialists and project managers seated, each man dedicated to the latest technology of weaponry and defensive systems.

They were not alone. Around them were IT communications technicians accessing computer data searching live feeds and selected systems. In this room, like any crisis, they were insulated.

Only plasma screens, laptops and lithium devices tinged the room with intra-agency intelligence. They waited, once again.

Slowly, the satellite imagery tracked through the event, frame by frame.

Finally Arguetta stood in front of the imagery, a heaving sea cutting across his chest instead.

"Thank you Gentlemen..." he said. He walked out of the small viewing room and was followed by his retinue. The entered the conference center next door where overhead office house-lights filled the room.

They gathered around the oval table.

"So...the question is *what was this*? How did it happen, and why?" He paused. "Tell me what you've got!"

Arguetta had picked his team well. Avoiding some, he had experts of deep experience, drawn from resources of key personnel best suited to this task.

Certainly he understood the need for political advisors and strategists, they had their place. But not here. Not today.

Not amongst these engineers and scientists. What he wanted were brains. Iterative talent and uninhibited free thinkers. This was strictly a technical code thing, as he put it. And he'd been highly selective about whom he chose to work on the project.

Mostly, these were men he trusted. And more importantly, men who trusted him. Men all bearing grey beards, or Greybeards, as they were called, but men not afraid to think wisely and who had visionary intelligence.

Arguetta spoke.

"The bad news is... that the senior ranking contractor with the technology know-how seems to have gone AWOL. We assume that as a retired executive, the reason given is that he's detached from the core business and simply out of touch. I know the man. He's a British national and a man of integrity. But since his spouse doesn't even know his whereabouts, we have to assume there's foul play and hostile intent to harm.." He leaned forward into his knuckles on the table and whispered. "Gentlemen: We have an enemy close to ground!"

"...If so, what is the source?" asked one...

"Or the motive..?" asked another

Arguetta paced with his thoughts.

"We think globally. We think strategically. Who has *what* technology? Where is the *commercial* scientific research? So, we examine development research, technical advances...scholarship stuff.

After that, its political strategic analysis: Is there a perpetrator? What is the motive? Can this be a random accident... We must assume it's a Class-One threat!

More. Is it a social threat...So, what impact? What consequences to societal destabilization?"

"There is some technology out there, mostly student projections of imagined development, but nothing real or hard...I'll run a survey on who's playing with lab toys"

"Right" said Arguetta. "Thanks Bill. If there's anything worth knowing, we know it. I don't like discovering stuff that we *don't* know!" He paused again.

"We look under every door mat; every basement experiment, every possibility of chatter and communications. We examine every connection. Got it?"

"NASA is a good place to ask first" said Dave, the last man to speak. "They inspire innovative thinking and research in the heart of every tinkering plebe.."

"Good man!"

Arguetta consulted his watch. They'd been cooped up at the Pentagon for two days. There would be no retreating from this problem. He continued. "We've watched with our own eyes something terrible. And here we sit. We can't figure it out! So we start from the beginning..."

He glanced up at the clock on the wall.

"Short lunch break. Hit the books for an hour: Tap all available data intelligence. Then we regroup with more questions at 1500....Bring your best analytical thinking!" said Arguetta.

It wasn't long before they were seated at the same table.

"So...we've got one Russian ship asking for our assistance?" said Tom Stewart, a specialist from the technical code of ship systems. "The problem? A nuclear cruiser with *radiation-decay*?"

He looked around the table and someone spoke up. "That's the lamest reason to beckon for our assistance! I mean, don't they have contingency plans?"

"Of course they do..." said a voice in the back. He was from HM&E systems. "There's a mechanical tone..." he asserted "but no sense of alarm or fear for the safety of the crew? It's a honey pot."

Arguetta looked up. "Possibly. Let's listen again to the technical assessment of Captain Jennings. He's pretty goddamned well informed about his ship. He never fell for it. What does he relay?..Replay his feed, Mark?"

"It should be contained. At the core of a power reactor, the probability of a nutron intersection with a fissionable nuclear moment before it escapes into the shielding is much lower: Their reactor runs on a highly enriched uranium. One of the technical difficulties is in designing fuel elements which will withstand a large amount of radiation damage. Fuel elements may crack over time, and gas bubbles may form. This, they claim is their problem."

"So, what else could have caused that kind of response from the Russians to pose such a situation? They must have known we'd figure out their design capabilities. No He was bluffing. It was something else."

"Something unpredictable. Something *improbable*?" asked Tenley from Engineering. This is his ExO. Not his ship's mechanic asking for a spare wrench!"

Play the tape on the next sequence Mark

"Marine reactors are designed for long core life: Enabled by the relatively highly enrichment of uranium, and incorporating a "burnable poison" in the fuel elements, the process serves as a throttle to slow depletion of the elements with age to become less reactive. The increase/decrease of this burnable poison is the speed with which they can lessen reactivity..."

"That's a load of crap!" said Arguetta. "We know precisely down to the hour the longevity of our ship's engines and energy source. Right?"

"Well, he was explaining the situation to a room full of non-technical staff, remember. He had to explain it in simple terms?"

Arguetta stared. "And...?"

"If the Russians knew enough about their burn rate, excuse me, that is, their high enrichment of uranium combining with their burnable poison in fuel element - they knew *exactly* how to throttle their burn rate to depletion. In fact, every sailor on board the ship would understand that concept."

"So why spell it out..."

Arguetta stopped pacing. "Because of what they're *not* saying!"

Tenley's voice came forward. "Was it really that they ran out of reactivity, and like a scout camp stumbled into their crisis, or did something else surprise them with the *management* of the propulsion?"

"Sabotage?"

Tom picked up on the thread. "They knew exactly how to throttle their burn rate of reactivity. Something that surprised them could well have been unforeseen in their calculations of the *rate of decrease* in burnable poison..." said Stewart.

"Or *rate of Increase*?" added Tenley.

"What does that suggest? That something unexplained was draining off their reactivity resistance in spite of the controls for poison metabolism?"

"Possibly. Then again, Jennings was suspicious! Did they just want to test our assistance, or to warn us of outside *intervention*?"

"They wanted to test how far advanced we were with our tech solutions for nuclear energy..."

"Possibly..."

Arguetta, who had been perched on the table, lowered his legs and walked over. "He's trained to think that way. That's why we have Captains like Jennings..."

"The Russians knew what they had to do: They alerted Jennings to keep his distance. They *knew*... If their reactor pressure vessel was exposed because their shield was damaged, they were at sea awaiting the gradual degradation of their reactivity."

"the greater impact of fallout failure?"

"Possibly. Yet they were at sea in a low impact zone. And they were trying to alert Jennings without revealing the bigger Russian problem...Something that was about to become potentially *our* problem?"

"They clearly suspected foul play! They were...warning Jennings of a deeper issue in talking about a technical failure with measure demure?" elected Tenley.

"But from whom? What *else* do we have?"

Nobody spoke, thinking.

"...Two Navy cruisers with nuclear propulsion in close proximity having similar engineering parameters, and yet *one* cannot explain the loss of degradation from their contained system? How inconsistent is that?"

"What comparisons have we made with everything else?" asked Tenley "Ships Crew. Training. Weapons systems. Technical capability. Repair history. Ship design...We've looked at both ships and found pretty much an equal risk weighting, right?"

"So...then..." said Arguetta "if it isn't adversarial, and both ships are compromised by sudden severe sea conditions?"

"Unless... unless, we have an anomaly that we aren't reading" said Stewart. "Mobility. Both of these vessels are kinematic."

"If they are linked in some way, that means they approached danger without knowledge. Or, if the sea state is responsible, what lured them into the same state?" said Tom

Arguetta reconsidered. "Ok...Let's look at some of those wave disturbances again"

Tom continued "Hydrostatically, they appear as little more than two ships in a storm, but here occurs something with sufficient energy to destroy both naval frigates..."

"That's a powerful statement, right there..." interrupted Arguetta, his mind on the lookout for signals of willful assault. "Are we thinking...too conventionally here?"

"Perhaps. But if we examine this for a third party assault, where is there missile disturbance by way of wave action? Or if subsea, sonar... Or a firing target resolution, we would have detected the heat radiation in the advance wave action. Or *any* dispersion pattern of impact stream. Hell, even the assault device itself...*Something*? No!"

The room fell silent.

"Cavitation?" asked Tenley.

No response.

"Unless its ...supersonic?" volunteered Stewart.

 "I wish! No. We don't have that kind of technology yet. Besides, we're not at war! Even the research is sketchy. No. We're missing something..."

Again the room fell quiet.

"So, what's in a display of taking down two cruisers from two navy fleets..." Arguetta's voice trailed.

Arguetta's face went pale.

The thoughts that ran through his head took him away from the crowd and deep into his consciousness. He'd need to think.

Surely not...

He left the room. He needed air "Excuse me Gentlemen.."

* * *

Philadelphia, Pa

"The Flood is one of the most re-told stories in ancient history!" said Sandra at the podium of the lecture hall of the historic society in Philadelphia, Pennsylvania. She smiled, then looking up at the audience, added "Children love the story as they imagine Noah taking *all those animals, two by two, into his great big ship, Noah's Ark...*"
Laughter.

Sandra looked beautiful, thought Amanda. There she was... standing at her podium presenting a paper for this academy of science about paleontology, playfully entitled *"Did Noah's Ark sail?"*

"Indeed it is one of the most remarkable accounts of the ancient world that we know of..." Her blond head fairly gleamed in the spotlight, if the rest of her was hidden by microphones and amplifiers for sound and audio. And her melodious voice was mesmerizing, she held her audience spell-bound.

Much to the surprise of the Academy, the seating was filled to capacity. Many had booked months in advance. Already the Board of Membership had gathered for an advance reception, a private fundraising event in the grand foyer of the historic building.

Many wore gowns and shawls. Some came with friends, and others had travelled from across the country for the occasion, like Amanda herself. All were donors of the charitable foundation, this was clearly a popular event.

And in this moment, it was clear why.

Amanda too was swept up with wonder. This was one of Americas most venerated institutions, founded in the 18th century by none other than Thomas Jefferson himself at precisely the historic site where those early colonists – many of them merchants of venture with ships at the city docks, who had signed the Declaration of Independence as the American Constitution.

Philadelphia, this city of a nascent nation, had thrived. Much of it related to early days of mercantilism and finance, but later developing to shipbuilding through WWII. How many had passed through here holding and testing and refining the principles of early Founders?

Now a Foundation of charitable donations for academic research and scholarship, it invited guest speakers to display new thought and findings of their research. As it did today, for Sandra.

This dynamic forum resulted in developments generously rewarded with donations from benefactors. Here tonight were mostly senior citizens who relished a lecture on paleontology. But upstairs, the event held ceremonial flourish, if not celebrity status for city newspapers.

As for scholars invited to present their papers, the privilege of this prestigious event was noted. Not only was there a generous stipend offered to continue post-doctorate work, but also recognition for contributing to the greater humanities "intellectual body of perceived wisdom," as the official Award stated in its Letter of Invitation: For Sandra McDonnell, it was unspeakably exciting.

Twice, she had waved at her mother. Once, out of nervous fidgeting before being officially introduced, and then at the end, when she brought the audience to its feet in unmitigated applause.

Amanda looked about the audience. Nobody it seemed, was too old to hear the story of the Flood.

Sandra continued with her lecture as the house lights dimmed for a plasma screen.

..."Around 13,000 years ago, the planet was emerging from its last great ice age. The ice age covered all of North America, Europe and Asia for thousands of years...

And as the ice sheets were retreating, we ask, what was it like? ..

"Giant mammals — steppe bison, woolly mammoths and saber-toothed cats roaming, perhaps grazing - or hunted, across vast tundra and grasslands?

"In this image we see a Paleo-Indian group of hunter-gatherers...These people became known as the Clovis people who had antecedently crossed a land bridge from Asia.

"They leave us rare specimens of arrow-heads as evidence. Their spears have distinctive features for their size of game... Even as the ice age was receding!

Sandra paused.

"Then about 12,800 years ago, something strange happened. The weather changed. Earth went backward and retreated into another Ice age.   We know that temperatures in the Northern Hemisphere plunged 8 degrees Celsius. We view it now as a cold snap. A blip in the passage of geologic time of 1,200 years.

She paused again

"Then just as abruptly, earth began to warm again!"

The audience gasped. An adventure in the making...and they murmured softly.

An image lit the screens.

"Here, we now see that giant mammals were dying out. Clovis people had apparently vanished..."

Another image.

"Geologists call this the Younger Dryas, and it's cause is a mystery. Possibly, freshwater infusions from a melting ice sheet entered the body of water and disrupted earth's heat-transporting ocean currents."

A bright image of NOAA appeared.

"NOAA has done some remarkable research in its prognostications. One theory suggests that About 20,000 years ago, the melting Laurentide Ice Sheet of North America released sufficient   freshwater into the North Atlantic Ocean to change ocean circulation patterns -- like a conveyor belt of warm circulation, and it was that event that triggered the Younger Dryas cold period of 12,800 years ago."

"But what evidence do we have? What folklore narrative suggests that something traumatic occurred?

We have no clear indications!

"but was *that* the story of Noah?"

Sandra paused, knowing that they were aware of the cultural conflict that followed: That is, the difference between cultural accounts of ancient Christian-Judaic epistemology as Western Civilization, and the facts of science.

Furthermore, Sandra knew that somewhere deep in their hearts reigned a sweetness of childhood that made them human, God's children...as it were, per Noah's Ark

The house lights went on.

"So, Ladies and Gentlemen, we have a raging war amongst scientists about what happened!"

Laughter.

"One theory suggests a cosmic event hit the earth and caused the sudden deep freeze. At 12,800 years ago did a comet entered the atmosphere of the earth? Perhaps exploding over the Laurentide Ice Sheet of North America. Is that possible, we ask... And, how long did it last?

"Did such an event   trigger wildfires? Did subsurface resonance induce volcanic eruptions?

 Could those fires/eruptions emit enough soot and carbon compounds into the atmosphere to block-out the sun and cool the planet once again, thus reversing the warming of the ice sheet and cause reversal to cold. How long did that period of sun-blocking last before an equilibrium was regained?

"We know that a similar "airburst" effect did happened on a far smaller scale in 1908 over Siberia's Tunguska region, if you recall. We see a pattern of heat dispersion in the lay of the trees leveled as it hit the planet. We suspect that the earth is still feeling that impact.

Similarly, a cataclysm at the onset of the Younger Dryas, according to the hypothesis' proponents, would answer the cause of large animal extinction...or even the disappearance of the Clovis people..."

She paused.

"For more than a decade, scientific journals have been the battleground for skirmishes over this 'impact' hypothesis. The idea has drawn opponents from a spectrum of scientific fields, including paleoclimatology, physics and archaeology..."

"Critics contend that there is little to no reproducible or incontrovertible evidence for many of the key arguments of the hypothesis.

"There are ...proxies for an impact," says Vance Holliday, an archaeologist and geologist at the University of Arizona in Tucson. "And they're *all debatable*, every single one!"

"In North Pole core and fossil samplings, we do see carbon evidence in the ice pack to show a definitive heat impact of some kind, possibly coinciding with, and resulting in...the great floods of ancient account?"

"Could this have caused an increase in sea-level and climate changes that caused water infusions as consequence? Could the great flood have been a true event and that gave rise to narratives laced with deity inference of that era?

Regardless, we do see evidence of a carbon deposit and resulting melting that is consistent with the time of the flood account.

In conclusion, to answer the hypothesis that Noah's Ark set sail then, we can say with some degree of certainty, based on ancient accounts of legend and writings...

She paused, adding softly, *the story of Noah is safe! "*

The room erupted with jubilant chortlings and laughter. *Hurray!*

And leaving them, like children, to enjoy the moment of their favorite storytelling, she smiled and brought her lecture to a close.

* * *

Amanda and Sandra spent the whole day together in the city of Philadelphia.

"Your talk last night was *wonderful*" said Amanda. "You're a natural..."

Sandra sipped her coffee and grinned. They had stopped at the bakery. "Well. I kept it light. It's what any basic lecture must provide, I think. Some levity!"

"And ...really, they were all very engaged...Yes. It's a lively lot up here!" chuckled Amanda. Adding, "you left them weighing science against conviction, and you gave graceful legitimacy to individual interpretation."

"Thanks!"

They shopped. Specialty shops, bookstores, art galleries and gift stores in old churches, most of them down narrow cobbled streets of a bygone era.

Finally reaching the historic Square of the old city of Philadelphia, they found it teeming with tourists. Mostly, it was families showing children the sites of celebrated colonial structures like Carpenters Hall and Constitution Hall. Others were taking guided tours on horse-drawn wagons, happily wending their way through the city under fringed tarps as taxi's honked for speed and a background of noise from Interstate I-95 hurled traffic at top speeds.

Clip clop... Clip clop...

> *"Here, the Liberty Bell was struck on the day that Benjamin Franklin struck his press to publish the first copy of the American Constitution..."* announced one tour guide to his passengers.

Philadelphia was an old city flaunting its new world. Flowers flourishing from old brick structures with uneven pavements held firmly their ground, if dwarfed by towering modern university buildings.

Jammed by pedestrians, bicycles and traffic moving from markets to training labs, professionals walked from

Georgian municipalities to office skyscrapers glimmering in chrome and glass. Incongruity in this city displayed a weathered patience for multi-generational uses, like the elderly walking in parks as students vaulted hedge rows with 20lb backpacks to attend class.

Philadelphia was a center of training institutions. Old city contained the School of Podiatry. School of Veterinary Science. School of Medicine. The Center for Architecture. School of Dentistry. The Culinary Institute of America. Penn University School of Law. Drexel. The Center for the Performing Arts...

Underlying such endurance was a century of finance for an emerging America. During the industrial revolution, here was the center of finance and trade, the early days of industrial tycoons and financiers who ruled the bond markets, built the railroads, created the textile mills, chemicals, steel, minerals and coal for energy. Here, rhe center of capitalism took root not meters away from the historic structures that framed the constitution and envisioned such progress.

It had been a long day for Sandra and Amanda.

Finally, at dinner, they sipped wine together, mother and daughter. Seated at a corner Bistro beneath twinkling city lights, the colors of dusk brushed over the city, and the soft sounds of a lively nightlife began to appear.

Sandra smiled. She watched a couple trip by with unfettered giggling, the girl wearing ankle boots and tights, the guy in jeans and a dark shirt covering a body fit from exercise.

It pleased Amanda to see her daughter look happy. It was more than just a grin. Sandra was savoring her accomplishment, satisfaction from a work of scholarship. For too long her world was filled with the life of her husband and his career.

Amanda recognized something more in her daughter's lecture. And she spoke.

"You responded well to your audience. They were not young students. They were people who had lived on the beliefs of childhood...something which you did not trample on!"

Sandra rolled her eyes.

Amanda leaned forward and spoke softly "You cared!"

Sandra looked at her mother, unsure of whether to consider that as a good thing or a bad thing. In academia, you were not supposed to care, only to analyze. She sighed.

"No. I'm serious..." continued Amanda. "You could have crushed their notions of old biblical flood tales..."

Sandra found a quirk and come back at her mother with a retort. "Well, from a purely anthropological point of view, you could argue that the power of suggestion in God's punishment for the earth with a great flood *did* advance the human condition toward modern technical knowledge of geophysics!"

"Hmm" chuckled Amanda.

"Anyway..." sipped Sandra, indicating that time was short and she was flying back in the morning. "How's Dad?"

Amanda met the question with a pensive frown. Then she looked directly at Sandra. "I've been called in for research in Washington..."

"Oh no mom.. You're *not* thinking of returning to your work? ..."

"Just for a few weeks..." Amanda paused. "I'm retired. Just some technical research and documentation findings at Fort Mead for some new R&D..."

"For Admiral Arguetta?" shot Sandra. "My God, mom. Is your security clearance even valid?...I mean, *What are you doing*? Why would you agree...?"

"Because...Dad's gone missing! His contract with the government is in turmoil. I'm on the Company Board. I agreed to engage *on his behalf*..."

Sandra stood up. "Where *is* Dad?"

***

"Will this help?" asked Penny Andrews, a female midshipman doing duty at the Pentagon Archives for the summer.

Penny had been Amanda's assistant for two days, and they had filtered through message traffic dealing with the servicing of ships' alterations to solve a dysfunction. Between active ships and civilian technical codes by specialization, topics ranged in size for everything aimed at optimum engineering, performance and updates. Lubrication pumps. Coils. Engine compartment kits. Deck surfaces. Gun mounts. Intakes. Turbines. Speed capability. Anchors... Nor was there any dearth of need by ships' class. The United States Navy was active on all fronts and in all seas, requiring any design improvements for a ship's hull, maintenance and engineering systems.

It was a handful of a task.

Penny and Amanda became pretty adept at spotting sleepers, as they put it, messages or occasional underlying assumptions that would hand them what they wanted. And they were thorough in sorting material.

But nothing containing material relevant to propulsion systems was showing up. It was all routine correspondence. Nothing had turned up for their search criteria within two years of traffic.

"...It's a message from the Pacific Fleet detecting a malfunction in propulsion systems during turbulence only, right?" wavered Penny's voice from the bottom of a box somewhere, as if the quest had to be recited periodically for veracity. "So..." she added with another jerk to dislodge more files "if ...it's *not* found to be a dysfunction by Navsea..then it's *not* in development as needing a technical solution either, right?"

"Hmm" nodded Amanda delving deep into digital data files of a computer. "Good thinking..."

She pushed back, her eyes dry and bleary.

"You know what, I think it's time to abandon this line of enquiry and focus exclusively on the FOI docs only! For some reason, these messages on propulsion seem to elicit distress by the ship's commander. Propulsion malfunction is not your garden variety routine request. Though it's nothing more than a propeller. It's...it's..."

"...like a macho thing?" volunteered Penny.

"Yes!" laughed Amanda. "FOI is where it must be told then..."

"Right!"

They had fun. And judging by the pile on their table, there wasn't a single Ship Alteration Request for Service that evaded their scrutiny for the past six years.

They went through another stack of records.

Finally Amanda leaned back and pulled off her oversized glasses.

"Nothing! Nothing. Nothing out of the ordinary..." she muttered.

Across the room Penny leaned forward. She had read dozens, no, tens of dozens of Requisition Slips for Amanda at the Archives; plus reviewed more files - and service reports on other matters, more that she could have imagined...

"Shall we take a break and get a bite to eat Ms Wells?"

"Good idea!" sighed Amanda.

"I can see why Admiral Arguetta has you examining this question Ma'am..." said Penny over a pita sandwich "You are exhaustive in your searching!"

"Umm" swallowed Amanda, a tuna sandwich in her hand "You mean compulsive-obsessive...?"

"No!" chuckled Penny. "Just thorough. You make every topic interesting to look at!"

"I search for Gremlins" said Amanda "It's what warrior pilots perceive on the wings of their plane before entering battle..."

"*Gremlins?*"

"imagined jinxes..." she grinned. "But sure, archival searches can produce real evidence. That's the difference between solving something urgent or just answering the mail."

Penny gazed at her, saying nothing.

By the end of the day, they still had found little to add to their Research Report.

Amanda was getting frustrated.

It was close to quitting time, and they were glad of it.

"There you are!" called out a booming voice from across the Archives of the Pentagon. Amanda looked up.

"You look like Arthur the Aardvark in those glasses" said Admiral Arguetta, grinning.

Amanda smiled.

He nodded at Penny.

"I hope you've got something meaningful by now?"

"We're close.." said Amanda much to the relief of Penny who could show little for hours of reading through classified communications.

"Oh good..." said Arguetta. "Then let's wrap this up. I'll drive you to Capitol Hill" He glanced at his watch.

"Learn anything Midshipman Andrews?" he said to Penny.

"Yes Sir"

Penny's car was in the main parking lot, she was going out with friends tonight, Amanda knew.

"Have a good night!" grinned Amanda, allowing her to leave promptly.

Amanda took a big breath.

"Long day?" said Arguetta, perching at the far end of her desk, one knee free.

"I'll say!" she said, piling up one final stack of documents for Penny's desk to review in the morning. And she explained their method to Arguetta.

Culling through Finding Aids, the archival retrieval process was marked by hourly Pulls by personal who must find and process the boxes from the storage shelves containing original materials: One wrong annotation, or box number from any number of equal possibilities, and the time wasted could be strenuous. Working on a tight schedule, there had been no room for inefficiency. "How do you know what you're ordering?" asked Arguetta, his tone casual.

"Well...you don't. Not really" she chuckled.

Neither could anyone be sure what was to be found in any box of correspondence, nor were all documents equal in value - or even accessible, given their level of classification and sensitivity. No, she told Arguetta, the process was not fast.

"How long does it take?" he asked.

"Twice daily, box-loads are wheeled out on carts. Restrictions apply. You are limited to number of boxes. Content. Space. Topics. And worse of all, limitations on reading time!"

Arguetta laughed. "That's worst than taking a goddamned test!"

It requires a clear mind, analytical thinking and knowledge skills to be a good Researcher..."

Amanda got up and stopped. She was ready to leave for the day.

Arguetta waited. "Here..." he volunteered, jumping for a stack that threatened to find gravity.

"Got it!" she responded, just in time.

"I'm glad I found you someone who could help!" said Arguetta.

"Penny has the skill. She's terrific. Thank you!"

"I'm going to get you a higher security clearance.." said Arguetta, pressing the elevator button down to the garage. "Do you need more assistance?"

"No. My two reading warriors are sufficient. I'm wearing them out!"

"Good training for a Mid!" said Arguetta, offering her to exit the elevator.

With an apartment downtown near the Navy Yard of Washington DC, Amanda routinely commuted by Metro. But Arguetta had offered to drop her off, and she accepted.

He opened the Fire doors to the underground garage and they walked the length of the hall before entering garage parking Level G3.

"I know how capable you can be for research...So we do appreciate what you're doing.." Arguetta said as they walked across the concrete level lined with parked cars, and Amanda recognized his old pickup truck. She smiled.

"You're still driving that thing?" she teased.

Arguetta, as far as she could remember, had never bought the latest car. It was his wife Ellen who owned a Volvo. He treasured that rusting trailer-hitch, hauling their sailboat around for years. That is, before Ellen died. Now, clearly, the old vessel had long lost its attraction, and Arguetta no longer went sailing. Somehow, the joy had left his step, she noticed.

They stood now just outside the perimeter of the premises, and he paused.

"I have to tell you Amanda. Trevor's company has put us in a hell of a bad place at the moment. I can't imagine what happened up there...But his absence looks bad."

He faced her. "I know his technical staff is as good as it gets. Trevor is not slack on hiring the best. But Jesus, Amanda...A ship down on his watch and he's *absent?*"

She averted her eyes.

"What's he doing Amanda?"

She was about to say something when a screeching of wheels veered in through the outside barrier.

It came out of nowhere, racing as it roared by, and from a lowered window a semi-automatic gun nozzle took aim at Arguetta and released two rounds of short bursts.

The vehicle left in a blur... Arguetta was on the ground, blood spluttering from his upper arm and neck.

She knelt beside him, put one hand to his wound and with the other searched for her cell phone to call for Emergency Help.

She had his fingers in her hand, all bloody, and he squeezed slightly. She understood. Assailants were recognizable enemies world-over who would stop at nothing.

Yes, she understood. This was to be no defeat. She would be relentless in her work... And here, he was saying something different. He did have confidence in her abilities to lead Trevor's firm. That was his signaled meaning. She squeezed back.

He was still conscious when the Ambulance left. Amanda was denied access to the hospital.

The next day it was found that Arguetta would make a full recovery from a flesh wound and a broken collar bone.

She called him repeatedly at the hospital, asking about his condition. Usually the Nurse station took the message. When finally he talked, he said "I am...too tough to kill these days!"

Amanda looked out the window of her apartment building, a view distorted by the silver glyphic of rain.

Rooted in her thoughts, she felt a tangle of frustration and resentment. This was not the first time that Trevor had gone missing...

Once before as British minister he had put himself on the wrong political side of policy here in the United States. And if quickly sorted by inter-government arrangements which put to rest the circumstances of his tactical decisions, she knew this city liked things to be clear cut and rational. Her eyes strayed to the iconic roof tops of government buildings and the dome of Congress, the Supreme Court and the Smithsonian.

But not all things were simple.

She and Trevor were retired now. He had aged, and she more preoccupied with the things that gave meaning to a lifetime, relishing those years that remained... It was a natural place to be for all who had accomplished so much. She and her family - and their activities, were everything!

This world was very far from the professional years of academic research and analysis – a time when she worked here with her small business years ago, before she settled to have a family.

Yet it was Trevor who framed her world. After she finished with her career, he had taken her little firm and put it on a corporate stage, amalgamating it into a well capitalized engineering and research company competing for global contracts. And now she was having to take Trevor's place at the head of that company, a company accountable to the government.

But it was the last place she wanted to be...And more than anything, she cared deeply about Trevor's wellbeing.

Where was he?

This had become an impossible situation!

She had heard nothing from him. His office in London had reported him missing. They continued to investigate his absence, they told her.

Was he alright? What if something happened to him? He was no longer a young man, she worried. What kind of distress was he under?

She had called repeatedly, and everyone was doing what they could: Jacques. Rosamund. The local departments of investigation. The police. Interpol...His disappearance had occurred on European soil after all.

But one thing was certain. Her role was not there in the fray of things, but rather here, holding up his interests on his behalf, she knew.

The rain gave way to brighter clouds, if low on the city.

But her thoughts held fast to Trevor. They had been through so much together – he, in his wonderful manner, his tall stance and reassuring gate. How often he had gazed down at her, his hair now grey and still stubbornly curly.

He made her feel elegant, she decided. In finery threads, with silvering hair gracefully pulled back and long down a back, she framed her life for him, she realized. How she loved to be going out with him wearing an elegant gown with pearls at her neck. Or seeing him next morning, together on a travel trip, coffee in hand, with that facetious smirk on his face as he read the newspaper...as if nothing at all had happened that night.

Oh, God. She missed him!

Yet here she was. Responsible for a firm that held a contract to the United States government. A contract that had just suffered a massive failure, and now she was left to solve the crisis...

Worse. Her former boss was the senior liaison government official with whom the company must be accountable..

How could this have happened?

Not only was Admiral Arguetta to oversee the task of solving the crisis, but he had just been gunned down.

Instinctively, she shuddered.

The drizzle was now relentless.

She must focus on the situation at hand: Was this shooting suggesting political overtones? Was this a targeted focus of some nature on secure premises, a leak an informant? Who had access? Who knew?

How to solve...

Especially since there was more to the event than she knew. Clearly, she had not been read into the whole picture.

One this was certain. Trevor's firm played a key role in solving a problem. A situation had gone wrong, and there was no evading that responsibility. He was the contractor who must support that failure...

Further, Arguetta's assault showed the hand of a real enemy.

She had work to do.

She would sift through the evidence first, then come up with a working plan of action. Monday morning she would set up an emergency task force at company headquarters. Together they would set up a place as ground zero.

Next, she would talk to all essential personnel, recruit the best and develop her team of active participants, with a team leader. She would delegate most of the tasking to him, and filter through as much intelligence as she could get for him to disseminate.

She spent most of the weekend making notes, following leads and exploring any findings from company research and technology. She was shaping her thoughts, finding less a fog and more a direction, she felt certain.

Finally she stretched, her neck aching from close work.

She should rest. *And eat!*

She turned away to make herself a fresh brew of coffee. She would give it her best, of that there was no discourse. That was Amanda Wells.

Monday morning a solid management plan was clear. Amanda showed up for work at *Research Technologies Inc* dressed like the CEO of the company.

She was welcomed at the Lobby by an Executive Assistant and taken to HR and Security offices to get her clearances and badges.

Then she was escorted to the 11th floor to meet and greet the staff. They briefed her.

As the day wore on, it was evident that there was not only a technical crisis at hand, but almost a management meltdown. They embraced her role of leadership.

Amanda knew what she had to do first. She had to pull them together.

Moreover, if there was one code of conduct that Amanda understood about the defense industry, it was professional conduct that did not allow for silly speculation. Too much was at stake. Too many people depended on the right choices of management. And mistakes were costly. Often, decisions had the consequence of life or death in the balance.

You did your duty.

For today, problem-solving had a slow start..but she gained steam, and this she would tell Arguetta later that evening at the hospital.

She found Arguetta in his room laying there, frustrated as hell.

Medication, and a few stitches had kept him in a semi-dozing state for a couple days, even if lines of grey remained etched across his face. But he looked fairly unscathed.

Still, for a man like Arguetta, nothing was more frustrating than being debilitated at Bethesda Naval Memorial Hospital.

A scowl on his face told her he'd read every booklet, every Travel Guide and Real Estate magazine found in the waiting room. And yes, he was *mad.*

Mad as hell that a gunman had breached security, took aim at a uniformed officer of Navy ...*and got away!* Someone, somewhere would be held accountable.

Amanda was patient, and Arguetta finally calmed down.

He felt fine, he assured her, apologizing.

Mostly, they were waiting on test results that might suggest brain damage. But none was anticipated. Lucky, he was... indeed!

He talked, sharing his mind with Amanda.

How could he have not seen this coming?

He knew better than to walk about without taking precautions in public spaces, he told her. The new protocol, as they called it. These days, all military personnel were cautioned to show vigilance...to be alert to *every* dark passage – or *oncoming* vehicle!

Amanda persuaded him not to blame himself. He was, after all engaged in the normal business of his job, she reminded him. On secured premises.

He grunted with another scowl, arms folded.

"No assailant would be deterred if he was *that* determined to seek you out, regardless. All milieus are penetrable!"

The prospect left them silent, assessing.

The question, rather, was *Why*...Why was he targeted?

They discussed the matter at some length.

Arguetta was an official figure. He held the rank of authority managing a crisis that had just occurred and been reported by the press.

Was there some connection? Or was it coincidence?

The more they thought about it, the more they realized that this was no accident. He was indeed the intended target.

But for now, they had arrangements to contend with.

Sergeant Morris was to make an official statement on the matter from the Anti-terror office at DHS. That was their jurisdiction since no declaration of hostilities had been issued, officially..

"An unfortunate mishap aboard a US Navy ship," as they put it. "A technical glitch with an unplanned outcome. An investigation was underway."

Far from conclusive, there was another suspicion developing. Definitely. This was a hostile act of terror.

Moreover, as far as Arguetta was concerned, the enemy had just shown his hand!

The wound was not critical. Because Arguetta was fortunate to have had no vital organ damage, his recovery was easy. He was discharged and sent home to rest for two weeks.

What that meant, in effect, was that the team he was working with came to his home for discussions. And like it or not, Amanda was frequently the one sustaining them with tea and coffee from his kitchen!

Still, it didn't bother her too much. Ellen had been her friend for years. And it was the least Amanda could do for her. Bill Arguetta clearly felt lost without his wife.

As the weeks wore on, the schedule of long days of work in Washington and nightly visits to Annapolis was taking its toll on Amanda.

At the office of *Research Technologies* Amanda was delving deeper into the support work for the contract. It was their task to conduct an official investigation and make their report on the ship's failure. Repeatedly she received calls from key officials in government; twice from the Chief of Staff at the Whitehouse.

Under no circumstances was she volunteering much information. In fact, it was Arguetta she was accountable to, and she deferred most queries to him, if receiving increasing demands and impatience over the phone.

"Never mind!" he assured her. "For all you know, it's the Washington Post you're broadcasting to. They're positioning for political polarization mostly!"

Amanda knew. Trevor had warned her enough times.

Arguetta was insistent."It's how Big Tech works!" he told her. "Keep the eyes down and mouth shut, as I tell my staff!"

With resources available and all essential staff at hand, whatever time had been used up regarding the assault on Arguette, operations were quickly evolving with new findings.

And the more they reviewed the event, the more aware they became of having been watched.

Even before the shooting incident in the garage, it was clear that there was a leak. Who had access to critical information?

More importantly, why?

Arguetta was getting frustrated. Was interference coming from his own investigation at the Pentagon?

He was assured that it was not. There were others taking his slack, as they put it. But increasingly, he relied on Amanda to keep things "in-house"

Gradually, as the technical staff from the Pentagon dwindled to two persons driving to Annapolis, it was becoming increasingly obvious that both incidents were related, if never stated by any of them.

Nobody wanted to risk thinking strategically, he later admitted to Amanda. Career politicians in Congress were itching to make mischief, somewhere...as he put it.

Amanda, for her part, worked hard.

Not only was she steeped in the analysis of the event from a technical point of view with a lot of startling innovative development, but Arguetta's concern were adding stress to something that apparently, should be hushed up.

If so, it would serve the enemy well if his absence from that circle was concluded. Thus, taking him out of circulation was an assault that was possibly synonymous. *Delay and disrupt!*

Worse. That made it a clear act of terrorism against a US target. This, they knew.

Further, the finding of *Research Technologies Inc* was an event clearly being watched.

And, how should she mask any prejudice, she wondered.

Increasingly, he relied on her to run cover for him. Plus they all looked at Amanda for answers.

Thankfully, the research of her team had remained sealed and silent. And she was dividing her time between his office *pro tempore* and her own corporate headquarters. But she was walking a fine line. And she recognized the danger.

On evening, alone in her apartment, she stood at the window thinking. There might other possibilities... She had been standing at his side when the shooting occurred. Was it possible that *she* was the intended target?

This, she told Arguetta. Was this altogether an ongoing assault on key personnel?

Had they been naïve to think it was coincidental?

So now they questioned another aspect even further. What if the corporate senior executive CEO of *Research Technologies Inc* was abducted? Wasn't Trevor MacDonnell after all ... What if he wasn't lost on a travel trip, but missing for other reasons?

No!

Amanda gasped with fear, and took a step back.

What did all this mean?

Had they underestimated the threat?

* * *

Arguetta had made a startling discovery, and he was back in town - if with him arm in a sling, giving orders and abrupt as ever.

In the Washington office of *Research Technologies Inc*, the analytical team of experts continued their work, and with a few delicate prompts from Amanda, they were presently assessing energy industries who might be competitors. However, that's all she revealed.

Or, as Arguetta's put it - she was the contractor conducting team support to brainstorm possibilities following daily briefings and intelligence from the Pentagon. Truth was, her team could have done better if left to their own devices of analysis. Arguetta was getting in the way. He was nervous.

Moreover, he was getting belligerent, chiefly because he was under pressure from his superiors, and because the answers were not clear.

For her part, Amanda was on the team of her husband's company, officially head of a task force to deal with a crisis. But she quickly absorbed the greater need to babysit Arguetta and run interference for her team, just so they could think!

They appreciated her good graces, and worked around the clock for her.

Amongst them were two civilian contractors supporting engineering, and they knew engine design systems; two were researchers from a private firm developing energy sources for propulsion systems, and one was a development engineer from the aerospace industries. One thing became immediately clear. This problem was related to energy, with intonations of global reaching.

Arguetta disagreed. He wanted all kinds of other technical specialists, including weapons development. And much as they felt increasingly sure of their own suspicions, they could not discount his assertions.

Amanda's only tactic was to persuade him that energy propulsion was something that could easily be weaponized. In fact, it was already ahead of the curve of conventional thinking...

Later that night, alone in her office with a desk full of reports, Amanda sighed deeply. Her life was not at all engaged in a world of technology, conflict or weapons of war.

Yet here she was. Like it or not, Amanda Wells was representing the company responsible for the development of technical systems in the aerospace industry, and she was thrust into the epicenter of the investigation!

She pushed back and looked down toward the coffee machine at the end of the hallway. She stood up and picked up her empty cup. She had to just dig in. It was 9.30 pm.

One thing was certain.

They had underestimated the scope of the problem.

How could this have possibly happened? Each of the respecting areas of experts took them further from the core question. She reviewed their findings.

There was no one-single crisis-point of ignition! Rather, a convergence...

Two ships, from two navies, had been drawn into an anomaly that damaged both, together.

Was this internal or external?

Was this a tactical assault with a wider agenda, or was it a random incident?

Occasionally, an expert was called away from the team to answer to Arguetta. He was carefully chosen, and with each of them holding duties of their own, there was little he would add to complete a whole picture. Only parts of a picture.

Why? Was it *planned* that way, she wondered..

She read the most recent conclusions of the day. They had one week. Already this was day three.

It almost midnight when she stood up. She walked to vending machine and started munching on a ham sandwich. Then back to her desk.

Amanda had made arrangement for the team to work at the top floors of her corporate headquarters where an open conferencing space was dedicated to the project exclusively.

Up here it was private, insulated, well-lit and calm. They could get up and walk about, share, talk, collaborate. Or they could turn back to their quiet corner for privacy and concentration. Above all it was secure. Downstairs was an armed guard.

Tonight, Arnold was the duty officer.

"You alright, Miss Amanda?" he called from hallway.

"Yes thanks, Arnold. I've got a sandwich!"

He chuckled and moved on. He was checking the building.

She looked at the clock. It fell increasingly upon Amanda's shoulders to delegate the strategic direction of the day at the morning tasking session. She became *de facto* the ranking authority of the investigation.

But she got help.

While they all knew of her affiliation with the company as a Board Member, few were cognizant of any details relating to the absence of the CEO. And that was the big question that went unanswered, they all knew.

 Perhaps he was overseas, they told others. Perhaps on another investment of the company. But they left it alone. And they all knew it was their responsibility to find answers.

Amanda Wells made their crisis management seamless. Her readiness to assist worked simply from an executive standpoint.

They had the security clearances to review intelligence. And already they had dismissed dossiers and profiles of standard assailants. Then they had turned to technical details. By now, they were already deep in the weeds with innovation and unpublished developments...

And no stone was left unturned.

Forensic failure. Metal fatigue. Friction. Energy shield decay. Composition of metals. Shock tests. Chemical reactions. Fusion poison controls. Design parameters. Hours on the engine, hours in personnel maintenance. The possibilities were endless.

At the same time, calls and enquiries were being made to source manufacturers, designers. What were they developing? Who was the client? What parameters were requisitioned?

The floor of the office was littered with engineering drawings. Amanda had put a hold on building janitor services for that floor. And they could jumble like monkeys, observed Amanda.

Desks were cluttered. Computer images danced through digital curves modeling anomalies, patterns, signatures, each sending computations like lightshows on LED screens. A day's computations could pass with breathless speed.

For Amanda, her work in one day was marked by people, phone calls, conferences, queries, and personnel popping in and out of her office. If not given to formality, she was nonetheless meticulous and detail oriented.

And she was relentless. She had cleared for action, sleeves rolled up and everybody sucking in with a high degree of intensity. This was a problem that needed solving. Period.

But at night, she roamed about and picked up. If untidy, the premises were clean, professional and exquisitely outfitted, of that she was sure.

After that, she spent hours at her desk alone, searching, thinking, collecting data...

Every day she faced a phone call from Arguetta. Mostly, it was with little breakthrough.

She felt frustrated, exhausted and for the most part, isolated.

She lived downtown. Not far from the Navy Yard at the apartment building that offered easy access for a few hours sleep. But only a few.

Fortunately, with secure parking and full facilities, she felt safe, especially with the hours she was keeping, even as it was close to company offices.

At dawn, from her floor she could look out the window and see a city of lights. The Potomac River, the Washington monument illumined the sky, it seemed.

Showered, dressed and ready, she showed up in the morning as fresh as a morning jaybird. "Morning everyone!" she began, a smile on her face.

But they all knew. Her effort was enormous.

Less than a week before, she had stood in her apartment at the end of the day, just before Arguetta was shot. She had been working on research for him...

She remembered her after-hours time of solitude and rest, standing there with a sandwich in one hand and a small glass of wine in the other for dinner.

She recalled wondering how this situation could have ever happened? And at this point in her life? Who would have thought that Trevor's Firm would suffer the consequences of a massive failure? Or even that it was *she* who had to stand up!

From her place she could look out across the darkened sky. Save for planes landing at Reagan Airport, it was remarkably calm.

But little in this city held her attention now. Those early years here had passed. Their house investments had long ago been managed. No matter which way she looked at it, the fact remained that Trevor was absent. And Amanda was by default head of the company..

That left her with little or no option but to carry on! She should hand it off to the CFO to manage. And this she would do at the first opportunity.

The company was viable. It had payroll, debt, assets, contracts and above all, personnel and workers with families who depended on its overall success for their future and aspirations. It gave meaning to their existence.

That also included its corporate investors. Bankers. Insurance, brand and countless support services. Then there was their research and development in technologies...

More than just numbers for future profitability, the company had made potential advancements and contributions to society as a whole...

She had an obligation, she decided.

And you did what you could in the best way that you could.

She had to smile. How often she and Trevor had shared those sentiments!

Especially now, she decided, and she took a deep breath.

Her chores were no different from any other executive with responsibility.

There were company briefings to prepare for the staff daily. She must consult with the Board. Delegate, prepare and be informed to give Press Conferences. She must frame the issues for company subcontractors! She must call her suppliers.

And she cared for all those who worked with her... She must meet with her personnel.

Still, all this would pass too, she decided. She wanted nothing more than to get passed this crisis. Her feelings, if she had any left, were on hold for the moment.

There was enough to deal with.

But first things first.

Of course she understood the crisis.

A catastrophic failure of her husband's firm was bad enough. But added to Trevor's absence, plus Arguetta's incident was almost inconceivable.

How could this happened...

Were they not all of them gathered in Switzerland just weeks ago?

No. Best that she keep her feelings on hold.

...That she not breath. That, she just stay *focused*.

* * *

Amanda must have examined the image over two dozen times. The utility of Spy satellites operated by the United States to defend its borders was necessary. Here was something different.

Arguetta had warned her...

From hundreds of miles in space, transmitting images in real time, a sequenced trail of frames showed the event unfold as it happened on the surface of the planet.

She picked up two images in particular that relayed, from space, the sectional moments before impact. Electronically recorded, she returned and replayed the sequence. .

She took off her glasses and rubbed her eyes, some of the imaging less than clear, and defying logic.

She had long kicked off her shoes, finished her coffee and nibbled on crunchies. The office was now empty. The staff had long since come and gone.

She stared, an office lamp illuminating an oasis of tossed documents, maps, charts, reports, images and technical manuals.

Amanda knew what she was looking at.

Spying on something was only half the story. The real mission was understanding *why*.

Intentions spoke volumes. Only one determination could be made. That was the challenge. Or so it would seem. But here, something else had happened...a metaphysical condition had been summoned up to create havoc?

Impossible!

What was it that Arguetta had said to them when he joined them in the Swiss Alps?

"Nuclear energy is a growing and dynamic part of our strategic defense planning. We're in development for a number of breakthroughs..."

She turned to her notes and scribbled.

Item 1. "One Russian ship asking for assistance. A nuclear cruiser with radiation-decay..."

Item 2. Captain Jennings' assessment:

> *"It should be contained. At the core of a power reactor, the probability of a nutron intersection with a fissionable-nuclear-moment before it escapes into the shielding is much lower: Their reactor runs on a highly enriched uranium. One of their technical difficulties is in their designing fuel elements unable to withstand a large amount of escaped radiation damage in their shielding. Fuel elements may crack over time, and gas bubbles may form. This, they claim is their problem."*

Amanda underlined the first four words of his brief. She read on, noting the interchange between the Captain and the Naval Headquarters in Washington DC: Evidently, something had sufficiently *"scared"* the Russians into asking for assistance...?

> *"the process serves as a throttle..."* ?

"Rate of Increase?" she noted, a comment made by the Contracting Officer in Washington.

So, was there "...something unexplained *draining off* their nuclear-reactivity resistance in spite of design controls?"

She observed the comment made by Captain Jennings, his posture was one of suspicion about the Russian's call for assistance. Was it rather, as he put it, a ploy to see

> *"how far advanced we were with our tech solutions for energy..."*

Amanda braced herself. She knew what she had to read. She'd read the report a dozen times already.

But here it was. This was what she must solve.

Item 3. "Russians ... *alerted* Jennings to 'keep his distance.' Why? They knew that if the life of *their* compact reactor pressure vessel was being expended...then, their shield was damaged! They were at sea *awaiting* the gradual degradation of their nuclear reactivity...

Why?

Sabotage?

Amanda thought about it. Was the Russian ship trying to *alert* Jennings without unraveling the ... bigger Russian problem?

Friend or Foe?

Two Navy cruisers with nuclear propulsion in close proximity to each other having similar engineering parameters, yet *one* cannot explain the loss of degradation from its "contained system?"

She closed her eyes, the images were clear.

Then, suddenly *both* ships are destroyed by a violent "disturbance of the sea?"

No, she decided.

These were two discrete events!

Neither ship was expected to fail. Therefore, was it possible that something *external* had lured them into a mirror situation at precisely one position of pinpoint inline latitude?"

The earth, her technicians had told her, was prone to better exposure from space observation at that latitude.

Amanda got up. She walked, rubbing the back of her neck, stiff and uncomfortable. The injury she'd sustained at Warwick University seemed to throb unexpectedly, especially when she was fatigued. She gulped down a painkiller.

The team had been over this part of the discussion. Too many unknowns; too many unexplained connections! It was frustrating. Especially since they now had the analysis of the forensic report.

Satellite imagery left little to the imagination. A weapon had been deployed.

A pulse? A beam technology? *From where?*

A condition that had "managed to agitate the sea state" was evident. It vaporized two military nuclear-powered vessels of the Line belonging to two different navies..."

* * *

Chapter 7

Admiral Arguetta was pleased to see Amanda. He had collapsed and was readmitted to hospital for more tests. But it wasn't as serious as before, and he was relaxed about the whole affair.

Amanda stood at the door of his room with a box of Scottish biscuits wrapped in gold paper with a blue ribbon. "For the crew!" she said.

"Come in. Come in!" he grinned. "Without you and the rest of your motley crowd aboard my vessel in Annapolis I haven't been able to win a thing..."

She came forward, grinning. "So they threw you out of the Eastport Yacht Club, right?"

"Damn right they did..." he said, opening the box.

For ten years, Admiral Arguetta had been their most loved Commodore; Acting Commodore; or Substitute Commodore – as they called it for lack of titles. He and his wife Beth hosted most of the Ragattas as *Race Committee* for junior sailing teams where kids raced their little boats on the windy Chesapeake Bay off Annapolis. Today, the tiny community yacht club was known as the Eastport Yacht Club, fully subscribed by big boat skippers, and logistically position at the extreme end of a promontory.

Now one of the most vaunted lands in real estate on the bay, it held commanding views across the Chesapeake Bay, all the way out to sight the occasional battleship grey of a combat Navy ship slipping out to deeper blue water seas.

Arguetta chewed his cookie. "I hate these damned things. They're dry and crumbly. Just like the Scots. But they are my favorite, thanks!"

Amanda sat quietly.

Truth was, after Beth died, Bill lost interest in most things. He resigned his membership from the Club.

"So, what've you got?" he said finally.

"Well, it's been an interesting research project, that's for sure" she began, opening her briefcase. "Everyone at the office - *your* Project Manger's team have been working 24/7. .."

"Huh!" he grunted.

"We're down to two possibilities. The nuclear reactor decay reported by the Russian ship was disabled for reasons that... caused concern to Captain Jenkins, right? Especially since he had orders to Stand By and make an assessment."

"Right"

"So. Jenkins was cautious. But not *alarmed...*"

Amanda placed an assortment of images and analytical findings before him. One after the other, he picked them up and nodded with understanding. Before long he was up to speed on the foundations.

"...the technology in question was at the center of the verbal exchange between the two ships" continued Amanda. "Clearly, Jenkins was protective about our nuclear technology systems, yes?"

Arguetta nodded.

"Yet.. it's quite the reverse! The Russians wanted to share something with Jenkins. Their readings has been altered. Someone had *tampered* with their systems of reading their ship's rate of burn, which as you know, is their throttle control. They were messaging to Jenkins that they were held under duress ..."

Arguetta looked up at her. On his face was the expression of *'I knew It!'*

"Who?" he said finally.

"Rather, a *What..*" said Amanda, pausing "An anomaly was upon them both, but the Russians were expressing a certified warning: After all, Jenkins understood what a slow decay meant."

She pulled out her images.

"But here we have imagery of someone leaving the Russian ship to parlay with Jenkins. It was the skipper of the Russian vessel himself."

"There was intelligence that he wanted to pass on. Because two hours later, with no sign of the dingy returning to the Russian ship, we see the dingy being scuttled by one of the crew...(I checked with the Air Force and with the new Space Command -they have a log of several overpass flights at extreme high altitudes over the ship during those two hours...)"

"Someone *else* was watching?"

"Yes" said Amanda, adding "Well, it looks as if they had tapped into their ship to ship transmission, with warning not to cause alarm. Yet here is a Russian skipper is *boarding* your ship!"

"So, what were the Russians telling Jenkins when they came aboard?"

"That's the real question. We do know that Jenkins transmitted nothing further. But we're thinking the Russians wanted to tell him that the excuse of decay was no accident...They were held hostage, in fact."

"By whom?"

"Well...." said Amanda, hesitating.

"A Russian Command of some kind? An observer? A splinter group?"

"What they said is not heard. But we did tap into Jenkins computer..."

Arguetta looked up.

"Antimatter. Space propulsion fuel. I analyzed Jenkin's laptop notes. He was online, and I intercepted his feed. He video-taped a meeting. I believe it occurred in the confines of his cabin. This man was a scientist making a presentation to him. See the background calcs and drawings? He suspected that someone was playing with space energy propulsion systems."

Arguetta scowled.

"See, when this research project was funded by NASA, it was estimated that it would require tens of grams of antimatter to enable an interplanetary mission. However, being limited to 2 nanograms per year..."

"Too slow. Not in the lifespan of humanity..." said Arguetta.

"The Russians knew that in order to produce a propulsion system fuel, positron (anti-electron) a production system would also be required. See that formula? Since Antimatter can be any combination of antiprotons, antineutrons, and positrons (antielectrons), the need was for the *production* of antiprotons. Given that it is much easier to create positrons than antiprotons, my guess is he knew of *another* party making antiprotons...And, given the implications of such a danger, he figured all parties were are high risk. *This* is what he wanted to communicate with Jenkins! Not his propulsion system. But rather, a highly innovative and sketchy propulsion system for space travel"

"And...?"

"And then this happens..."

Up came the picture of the sea state that sank both ships in less than one hour.

They both stared.

First a transmission of distress followed by an alarm.

"All this..." said Amanda "in less than 9 minutes!"

"What kind of research do we have on altered sea state?"

"...Oh, there's some stuff being developed at NOAA, NASA, Talylor Lab, MIT and several other nations...."

Arguetta nodded his head. Then he looked up.

"Trevor's firm has some R&D on this. They've been at it for a few years." He paused. "You're holding something back. What is it?"

Amanda was not surprised. She opened her mouth to say something, then looked down.

"I know. You've got a hypothesis. But you don't have the confidence to bring it forward...Is that it?" insisted Arguetta.

Amanda looked away, a little embarrassed, but not offended.

"Oh hell, Amanda!" said Arguetta "I'm getting too old for this stuff. And frankly, I've seen better results from you and your team than most of my highly paid navy technical staff...Now, I'm sorry to be a little gruff. But I've been shot for a reason, remember!"

She smiled. "Serves you right! Your manners are atrocious, as Beth often had to remind you...." She chuckled. "No" she said. "It wasn't a natural phenomenon. It was a deliberate assault that sank both ships!"

"*What?*"

"Think about it. Two ships, from two different Navies, sunk at precisely the same time, and just as they are dealing with nuclear energy propulsion development, perhaps confabulating or sharing intelligence ..."

"Who?..." Arguetta's face lit up. "Of course. I should have known...It's space propulsion technology development, isn't it?"

She nodded.

"Space satellite and energy systems are vulnerable to all intelligence..."

"We don't know what *caused* the sinking...A meteo-tsunami or a seismic tsunami. It can also be confused with wind-driven storm surge or a seiche..."

Amanda paused, giving him time to process the possibilities.

"And...?"

"Try this" she said finally. "It's an old friend."

"Torpedo attack!" he blurted out. Adding "Now I know you're off base. If the whole event was being monitored by a submarine with a firing solution, then that's impossible because we have the ability to detect any approaching threat..."

"Hmm.."

"What then?"

He face paled.

"A *sonic* technology cyber weapon?"

"Underwater..."

"An *underwater* sonic weapon?"

"Hmm..."

"There is nothing that could move that fast! Again, we have advanced detection sensor devices ..."

"Hmm" she said, adding "Try this..."

Amanda pulled out a folder and placed it on his lap. He sat up in his hospital bed to gain purchase for reading. It was marked *Eyes Only*. He put on his spectacles and was about to open it up when a pretty voice sang out from the doorway of his room.

"Knock! Knock!"

A nurse wheeling a trolley stood there with a big smile.

"Come in!" hollered Arguetta, happy to see her.

Tall, with African-American features that accentuated generous almond eyes and wide nostrils, she paused and gave him a moment. "Sorry to bother you Admiral Arguetta, but it's that time of the day for your tests!" she said.

He grinned.

It was impossible not to be impressed by this imposing figure, her face accentuated by an appointed colorful band that held a corona of shiny hair, and she approached his bed with a certain pernicious sway.

Everything was moved out of the way for the tray.

Amanda knew it was time to withdraw from the room. She gathered all materials. "I've worn you out!" she said to Arguetta. "Please forgive my over-abundance of materials here...." she added, as if to emphasize the need for some measure of security with the intelligence at hand.

"Not at all..." he said. "Thank you! I'll read every word, and I'm glad you've kept me in the loop. I'm informed with something to work on. I'll be in touch with you shortly Amanda. Thank you!" he said.

Amanda was concerned at the situation she saw unfolding. She would have liked to secure all the documents now. To do so would infer that he was too incapacitated to do so.

She glanced about the room, hoping to find a locker into which she could stow some of his papers. There was none.

Arguetta was now chatting with the nurse.

It disturbed Amanda to walk away from so much sensitive material. Security was something you wore like a cloak. It never left your consciousness. Yet here she stood, displaced by a nurse and a happy patient deep in conversation...

She eyed the door to his room. Two armed guards were standing as protection. There was not much more she could do.

She looked at him, as if to remind him...But his attention was elsewhere.

She had to withdraw. She turned and left the room with her briefcase and her laptop, hoping to God he was alert sufficiently not to let the interruption by the nurse compromise the necessity for discretion.

"Thank you gentlemen!" she said, passing the two men on sentry duty. "I trust you'll watch over anything that leaves the room..." she added softly, looked directly into their eyes.

"Yes Ma'am" one said.

Were it not for the interruption... she'd have had collected all the material herself. Especially the last document that she had placed on his bed.

Amanda walked away with some apprehension in her heart. She would call him later, she decided. In fact, she put in a request to her team at Advanced Technologies. All documents were to be delivered to Admiral Arguetta's office by tomorrow noon. Special delivery by secure courier only.

That way, he'd be briefed in quarters where he had complete control.

She punched the elevator button at the end of the long hallway and several parties entered.

She thought about the visit.

Arguetta was certainly to be commended for his energy and interest, even if fatigued. Clearly, he was determined not to let an incident like this slow him down.

He had a crisis to solve. And he was not going to be thwarted. Certainly, he had a team working on the problem, and he trusted his Project Manager to oversee the investigation. Two more days, he told Amanda. Then he could be discharged.

Further, what seemed to gratify him was that he was the one hurt, and not Amanda! After all, she was standing at his side at that particular moment.

Still, more than once she saw his gaze shift about, as if disoriented. Perhaps he was on medication, and this she completely understood. Not that it was her place to ask, much less probe. But something worried her.

Trevor would have expected nothing less of his wife than to express sincere concern for the recovery of an old friend, let alone a former employer.

Nonetheless, he looked very tired. Especially towards the end of her visit.

She did not broach the matter of the sea state lightly. It was just too much, she felt. So she left him with the file.

But as the hours wore on, Amanda felt unsettled and uneasey..

The elevator stopped at the second floor, and Amanda walked around to the main entrance of the hospital before entering another lobby of elevators. Those elevators were allocated to the garage. She had been parked for over two hours.

Level three Underground took forever to reach. Everyone and their uncle was on the elevator, she felt. Nurses. Doctors. Visitors. Crying children. Janitors. Change of shift hour, clearly...

Anyway, her duty was done. She heaved a big sigh of relief as she walked to her car.

She found her key and got in behind the wheel.

It was just at that moment that she saw a glint of a silver flash to her far left. She turned. With its rear lights on, a dark SUV had started its engine and was slowly reversing from its parking slot.

It turned, and slowly drove out of the underground garage. She following it up three floors and out the building. She noted the tag number. Local.

Nothing eventful. Except for that silver flash, a glint, reminiscent of the seconds preceding the incident where she and Arguetta was shot?

But that glint...Perhaps nothing. Perhaps something. A reflection of some kind, from behind a smoked glass windshield at the wheel of the car. A driver's hand across the wheel? A metal rim to eye glasses...

She was getting paranoid, she decided. This city was filled with official cars delivering visitors, guests, tourists, diplomats.

Yet the glint flash, just here, in that parked vehicle had made her flinch instinctively. She thought about it later.

 She wanted to be alone, and she sipped a scotch on the rocks at her apartment, looking out into a city glittering with lights and monument, as she liked to do.

But the more she thought it, the more she realized it was something. The flash of a ring from the driver perhaps. Or perhaps a glint of metal like a watch, or jewel that flashed roughly at the position of the steering wheel?

If it wasn't the same vehicle, then it was something.

Finally, she knew she must let it go. Enough with the stress! The visit to Arguetta...

She shuddered, as if feeling cold. She thought of Trevor.

She'd call Jacques in the morning again. He was the last person to talk with Trevor. They'd had a rendezvous in

Calais, she knew. *Then what?* Again she'd talk to Sandra. And again she'd call London...

She felt exhausted. At least the company had responded appropriately. She'd led the effort, and the tech staff were up to speed.

Amanda finally lay down in a dark room, as if her eyes could rest without closing. But her mind was in turmoil. It had been days since she'd had a decent night's sleep. The hours at the office had been long and the stress relentless. On two nights, she'd stayed in all night. One dark skirt and change of blouse could do wonders to greet the next sunrise, she'd discovered.

She'd just presented Arguetta with her preliminary findings, and basically, she was done.

Relieved that she'd been on the team, at least, she'd shown the leadership within the company that was responsible for the performance of propulsion systems. Not that she was any expert qualified to deal with technical issues, but she was on the Board, and the technical analysts had kept her informed...

In the absence of her husband, apparently called to another mission as they put it, she represented the Board of Directors who were the primary authority of the firm.

Moreover, Amanda had more than appeared as a show of leadership. She had stayed in the kitchen to take the heat. She'd contributed to the inquiry with research. That much she could do to help...Certainly, there was more to do. But she could back off now. The investigation at Advanced Technologies was fully underway. This, she had told Arguetta before leaving today. The staff at Advanced Technologies were on it! She wasn't needed anymore...

That was the sum of a call she received from Arguetta on her way home, an hour or so after seeing him. Arguetta was courteous, of course. But her mission was complete now that the crisis was getting traction and management. He had commissioned her help rather abruptly, after all. It was her responsibility to account for the contractor, certainly, being on the Board of Directors and in the absence of a CEO.

But now the pressure was off. She was being dismissed. Not in so many words, but Arguetta was informing her that she was relieved of her responsibility.

Clearly, Arguetta read the report. A preliminary draft, a forensic opinion that would need lots of work and verification, she knew. But it was fruitful, and it would give him something to work with. She had wanted to personally give him a Heads Up.

She was relieved. She could go home!

Later that night, as Amanda closed her eyes momentarily, she awoke suddenly. Had she dozed off?

There was nothing she could identify, yet something had alerted her instincts. All was well, given the circumstances. The research was done, if only her contribution.

Arguetta was recovering. He had two armed guards at the door...

Then *what* was bothering her?

She got up, fixed herself some orange juice and drank thirstily. She dabbed her face, letting the cool water calm her thoughts...Then she looked up.

Definitely, the 'flash' was reminiscent of the hand of the driver at the wheel of the same dark car that had assaulted them earlier in the week...

The hand and its flashy ring – only now recollected in her memory, was that of the driver of the vehicle who shot Arguetta.

Also the same hand at the wheel of the vehicle that had just driven by her, tonight..

And it suddenly struck her. Was she was being followed?

No!

Possibly, it wasn't Arguetta that was of interest...She swiveled around. Instinctively, she knew it was not about the issues at hand, even.

With a cup still in her fingers, she thrust one hand to her face as an idea burst upon her and made her spill orange juice.

It was not Arguetta...It was Amanda who was the target. And...

Neither was the University of Warwick girl, an *accident.*

Trevor?

These were his assailants...shadowing her movements!

She was the target.

Was Trevor dead?

* * *

Amanda unbuckled her seat belt. The warning lights went off. The plane was in flight! For some silly reason, she never really felt that she was aloft until the plane had switched off all its warnings. She relaxed.

Now she could truly breath freely.

London!

She ordered a drink, and food came out.

Her thoughts went back to her office at Advanced Technologies in Washington DC where she had spent the last few weeks.

She had taken a flight to the United States, ostensibly to attend a lecture in Philadelphia where her daughter was giving a paper.

She had planned to return to London and join Trevor.

The panic was over. She got a message from Sandra that the office had contacted her with news. All good, she said.

Apparently, Tevor had left for Paris to meet with Jacques de Torraine. An urgent matter, he had told her in a message. 'Back in two days...'

Amanda however, was met with a crisis. Rather, a crisis that belonged to her husband's company!

Presumably, Sandra's message was current.

Bering retired, she had long abandoned her professional work for the company, especially knowing how many able personnel worked at the firm today. Its brand of operations was well established.

Truth be told, Trevor was the owner in name only, he too had long retired from its management, save for occasional attendance to the Board where he held a large stakeholder's position.

Nevertheless, for Amanda the calamitous event came as a shock. Especially since nobody could locate Trevor...

But how could she forget that first week? It had came as a total shock!

Officially, the company was contracted by the US Government to manage a defense project of prime sensitivity in technological development.

What occurred instead, was a catastrophic failure – an event for which they were the responsible party. A disaster, they called it. The US Navy was facing the sudden and mysterious disappearance of a ship at sea! Actually, two ships had simultaneously been attacked and sunk. The second ship belonged to the Russian navy.

Amanda had propitiously landed on US soil just as the crisis unfolded, and in the swirl of things that followed, she was cited as a ranking Board Member and stakeholder of the company, now called in to account for what happened and appoint the lead forensic team for technical diagnosis of the crisis.

Or, as the Legal Council for the awarded contract explained, she had both the authority and the obligation to do so...

Luckily, she still maintained her US Security Clearance. And while her concern for the welfare of the personnel and loss of the ships was bad enough, stepping in as a lead representative was hardly the reception she had expected!

Even if Advance Technologies held the best reputation as a highly venerated technical, engineering and design firm.

It was unthinkable! Not only what happened, but what she discovered as the cause for the incident. It was now up to government officials to explore the scope of damage to political and military affairs.

Nor was the revelation of the technical problem any less comfort. These were definitely unchartered waters, if not cutting edge development in strategic warfare potential. And it was dangerous stuff...

The next question was why? Or who?

None at the office could have anticipate such a catastrophic plot, for that is what it was an assault purposely delivered with intent of harm. And the consequences were horrendous!

She shuddered, glad not to be the one to ponder such matters.

She sipped her drink and began to doze off, but her thoughts returned.

Was it surprising that she had to answer to her former boss? Someone who had hired her years ago for research work, back when she and Trevor lived in Washington DC.

Bill Arguetta, now almost retired himself had become a good family friend, yet holding the position in government that oversaw the technical performance of certain company contracts...

Not, not surprising at all, she decided.

She sipped.

Neither did it leave the company less culpable, nor did their relationship with Arguetta alter their obligations to the government.

Still, she was able to report to him in less official ways than formally required, especially since the research itself require around-the-clock investigative hours. Crisis management, they called it.

But what Arguetta frequently had to remind her was that the quality of her professional standards were beyond reproach and still highly viable, something she doubted. It had been years since she'd been engaged in technical intelligence...

Still, she had managed a weekend up in Philadelphia!

Moreover, what caught them entirely off guard was the shooting of the underground garage in a government building. They had enemies.

Admiral Arguatta was hit. And the matter was listed as a domestic incident, but it nevertheless had ramifications.

That an assailant actually occurred with intent to harm was threat enough: But that the perpetuator had penetrated a secure building and targeted an official made him a terrorist.

And Amanda was standing at his side when it happened...

Sandra called The message she had just received, it turns out, was dated. Sandra had misunderstood the words of Rosamund from the London Office. Trevor McDonnell had left a message for his daughter, Rosamund explained, but two weeks ago!

For Amanda, that meant one thing.

He was still missing.

His disappearance was no coincidence. Rather, it was a critical aspect to the assailant's plan...

* * *

Admiral Arguetta walked stiffly into the White House in full uniform, his cap under his arm. Striding beside him was the Secretary of Navy. Navsec, as they called him.

They were shown into the offices of the Chief of Staff, joined by Head of National Security Bill Robinson, Secretary of State, Paul Reynolds.

"Gentlemen, please make yourselves comfortable!" said the private secretary Stan Olander as he entered the room. "Coffee anyone?"

"Sure!" smiled Robinson. "Any donuts?"

"Yes, thank you ..." added Paul.

"Mr. Reuben is with the Present now. He'll be wanting to brief the President again later in the day" said Olander. "Is there anything you might need? As you know, over here is the lighting panel... Keyboards for screen plasmas; secure communications above the deck, and stationary at the end here... Just let me know."

"Thanks. We're good Stan. We're all set with our papers...."

They waited.

The door opened.

"Good morning!" entered Stewart Reuben, angling as Stan made his exit.

"Everyone comfortable?" He paused, his face dour. "Then let's get to it. The President wants an immediate update. And...the Russians want us to inform them of course. *Our version.* So, what've we got?"

Navsec spoke. "It would appear that we've been blindsided..."

"I'll say!" scoffed Reuben. "We've had a contractor screw up..." his eyes angry. "We're supposed to be leading the world in R&D and here we have a lame rusty Russian ship take us down in a wind squall at sea! What the hell...?"

It took Reynolds to calm him down.

"Our Frigate had instructions *not* to interact..." "Oh *really?* You could have fooled me! From what I've read, they were sharing notes about nuclear propulsion technologies. And they both went down holding hands... *Jesus..*" he pounded, "tell me *what the hell*...gentlemen, *Please!*"

Reuben was hard to mollify.

His perspective was one of containment of damage done to the reputation of the White House. His patience was thin, and his temper flaring at the nostrils.

Only when Arguetta was invited to speak by Navsec did the situation gain gravity. This was no screw up, he explained. It was a deliberate ploy far greater than anyone had expected.

"With all respect Sir..." he said "it wasn't just *Advanced Technologies* that inspired the crisis. If anything, they have moved a few mountains in assessment of the situation. They've earned their keep with quick responses to some very complex issues. Without them, we'd be weeks behind still searching for answers" he said.

The others nodded.

Reuben waited.

"The nuclear propulsion was not the problem at all. Sure, the Russians had a malfunctioning meter that inaccurately measured their rate of decay of fuel, but this was designed to embarrass us politically. Captain Robinson and the Russian vessel had to talk, our skipper made a critical judgment that only he could make at the time. This was sabotage. The Russians were aware of a saboteur with intelligence that needed to be shared. Robinson was smart enough to pick up on the nuances" "Who? Some splinter group...?"

"No. Not internal. That was the surprise. The threat was from an outside party. A commercial competitor seeking to make his point about space propulsion with technology that would far outpace space travel fuel propulsion...."

"meaning..?"

"An advantage in space satellite warfare; waste disposal and colonization efforts by far..."

"How damaging is this to our long term projections?" asked Reuben

"Nothing we can't recover from..." said Reynolds.

"But...?" interrupted Reuben

"Well. This is where we can't verify the details" said Navsec. "The phenomenon that took down two ships was not a freak event. Nor a storm. It was an external assault...with a message!"

Reuben looked up.

He knew enough to realize that the United States had supremacy in sea combat technologies. Now he was concerned. "So go on, Bill"

"..the two ships were close enough to be targeted by a subsea weapon. They both took damage from one impact..."

"How?" Reuben paused. "Who could get *close* enough to launch an attack?"

Arguetta stepped forward. "We do know that there is a developing technology that would allow submarines to travel more than 750 mph...Unbelievable, I know..."

"What are you saying? That's faster than commercial aircraft fly..." scoffed Reuben.

"It's *possible*, if sketchy. The technology is called supercavitation, and it's been around for decades. The idea is to increase the speed of an object like, say, a submarine or torpedo by creating a bubble around it, reducing drag as it moves through the water. The nose of the projectile typically is designed to *create* the bubble, and gas often is used to *shape* the bubble. In essence, guidance throttle.

The Soviets used this trick on the Shkval torpedo in the 1960s and '70s; it was capable of 230 mph but for no more than a few miles duration."

"So..."

"Steering a supercavitating vessel requires having control planes of field that pierce the bubble, producing drag. These planes also would be under tremendous force and pressure at speed, and would need to be extraordinarily strong...." Arguetta paused and lit up the plasma for a visual demonstration.

"High speeds, around 45mph, depend greatly on the size and design of the ship. It's tricky just to reach a speed where a bubble can be created in the first place." Arguetta paused, looked up, then proceeded.

"Chinese Researchers at the Harbin Institute of Technology's Complex *Flow and Heat Transfer* Lab have made a breakthrough in supercavitation. They describe the limits of standard underwater propulsion that will hold them back—especially if they want to make a real submarine."

"They've developed a solution?"

"Yes and... No. An underwater rocket capable of giving a supercavitating vessel *long* range doesn't exist yet. The Chinese have developed a "liquid membrane" that tackles both issues. They use a continuously-sprayed-on membrane to reduce drag and help the vessel reach speed. The membrane *could* allow various amounts of friction to be applied to different sides of the ship, creating a steering mechanism.

"Un...*believable!*" muttered Reuben.

Arguetta proceeded "We do know, from our own research that by combining liquid-membrane technology with supercavitation, we can significantly reduce the launch challenges and make cruising control easier."

Arguetta flipped on the house lights. "Details on the new developments are few. How to leap into supersonic submarine speed is something else, however" he finished.

Robinson stepped in. "That's the good news. The bad news is we have no idea what other capability this technology as developed!"

"*For real?*" asked Reuben. "Are you saying someone or something approached us at high speed and sank both the ships?"

"If I may say Sir. It was *Advanced Technologies* that came up with the answer themselves..." said Arguetta.

"So. What have we got? An aggressor flushing out two vessels sharing intelligence on fuel propulsion technologies related to supersonic warfare....then *sinking* them?" Reuben's eyes bulged with incredulity.

"We've got the Russians asking us what happened, and you're saying the Chinese sneaked up on us and sank both vessels from two of the world's navies?"

This time it was Bill Robinson who spoke. "As far as the National Security intelligence can find, it was not the Chinese. It was an outside source. A commercial competitor from the space technologies sector..."

"Ok... *Why?*" said Reuben.

"To embarrass us. To show his presence! He tested us. He has no sovereign power to answer to. He has no diplomatic authority to restrain him. No accountability to anyone. He has his own agenda!"

"Are you *kidding?* Anyone with that kind of power could stampede his way into world supremacy! Let's identify this party."

"Yes Sir" said Paul

Reuben looked at them. "Let's find out his motive. Any ideas?"

The room remained silent. He turned to each one of them. "Bill...?"

Arguetta looked up and hesitated. Then he said "I think... it's a message!"

"A *message*?" repeated Reuben. "My God...didn't he leave enough damage as signature?"

"He had resources, and he manipulated the crisis. It's not about technology. Or even industrial superiority in space capabilities. He damaged not one but *two* ships of the line from *two* superpowers..."

"What are you saying...?"

"He's defying global stability: He delivered a message *beyond* the balance of power or sovereign authority. He's making a larger geopolitical statement...as a global movement, evidently!"

The words filled the room, and they stared.

"If that's the case..." said Bill Robinson "from the perspective of national security, he isn't done yet. There's a real probability that he plans to inflict more damage. If he's angry enough to pull this stunt, he's wanting to hit pay-dirt for his grievance..."

"Or establish his own agenda" added Reuben, putting down his pen, choosing his words.

"Ok...Gentlemen. I'll brief the President. Meanwhile, we start with asking who'd want to overthrow the ecosystem of the free world, if I'm hearing you correctly, especially if he has technology of this scope..."

Reuben rose from his chair, his face pale. "We habitually keep our friends close, and our enemies closer. And we do know them all. This... is a rogue player we *don't* know!" He paused. "Gentlemen, what we most likely have is someone with a radical agenda - happy to overthrow civilization if he needs to..."

They all stood as Reuben crossed the room. He looked back.

"Good work, gentlemen…" adding "keep me informed." Then he turned to Arguetta "Yes. Err…you can commend *Advanced Technologies* for staying on top of this."

He walked through the door saying "…the rest is nothing we can't solve with some R&D…"

* * *

King of Prussia: PA

Sam was retired from LM.

Determined to complete his design before the end of the year, he opened up his basement. His problem was propulsion. He scratched his ear. He had experience...

Meantime, he was busy with something else.

He went back up to the house, made himself a cup of coffee, and then walked around to the garage of the house.

He faced a display of tools along the rear wall. Saws, hammers, jars of nails, screws, nuts, bolts, cutters, pliers, blades, hack-teeth and tool-kit bits.

He lifted one lever and popped behind a closet hallway where additional garage implements hung. Garden tools, mostly. Weed-whacker. Rake. Scraper. Blades and Bites and shields for his lawnmower. He turned. To his right was a concealed false door and he slipped behind it. He descended the steps underground where only an old Boiler, Air Conditioning unit and electrical box hummed. He threw open the main switch for lighting.

What should have been a dark and dusty subterranean utility room was white, clean and glossy-floored.

His office was well equipped, a picture on the wall.

Before him was an oasis of plasma screens, rules, mapping tables, cad modeling devices, print machines, scanners, cabinets and sketch drawings cabinets.

At one end of the office was a lab with gadgets for heat testing, sinks, burners, ovens and insulated refrigeration for vials and experimental chemical components. He walked by them, and the lights switched on.

Beyond them was a compartment that required a key pad.

Within was a steel grid-cage surrounding a stand-alone IBM data storage capacity computer console. It hummed softly, live.

He sat at his drawing table within the cage, and opened up a laptop. He checked all messages on his decoder.

He had helped design an aircraft years ago. That was at the time of his subcontracting days for *Skunk Works*.

Blackbird. And it was a legend.

Known as "Blackbird" SR -71, the black project was a long-range, high-altitude, Mach 3+ strategic reconnaissance aircraft operated by the United States Air Force. At that speed, the plane sustained over 2,000 miles per hour. It was the fastest aircraft ever designed.

Even in retirement he knew that nothing had been designed for those parameters since!

But he chuckled, the memories flooding back.

Back then, the challenge was to maintain an aircraft flying at high altitude that had the endurance to withstand heat deflection at those speeds.

Titanium was the design answer, and they had re-tooled its manufacture to solve for the aircraft's leading edges which exceeded 1,000 degrees Fahrenheit in heat resistance.

He smiled then, as he always did.

Since black paint was known to emit and absorb heat at the same time, the aircraft was painted black. They called it Blackbird.

The picture on the wall of his office lab said it all. The original Blackbird was built by Lockheed Martin and designated as the single-seat A-12. Later, it evolved into the larger SR-71, which added a second seat for a Reconnaissance Systems Officer and carried more fuel than the A-12.

Mainly, it could be refueled in flight. But at that speed, it had to slow down for anything to approach it with fuel...

Yes, the aircraft was retired. Only 32 had gone into production.

But then again, so had he retired!

Now he had a small contract to do some design-work.

So he was working on the next generation SRA blueprint before him. In fact, it was being built for the United States air defense systems. Nobody knew that of course, except for a few. Those sending the messages on his decoder, of course. But that's it. And he did not know whom. Except for one.

As a matter of fact, tonight he was due a call from his point of contact at the DoD. When the call was due, he would use an encrypted decoding medium. His contact would want to know the status of any latest development.

And for good reason.

He was a specialist in design parameters. He and his IBM machine could compute fuel consumption at various speeds; maximum power acceleration rates for high altitudes, optimum cruise altitudes, deceleration and decent air speeds; endurance burn-rate and turn rates. He had at his fingertips the computational solutions for burn rates by Special propellants, including LOX/LN.

His was a highly specialized area of modern engineering design and performance testing. At the very least, it was a spy ship. At best, it would be a ghost.

That said, this aircraft was a weapon system, complete with sophisticated integrated communications.

The phone rang. "Hello Bill..." he said.

"Hello Sam" said Admiral Arguetta. "How are you doing...?"

* * *

Amanda peered out of the porthole window and saw the landscape of a sprawling modern city. The airplane was about to land at Brussels. She smiled, sunlight reflecting off her face as it bathed the fuselage.

Belgium, heart of modern Europe was the seat of power for the European Union Government.

It was hard to believe that this country was one of the smallest and most densely populated nations of Europe. Since its independence in 1830, it was a sovereignty ruled by representative democracy and, because of its history, a hereditary constitutional monarchy.

What a remarkable combination, thought Amanda.

Belgium had seen its share of military battle on repeated occasions. Wet and drenching trenches of WWI were followed by WWII where every manner of wheeled vehicle and gunnery machine along front army lines had left its mark. Neither had its earlier history been any kinder, being a landscape free of mountain terrain.

Today a composite of three linguistic communities, it thrived. Flemings, or Flemish of Dutch decent; French-speaking Walloons; and Germans of Eastern Liège province, held a federal state of sharing power among the regions of Flanders, Wallonia, and the Brussels-Capital Region. And it bustled with fast highways, packed cities, and chrome construction along modern architecture.

The plane landed and they disembarked routinely. It had been a short flight from London to Brussels. But she felt ready to move forward with her plans.

After her return from the United States, she had made up her mind where the first destination should be. Rather, the place from which her search for Trevor should begin.

She did stay-over in London for three days, to regroup her affairs and to check in with the London office. But Brussels was the destination. She would track his trail, having found little in London to enlighten her footsteps.

The airport was busy. She made her way into the main terminal signed by *Airport Benvenuti!*

She looked up and realized that she had not eaten much in two days. Amanda stopped at the Italian *AMO*. She ordered pasta and salad, but the food tasted bland. Or was it that she had lost any sensation of palate in her mouth. She felt uncomfortable, dehydrated, fatigued.

No return calls registered on her cell from her daughter Sandra. Nothing from London. And only a few staff calls pending from Washington...

Not exactly promising. Amanda took a big breath.

She walked about to stretched her legs. She had just crossed the Atlantic, stopped in London, and would put everything behind her, she decided. Everything was under control.

Advanced Technologies would make it, she smiled. That much was certain.

And she felt particularly pleased with her time on station. She had pushed them. Not in theatrical ways, or even by virtue of rank of executive standing. Rather, she encouraged them to think freely, like experts. Especially the technical staff and their scientific findings. What they achieved impressed Arguetta, and clearly he was able to use the intelligence to make advances in his case.

He told her he was pleased.

.

The investigative findings of the company team had produced exceptional results, if at first highly improbable. But they did result in higher probabilities; logical conclusions and imaginative solutions...

Deductive reasoning, she found, had ways to surface unpredictable conclusions, if allowed.

Yes. Amanda felt satisfied that she had done her duty. But she was tired.

Amanda checked the overhead airport monitors. Arrivals. Departures. Time. Gates.

She was there physically, but she felt that she was in another dimension. Jet-lag, they called it.

Her mind was still miles away.

Clearly, she had stepped away from a crisis. That she had managed to make a significant contribution meant everything to her right now. Trevor would have approved, for sure.

Trevor...

Where was he? What had happened to him?

Her husband was missing! And now she must face this problem. Tired, annoyed and irritable, she wasn't sure how best to begin?

She turned her thoughts to his activities. They had many areas of management that sometimes took him away, she began to think...

But her concentration wandered. Now she must face new challenges - almost like a new problem, and start from the beginning.

Why?

And...why was she feeling so exhausted?

Trevor MacDonnell was the head of bank that took him world over. That is, until he retired and scaled back his official duties. Semi-retirement, he called it.

But where was he now?

He had served as a Minister for Her Majesty's Government. On occasion, he was called out of retirement and into consultation for diplomatic developments.

Further, Trevor was not only a philanthropist but an adventurer who explored various interests, often taking field trips for days...

But Trevor always - well, *almost* always was reachable for Amanda. But not now!

That profoundly worried her.

She sat in the great lounge, and with a coffee at her side, took a moment to write in her book some items of sequence, to jog her thinking...

Initially, he had left for Paris, or so his London office had told her. Then he went to Brussels, where he had a bank branch office. From there he was to return to Paris. The last person to see him was Jacques de Torraine, a longtime and trusted friend...

So, when Jacques recently told her that he was leaving Paris for Brussels to ask about for him, that's when she decided to go to Brussels also. She took a plane hop from Heathrow to Brussels, less than two hours...and here she was, waiting?

That was their plan. They were scheduled to meet here today. She looked down, her phone posted a contact.

A message from Jacques.

 "Still in Paris... Delayed 24/hrs. I have info. Meet me same time/place tomorrow!"

She sighed, looking up. The Airport was filling with another flight of passengers disembarking, and she felt tired.

Just as well, she thought. She could use a good night's sleep at a nearby Airport Hotel.

She booked.

Chapter 8

Amanda walked about the Grand Place of Brussels, a UNESCO World Heritage Site.

She had time to use up...

The large square of baroque architecture rimmed the perimeter like a magic box of historic jewels.

The *Church of Saint Jacwques-sur-Codenberg;* the *Palace of the Nation* - a Parliament building and now called the *Academy Palace.*

Brussels, famed for its delectable chocolates; petit fours, sweets and custard pastries enabled Amanda to stop at various patisseries and sample her way from *Palace of Charles of Lorraine* to *Eymont Palace* on the other side of the square.

At the *Saint-Hubert Royal Galleries,* one of the oldest covered shopping arcades in Europe, she came to a stop. She consulted her tour guidebook, and circled the *Congress Column* - a monument built in the middle of the 19th century, the page informed her, before finally reaching the articulated *Brussels Stock Exchange* building, built in 1873.

She stared, awed.

Here, history was unfolding around her. From here Europe was demonstrating centuries of effort and culture to create the great modern Western Civilization of the free market economy of today.

This achievement had come at a cost, considering the conflicting interests and armies which had marched through the region. Nonetheless, here was man's inventiveness at its finest; industry at its most robust and fecund.

Brussels had evolved into a commercial center for good reason. It was said that all the goldsmiths of Amsterdam had lost most of their Jewish diamond-cutters to Belgium when offered better terms than the Guilds of their home.

From here, the supply chains for Europe had centered, included fabrication, transportation and processing of imported raw materials like gold and ivory from Africa. Equally, the export of finished products flourished, routing into outbound destination using sea ports and international broker markets for wider trade.

Further, Belgium had advanced to be a major steel producer in the early 19th century. This, Amanda knew, for they had seen rigorous monetary reform in the post-World War II restitution. Especially for the manufacture of tools from Flemish regions, and chemical industries developed up north: Belgium, so badly burned by the war zones, had reconstructed itself to establish a favorable balance of trade market in modern Europe.

Banking was not far behind. This, Trevor had explained to her, as the history of his own bank opened an early branch there.

Amanda looked at her watch.

She still had time, and she consulted her tourist guidebook. *The Palace of Justice* was built in 1883, designed by Joseph Poelaert.

At some point in its development, as heavy industries depleted their resources, it became necessary for Belgium to invite foreign investment.

That is, because of heavily subscribed social welfare programs demanded by labor movements of the late 20th century, such that the government had to reduce its budget deficit with extraordinary measures of "belt-tightening austerity." Eventually, as socialist subsidies dried up, many people left, and the scars of that conflict was somewhat evident across the face of homes once inhabited but left abandoned.

Today, Belgium was a major financial sector with foreign banks operating under the financial security of a central bank. The legends of its past had become the sinews of a vibrant modern *European Central Bank*.

Vibrant, dynamic and chrome-plated on every electronic platform, the ECB was apace global economies, shaping monetary policy; merging its stock exchange with Amsterdam and Paris to form the *Eurnext* – the first fully integrated equities market.

Neither had foreign investments shrunk from investing in energy, or other support sectors of the modern world of Belgium now the brokering capital of Europe.

Amanda pulled down her wool hat. The air was crisp for March, and she drew in a deep breath as she looked between golden domes and spire parapets to see a glimmering blue sky.

She had one hour left to pass the time before her rendezvous with Jacques. She picked an outdoor café and sat down. She sipped at a cup of coffee, the sun warm on her face, and she watched pigeons flutter at her feet.

It did wonders for her soul, gazing at neoclassical architecture of the 18th and 19th centuries of the Royal Square. How too it must have empowered those who early plied their trade across these streets!

It did her good to be so uplifted.

For her own life, the events of the last few weeks had taken her down to ground zero – averting a disaster that might well have caused an international incident had they not worked so tirelessly to find quick technical answers in Washington.

Life, clearly, had its battles for every person, she knew. She sipped. Where was Jacques?

Strolling tourists passed by, children chasing pigeons. What would be the battles of their next generation, she wondered.

From inside the Café, a news broadcasting screen could be spied. It displayed a litany of malcontents with strife in the other regions, chiefly to raise audience metrics, she mused.

Water pollution was a problem, apparently. A small hydroelectric power industry had developed along its fastest moving streams. And now that nuclear reactors generated half Belgium's power grid, the use of water for cooling nuclear power stations had become a deeply grave situation...

"Hello Amanda!" called out a familiar voice.

"Jacques!" she jumped, surprised.

* * *

"You could not have picked a prettier time of the year to visit the city!" said Jacques, seated at her little table with coffee and a gateau. "They have occasional garden festivals here..." he was saying "I'm told their next exhibit will feature *Blooms of Amsterdam*, the Tulip..." he grinned.

Amanda laughed "That must be lovely!" she said.

But her eyes gave her away.

Jacques softly put down his fork. "There is much to tell you" he said quietly. He picked up his coffee cup and sipped with an innocent smile.

They both knew they were being watched. Jacques lived in a world of antiquities and great collections, a world filled with rich and rare articles named as priceless commodities, much of which moved in markets of anonymity, secrecy and shadow.

Occasionally, it was the intelligence about certain commodities that helped recover stolen goods from black markets. For insurers, that was good news. Or, if they were ultimately found and returned to their legitimate owners. Such gestures of civic responsibility Jacques was glad to oblige. But not always was it safe.

This was a tenuous world. It worked both ways. Not all was without risk. Where Jacques went, and to whom he communicated, was always of interest to third parties...

Jacques looked at Amanda quietly, his eyes lingering on the shine in her hair as the sun fell on her face. He knew she'd been under stress.

"Come" he said, gulping down the last of his gateau. "I'll take you somewhere...."

"Heron district" said Jacques to the taxi driver. One man listening in a taxi cab was better than an open audio feed to eves-dropping software technicians able to discern spoken syllables from half a mile away.

Jacques turned to Amanda put his arm around her shoulder, drawing her closer. He gave the top of her head a kiss, like that of a sister who was enduring an ordeal.

"Keep smiling!"he said

The cab driver noticed.

"So, three things to tell you," he said.

"In 1935, a British ship rescued items from Russia that were transported to Britain for safekeeping. They included royal collections, valuables, paintings, bullion. But also ledgers of industry and advances producing minerals and drawings of technological improvements for manufacture techniques, like smelting of special fossil fuels for industrial process..."

The cab turned a corner on two wheels.

"Much of it was used for re-building Europe and making great fortunes for those in positions of power and leadership" He paused, looked out the window, and smiled. He looked as if he were admiring the weather when in fact he was checking for a tail.

"One such manufacture came from the coal mines of Russia and belonged to a family who had been once loyal to the sovereigns..."

Yes, the driver noticed them. He smiled in the mirror, listening.

"Much of it was stored for safekeeping in the Bank of Sterling, Trevor's, by royal mandate, a place guaranteed by the British authorities. But those ledgers were appropriated and stolen. They had been given in Trust, and that trust was betrayed to the enemy..."

"what...?" she muttered, as if hearing for the first time a delicious secret recipe for baking a gateau.

Jacques continued soberly. "That inventory disclosed the identities of those who owned the mines and minerals and wealth of raw commodities for manufacture..."

He gave the top of her head another little kiss, before continuing.

"They became targets for the socialist revolutions that swept through Europe and toppled the governments. Their inventory and technology industry know-how were trampled and lost. Even the British social, political and economic upheavals were threatened. The industrial relations between Europe and Britain....they were not good."

The taxi veered left, and stood idling in traffic. He hit the horn and then jerked forward into a side alley.

The driver peering into his rear view mirror, and then touched his nose. They were safe with him, he wanted to say. But Jacques became uneasy.

"I have reason to believe..."continued Jacques "that is the cause of the disruption today we see in our theft and vandalism..."

"But that was years ago..." said Amanda "surely..."

Jacques lifted his finger to his lips, inducing quiet.

He turned, gazing out the window, his eyes scanning the street with sharpness. He leaned forward.

"*Merci Monsieur!*" he said. "*Nous nous disembarques ici... il y a un petit restaurant pas loin d'ici...*" he handed over a wad of money.

"Come..." he said, fairly pulling Amanda from the rear seat.

They walked away down the remote alley and turned the corner to re-enter the mainstream of the main boulevard, northbound.

The temperature of a cold March blast hit them, and they turned up their coats and gloves, walking briskly.

"It's safe, here!" he said, adding "I'd like share some information with you. I know of a gentleman who was once famous in Europe for his political connections with the new elite of this city. He created a technology company, and they said he had potential as a political figure. He was born Russian, and his father served in a movement of socialist liberation..."

They walked on briskly.

"His name was Victor Alexandrovich. He was known as a radical progressive socialist. They venerated him into sainthood. I rather think rather, that he was the father of European terrorism!.."

"But his son is Uri" Continued Jacques. "He inherited his father's company. He is also well recognized here at the NATO headquarters. Today, his firm has a service for the development of energy and thermal-nuclear reactor generators. He wants to drive policy away from fossil fuels..."

"Well that doesn't work for America, right now" said Amanda

"Precisely!" added Jacques. "But it is what Trevor's bank has financed here in Europe!" he said.

"*What?*"

"Yes. You didn't know because Trevor's bank keeps that account very quiet. Nobody but the British and American authorities knew..."

"No. Jacques. You must be mistaken! Trevor's firm is ..."

"Yes. Yes. I know! But his bank has some very old accounts and contact legacies on its books..." he grinned at her, adding "Eh bien. Before our time..."

This took Amanda totally by surprise. "Are you sure...?" she began.

"Your husband's bank" said Jacques, ignoring her "has founded many projects since the early 17th century in the development of European expansion."

This, Amanda knew, including the merging of the Scotting and British sovereign rights and economies centuries ago:

The Darien scheme, later called The Panama Canal. The Suez Canal. The shipping industry. Insurance. Others.

"So what are you saying?" she said, getting breathless as his pace of walking.

"Come inside!" he said finally "We order another coffee, yes?" And they entered a small bakery in the Heron district. "We are safe here!"

"Safe...?"

"Bonjour!" sang out the proprietor.

The warmth of the ovens filled the tiny restaurant, now redolent with baked goods and savory dishes. Amanda took a minute to recover, and they sat at the far end of the tables. Jacques too was able to relax a little.

Amanda's head was spinning, and she felt weary enough to end her patience.

Where was Trevor, she wanted to know...

Jacques took her hand. "I know...I know you want to know where is Trevor. He is alive, that much I know. But my envoy Yvonne Destin - whom I had sent to greet him when he left for Paris...she never met up with him!"

"What...are you saying, Jacques?"

"Yvonne Destin was delayed by a flat tire... One witness says that he saw Trevor talking with a lady, much like Yvonne. But they got into a car and left together in Normandy..." His turned his head, then added.

"That was not Yvonne!"

The words took a minute to sink in. *Trevor was still in Normandy?*

That could mean only one thing. He was detained against his will.

"Is he...is he alright?" she said the words, almost afraid to hear the answer.

"Yes. That much I am told. But I am to wait for instructions..." He looked away. "I am the point of contact, clearly. They know that I talk to you..."

"Who is *they*? Who are these people? What do they want? And *why*? What are you saying? Why did they pick you to convey..."

Jacques looked at her gravely, sensing her distrust and fear. He looked down at his two hands and hesitated.

"What?" insisted Amanda..

"Yvonne, my associate broker...She was found dead in the stream not far from where she used to jog..."

Amanda's faced paled.

Now there was no doubt. This was a real threat. Trevor was in the middle of it...

Amanda cleared her throat, her lips parched. "I'm so sorry..." she began

Jacques nodded somberly. "For sure..." he continued, without raising his eyes "Yvonne's death was a message."

"A *message*?"

Amanda could only stare at him, almost dumfounded. Jacques was definitely their point of contact.

And Trevor... was at the center of it all.

They left the dry hot restaurant and just stood outside in the cold, as if their minds needed refreshment. And they were both looking up at the daunting edifice of the NATO Headquarters of Brussels in Heron.

"We shall go to the Opera!" he said.

They had a plan.

* * *

Amanda was ready by 7 o'clock.

"You look stunning!" said Jacques, his eyes sweeping over her.

Accustomed to Europe's celebrated events in the high stakes world of Antiquities, Jacques knew beauty when he saw it. Certainly, many had laid their charms and splendors at his feet. But Amanda had aged beautifully. And she enchanted him. Since his earliest days of knowing her, he held a torch for her deep within his heart.

"Thank you" smiled Amanda in her floor-length black organza skirt and jacket from the runway collection of Ralph Lauren.

"And Trevor...is a lucky man!" he added

Amanda had agreed to go to the Opera that evening with Jacques. The performance of *Aida* was in Brussels. It was to mark the official opening ceremonies of the EU Parliament.

Taking her seat at *la Monnaie*, Amanda felt like an ornament in a bejewel time capsule. The *Theatre Royal de la Monnaie*, Jacques explained, had been commissioned by Maximilian II Emanuel, Elector of Bavaria, Governor of the Habsburg Netherlands.

He paused and turned to her to say "He was an important man. Historically, as "Elector" – one of seven princes authorized to elect a Pope. A Pope was the not just a religious man. But the leader of an empire, the Holy Roman Catholic Empire of medieval Europe, as sovereign power, complete with a treasury and military arsenal to vanquish lands, nationalize and colonize!"

"It mattered, surely, that burden?"

"Oh absolutely it mattered! The Pope was the one who ordained a monarch. He chose the monarchs of Europe: He managed the line of dynastic kings across several ruled territories within the Holy Roman Empire! Not only did they hold armies to defend their own lands, but that of the Holy Roman Catholic Church…"

"And that didn't go so well for Henry VIII…" chuckled Amanda.

"No, poor fellow. All that sex life and not a male heir to be proud of! But when he split from the Roman Catholic Church, he created the Protestant Anglican Church of England, breaking up the dominance of the Roman Empire over Europe."

Amanda nodded. "Including the Netherlands, yes?"

"Yes. Thanks to Martin Luther. They became the hub of commerce for themselves…" grinned Jacques. Adding, "Mmm…judging from the jewels here tonight, I'd say most of them were cut in Amsterdam during the 18th century!"

They climbed the grand stairways together, he holding up her hand and she holding up the hem of her gown for a splendid appearance.

Jacques was well known in these parts. He chatted, waived, smiled….

"But by the 18th century, however…" he said, wanting to capture the ending of his tale "Lutheranism had taken root in his territorial lands, and this Elector would now re-shape the destiny and culture of Europe with his Protestant predisposition!"

"Ah" she smiled

More grand stairways.

The baroque architecture was lavish. Rebuilt by Venetian architects after the bombardment of Brussels by French King Louis XIV, the city, it was told, received the rescue of its enemies. It had been leveled by artillery and firepower, heralding modern of military might.

The attack on Brussels wiped out centuries of medieval and artistic heritage, such that the Master of the French artillery wrote in his report *"A more appalling spectacle has never been seen, and nothing else comes as close to the sack of Troy."*

They entered the Opera theater.

As the orchestral strands of music soared, Amanda felt touched that this Opera had risen from the ashes of the iron century.

Relentlessly, the *Seven Years' War* – as it was called then, had engaged Great Britain and France in a struggle for the control of colonial North America. India too, was at the heart of the conflict.

Colonial continents beckoned for their commercial wealth and political concept of Protestant freedom for individuals.

Further, Britain's alliance with Prussia was to protect the electoral Hanover dynasty that was of the British Protestant culture.

France was Catholic. All Continental possession should be kept from the French...

This city and its legacy spoke of lost empires and broken wars, and today remained a capsule of philosophies still rampant in global disputes.

They raged, conflicted still between free market economies espousing decentralization of wealth, and socialist centralization seeking the redistribution of wealth as progressive movements. Europe was still torn.

"There he is..." nudged Jacques, nodding down to the front row of the audience below their box.

Amanda followed his gaze, and lifting her opera glasses, she viewed carefully the focus of interests.

She scanned the facial features, expanded her zoom, magnifying ...Then methodically imaged them with a button in the handle of her small binoculars.

She was collecting a database through the lens of her optically designed device with digital memory embedded within the opera glasses.

She looked up at Jacques.

"Got him!" she said with a sly smile, and she tucked away the glasses.

As far as she was concerned, their mission was complete.

* * *

"So, are you telling me that this man... is *afraid* of heights?"

"That's right" grinded Jacques, his eye glasses perched on his nose as he perused the photographs on the desk. In his right hand was a mortar and pestle where coffee beans were pounded into powder.

"...And he's sending rockets into orbit?"

"Yes"

"You don't find that strange that he can't fly a plane and he's in the business of high altitude missile technology?"

"He won't even sit in an Opera Box at the theater..." said Jacques, pouring over the images.

 "And...who is this, the woman beside him in the seating?" asked Amanda

"She's his sister in law. Madam du Luc Alexandrovich, descendant of a grand Russian princess, they say in a fashion magazine.

"Oh really?"

"Yes. Apparently, she inherited a diamante tiara that was photographed in 1911 on the head of the Grand Duchess when she visited her sister, Queen Alexandra in London."

"Well, I doubt that very much..." said Jacques "I see those tiara's too many times in my business!"

"Oh?" said Amanda. "As collectable valuables?"

"Well, as baubles mostly... There's work to do here. I can see that you've done a good job of identifying many people in those images."

"But...who are these people, *here*?" said Amanda, her finger on one.

"Umm. Security? No. An official known in the EU?"

"He's clearly a popular man with them?"

"Yes. Others, let me see, may be his henchmen" muttered Jacques. He straightening up from the laptop. "Let me know what other data you find on them!"

"Working on it..." she grimaced, stretching.

Amanda had changed into jeans and was wearing a white T shirt, the coffee cup by the computer was freshly brewed, and her evening gown was strewn over the back of an armchair.

She peered into the pestle.

"Ah! Wait 'till you come to my place for dinner, Amanda. I like to cook..." Jacques was saying.

Amanda moved to the desk. "I'm very impressed with these" she said, lifting the 10x22 Mini Military gold ringed binoculars.

Delicate, simple, these opera glasses were modified lightweight high powered binoculars with telescopic lens. Popular with Bird Watchers, they were seen in travel journals for sightseeing. And they were also advertised for use at concerts, theater, Opera, camping and hiking. Some models were outfitted with night vision capabilities. Inside was a digital lightweight camera with video recorder as an electronic device. Amanda had downloaded the camera chip onto her laptop immediately upon returning.

"Mmm" said Jacques, picking up the binoculars. "In this business, anything is possible...I keep them handy!"

He walked around the table of images and said "anyway my dear, you impress me immensely with your work. There is much to be identified still. I doubt he travels in circles like these without "eyes" everywhere!"

"It's best to be cautious" he continued "watch for anyone who might be a danger. Be circumspect. Be discrete. Eyes down and mouth shut, to be safe. But miss nothing around you!"

She grimaced

"I know you have your sources of discovery and intelligence Amanda. So keep at it....He is the one behind Trevor's abduction. I am certain."

Amanda looked up at him, her eyes full of apprehension.

Jacques approached her. "You've been at this for days. Get some rest. I'll see you tomorrow afternoon at four o'clock. We'll go out for a light tea and bite to eat at a bistro, then back to work. OK? You have all you need here at the hotel?"

"I do, thank you!"

"Ok then" he said, pecking her on the cheek. "Rest! Keep this door locked...I'll call you, undersood?"

Jacques, Amanda knew, was about as harsh as a soft boiled egg. But this was Europe. Over here...things could turn frigid very quickly. He had savvy. He was a trusted friend.

Amanda worked into the early hours. One image in particular gripped her with suddenness.

As tradition would have it, the audience dressed up for the event. Tonight, there had been no end to the silks, shawls, long gowns and dandy assortments of ornaments, jewels, soiree bags, sparkle and pins in the audience – both on men and women. One set of necklace sequins or spectacles could catch a glimmer from a stage light and blaze like a star. Some dark images had mixed shapes, small. Other features were large and dramatic.

But one black pair of earrings caught her attention. Or, they could have been lost in the shadows of baubles? Yet they held very still, like two glassy identical rings. Fixed in position by someone seated behind their person of interest. Amanda realized they were not jewelry.

They were BAK-4 Optics Lens with FMC green film, a prism material with fully multilayer-coated objective-lens used for weak light conditions, if not totally darkened conditions...

This "lens" were focused squarely on her and Jacques. Amanda had caught them! She spotted them by refraction of the light, and they were held up by someone looking up at the box directly.

She and Jacques had been clearly identified.

They too had been watched.

* * *

The next day was no better for Amanda.

An urgency to locate Trevor was mounting with every hour. That he was in the hands of an assailant was almost impossible to refute. But...

Who was this enemy?

What did he want? Could this even be substantiated?

One person had been killed. Yvonne, a trusted associate whom Jacques had sent to rendezvous with Trevor in Normandy. She was found dead. And though the incident was not yet ruled a homicide, Amanda and Jacques were distressed beyond belief.

Jacques blamed himself. He should have taken more care, considering the sketchy characters that populated his world of Antiquities.

Further, the matter developed deeper substance when Jacques explained to Amanda that he had agreed to meet with Trevor in a private place because of some intelligence he had about the painting... and its bidder!

As confidential as that rendezvous was, someone had yet managed to intercept the message and abduct Trevor.

Had they attempted to communicate with Jacques? That was the question. Why?

It was too awful to imagine.

Jacques was about the call in the police. He chose to consult with Amanda first. And they had to be sure...

"Who is this man?"

"The images are consistent with his entourage and family..." replied Jacques. "Identification verification can be made for each of the family players and partners, all of whom had become agents for his business in drug trafficking..."

"What are you saying? Who is he?" asked Amanda, her mind still processing.

Jacques raised his hand, spectacles perched on his nose, un-muddling thoughts ranging through his head as he paced.

"...That's not all that he is involved with..." he muttered, pausing.

"Well. That's all the information I got from the United States...the, umm, you know, the, the.. New York Department of Justice..." he finished

"Should we consult the FBI?"

"Let me see these images" said Jacques, a large pastry filling his mouth.

The assembly of photographs passed his scrutiny. He picked up one photograph, not speaking for a few minutes.

Finally he said "So. European intelligence has a dossier on this man. This is George his nephew aged 27; and Alicia, his sister's daughter, aged 22 And there is his ...brother in law Leo. Leo's new wife Lucinda is age 45. She is Polish - enjoying an upwardly mobile social society. With Leo in the Construction business, Lucinda is recognized. She has a chalet in Normandy France!"

Amanda looked desolate.

Jacques reached over the table and took her hand. "We will find him Amanda! I promise. My guess is, it is *she* who has Trevor in her house. She's been known to play the strong-arm at times...But never a murder, if that's what you're thinking"

Amanda's eyes filled with tears. "It's not that he's a young man anymore! He's getting on, you know, slower.. and I'm not sure how strong he can be..." Her hand flew to her mouth.

Jacques looked at her. "You've been together a long time Amanda..."

"We have. Yes. And we've had a good life, for sure. But he is a dreamer, Jacques. A man who sees no danger..."

Jacques leaned in. "He is a rare breed of man, Amanda. Trust me, I've seen my share of humanity in my business. But it is not danger that he does not see, it is love for others that he *does* see...There is nothing in the world like that quality. Nothing competes..."

"And he would die for it!" choked Amanda, frustrated.

Jacques did not contradict her. Instead he looked away. "We will find him. In fact, these images are good work. They define the players..."

Amanda sat back, her anger abating. They rays of late afternoon sunlight splayed across their tea and sandwiches.

"Thank you, Jacques" she said "I *am* nervous!"

Jacques sighed.

"I wish it were that simple" he said. "This man....this man Victor is no longer playing at ordinary crimes. He is a vendor of high stakes technologies that belong to the world of cyber-space arms and defense...He has not quite managed to get his hands on advanced research, but he has bidders begging for his commodity when he attains it..."

"Didn't he serve in prison?"

"Yes, he did. But he lives in Croatia now, and his father's family were Russian - Bolsheviks to be precise. They played at activism; crime opportunism; propaganda and political movements -- toppling monarchies across Europe with revolutions and anarchy." Jacque's voice waned. Through these very spectacles, he had seen in his business too many legacy collectibles originally belonging to the afflicted, the fallen and oppressed of the past century. He sighed heavily.

"Today, he carries on with a younger generation hoping to overturn the free market economies of the world. He is continuing the legacy of his father, a hardened socialist with doctrines of redistribution of the wealth..."

"He is a terrorist?"

"Yes. No! He's not interested in gorilla warfare. He is more refined. He is intellectually interested in overturning governments, inducing financial instability.."

Jacques paused and sipped on his coffee, offering time for Amanda to digest.

She fell back into her chair. "Is that what he's is doing here, now?"

"It is what he has been doing for a while. All those people around him, didn't you find, are ministers and senior Leftist officials at the EU?"

"But surely, that's a legitimate Parliament with constitutional obligations to uphold the law?"

"Hah!" laughed Jacques. "This is Europe. Progressive socialism will declare for enough environmental hurdles to stop at nothing if they can seize individual opportunity and shut down all free market capitalism. This is a hungry, unionized world! He can achieve power as a social reformist and make it look like democratic campaigning!"

"Oh! You mean, like Brexit...?"

"Well, that's the simpler version. The Brits are sincere people. But they have no clue. Ever since Churchill had to surrender the British Empire's holdings to Roosevelt for the American contribution to WWII, they are without merchant power. Ah, *mais oui*, said Jacques, knowing that it was the French people who had to be liberated. He smiled, as if to say that the conflicts between the French and English were old indeed. But so were the bonds.

"Anyway" he said "This man...He wants to terrorize the world with a doctrine of "egalitarianism" which officially only a central bank and central government can control on a globalist level..."

"Surely you don't mean that, Jacques. I mean, that would take a lot of resources?"

Jacques leaned forward. "It's *socialism* Amanda! I am not a religious man, and virtue is not my greatest gift. But since biblical times, it's been proved to be unsustainable ...It's a religion."

Jacques looked down and became serious.

"Look. This much I do know. The men in this photograph...Here. Here. And here... they are avowed Leftists. This man, he dictates the agenda of his party in the EU Parliament. He will not even bring to vote matters of business enterprise! Let alone finance. He opposes independence for individuals. He wants to redesign human rights. He wants his party to own it all..."

"What constitutional rights..?" began Amanda.

"Rights? He shuts down his opponents for free speech! He despises the military of NATO, and he has murdered at least 6 men that we know of... with ties to financial banking...His tech company collects data on accounts."

Jacques pulled out the next image. "See this man? He is an intelligence officer for the fringe elements of an Asian ring of cyber hackers who intercept intelligence. Especially, they trade in new patent technology; microchip remote technologies manufactured in Asia. This man... is Iranian. That one... is known for his research of missile launch codes and cyber space satellites...They are passing information to him to sustain his globalist aspirations with intelligence!"

"And Trevor?"

Jacques looked at her somberly. "And Trevor" he repeated.

Amanda nodded. He was being honest.

Then Jacques leaned forward and said quietly "It is Trevor's firm in Washington that they are after..."

She stared at him.

"*What?*"

"Yes. It is what you are planning to provide as a subcontractor for the US Government."

"The accident that just happened...that was military grade..."

"sabotage" he interrupted. Adding, "that was no accident. And besides, that's just the beginning: When you can embarrass two major powers with the disaster of their ships, then you have announced that you are a threat..." said Jacques.

"My God..." said Amanda, her hand to her mouth.

"No. But it's what he wants to *sell* that is so troubling" added Jacques "The US Department of Energy is hoping to develop a space-ready nuclear fission reactor, known as Kilopower, that could provide up to 10 kilowatts of power and be deployed on other planets and moons. NASA has employed radioisotope thermoelectric generators — batteries that run off the heat from radioactive materials..."

"Those two ships each had nuclear reactors..." interrupted Amanda.

"Precisely!" said Jacques "Countries like Germany, South Korea and Taiwan are looking to renewable energy or cheap natural gas instead, leaving China and Russia to take the lead in the development of new nuclear plants."

Amanda stared.

"But it's the long game that he's playing. He wants cultural control for social manipulation. There is a power struggle."

"What does this have to do with Trevor's firm?" asked Amanda

"NASA faces competition from private industry. It's had its hopes pinned on atomic technology to power human colonies for habitation on other platforms...These are long term future strategies for investment and new horizons well within our capabilities... "

"That sounds a lot like what my son in law is doing at his Lab in Berne...' supplied Amanda.

"Yes. Our capabilities for manufacturing systems for space applications is a ready market for technical development. The size of the market is directly tied to how easily these systems can be manufactured. In-space nuclear power systems for electrical and propulsive power is leading to interesting things...It will put them in space as satellites for tracking..."

Amanda's face changed as a thought crossed her mind.

"Wait...You don't think that Jack and Sandy are also implicated in this nefarious plot for technological superiority?"

Jacques said nothing.

"*Do you?*" repeated Amanda

Jacques looked at her gravely. "Let's not speculate, Amanda. We don't know. We are only being analytical. That is hard to do dispassionately. This may be totally without meaning, just a happening of the events...We'll need to examine more findings before we know for sure..."

"Jack is...Jack is out of touch with Sandra!" Amanda said quietly, adding "What is going on? What else do you know?"

Jacques paused. Then he said "Why not consult with your boss and ask him if he knows anything Amanda. It may be a lot of badly timed events. Perhaps he will know more than we can discover?"

"Admiral Arguetta?"

Amanda knew not to press. This was not the time. She'd be patient.

Jacques took in a big breath.

"I'll set up a secure connection with Washington for you to work from here, Brussels. I have a client with an apartment close by. It is a safe place. He is gone for the winter, and he has it periodically swept for electronic surveillance. Do you wish to occupy it, or is the hotel sufficient for you?"

Amanda considered. "Does it have a kitchen?"

"Oh Yes! He is a culinary savant...Especially his wine collection. He has everything!"

"I like to cook. And if that's o.k. I'll be happy there!"

Jacques nodded, pleased. "Excellent! I may bring my staff with me then...to work there?"

"Yes" said Amanda, a pale grin on her face.

"In the meantime, let's focus on Trevor. Yes?" said Jacques.

"Absolutely"

On his way out Jacques paused by the table with the photographs. He pointed to the profile of Victor Alexandrovich. "This man..." he said half to himself "is more than a dangerous man. He is deadly."

Amanda went back to the hotel that night feeling like she hated Brussels.

She looked at her cell phone. No message from Sandra, either.

The thoughts of their conversation kept her tossing all night. The more she thought about it, the more she understood the scope of this man's ambition. This was not just one venture's aspiration...This was an industry that he had appropriated to service his life-long mission to overturn government and revolutionize the world!

If Jacques was right, the assailant had abducted Trevor to stop the development of technology and eliminate competition. This, *Advanced Technologies* was conducting. Except...

He did not count on Amanda. She had stepped into Trevor's role and filled the gap of company leadership!

Now, her family was now implicated in technology associated with this man's ambition.

She felt angry. Clearly, she would become his new target.

Perhaps... that is worried Jacques most.

Chapter 9

Sandra was delighted to learn her mother was in Brussels. She had left a text message for Amanda on her phone.

Sandra wanted to meet her mother. She and Jack had returned to Switzerland, perhaps for reconciliation. "When are you free?" she had asked. "Call me!"

They were so excited.

Sandra came to Brussels and stayed with her mother at Amanda's new living quarters.

They had lots to talk about, and the days passed easily. Especially since the accommodations that Jacques had provided were safe, private and fully provisioned. Jacques' client was clearly a man of financial means, occupying a penthouse apartment with its own terrace.

It was cool for March, but these were conditions that Sandra and Amanda loved most. They lunched outside on the terrace, with a view of the city at their feet.

Amanda produced a lunch tray of bisque soup, fresh salad with peas and pesto sauce, and a slice of rustic bread.

They ate, sitting outdoors in the cool breeze wearing scarves and heavy sweaters, and they basked in the midday sun as if they were Nordic skiers.

Much as they had to discuss, it was a comfort to be together as family. Then when Amanda came out with hot white chocolate on frozen fruit for desert, they savored their coffee in total solace.

Amanda spoke of Trevor. That is, all but some sensitive details about his assailant that were best left unsaid. There was no need to expose all, and besides, it would only leave Sandra worried and vulnerable.

Amanda asked about Jack.

"Well..." said Sandra, tucking her legs up in the deckseat, "you know the US Geological Survey hosted a Space Resources Roundtable at the Colorado school of Mines in Golden, Colorado?"

"Oh?"

"The space-resources community want to work with them - I mean, his lab... to assess the location and value of minerals, energy and water on the moon, Mars and asteroids."

"Wow!" said Amanda. "Well that would be Jack's area of interest, of course!"

"Yes. It was very interesting. It's refreshing to find that the USGS offers proven expertise and unbiased, quantitative research that acknowledges terrestrial resources..."

"Whoah. Slow down! " teased Amanda

"Ok? ...Because everything you read is framed in polarized political overtones?"

"Hmm" said Amanda, her thoughts running to the activism debates at Warwick Library. The was different, she thought dismissively.

"So..." continued Sandra, sipping her coffee "This USCG collaboration can also lead to reliable and much-needed geological maps for more precise landing-sites and resource-deposit selections..."

"Here on earth? Or do you mean space landings...?" chirped Amanda, puzzled.

Sandra sighed at her mother. "Space! Here, this is their program, and I must say, we had a great time meeting colleagues and friends over there. I was surprised at the interest by private industry though. Some investment firms were very seriously deepening their ties to the movement."

"Well you know how it is. They are convinced that space travel is a necessity to resource-abundance platforms for mining..." said Sandra.

"I see..."

"The U.S. human space program seems to be focusing on missions into deep space where space resources are extremely valuable. So commercial efforts able to extract space resources, are growing"

A small shadow flickered briefly across Sandra's brow. "You concur?" asked Amanda, pouring fresh coffee.

"Actually, I do! But it's almost uncomfortable for the rest us doing research...As if we have to apologize for developing foundational principles of sound research and policy!"

"How does Jack view this?"

"Well that's just it, you see. He's persuaded the planet is under siege by pollution caused by humans! He thinks space resource-mining is restricted by barriers of cost; conservative restraints and/or fraught with geo-political antagonism!'

Amanda nearly paused at the rising tempo of Sandra's voice, as if telling a good joke. Then she saw that her daughter was far from calm.

"Where is Jack?" asked Amanda softly.

"Well...I'm not exactly sure. I think....I think....well, I don't know *what* to think!"

"I get it. You think he's under the influence of his international colleagues at Berne – most of whom find social injustice under every bed?" chuckled Amanda.

"No" said Sandra, abruptly rising. "More like the battle cry of every charge..." she blurted.

Amanda stared at her daughter.

This was more than a social visit. This was a crisis in Sandra's life.

"Wait..." said Amanda.

Sandra was already in the kitchen putting away the dishes. "What I mean is, there's something very odd about his company and he's having to be *secretive*. He's espousing stupid socialist manifestoes like he's recruiting for world-change, and it makes me uncomfortable...I just don't know *what* he's up to!" she blurted, her eyes troubled. "He's not himself anymore..."

Sandra disappeared into the bathroom and emerged with her face refreshed. She reached for her coat, gloves and bag.

"Now look here..." said Amanda. "Perish those thoughts! Jack is devoted to you...He's busy sorting out the motives behind a fast and furiously developing new industry. There is technology...intelligence...sovereign security and political stability at stake, perhaps. To say nothing of the financial risks and investments necessary... Give him time!"

Sandra smiled.

"It's a political capture for any industrial competitor" continued Amanda. "Especially if he's working on defense. Stick with him. Work it out. Don't fret..."

Sandra gazed at her mother, then reached down and kissed her on the cheek.

She left, the door barely closed when Amanda realized she had left her folder behind with the program catalogue of Jack's convention.

Later that night, Sandra called. She apologized for being so edgy. She had to get back to Switzerland, she said, but she asked if they could get together again next month.

Amanda agreed, both of them chuckling as they signed off.

The catalogue of the Convention was strewn on the table. Amanda had viewed it briefly. She stooped to pick up from the table and clear away the tray and china cups.

The brochure flipped over to the back page. One of the key industrial investors, she noticed, sat at the head team. Then she froze.

He was a face she recognized. He actually gave a speech, evidently. At his side was her son-in-law, Jack Lucas. The figure was someone she and Jacques were following closely.

Victor Alexandrovich.

* * *

It was early in the morning. For business, that is.

Amanda had fretted all night, and she couldn't wait to talk to Jacques. She should wait another hour, she thought. Then as Amanda picked up her cell phone and was prepared to dial, he called her.

"Oh hi!" she said "I was just about to call you!"

"Yes. *Bon Jour!* Look Amanda, I am pressed today, in fact I'm on my way to the rail station to take a train to Paris. But there is something I want you to see: I have left an envelope for you at the Concierge in your building. Open it up. It has a computer app with some footage on it. I've been watching the home of the family in Normandy. Madam du Luc Alexandrovich was there this weekend. Tell me what you find? Survey the feed. I'll be back in a day or two..."

"Yes, will do! Oh, there is something else Jacques..." she said. Should she tell him that Sandra came to visit? Was that necessary, she wondered.

"Err..." she started, thinking to tell him of her son in law Jack collaborating with Victor Alexandrovich? Or even, that his interest was in space technologies...As a family member?

No. Not over the phone, she decided. The less said the better. "That's ok, no problem. So, have a safe trip!"

Amanda was not confined to quarters. Neither was there anything wrong with having family as a guest – such as her daughter. Jacques of all people would understand.

Then Jacques said one more thing before closing. "The minute you read that file, Amanda, I'm going to call Trevor's office and ask them to open an official investigation about his disappearance. Is that alright with you?"

"Let me call you back on that decision Jacques. Trevor would appreciate the privacy before we sent out the troops, I know him. But soon...I promise."

"No! Forgive me, but I must insist Amanda. The police must be involved"

When he hung up, Amanda's hands covered her face. That would mean the Press would advertise that Trevor was missing! Was that wise? His office would be the focus of an audit and a full Enquiry. She had better warn his lawyers, now.

Further, that meant exposing their own hand, that is, their private investigations of the assailant. Perhaps alerting him of their suspicions and search?

Jacques was right, she decided. Of course they must alert the Police. His safety should come first, come-what-may!

How could she even hesitate?

Should she warn Admiral Arguetta?

She took a big breath and walked to the window. The rain of Brussels drizzling into the terrace, and her thoughts wandered.

Truth was, they lived a quiet life of discretion and privacy, she and Trevor. They were accustomed to no fanfare or celebrity status, though clearly Trevor was an icon in his industry.

Clearly, they had their reasons. Out of respect for the sovereign authority that they served, foremost. They were in a world of cutting edge developments and not only was there a high level of security required, but a higher risk of espionage and intellectual intelligence at bay.

Yet it was more. They could easily live the high life, Trevor and Amanda were people of considerable financial means. But simplicity, and what was described as an 'attitude of gratitude' prevailed. It demonstrated love and fidelity. It showed tradition and values to their children – from big events of social responsibility to the personal recital of saying Grace and giving thanks to God at every dinner meal...

For Amanda, she too could afford to be a personality of recognition. But it was Trevor who gave her shelter and security, and she chose to vest her allegiance to him alone, not to the media or the money that chased them! It was a personal code of ethics and understanding. It was a trust in the authority of the family, where they all flourished...

Trevor would have it no other way, she smiled.

Yes. Of course Jacques was right!

No matter what, it was the right thing to do. And for the right reasons.

Meanwhile, there were issues she had to deal with.

Like, how could Amanda tell Jacques that Sandra's husband knew Victor, a known felon?

Or that Jack was informed of intelligence by the US government for deep space travel? Well, that is, everybody knew...

She thought about it. Was she overreacting? Jack's company was a private corporation. His lab was in Berne Switzerland.

And, why was Jack in his sights? Had he not already murdered Jack's associate, Sophie?

Yet... the development of his research was now of interest to the defense industry! Was there any connection? A conflict of allegiances..?

Was that even her concern, she wondered.

* * *

Never was Amanda more certain of her decision to return to Washington than later that night, after she had analyzed the tapes on the electronic device that Jacques had delivered.

The house and grounds of the luxury home on the coast of Normandy appeared pastoral. The imagery, captured by camera from a police drone the size of a toy plane, showed the premises shrouded by a gloomy-grey rainfall coming off the English Channel. But the features were definable.

The main residence was where Madam de Luc was staying. Staff and guests came and went. Occasionally, a few pets ran out.

The adjacent guest house however, was the focus of attention for Amanda. It was across the courtyard and along the walkway of a green, facing the sea. A meal, a delivery of food moved from the Main house to the guest house daily with the groundskeeper, often with a family pet bounding at his side.

She knew the breed. The animal that attended the groundskeeper was his. Brown and white, it was clearly a Welsh Springer, and it rarely left his side as he came and went. The Springer in the imagery reminded Amanda of their own pets at home in England.

Trevor had one, Trigger. It never left his side. Trevor would feed him dog scraps under the table -as if nobody knew what he was doing! The dog was devoted... As a retriever, the dog pointed well and ran with some speed to fetch fallen game. It was not given to sluggishness, or dainty footwork. It was a fast runner.

Trevor had trained it do a trick that was quite remarkable for its breed. He made it recline on its back, and roll over three times. This was a unique trick for his breed, denoting total trust in his master.

Amanda replayed the tape. And again.

Amanda watched the pet beside the groundskeeper. On the last trip up to the house, the dog reappeared. The groundskeeper stopped suddenly when his cell phone rang, and he disappeared.

But the dog stayed. He was attentive to a sound. Then just quite suddenly, the keeper's dog reclined on its back, and rolled over three times: Only one person could have instill that kind of trust in a dog.

Trevor was alive!

Trevor was in the guest house. The dog gave him away.

Amanda must have replayed the sequence a dozen times. And now she was certain she must return to Washington. Her reasoning was lucidly clear.

The Firm in Washington was compromised. If the CEO was revealed as being held hostage, then the data of the company was at risk. If not by direct means, then by indirect means tantamount to a leak bought for a price from someone under the counter. Not that security was inadequate - they had all been vetted as employees and they were loyal But third party tech surveillance could find ways to infiltrate a system using hackers. That much she knew. Big tech was competing in industry using high stakes digital data-mining, refractions and encryptions.

She packed, her mind a whirl.

She opened her computer and drew up a list of factors and observations. Next, she would deliver a preliminary report to Arguetta. Then she would book her flight ticket at the Airport...

She paused suddenly, determined to bring her thinking to order. Was she being reasonable?

She itemized the events with jotted notes.

A disastrous failure at sea had occurred: The US Government was justified to consider *Advanced Technologies* as responsible.

Now here was Trevor, held captive in Normandy France!

Had Trevor MacDonnell been the target as CEO of a major company developing a technology for the US government?

Further, had his reputation been impugned by an Auction where the media suggested fraud...

Was it possible that he was designed to be the subject of a public scandal, as if he had rigged bidding at the Auction? Was his character besmirched to damage authority and brand?

And, what of the painting itself? The painting reflected a family legacy in a period of history defending the Empire, if today scorned by modern culture of populism?

Was this a rabid socialist with a plan?

Next, the probabilities:

Did he have the money? As an industrial leader in the technology sector of the market, was he truly viable?

Yes. Based on her observations at the Opera, and later in the imagery of a home on the coast of Normandy, and that left no doubt as to his means!

No question. Trevor had been abducted.

She paused, thinking. How to frame the question of motive?

If Trevor was held hostage, and Jack was in his embrace, did this man have the technological capabilities to stage the spectacular sinking of two ships?

Worse. *Did he have bigger ideas of technological conquest?*

It was a horrific picture now developing. What if she was mistaken?

Regardless, she had an obligation to speak. What was the old adage: *Oh! Watchman of the Tower fail thee not to sound the alarm - lest ye be the one responsible for the battle...*

To whom could she talk?

Was she being logical?

Analysis, that is, critical analysis was based on assumptive thinking; insight and qualified quantitative evidence...

She paced the room.

...Private and public sectors, both held boundaries to reach. Space travel, she knew, was the next new frontier.

She paced.

From a practical point of view, this was clearly a potential resource for commerce. The industry was promising, if fraught with danger.

Much development was already expended. Large investment strategists were interested in this technology. Mining interests. Banking interests. Risk and Planning were at early days yet, but even sovereign governments were involved.

For futurists and capitalists, it was prospect for exploration. Leading-edge advancements, with global ramifications was a new frontier for trade and world stability, and cyber security.

But...What if he was a *rogue* player? Or more importantly, to what end?

Her thoughts flew to what Jacques had said. This was a different sort of enemy. Revolutionary. In fact, if left without sanction, he had the means, and the methods in technologies...

Her hand suddenly flew to her mouth.

This man had the motive of an angry, secular heart aimed at overthrowing the free world and redistributing capitalism!

She stood up, backed away from her notes, ugly.

History was replete with misguided liberal reformists who failed to survive the test of time.

Inevitably, it was unsustainable. What followed was usually filled with darkness and evil...

She paced.

Finally she paused. She washed her face with fresh water and took a big breath.

The day had waned. She looked at her watch.

She scribbled a personal memo for Jacques. The Concierge would arrange to have it delivered to his private residence by certified courier. In it, she explained her reasons and her movements.

She would be ready for the morning. She would get some sleep for the night.

This man, Victor Alexandrovich had defied the Navies of two super powers in a display of power, without apology.

What was his next move?

Definitely. Arguetta should be warned. Yes, she decided. She did have to go to Washington.

For now, Trevor's crisis was better managed by Jacques.

Trevor, after so many years or doing so much for so many... a man now in his seventies, was a captive!

She wanted to weep for him.

Trevor MacDonnell... deserved so much better that to be subjected to such sordid games. How was he holding up in a cold cottage... off the coast? A sudden choking anger swelled within her. How dare someone target him in such fashion?

She must control her impulse. This, she knew from years of discipline. This was the only way to be effective.

But her moment would come. Of that she felt certain..

She calculated her best offense.

Yes, she decided. She would send a message to Jacques. And she would keep him on track for Trevor.

Yes, she was packed and scheduled to leave the next day. There was much to do in advance.

There was more intelligence to coalesce. Information and investigative thinking had to be marshaled and coordinated. But she had to be careful.

No sharing ... on the internet. No use of electronic device on unsecured browsers. No indiscrete information over the phone. No images by cell. No location Apps. No trash, unsecured papers or files left... for trash collection.

Only the *right* date for the *right* contacts....

She was a pro at the protocol of security. But it had been a long time since she held a job. Still, the same protocols held true.

And, above all, it required concentration and a clear head.

Rest. Get some sleep.

It was dark. She lay on her bed, thinking...

What was his profile? Was this the same arsonist who had sabotaged a coal mine in Pennsylvania?

Was he protesting, or generating an incident? The establishment that relied on fossil fuel, what was that about? Was it activism? Against whom?

Socialists held grudges. By and large, they were an angry, bitter breed of people. There was little joy in their heart; rather, given to selfish neediness, allowing the seeds of malcontent to take root, usually without thought to the consequences...

Had all that hard work by unionized coal miners not served to ignite the industrial advances of the last century? No. There was no rationalizing with them...

For them, neither was today a new world full of hope and wonder, nor was the West inspired by innovation to reach frontiers of space travel, or exploration for resources, trade and general advancements...

What exactly was this malevolent man doing?

Was he challenging national security? Sovereign entities? Market economies? *What...?*

Clearly he had ambition. He was a dangerous man. A terrorist, at best.

America not a beacon of hope...

Worse. Was America his target? Did he plan to shatter global order into disarray by the hand of this terrorist? Why? Because he launched a competing technology?

She could not sleep. She tossed. The hotel was quiet.

She put on her jeans and a heavy sweater.

She would stroll downstairs and casually enter the cybercafé. There, she would go online and consult the flight schedules for the next few days. She followed the trail of bookings as if shopping in New York City.

So. A stop at Macy's for bedding. Tiffany's for earrings. Talbots for a couple blouses. Pietros' for a leather handbag. A hair cut at David Mallett's Salon. Tickets for the Couture NYC Fashion Week...

She got what she needed.

For the week, her footsteps and destination of her trail would untraceable.

* * *

Amanda got up early, sipped her morning juice and finished her toast. She poured herself a cup of coffee and opened the newspaper. It came daily with the Concierge service.

Today would be a long day.

Her cell phone pinged. It fairly danced along the marble countertop. Normally switched on for the vibrate-mode, she wanted to hear it ring - to be sure she wasn't missing any calls. An old habit really, from the days of guarding the children when they went on a travel trip. Or even when Trevor was on the road, her cell was close in case he called for support of information, documents or tasking. And she had received a few over the years.

Once, Sandra once called from India to say she'd run out of money. Tray even called from the airport in Chicago where he was detained by the authorities for carrying a can of shaving cream onto the plane. And Trevor had called to say he'd lost his wallet, unable to pay the taxicab fare...

Amanda reached for the ringing phone. *Oh God Trevor... Where are you my darling?*

She did not recognize the calling number. "Yes?"

Her fears quickly dispelled when she heard a familiar voice. "Bill..." she said, totally surprised.

"Hello Mrs. MacDonnell. I'm in Brussels on business for a Conference. I wanted to see how you were doing?"

Bill Arguetta knew her number, of course. They'd worked together in Washington DC.

She did not discuss the developments of the last few days, and she waited.

Unless by political design, the movements of ranking officials were not necessarily announced. This was an unscheduled stop.

"How's your arm?" she asked

They chatted. He'd told her that he'd be in town for a couple days, three at the most. Was she free to meet for lunch, he wanted to know.

She looked at her suitcases packed by the door, thinking airline tickets and booked flights were easily cancelled, if necessary.

"Delighted!" she said.

Arguetta commended her for the professional commitment to her husband's firm, thanking her again for her duty in Washington.

Trevor's absence, and the role she assumed, was clearly putting things on a different footing. She was now in service to him as an official capacity. This was no social call.

Yes, she was nominally on the board of director's of the parent company in London. Not that she ever engaged much - that was Trevor's world. But Trevor had insisted, and the banking community had come to trust and respect her. By default, she was a stakeholder.

Certainly, as a Department Contracting Officer, Arguetta was responsible for the oversight of the company under contract to the government, and he was informed about the company's internal affairs.

He was here addressing not Amanda, but the company. And he had to make his new requirements clear. For this, he wanted to meet with her.

This posture, in addition what she and Jacques were doing here in Brussels, put Amanda in a awkward position. She was obliged to keep him informed.

There was pressure, but she could not flinch.

If Trevor was taken hostage, her every move and word was being monitored, she knew.

Her decision to fly to Washington, for example, would not go unnoticed.

Even her call from Arguetta was being monitored.

She closed her eyes.

Trevor...

She spent the morning preparing. There was much to disclose.

She collected her thoughts, and would make an assessment of the situation with a short briefing. Then they would determine the best procedure.

But her thoughts wandered.

Trevor. Where is he held, by whom, why? Already, she was on a different track of thinking. She was certain he was being held against his will by Alexandrovich.

Might Trevor have been hurt? She could not know.

At lunch she would explain their findings to Arguetta. But not until they could talk.

Still, she had to be cautious. She could reveal nothing. Intelligence on what had developed in Washington had them all under secrecy.

No question that she was being watched. But... how to *prove* who was behind this?

She must show the utmost discretion. Of course he had surprised her. She was at a disadvantage.

She had few resources at her disposal, and while the business of the company operations ran smoothly, Trevor's absence was increasingly at issue: Should there be a newly elected senior officer to replace him, she wondered.

That would be noticed by the Media, if nothing else.

Should they issue a Press Release?

True, for now the Acting Director of the firm was filling his shoes admirably. But what of the Annual Meeting upcoming? Should the police be involved in a formal investigation at the company? Would that mean an automatic audit? Would it jeopardize their performance rating...Would the investors become alarmed?

These were questions coming in all day. Her email was full of questions by staff. Questions she chose to stall... in the hope of locating Trevor with a private investigation of her own. Jacques knew this, of course.

Chiefly, she wanted him alive!

The rest... would sort out later, she decided. Surely, the assailant would show his hand soon? They were waiting. But for how long?

And still no word. Not even from Jacques... Amanda's nerves were on edge. She tried to stay relaxed.

She looked again at her cell phone.

Nothing.

And now here was Arguetta in Brussels!

Should she tell him about a mad man in Europe, a respected minister of the EU with a tech company – Alexandrovich? A man who had targeted her family; killed a research scientist; ignited a coal mine incendiary in Pennsylvania and now kidnapped her husband Trevor?

Speculative! What if she were wrong?

No. Of course not.

Besides, she suspected that Arguetta knew.

The lunch was postponed. He was busy with meetings. Was is possible to have dinner, he later asked.

He was being cautious.

She agreed. Her place...

Amanda had lots to do before her dinner for her guest, Admiral Arguetta, USN, retired. A family friend, true. But here on business, for sure.

She dashed through her tasks: There were messages on her email. New information about the painting had come in. It's restoration and condition, mainly.

Another message came from Trevor's London office.

Then, scheduling a local meeting with a member of Jacques staff...Later in the day, she was to meet with an editor from a publisher. For *Brussels in Springtime*, they told her, lying through their teeth.

Tray called.

The concierge called. An envelope, downstairs was waiting.

Others called.

But not Sandra, she noticed. That shadow of anxiety that had crossed her daughter's face was not lost on Amanda: And though she would not meddle in a personal life, she was concerned. Sandra's state of mind seemed unsettled. Something about her demeanor was worrisome. She knew her daughter.

Clearly, Jack was under pressure. He had been deeply affected by the accident where Sonya was killed. Moreover, he'd been on travel, his work kept him away, Sandra explained.

Amanda gave her a call.

Sandra picked up. Yes, Jack was with her. Yes, they were fine and on their way to London. But they wanted to stop over in Brussels for the night, if that was ok... Just to visit, as it were.

They'd arrive late. Their flight was scheduled to land around 7 pm.

Welcome!" said Amanda, a big chuckle in her voice. "Arguetta will be here too. He's coming to diner!"

Amanda could have easily have called the Concierge for help with catering for the dinner party. Or she could have ordered something to be delivered. Instead, she searched for the address of the local vegetable market and decided to go there herself. She'd pick out her favorite fresh greens, then a delicious cut of meat from a butcher and, even commissioned a chocolate gateau from a local Brussels *Patisserie*. For drinks, she'd serve wine and cognac for spirits, along with delicious coffee for *apres* dinner.

It was almost five o'clock when Sandra called. Their flight had been postponed and they'd have to change plans. She apologized. But their visit was cancelled.

"Bill Arguetta will miss you both!" said Amanda.

It was a sudden change. Much as Amanda wanted to serve her beautiful dinner, she felt deflated and exhausted. She sat down into the great white divan and closed her eyes.

Less than ten minutes elapsed, Bill called.

Amanda explained that Sandra and Jack had planned to come...

Bill insisted on taking her out. "Come on. I'll do you good to get out..."

Amanda conceded.

It was raining when Amanda emerged from the Lobby.

A black powerful looking SUV stood waiting. Inside was Bill Arguetta with a phone to his ear as he held open the door for her. His driver was a corpsman from the US Marines, a security detachment, certainly.

"Hop in!" he bellowed. "How's the family?.."

She gave him a cheerful hug and they laughed at the rain.

"Carry on" said Arguetta to his driver.

They stopped.

The city was a sheen of night lights as they reached a casual restaurant, a pub with a good Grill and Bar menu, as he put it.

Periodically Arguetta responded to his cell, sometimes with a curt summary dismissal.

Amanda understood.

Europe was a friendly place to be, and certainly Brussels was the official headquarters of NATO. But no military personnel were without escort if they were of ministerial rank, and especially when mobile between secured premises. This was a new world.

Once inside, Amanda relaxed.

Behind them, a dance floor lit up with colorful sparks and a lively band blew out the acoustics.

Arguetta ordered two bottles of German beer, smiled, then looked about casually. There was no question that they were being observed.

Being in town, and taking a family friend out for a casual meal was a good excuse to get together.

"A good place to talk..." he said, over the din

They finished their steak and drinks.

He asked "no word yet?"

Amanda shook her head.

She told him everything she knew about Trevor's whereabouts. That much she could share.

He took it all in.

"We have a number of inquiries made to the French authorities. They are investigating. As are the Brits. But it's not public at this point you understand. Trevor is a large stakeholder in a big game. His disappearance is of great concern."

Amanda looked up, a small nod told him she appreciated all that he was doing.

"Look. Amanda, I want you to be prepared for anything! I may need you in Washington to ratify some rewritten procurements for the company. You ok with that?"

She nodded.

He covered her hands for encouragement. "Good spirit!"

She briefed him. "But it's all speculation..."

"This man....you say, he's on some kind of a greater quest?"

"Yes. He will make his intentions known. He will show his hand soon, I'm sure of it...Jacques tells me he has a construction company with a large workforce, many of them union members. He intends to subvert the EU Parliament with radical reformism...Again, speculation?"

"Yes. You are right. We are aware of him. He is on our radar"

"You are aware of his aspirations for space travel as a technology competitor?"

"I'll show you some images of a conference we just had in Washington. You'll recognize some of the faces."

She looked at him, her face full of apprehension.

Bill opened a dossier on the man Alexandrovich.

"He may be entertaining a bidding war for space defense systems" said Arguetta.

"And I thought he was interested in Art and Auctions!" said Amanda.

"Hardly. He's been setting up an agenda for some time. It's dark energy sources for space aviation he wants to corner...He's made a mockery of our nuclear-powered propulsion technologies."

Amanda looked at his face, it was set in a grim line.

If that was the prize, Amanda realized, then the threat just became larger. Aviation propulsion technology could be used for experimentation. Or, a new social order.

He dropped her off.

"You've been terrific.." he said, squeezing her hand. The SUV disappeared into the night.

* * *

Brussels, Belgium.

The meeting was held on the fourth floor of the American offices of NATO. Admiral Arguetta had just completed liaison meetings with several counterparts in Europe. He was dressed in full uniform and surrounded by several commanders and Lieutenant commanders. Some civilian personnel were there, two from Trevor's firm. George Anders and Steve Smith. As technical specialists, they had accompanied his group, and they had just been instructed to brief their stand-in CEO, Amanda Wells.

Arguetta was here, in fact, to give them an update of the situation on all new developments.

"What we have is two clear launches: One in the United States. And one here in Europe" he paused.

"NASA reports that all the test and launch preparations are in full readiness" he said.

"To test our new avionics technology, we've distributed payload communications sounding-mechanisms that will give scientists soundings from rocket-based research. Sound, in the dimentions of space, carry history. We'll be one step closer to hearing "history" if you will. Picture this, if successful, we'll have been able to trace back the origins of what happened to our ship and that of the Russian nuclear frigate."

He paused, then proceeded.

"Retracing a source of threat is significant as a deterrent. NATO views this as a potential threat, and one to avert: It anticipates a possible impact for our response. So, this leaves tracers in place at intervals to give a fuller data spectrum that informs that picture."

Amanda listened by electronic means.

"These instrumented sub-payloads, once deployed, will form a distributed payload communications technology, or a listening network. The devices should collect and transmit feedback loop of about four minutes of data - before reentering the atmosphere..."

I'll let the team experts explain.

"The capability is just one of several to be tested in this technology-demonstration mission known as Suborbital Technology Carrier-8, or SubTEC-8, a payload," said George, opening the schematic.

"SubTec-8 will be integrated onto a Terrier-Improved Malemute sounding rocket on April 1st . So far, this is on schedule and good to launch. "

"We at *Advanced Technologies* will be in the lead" he said.

"However, there is a second launch scheduled.." he paused, checking with Arguetta's nod, and allowing for everyone in the room to absorb the information.

Some were surprised.

"It's in Europe. The second launch is almost simultaneous. Here, colorful clouds formed by the release of vapors from an AZURE rocket will, ostensibly, allow scientists to measure auroral winds. The concept is similar to the distributed payload communications technology of the SubTEC-8 sounding rocket mission."

 "Nobody told me..." said someone.

Two hours later, Amanda went in to see Arguetta herself. He was the Project Manager of their contract. And he was coordinating with the Europeans.

It was noon, and she found him on his way up to the cafeteria of the office building. Together, they chose a lunch, and found a table to sit with their lunch trays.

She faced him squarely. "Nobody told me at AT that we were in aviation technology as well as naval engineering support!"

Arguetta remained silent, chewing.

Clearly, Amanda had been left in the cold.

He took another bite.

"Did you know that this man Alexandrovich is planning to launch an avionics mission, shortly?" she said.

"That's what we learned. He may be playing a bidding war. His company has license for a launch at the North Pole. A 'summit launch.' It's feasible."

"So. You *did* know!"

Arguetta finished chewing, and pushed away his tray.

He looked at her and spoke quietly.

"Not only is he launching his own rocket, but he plans to land it on ST87, an asteroid. There, he plans to plant a long range missile as his platform.. Gyroscopically it's aimed at the US."

"*What?*"

He reached for his salad.

"Actually, he plans to sabotage our launch sequence altogether...." said Arguetta.

She stared at him.

How could he have kept her in the dark about her husband's firm on *other* developments? The answer was obvious. She had her hands full with the task at hand. The company was conducting multiple aspects of research for the government, including support for naval propulsion systems. That was her main task in Washington.

He put down his fork.

"It's just that the two items now become one agenda. They were two independently and mutually exclusive task orders...AT was best qualified" he added.

Then he added with a grin "I didn't get this soldier's battle wounds for nothing..." he said. "I was targeted by a gunman for a reason Amanda. I stood over the management of the projects that impeded the assailant's aspirations!"

She got it. She was only on a *Need to Know* basis.

He read her thoughts. "I'm sorry I did not read you in on the full intelligence Amanda. You did your job commendably. And I thought it wrong to overburden you with other matters...But as it turns out, they are now connected. And in case you're wondering, we think you're the best party for the job. I recommended you!"

She looked puzzled, but accepted his acknowledgement.

He waited, giving her time.

"The assailant..." she began

"Ah! Now he...didn't count on you taking Trevor's place in Washington! He counted on a contract cancellation and a meltdown of technical support..."

Amanda said nothing as he drank water, his face flushed and angry at all that presently filled his thoughts.

"Moreover, he... didn't count on *me* to be the Project Manager of the SubTeck 8 sounding rocket mission - following the failure on the ship's support task order..."

"Much as we hate to see failure, we know the difference between technical support by a company, and a strategic defensive failure by government: That obligation is *ours!*"

"Your Captain acted well within his responsibility..." recalled Amanda "did he not?"

"He did. He never saw it coming. In fact, he went well above and beyond his duty in his risk assessment for a parlay with the other ship! As it was, the Russians wanted to share intelligence, but were being blocked. Unfortunately, they never got the chance. They were intercepted. Subsonic torpedo action impacted both ships and they foundered."

The incident brought them both to silence.

Finally Arguetta said "This man...he has big stakes in the game. Alexandrovich!"

Amanda's hand went to her mouth.

"Did you have any warning predictions on this man? Any intelligence?"

"Do you mean, could we have *alerted* Trevor? No. Nothing substantial. But..."

"Actually Amanda," he continued "I did say something. I came to Switzerland to talk with Trevor. We were alerted when first the scientist was killed. Youknow, the partner to your son's work, his colleague Sophie. She was entering nuclear fusion and propulsion systems. We were concerned about possible foul play. Now we know." He paused, then added "I told Trevor that competition to find the next space propulsion system was heating up. His company was the best qualified to get the award contract. He was aware of how important this is to the government. He knew his company was going for SubTech 8."

"Are you saying that's why *Trevor* was targeted by this man?"

"No question about it! Trevor holds a key card in this technological game. He is a prize. That's why he's still alive! Even your son in law is in the field."

"Jack's research...?"

"Jack's Lab in Berne Switzerland has already launched a scientific test rocket from the North Pole, and they plan another.."

"the...the North Pole?"

"Yep! To measure various physical phenomena in Earth's upper atmosphere! It's a scientific project."

"You've got to be kidding! Alexandrovich is *funding* that research?" said Amanda.

"Yes. It's no mystery that we had a similar launch, as you just saw. The AZURE mission flew the same sub-payload form factor, but it carried only a programmed tracer ampoule. It did not have the telemetry avionics intelligence that we're now developing for distributed payload communications" he said.

Amanda swallowed her coffee. This was a lot of information he was giving her.

He proceeded. "This technology will include radio receiver, a sub-payload antenna no larger than a quarter; miniaturized transmitters, and a highly efficient power-distribution system. It's part of the Internal Research and Development program funding at NASA's Goddard Space Flight Center in Greenbelt, Maryland."

"So, what is the direction to take, now?"

Arguetta got up and carried both of their lunch trays to the side bar. He returned.

"Nothing" he said. "We know what he's up to. We plan to forestall his intentions...And we have plans for his schedule. You were not on the *Need to Know* list, Amanda. To be honest, you had your hands full. And I was concerned that you might be overwhelmed."

Amanda followed him down to the elevators. They reached the lobby.

He turned to her and said "I'll have our Internal Affairs chief get in touch with you. Her name is Karen Simpson. This is her contact sheet. She's got a full investigation going on Trevor. He is on her list as a top priority. We are following closely with the authorities in London. And I'll alert her that you're here, if that's ok? She's in touch with the French off the coast of Normandy. She has code clearance for his action. She'll call you. Consider her your point of contact."

Amanda smiled, her stomach in knots.

"Oh! And one more thing..." he said, as his driver pulled up to the curb outside "I'm told that Jacques de Toulane - your associate? He's held up in Paris. He's been called up for Jury Duty. That will keep him sequestered for at least a week."

Amanda knew what he meant, and why he was saying it. She was on her own.

"Be careful" he added, in parting. "Call Karen Simpson"

* * *

Honfleurs, France

The rope had wedged between the brickwork and pavement. It rolled as Amanda stepped on it. She lost her balance and as she teetered to fall she grasped the only vertical lever she could reach.

Her hand clutched a hawser that served as pully-hoist to lift buckets of construction cement to a workman's platform 100ft above her head.

The jerk on the hawser spun through the hoist-wheel, and catapulted one workman's bucket off its clip and tip to release from it's waterspout fluids that splashed down at her feet in a display of grey paint-wash.

The bucket followed, landing like a heavy bell from the tower, and rolling halfway across the road with a loud crash.

Two cars came to a sudden halt, one honking and the other screeching its tires in angry protest. Both drivers bellowed.

Amanda stood, wet from head to foot, her shoulders hunched over and her hands flew to her face.

"Hoh! Hoh! Attention!" yelled a man from above.

"Mon Dieu!" screamed another. *"Est tu foux àlors?"*

The police sirens were not far away. To her chagrin Amanda wondered how in the world she had failed to notice the rope on the ground. Or why she reached out to yank on the pully-hoist.

Two bystanders stopped to help. The workmen descended. The Priest came. The Church Warden came out, as did the resident archivist and, finally, the police arrived.

Was she alright, they all wanted to know.

She assured them all she was unscathed.

Only gradually did the Police officers bring calm and establish what happened.

St Catherine's Cathedral was having its roof refurbished and workmen were painting the soffits and repairing rain spouts.

Upon further review, it did appear that the omission was the fault of the construction crew working on the roof. Since the street fencing had been removed, and no safety barrier had been positioned where the ropes reached the ground, it was not the fault of the pedestrian, they agreed. And they apologized profusely.

Amanda would not press charges.

The Priest talked with her solemnly, and the officers proclaimed that all further construction should be done on the inside of the structure, not the outside.

The police took notes and used the car radio to report the incident to their dispatcher. But they signed off without making any official citation.

The priest lingered to protest that fumes from the paint remover substances were a liability indoors...

Amanda was free to go.

She crossed the road and slipped away, leaving them all in discussion.

At the very least, her name would receive no mention in the local news, let alone the church newsletter.

Returning to the safety of her rental car she drove straight back to the Bed and Breakfast of the Normandy coastal town of Honfleurs.

By dinner-time, as she took her seat alone in the small dinning room, it was already dark outside, wintery winds blowing hard off the British Channel.

Trevor, I'm going to find you!

* * *

Chapter 10

Amanda strolled down to the old harbor seawall.

It was grey and windy, if beautiful. Below her an angry sea reached for the gravel beach beneath a rocky ledge. Sea conditions told of a British Channel that could wind itself into swells so fierce as to topple large sailing ships, it was said.

But its past was redolent with epic voyages by sea. Vikings had raided Britannia shores for village settlements. Saxon and Gaelic kings had fought for their legacy on English soil, eventually shaping the destiny of the British Isles. And the Spanish Armada had failed to deliver England of her Protestant Queen, Elizabeth I.

For good reason were the British Isles a destination by sea, Amanda knew. She drew in the fresh air as seagulls screeched at sea prospects, and she looked across the Channel.

Throughout the centuries England had provisioned seaborne trade. With her fresh supply of water springs, winds, and woodland, she was a haven for traders, offering seafaring inlets, protective harbor and shelter. On land she was cherished for food in cattle-grazing and sheep products like wool, mutton and dairy.

Skilled were the worksmiths of ironware, gold and foundry makers as they developed skills for horse-shodding at post-inns for transport, tools and arms, linking manufacture to markets.

To the south at Salisbury Plains, five luscious rivers converging to make a basin of dwellings, settlements and the delivery of trade in a world of shipping supplied to Europe and the Mediterranean waterways.

There harvests of barley and hops in soils plentifully staved off starvation and pestilence of plagues that afflicted the rest of Europe. It was the their sea. The Channel protected her from advisories. She was an island that even Roman Armies could not vanquish.

But there was more to the English Channel.

Amanda took in the vast expanse of water, and for a moment, closed her eyes in wonder.

She walked.

Honfleur was a small town by the sea.

It had flourished in the 18th century due to maritime trade. It toasted epic voyages.

From this tiny port in 1503 Binot Paulmierde Gonneville sailed out to discover the coasts of Brazil.

Newfoundland was discovered by Jean Denis, and from this port, Samuel de Champlain sailed to be the founder of Canada.

Facing the breeze, Amanda could only imagine the excitement and anticipation that was carried upon those early sailing ships...

Yet even as she listened to the wind, she knew that she stood not far from the beaches of Normandy where the greatest battles of modern history took place, D-Day. There on those beaches, under heavy gunfire from enemy fortifications, entire platoons of men landed on foot off Allied warships for the liberation of Europe in WWII.

She walked. It had been raining, the clouds now reopening.

She reached the main street and walked back up the hill, and then suddenly splashed by a passing vehicle. The white van was driving too fast through mud puddles on the road. *Legacy Moving* was the logo across the van. A second van followed, and Amanda knew to move away before it swerved around the corner.

Less than ten minutes later, another moving company fled by. Blue, this was named *Seaside Moving*. Clearly, a local family was moving their belongings - perhaps relocation to a different part of the country? At any rate, a lot of effort was being invested in this house-moving event. And close-by, evidently, since the Movers could be seen wearing working overalls and utility gloves...

The sky closed again for a dark grey, and Amanda strode briskly towards the town center.

It was a popular place for tourists.   Not unlike the brochure at the travel agency in Brussels, the street showed houses with 17th century architecture in picturesque colors. Galleries, boutiques, bistros, bars and even a *pommes frites* stand offered beach fries and sandwiches.

Here, artists had come for inspiration. Gustave Courbet, Eugène Boudin, Claude Monet, Johan Jongkind, creating between them a collection of art known as l'école de Honfleur, a significant movement for Impressionism.

Moreover, as Amanda strolled on, came the Sainte-Catherine church whose bell tower was separated from the principal cathedral. Yet it was largest church made out of wood in France. Built early, made of timbers in the 15th century that were hewn by shipwrights, it demonstrated the work of stone masons and medieval iron-smiths, and it had withstood the test of time for Christianity in Europe.

Eying the pulley and hawser that she had brought down, Amanda cross the street. It was now fenced in.

Chiefly, there was another reason that brought her here. Amanda was searching for Trevor.

After all, this was the last stop he had made in this town, as Jacques put it. Plus, it was from here that Trevor had left her message on the phone. And then sent her a postcard. *"We need to spend a week here..."* he wrote.

She walked.

Another van came by, this time stopping at a little gallery. It unloaded two crates from the rear of the van and carried them inside the building. Its delivery completed, the van pulled away. The tags of the moving van were French, but stickers from Paris. Not local, noticed Amanda.

She strolled on casually. Then she crossed the street and sat at a little bistro, she ordered a *café au lait*.

She sipped, observing the shop.

For a Sunday, the shop was officially closed. But clearly the van had altered its route, and the proprietor and attendants were inside, unpacking the wrappings and bracing for the acquisition of new inventory.

A few American tourists walked by. Could they go inside, they asked...

Unofficially, they were permitted to browse through the gallery. But officially the gallery was closed. Their prospect of buying a piece of art however, looked promising, and the proprietor smiled brightly.

Amanda walked over, and she too was allowed to enter.

Softly, quietly, she toured the gallery. There was no one about. Then she froze.

Nothing could have surprised her more than the moment she saw the painting partially unwrapped and just placed on a carpet against the wall.

Amanda approached it carefully. It's frame newly added, it gilded.

She tipped open the wrapping with her finger and stared into the familiar eyes of her husband Trevor whose likeness held fast at the center of the canvas.

It was her painting, and it almost took her breath away!

She tossed back her hair and took a step back.

How could this be, she thought, eyes darting across the packaging.

She had put it up for Auction in London as a charity event. The man in the portrait was Trevor's grandfather - the family resemblance unmistakable.

She bought it, asking the proprietor to have it delivered to her Bed and Breakfast Inn at Honfleurs.

He agreed, a check in his hand.

* * *

With the painting secured in her room, she brought her thoughts to heel. She had placed it carefully under the bed, after hours of inspection. And she made a decision.

She would return to the Gallery.

The painting, the proprietor told her, was bought directly from an Estate in Normandy.

A local sale to a local gallery, he explained, was perfectly permissible...Payment, of sorts, for services delivered.

All the household inventory of assets and art collections had been assessed by them, and the items were now being taken to Paris for Auction. The owner was liquidating, he told her. The house was for sale. And the address was easy to discover...

Amanda remained as obsequious as possible, smiling politely and nodding like an American tourist.

Within the hour, she was in her rental car. It was raining profusely.

Found along the coastal driveway amongst a passage of lavish mansions built by wealthy owners from all across Europe, Amanda was able to locate the entrance of estate. The entrance was rutted and splashed by trucks of transport and construction activities.

No question. This was the place. She recognized the terrain, the roadside field hedges, the grounds and even the gravel of the main house and quarters. All of it consistent with the video footage Jacques had acquired for her some weeks before.

Evidently, Alexandrovich and his wife, whose resort home was on the Normandy coast, were on the move.

They had something planned, especially in removing all their household belongings and putting the house on the market.

Their prized possessions, all valuables were now going up for Auction in Paris. Except for one painting chosen by the

Appraiser of the art gallery for himself, if executed by a moving manager.

Clearly, the owners were liquidating!

But not without aim, decided Amanda. She thought about it. No. This was well orchestrated...

With money at his disposal, Alexandrovich had taken aim at Trevor by attacking his family reputation.

The family, which had historically contributed to society as a banking entity for early industrial development in Great Britain, had been targeted with allegations of dishonest transactions. The painting therefore, was not only redundant, but now best to be waylaid, if not swept under the rug somewhere obscure...

The family legacy of empire days was to be viewed as less than noble or iconic, the brand name besmirched. And the message was clear: Such nobles had exploited the blight of war and working classes of the early 20th century. They deserved no riches today...

Was Alexandrovich behind the bidding at Amanda's London Auction event?

A man of his wealth could easily afford to write off millions on company expenses. His firm was leading the new technological revolution, after all, and his investors could not give him enough money for the exploitation of his developments in a new world order of unopposed globalism, if without accountability!

Perhaps to embarrass Trevor, the run-away bidding demonstrated how the painting was poorly evaluated, or under-insured. It was not securitized with underwriting.

If damaged moreover, Trevor was to pay for the difference in valuation? The painting was vandalized.

Another strike at Trevor...

Would his bank cover the costs of its priceless loss and damage? Or would the claimant cite insolvency? Was there legal insufficiency? Would he deny the claim? These were all questions and allegations that were unfounded..

Regardless, the media had a field day and impugned his name across the tabloids.

Amanda paced the room. The building was old, its wall paper had been replaced many times. Nor was the lighting in the room ideal. A bedside lamp was all she had to read by. A small coffee table had to be pulled close to the bed to serve as desk.

She opened her laptop. Where was she, exactly, in this remote part of Europe?

How very strange that she discovered the painting right here!

So. Was Alexandrovich behind this, she wrote.

Clearly, hidden in his resort home, the painting was being disposed of on the sly, given to an unsuspecting local gallery?

Of course. *It might be recognized in Paris.*

Moreover, Alexandrovich was not planning to return, she decided. With his home for sale, he was leaving no loose ends. No. He was planning to vacate the region altogether. That was the answer!

That evening, Amanda looked out the window. It had not been painted in a long time and the window glass had seen more than its share of channel weather. It was drizzling.

Outside people walked, huddling to the closest parking space beside the old pub which kept its lights on, if in waning daylight.

Beyond the town, high-speed motorways bypassed villages and raced to Rouen, Paris, Calais.

Fast traffic. Fast cargo. Fast people.

She heard fire engines in the distance, doubtless responding to a car accident.

She felt sad. She felt alone.

Trevor, where are you, her aching heart cried.

She returned to the laptop, finding the files that Jacques had sent her. She opened.

At some point, she spotted the routine that indicated Trevor had been taken them at some point, to be held hostage.

Then it occurred to her that...

It was very still in the room. Even the rain had paused. Only the fire engine alarms could be heard in the distance.

What if she went there and took a look? Maybe some evidence remained on the premises? Even if the house was deserted. Even with all possessions gone? All occupants vacated. At the gate was a FOR SALE sign. It was posted by the Real Estate Agency, its telephone number unclear, really.

In the last video she had viewed, she had seen the groundskeeper of the house, taken from an overhead feed. And it had shown a woman come out to talk with the caretaker.

He was carrying a box, or a container of supplies. She objected, and he was turned back. But not without some argument. And the dogs at his side played, one of them turning three times... just as if Trevor had trained them?

She put down the lid on her laptop.

Impossible!

And, why not now... in the dark? She could always go tomorrow, in the day light. But she wanted to poke around in the shadows...If only to be in close proximity to where Trevor had spend some time.

She was in the car within minutes. She switched on her headlights and made her way to the highway.

The map had a side road clearly marked - a road for private estates. Surely there was an Exit ramp?

The rain poured down.

To her surprise, she was overtaken by two cars. They honked, then swirled past. A third followed them, this time an official car with sirens.

Only then did Amanda realized that there was a procession leading down to the cliff area and she saw where houses lined the coastal vistas. The sky was strangely lit, a pink sky billowing with clouds. Smoke. There was a fire!

She saw the house from the top end of the lane. Even then she knew this was the house. *On fire!*

She raced forward, police and fire trucks filling the lawn like a parking lot. She parked off to the side, and she ran forward. Bright at the incendiary, and busy as everybody was, she went unnoticed.

Yet something was not recognizable with the images she had viewed on her laptop. Was this the house, she wondered?

She tucked herself between the trees, and noticed the lay of land continued downwards to the cliff.

Was it possible that there was another level of structure partially concealed by the cliff side, like a sea-cottage in the cliffs?

If so, was it connected to the main house with underground tunnels?

It was dark. No sign of interest in that area. If the place was vacated, then she would explore without attention...

Down she went, the main house billowing with smoke and firemen still arriving.

A pathway steered her in zigzags, steppes occasionally, then a bridge of wooden planks flanked the side of the cliff. On she went.

Perhaps it opened to the sea. Perhaps it had a veranda at its destination. She could not tell. It too wet and dark.

Above the cliff there muted sounds of fire engines, distant noises if now fading behind her by a buffer of the cliff.

Before her, the path trail proceeded. Now she could hear the angry sea.

She was about to abandon her quest when she noticed a vague odor. Rancid. Smoke. Fire from a house with smoke all the way down here? How was that possible?

She looked back, above the cliff-top and she closely examined the dark chimney of stone in the abandoned cottage by the cliff.

It definitely belonged on the same estate, she knew. The stone masonry and wood beams protruded in the fashion of renaissance structures, with overhead eves shading heavy timbers within, tudor-style.

Again she turned, rain dribbling down her face. And almost before she reached the steps, her mind tugged at her sense of apprehension.

Long ago, Trevor had called her obsessive.

"My school training" she chortled back at him more than once. He would never clean up like she did, she told him. How he laughed at her fastidiousness! And when their children were young...Oh such panic it caused, when she insisted that only a personal assistant would do to support the family while on travel. She nearly drove him crazy, she knew.

But there it was! Again, a small acrid smell. Smoke. Perhaps drifting from beyond the cliff - odors carrying on the winds as they splayed from a burning structure, much of it oak beams and stone. She looked back. The fire soared through the night like a warrior's pyre...

No. She would remain to inspect the small structure. Then she saw a garden aperture built into the rock face – somebody's idea of a romantic access to the sea no doubt.

A separate garden retreat for the writer, or artist? She found the front door. Not a romantic fairytale door, but a mediaeval iron-wooden door of heavy construction, like the gate to a fortress. Yet it was not without grace since ivy crept up its angry black bolts, and sea moss stained it's brass-laced timbers...

There, at the base, from a small mouse-hole a curling fog emerged, then blew off in the seabreeze.

Smoke!

The place was connected. She looked up. Should she report it? Should she yell...

Then she saw something, something not far from the door. A dog's bowl. A dog's bowl of water. And beside it, a small bone.

Someone was here! But it was sealed. Solid. Locked.

Trevor?

She banged. She yelled. She rattled at the iron bars across the front. And then she listened.

Again, like a soloist in the choir, she called, then she listened. An echo? A sound? A reverberation?

Nothing. But she would not leave.

This place was connected to the main house with underground tunnels. Sooner or later, the main blaze of fire would start creeping down those old hallways, full of dust, debris, plant roots and rotting leaves...It was unthinkable. If he was...

Had they *abandoned* him?

She pushed back the brush. Did this garden cave have windows? Yes, it had a chimney. But windows?

She found one. It faced the sea. But it was impenetrable. It had tudor-styled iron-paned windows, and it was shuttered from the inside.

She looked around.

She ran up to the top of the cliff. She ran to the Fire Marshall and announced herself as a friend of the family. Could they inspect the gardens and the premises down by the cliff, please?

He looked at her, his heavy face suspicious, and he was joined by a member of his team. He turned his back, his heavy fire-proof jacket obstructing her view.

What did he say?

He turned to her, and asked her to stay by the police car and identify herself to the police officer. The other man went around to talk with an officer.

She was clearly a suspected arsonist, she realized, coming out of the darkness and calling herself a friend...

No. *What an idiot she'd been!*

She turned and ran back into the darkness. Noticing a tool shed as she reached the edge. She stopped, looked back, and saw the men talking, one pointing, another walking. They were both police officers, as their vests said. One was certainly French, the other appearing to be wearing the insignia of the Belgian National Defense. Had they dispatched for extra assistance?

Why Belgian? Was there a manhunt going on? Was arson a reason for investigating this region. Why? Who?...

Then both officers of the law returned to fire now raging out of control. An explosion erupted from the structure. The rafters were alight. And they conformed into line to assist Firemen with hoses. First things first.

Amanda pulled at the toolshed and jarred it open, everybody was too distracted to notice.

A pot fell and broke with a loud crash. She froze. Nobody noticed, the wind was blowing away from the sea. All sounds were muted by the howling of wind, she knew. She reached inside and saw an axe.

She raced back down the steps. If she fell, she'd die right here on the cliffs, she thought. But there was a bigger impulse that drove her.

She reached the door. "Trevor!" she screamed.

She lifted her axe, and she rammed it at the door. Nothing.

"Trevor!"

She lifted the heavy axe and nothing budged on impact.

Not only was the axe heavy, but it bounced off. It would leave no mark on this door. She realized that the door was as good as a prison door. No need to worry about unlocking the door. The most vulnerable aspect to this door, it seemed, was the wood itself. It was old, and possibly weathered strong. She could hammer at the wood, and use the metal bars to dig away at the wood...

She worked for twenty minutes, exhausted.

"Trevor!"

Then she saw it. A small rattle within. The wooden slats inside the window were being rattling, dust falling from them as they shook.

"Trevor" she said, under her breath. "I've found you!"

She lifted the axe with a force she never imagined she possessed.

* * *

Amanda awoke to a pale sunlight barely touching treetops with frosty mist.

It had been a cold winter in Europe, yet here nascent tree life emerged as new buds bounced up and down on spindly boughs in windy gusts. That's all she could see through the heavily draped windows of her room. She was in her bed at the Bed and Breakfast Inn of Honfleurs.

She turned her head and smiled.

Beside her was Trevor. His face was pale and his head grey with age, worry and dusty debris still. Yet he was reposed.

She touched the soft tuffs of hair on his forehead, and he exhaled a deep breath in a peaceful sigh of safety. How long had it been since they'd been so close together, she thought.

Life. It had a way of intruding on the precious years of a marriage until nothing was left but duty and work. Remarkably, their union remained vibrant. They shared ventures together, following endeavors and supporting exploits of valued causes. Both busy, both needed in various activities...

How alone she had felt! How lonely was the world she inhabited without him! True, she was surrounded by people, events, and concerns, but she had been alone.

She smiled.

Older now, certainly. Independent and working in separate spheres, yet he filled her life and framed her world. How she had missed him!

She had rescued him from a fire.

He'd been abducted and kept prisoner. No question, the plan was for him to perish. But something had happened in the household. They'd had to accelerate their plans and the owners had left abruptly. The fire was set by arson. Trevor was left in the basement to die...

He breathed softly. She watched. Seriously dehydrated and his skin scorched, he appeared frail. Burns, raw and painful marked is hands. Smoke had very nearly overcome him when Amanda pulled him from behind the double doors of the garden cottage by the cliff.

It took a long slow day to get on his feet. But eventually they dressed and went downstairs to eat, together seated at one of the white damask tables of the B&B.

For now, the building was uneventful and they were safe. But Trevor was exhausted. Hot and then cold, he was running a fever. His legs were unsteady, and he drank copiously. His appetite was all but gone.

Later that night, Amanda watched over him, she thought about what happened.

Trevor was in danger. And for good reason.

This was a contest of fierce competition between titans vying for unprecedented power and celebrity status on a global stage of technology and cultural strategy.

Trevor was old school. Alexandrovich was a vengeful radical, preparing to overturn the world. Not with terrorism. Not with politics. But with money and with technology.

This was a battle for space technology.

The free market world of capitalism was to be replaced by a new frontier of science and technology, led not by a legion of warriors, but those wearing sneakers and with software.

This was the new face of cultural socialism.

"How did you find a way out of the basement?" asked Amanda, both of them chewing on breakfast in the dinning room the next day.

"It was when I spotted the abandoned steps down to the cliff cottage, actually..." said Trevor. "I was allowed outdoors for an occasional walk. Mainly around the barn yard. But the housekeeper liked to talk on his cell phone. He let me wander a bit...as long as he could see me. I strayed. He let me smoke, and I gave him no clue..."

Amanda put her hand on his. He flinched. The burn was painful.

"No....It's ok. I can talk..." he said, his voice wavering. "When I ...when I saw the steps leading down to the platform below the cliff's edge, and the stone chimney, I knew it was an abandoned observation post. Obscured from view, that could mean that it had been used in the last war."

He chewed, and sipped his coffee.

"It had been used as a Look Out for ships, I discovered. It was a radio room hideout. A spy range-hole even, for sending light signals from the cliff." He paused.

"Of course, that meant it could be reached from within, underground tunnels...I searched them out. " He paused again.

"Later, I found clues in the concealed hut, I found old wires and an antenna abandoned in a dusty corner. They were once used on transmitters..."

Trevor looked up with a deep breath. "When the fire ignited, I knew I had to find a way out. So I meandered through the tunneling. "

"These must have been tunnels used by the French Resistance in WWII then?" asked Amanda.

"Yes. That's how I stayed ahead of the fire..."

Again Amanda put her hand beside his. This time, he did not flinch. His thoughts had returned to a war that roiled Europe into terror and conquest. "It must have been Hell…" he said, "all that punishment in a killing war to liberate the world of fascist dominion…"

Amanda realized that his nerves were on edge and his emotions raw. When humans are taken over by others, they find only despair and distress. His imprisonment served the same purpose, and Amanda feared for his return to normal. She waited.

His recovery was slow.

Up there in her tiny room above the dinning hall for almost a week, she watched Trevor attempt to get stronger and regain his balance. He slept long hours and he drank fluids. They ate in the dinning room, sometimes they watched a movie downstairs, like visiting tourists.

Occasionally they played casual card games. Twice they strolled through a garden where roses peeked through latticework and ivy climbed up stone.

By Sunday evening, as Trevor read the paper in the parlor, Amanda put a glass of cognac in his hand as night cap. He smiled.

He was looking better. And he began to take notice of his surroundings.

Gradually, she brought him up to date.

Only twice she left him alone to go to the Pharmacy for local antibiotic skin cream.

His normal face color had come back, and she found him playing Solitaire on her Laptop.

She did not tell him that she had a cell phone in the car.

* * *

"How strong of you to step into my shoes in Washington!" he said later that night.

"My God, I could have climbed the walls when he told me of the naval frigates..." he was grinding his teeth.   "...And he *knew* there was nothing I could do... Jesus Christ!"

Of course Trevor meant Alexandrovich. They had come face to face, Trevor captive to a gloating radical...They had talked.

And Trevor's mind was still traumatized. Once he lifted his head off the pillow, his face contorted with frustration. "*I was responsible!* It was our Contracting support office that had *failed...*"

Amanda waited.

She leaned forward and pecked him on the shoulder. "Well...Alright then. That's what you married me for, isn't it?"

He looked at her, his eyes fiercely caught up in anger, then suddenly his brow cleared.

He smiled.

He lifted his head and let it rest on his elbow.

"But of course!" he chuckled. "I just knew you'd make an excellent nuclear physicist one day!"

Amanda felt he had returned. She told him the general brief of the forensic analysis, of Arguetta's response, and the company's quest to find the solution...But she omitted the incident of the shooting in the garage where Arguetta was hit. She found it non-essential to the moment.

Trevor listened, his eyes full of wonder at her abilities.

Finally Amanda said "So, tomorrow My Young Naval Cadet... You report for fitness training with an early jog!"

"Thank God!" he said. "I was beginning to feel fossilized"

They laughed, and decided to stray outside the B&B for a stroll.

Amanda was not deluded. This man was in a very vulnerable state of mind. She would have to watch him very carefully.

"How can I thank Bill Arguetta enough?" chatted Trevor as they approached the harbor.

They sat at a bench in the sun and ate *pommes frittes*.

"You will, in due course. He's been a wonderful family friend."

She waited, feeding the screeching gulls.

He laughed, relaxed.

She had not confronted him about the level of work being performed at his company.

She had filled the gap, she simply told him. She had stepped in to solve a crisis of management issue.

He was quick to pick up the nuances. The company had been targeted for a reason. The technology that Alexandrovich was really targeting was at issue. Especially the avionics research that involved newer technologies.

Trevor was never one to talk much about his company activity. Less so by order of his classification requirements. Would he now volunteer an explanation perhaps? Would he disclose intelligence that might put her in the picture, she wondered.

She would give him time, she decided.

"Amanda.." he said quietly, "I've been less than complete in our tasking for the government"

She turned to face him. "Shhh..." she said. "That's for another day, when you feel stronger perhaps. For now, let's just take it one step at a time, and get you back on your feet!"

He looked at her thoughtfully, his eyes concerned. Then he conceded. "Right!" he said brightly. They looked out across the water.

The English Channel blew with white caps, grey waves and surged against the cliff. "Care for a swim?" he chuckled.

"How about a hot chocolate" she said, tucking up into her collar.

"I agree!" he said "Let's go!"

Inside the car they talked. "It's that I'm concerned about Sandra. Jack is immersed in this race for research in Europe with his academic grants. He's giving us some competition, and they are launching European excursions...I don't believe he knows what he's up against" said Trevor.

"I think he's been approached by others for his work expertise" said Amanda. "A hunch..." she added, without telling him of the intelligence photographs that Jaques had sent her showing him immersed in work for Alexandrovich.

"He was in Brussels to speak on the research developments of their space technologies propulsion systems..."

No. Amanda chose her words carefully. She should not overwhelm Trevor. He had to be ready and fully able to handle crisis management...This was not yet the time. He was still frail.

As they returned to the B&B, she spotted two men emerging from the Concierge lobby. Both were from the Police, one wearing the uniform of the Belgian Police force, she recalled. He was unmistakable.

Evidently, they had just walked out. The Proprietor was out. He did that frequently, noticed Amanda.

Just as well, she thought.

Yet there was something familiar about them. One, had a clip in his ear, like a jewel or earring...

That night as Trevor slept, she opened her laptop and searched the images which she had taken on the night of the Opera with Jacques.

Alexandrovich was surrounded by a large party of family, friends and bodyguards for security reasons, perhaps. And she was right. There they were: One had a clip in his ear, like a jewel or earring.

Clearly, they were searching...

If they were attempting to locate her cell phone from a local tower of wireless communications, they were getting no signal ping from her phone. She had turned it off and removed the battery. It was in the car still...

Mercifully, the Concierge had not noticed Trevor.

Amanda's advance payment of the bill every morning in cash was well appreciated. But the Proprietor did appear briefly as they were having dinner one night. A guest of hers for dinner, perhaps? He was now asking

Especially since Amanda had told him nothing.

* * *

They packed the car the following morning. There was nobody about. Amanda gave Trevor her Rental Car ignition keys and sent him out to the car with some parcels. They were leaving Honfleurs.

He opened the trunk and then got inside to wait for her.

Amanda told Trevor that she was checking out of the Room at the Concierge. Instead, she paid for another week. In fact, she went to the concierge and told him that she was touring a bit. She informed she'd be back. He grinned at the chunk of cash she gave him. She knew that her room would be reserved and considered occupied, with nobody to disturb. All they could say was that a woman was there, and touring...No. There was no man!

She picked up her purse and thanked the Concierge for his services. A precaution, she told herself. It might buy her some needed time.

She ran across the street, opened the door to the driver's side of the car, and got in.

Inside the car she found Trevor on her cell phone.

"Yes, Sandra. I'll tell her you called. And thank you for your concern! I'm sorry it took so long to get back to you...Bye. Bye!" He turned towards Amanda and smiled. "Sandra sends her love" he said. "I found your phone in the back.." he buckled up.

"What's wrong?" he said, seeing her face.

He had plugged it into the battery for a recharge.

Amanda looked in the rear view mirror, it was drizzling. She got into gear, and drove through town and onto the highway towards Rouen.

They stopped for gas, and then for coffee again.

She consulted her messages. There were several. Four from Sandra, asking her to call. One from Jacques. One from Bill Arguetta. One from the offices in Washinton, a colleague with some information for her...

"Trevor" she said calmly. "We don't have much time. They've probably located me by now by finding a ping off my cell phone. They're clearly searching for you!"

"Oh Christ!"

"Where is the last place you stopped before they found you?" she asked. "Let's go take a look!"

"They took me directly to the house, actually. No stops. No prevarication. It was only when they took my cell phone and laptop that I realized I had walked into a trap....Jacques was supposed to call me and..."

"Jacques' assistant, Yvonne was supposed to escort you to Paris. I know." She paused, hesitating, then said "I am sorry, but Yvonne was found dead. These people aren't fooling around Trevor...They want your technology and they aim to do damage!"

"You could say that again..." He looked out the window at the drizzle. "Any chance we can return to the house?"

"What? That's off limits, an unsafe zone, if not a policed scene of a crime by now?"

"I know. But there's a side road, down the flank of the farm next door...Can you make it?"

Amanda paused. "Are you sure about this?"

"Yes. It's a risk we must take. Trust me!"

Amanda looked out the window of the driver's side. She would have liked to flee the area. Run somewhere safe. Get out of France, something.

Trevor was safe!

She knew better. She switched on the engine and reversed the car into a side field road obscured by bushes to turn around. Just as she did so, two police cars raced down the highway, clearly in pursuit of a Rental car. They had missed her in the bushes.

She looked into Trevor's grey eyes. His face was set. "Go on!" he said.

The lane was slick with mud and runoff. But a few pebbles gave traction. She followed his lead, and they bumped down a cow path alongside the damaged house, still blackened and smoldering in the drizzle.

"Down there..." he insisted.

"I can't!" said Amanda. "It's too wet. We'll never get out..."

"Alright then" he said. "Turn around. Leave the ignition keys in the engine. We may need to make a fast exit... "

"Trevor, its dangerous for us to be here...Are you sure?"

"Yes!" he said definitively, and he opened the car door.

She waited. Two cars drove into the fire-damaged house, and she heard voices.

She crept out and tracked Trevor. She found him three hundred yards down the path that led to barn. She opened the door and it creaked.

"Trevor?" she called softly.

"Over here!" he said.

She found him in a cattle pen searching in the hay. A wide sweep of horse manure coated the floor, and still he swept it with his hands.

"What's in this horseshit?"

He looked at her, his face still. "You'd be surprised!"

She joined him, searching in the muck and slime oozed out between her fingers.

They heard voices.

"They're searching for someone!" whispered Amanda.

A cow behind them mooed with a ferocity that made them jump, then it urinated profusely.

"Oh God!" she groaned

Suddenly he froze. He dug a little faster and then stopped. "Here" he said. "Hold this!"

It was a plastic bag coated in sod and straw, water running freely down its folds. The contents were dry.

Trevor stuffed his pockets with a second package....

More voices.

"Alohrs! C'est un vehicule!" called out one. Someone had found their car.

"Ils son'la! Trouvez les! Marchez les chiens?"

Their police radio transmissions crackled. They were to return to the site of the fire...Immediately.

"Here!" whispered Trevor, offering Amanda a second package of paper wrappings, this time a little more soggy without plastic protection.

She picked up the wad and placed it into her pockets, mud spilling over her coat and pants.

"Let's go!" he said suddenly. Then, "No. Wait!"

"If we make a run for the car, they'll follow us relentlessly. Let's make them feel the car is a non item!"

Another cow moved closer. "Oh no!" muttered Amanda.

"Nothing like the smell of cow manure" grinned Trevor. "It's a wonderful smell...breath it all in!"

"In Scotland maybe..." she groaned

Amanda realized that he was actually enjoying himself.

They waited, the hours slow to move on. They lay in the loft, waiting.

By mid afternoon, the officers were beginning to abandon the scene. The breeze had picked up off the Channel, and a howling wind turned into a dry gale, sometimes gusting up to 50 knots velocity.

With no one in sight, they had given up hope on finding persons in the vicinity. Clearly, the owners had fled, they all said.

Chatting, the police officers proclaimed the weather unfit for police work. They were tired. They had families to go...

To their radio dispatcher they said it was too cold and windy for any further investigations...And certainly, there was nobody here!

They waited another hour, then drove off.

It was dark when Trevor emerged from the barn with Amanda.

They returned to the car, and without headlights, managed to negotiate the car up the lane which had dried out considerably in the wind. But mud had splattered against the windshield, and Trevor got out periodically to wipe it off with his sleeve.

Before broaching the road, Amanda looked at her phone one last time. A message lit up from Sandra.

"Mom. I'm glad you're safe. I'm in London. I want to catch up with you and find out your updates and whereabouts. Where are you? Jack is with me. He says he has a message for you. He won't tell me...Call me!"

Amanda unpacked the cell phone and stepped out. She threw out the Sims card and device. She sent them over the seawall just as a wave thrashed the rock and pulled everything back out to sea in a ferocious swill of tidal force.

"She brought the car up to grade, and stepped on the gas."

"Where are we going?" said Trevor.

"Back to the B&B. It's safe. I am still registered..."

* * *

Chapter 11

By the time they washed off and warmed up, Trevor and Amanda both had a hefty glass of cognac. Two brioches were left over from breakfast.

Amanda ignited the small electric heater placed in the fireplace, and together, they sat in the glow, unpacking leftover filth and grime from Trevor's barnyard quest.

"You were busy, I see...in your captivity" admonished Amanda.

"Hmm" he said.

"And this is *what*...exactly?"

"Hmm" he said again, unsure of what he could bank on quite yet.

One by one, he extracted electronic devices. One hard drive. Two computer sticks and a small book of passwords and key strokes.

"I made nightly excursions from the basement..." he said. "I found his ...err...his office and his computer" he said "Pass me your laptop!"

"The safe was untouched" he added. "So they didn't suspect anything. But I lifted his core files that contain the data to his mainframe. He was linked to his office technologies. I have a full schematic of his missile plans and payload schedule. What I *don't* have are his key codes and scheduled launch sequences..."

"My God, Trevor. Is this possible?"

"You have no idea... This man has plans!" said Trevor, his lips tight and his face grim.

"How is it that he didn't kill you? Isn't your company working on the same technology?"

"It is. But our work is legitimate work for the government. He *needs* us!"

"What will you do?"

"We know his social disposition. He is an angry, bitter man wanting to overturn free market economies for centralized and global market control. If I find evidence of his intentions, then I'll meet with the government for possible action. This is a strategy decision that only they can make..."

"You mean he's a terrorist?"

"He's a global threat!" said Trevor, his face pale. "If we could locate his sites, we could ready a target firing solution for his missile launch pad, or even alter his trajectories. But he could be launching from under the poles. So, no question. This man is a threat."

He plugged into to her electronic device and watched the apps open functions.

Trevor's face lit up in the glow of the firelight, and slowly the data began to download. The laptop hummed, she plugged into her European electricity transformer, to be sure of power.

"What's you're memory on this thing?"

Amanda moved to her handbag. "Limited. But I always carry a spare!" she said, producing a memory stick.

"Perfect!" he continued, his concentration focused on the downloads "They didn't have a clue. There was a lot of data I was downloading and copying. Much of the time he was gone. His staff were uninformed."

Before long her screens were filled with technical schematics, electrical grids, statistical data and cad drawings that would make anyone blush outside the defense department.

"My! My!" she said. "You've come a long way from WWII signal wires and antenna?"

"Hmm" he said finally, the downloads complete.

"Mind if I take apart your laptop?" he asked.

Amanda looked at him. "you're not serious...?"

He was already breaking into the keyboard and disassembling the frame.

"Wait!" she protested. "I have images on there..."

"No worries" he said, extracting from the tin foil and layers the screws that led deep into the heart of her device. He dug in and reached the hard drive. He pulled it from its connectors.

"And I have it all stored on this hard drive. Don't worry. We'll reconfigure it all on a new computer where we'll insert this hard drive..."

"Gee thanks!" was all she said.

He held in hand a thin silver square, much like an old cigarette case, and he inserted it into his pocket.

"It's indestructible" he said "I promise!" and he leaned over and kissed her on the forehead.

They spoke little, both laying in bed, half sleeping and half waiting for first light, each of them dressed and ready to leave the premises.

"Trevor" she said, turning to his ear. "You awake?"

"Hmm?" he said, his hand reaching for her body.

She snuggled softly, then added "It's just that I have a stop to make on the way out of town tomorrow. Do you mind?" She paused. "It's the local Gallery. I need them to send to London a certain painting..."

She held her breath, waiting. Would he possibly compute that the painting to which she was referring was her own?

Would he understand? All the trouble it had caused ...to Jacques... to the family...to the Insurance and to his bank: Her misplaced trust had been entirely without merit.

Would he be pleased to know of its retrieval...?

It took him a moment, the conclusion of what she might be suggesting. He turned, one eye peering at her askance. "You didn't find...?"

"Ahuh!" she nodded.

"Where? *How?*"

"Well, it's under the bed!"

"Under the..."

* * *

They left the Art Gallery and Amanda was at the wheel. She had a grin on her face at Trevor's latest remark. "That damned painting of yours has cost me a fortune I'll have you know..."

"Let's get out of Dodge..." she began, adding "Oh shit!"

Behind them was a police car.

She made a quick turn and entered the parking lot of the Cathedral. "Come!" she said.

They thrust themselves under the porch of the bell tower separating the two naves of the framed Cathedral. It resembled the inverse of a ship's vessel, having been constructed by joiners and ship's carpenters of the 16th century. But it was made to also serve as a market hall. Thus, from above the porch, a sculpture of St Catherine holding sword and a wheel looked down upon them in trade venture.

Trevor gazed, she tugged.

"They began this cathedral in the second half of the 15th century..." said a tour guide.

Amanda nudged at him and they darted into the second nave – "That part of the architecture that was built in 16th century" was saying the tour guide.

"There, the roof rafters emulate vaulted heights of early Gothic churches, and, being supported by bays and pillars.."

Trevor and Amanda found shelter from view.

The police lingered within the Cathedral and inspected the cloisters. They searched through a mob of visitors that roamed. With them, standing by at the entrance ere two muzzled dogs.

"You have that hard drive in your pocket?" asked Amanda.

"Yes"

They kept their head down and moved between the pillars of the nave.

The side walls were of unequal length, and problematic in construction, due to insufficient trees, the brochure had said.

Little comfort, thought Amanda ducking, and watching as the dogs strained and sniffed in their general direction.

Still, they huddled behind a pillar that uniquely had a footing made of a stone pedestal.

"I have to get these to Jacques" whispered Trevor, indicating his hard drive. "He was supposed to collect any evidence I found. That was the arrangement before I arrived in Normandy."

Amanda looked at him, the look of understanding suggested she knew what she must do.

"Forget Jacques" she said. "He's been sidelined for two weeks of Jury Duty in Paris..."

A noise erupted from the crowd, clearly induced by the police for people to move away. Trevor pushed Amanda against the pillar.

"I need to get this data to Arguetta, rather" she said, thinking ahead.

Trevor glanced up at the roughened beams where axe masters of naval yards had cut without the use of saws, just as their Norman ancestors had done of the Bayeux tapestry. Or Vikings. His eyes searched frantically.

A police officer surged forward as his dog tugged at the leash: No intruder should be allowed to darken such hallowed places with mal-intention, their eyes implied.

Amanda and Trevor darted across the church floor and into the bays for the choir. They waited in the shadows. Above them a Renaissance balcony, ornamented with musicians, was surrounded by stained glass windows of the 19th century.

"I have an idea" said Amanda "follow me!" and they climbed the choir steps to the upper levels.

She led down a hall and emerged on a ledge of window sills which were opened for construction.

Modern ventilation at the higher levels of the Cathedral helped the circulation of air for congregations. And for noxious paint fumes.

The windows were open because workmen whose construction project led to the roof for repairs, had access to the outside scaffolding.

A shrill whistle blew as they were spotted by the police.

"*Arretez vous!*" they shouted.

Suddenly the cathedral filled with sound and alarms and barking dogs.

Trapped and surrounded, Amanda and Trevor felt goaded like villains.

It was precisely that moment when Amanda reached into Trevor's pocket and pulled the hard drive and the two electronic devices. In one flash of a movement she thrust them behind him into a bucket that was on a rope pulley. Then she turned to cling to his arm.

By now all visitors were gawking, the staff running out with the priest to witness with horror the drama above them.

"Don't panic..." she managed to whisper as the police officer grabbed Trevor. "It's OK what I did..." she added.

The charges that were laid against them amounted to nothing much more than suspected arson. No linkages to any greater crime were cited, and none were found.

Trevor and Amanda played it safe. They said little, and kept things simple.

Later, both would be represented by intergovernmental attorneys. Meantime, they remain as low-key as possible and call for as little attention as possible.

Since there was no material evidence of any criminal activity, they were released.

They had strayed, they said simply. Adding that they were tourists, and they got herded and frightened by the police. Tourists, yes. That was it.

Before long, the sergeant lost interest and everyone drifted away.

It worked.

The following day, in the car ride to Paris, Trevor for some reason felt compelled to recite the historic details of the Cathedral. That is, after they had returned before dawn to inspect the workmen's buckets, all of them lined up against the garden wall within the grounds of the cathedral – something that Amanda had managed to know from her clumsy fall on the pulley ropes.

Trevor was impressed when she fished out the electronic hard drive and devices.

"So..." said Trevor cheerfully, "the first written record of Honfleur is a reference by Richard III, Duke of Normandy, in 1027. By the middle of the 12th century, the city represented a significant transit point for goods from Rouen to England" he added. He slowed just enough to let the traffic drive pass.

Amanda had to smile.

He had recovered, and adjusted well. "The Cathedral was affected by the wars of the French revolution and the First Empire" continued Trevor, now seated behind the steering wheel. "Naval blockades of this port caused the ruin of Honfleur." Adding, "then came my wife..."

They stopped for a bite. Amanda sipped coffee and unwrapped their croissants, listening.

"By the 19th century their chief trade was wood from northern Europe..." he continued.

He was driving quite well, and Amanda started to relax. "But the harbor was silting up! The modern port at Le Havre took away all its business. Still, it is a working port."

Trevor took a bite from his croissant and turned to Amanda, who yawned widely.

"Honfleur was liberated in WWII by the British army – 19th Platoon of the 12th Devon's, 6th Air Landing Brigade; the Belgian army; and the Canadian army..." And now Trevor looked away, his words lapsing into sadness as wind blew in through his open car window.

He turned to Amanda and found her fast asleep in the comfort of the car beside him.

He smiled.

* * *

Paris, France

"Jacques is a man full of surprises" said Trevor

"Err...how long has it been since we've been on vacation in France?" she asked.

He chuckled. "Well if you call this fugitive escape from the police on course to a vacation, then I like your outlook!"

He tucked his hand through her elbow. Retired or not, they were still having fun together.

"I'm still driving!" she protested.

"Hmm" he sighed happily.

Then he turned to look at her face, still young at heart and vibrant with sincerity.

He reached out to put his hand gently over hers at the wheel. "How brave of you to take up the mantel for me Amanda. You saved the company!"

She smiled.

"And, just as wonderful ..is how you see only the best in people and the happy side of life!" he exclaimed "It's what I have loved about you Amanda!"

"Thank you!" she smiled, adding "I'm glad to see you're fully recovered from your ordeal, yes?"

His turned away, his face now set with serious resolve. After a moment he said "You know. We have a very dangerous mission ahead. This man is tampering with a technology that has devastating potential. In the wrong hands...he's a serious threat. We must stop him! He's angry. Vengeful. He's without remorse or conscience..."

"And he's a thief!" added Amanda.

"Oh...more than a thief. A murderer. He could walk away from mass genocide with impunity!"

Amanda looked into the rear view mirror and saw no followers. "Just checking" she said.

Then she signed with a touch of drama. "Ah well...Too bad he chose the wrong Tech company to trifle with!"

"Damned right! I'll bring his world down about his ears..."

They stopped for gas, keeping a low profile, and held a steady pace until they reached the heart of France, Paris.

The traffic slowly changed.

Not far from the River bank, the boulevard filled with tourists, joggers, baby strollers and vendors. At each corner an event blared. Traffic honked and became as loud and busy as any capital city. Uninhibited, the French had a way of hailing and name-calling.

Trevor and Amanda persevered to their destination.

Jacques had a substantial apartment atop a four story Rococo townhouse. He greeted Trevor like a brother warrior, his eyes moist.

Amanda realized that she and Trevor were as close to family as Jacques had. Certainly, they had known each other for years, not of all if easy. But if there was one man that he could trust, Jacques once told Amanda, it was Trevor.

Trevor, for his part had come to appreciate Jacques for his devotion to his art, for his loyalty to his friends.

Further, Jacques was always an informed man of great savvy, if with odd habits.. to occasional intelligence from his traders. His business was one of many shades, colors and cultures.

They spent the evening over a quiet dinner prepared by Jacque's kitchen staff.

"It's one of the privileges I have for owning a small bistro in downtown. It's always packed with people, and I like my chef to deliver to me his specialties from time to time. Of course, I also enjoy my own view up here. It's an old house, with a history. And also its full of mice! But..." he said, raising a glass to toast Trevor's safe return. "Mon ami, *Bien Venue!*"

They talked late into the night. They discussed the situation and decided on a plan between them.

Later, Jacques led them downstairs and across a great marble foyer. His Library, he told them. But it was where he kept his collections...

At first impression his office was that of a high Renaissance French salon, especially the arrangements surrounding his Louis XIV desk.

Then he turned to face the rear of the room where the walls were filled with works of art.

At the center, a massive pair of cherry-wood paneled doors unbolted. Served by a small box of electronic key codes, they opened slowly for Jacques. Gradually, nothing less than a working forensic lab faced them.

Lighting, subdued and diffused, displayed glass counters exposing items under examination. Devices for photographing, scanning, viewing, and illumined computer screens with testing equipment for analysis and sampling flanked the perimeter of the laboratory.

"My lab for the conservation of works of art, some of them brought in for preservation, some of them for verification of authenticity...In my business, anything is possible!"

He lit up the far wall, and Amanda was staring at an assembly of photographs taken by them at the Opera together. Beneath it was a counter with digital applications for identification intelligence. Papers stacked up at the print machine, and records of catalogued items lined the shelves..

"Wow!" said Amanda.

"This is the complete record of what we did in Brussels at your friend's condo. Yes? " she said, her head titled. Then she added "...that apartment in Brussels? That does not belong to a friend. It's *yours!*"

Jacques simply shrugged.

"It is the seat of the European Union Parliament. How can I not have a *peid at terre* there?"

"I told you Jacques was a man full of surprises!" chuckled Trevor.

"C'est bien, Alors" said Jacques. "I wanted Trevor to see the full scope of what we are looking at. Also, I wanted you to see the men in this frame who are affiliated with the European Launch of the space missiles. It is scheduled for about the same time as the American missile launching..."

Trevor's eyes roamed to other images. "I see you also ...have the full satellite imagery of the ship sinkings?"

"Yes. And that's highly classified material" added Jacques. "Look, you know me. I need to be kept informed!" He paused, then added "One thing is certain. If I have all this, then so does your man..."

He turned back to the Opera set of images.

"Over here, you see Alexandrovich talking with this man. He is on the Board of European Energy Commission. He is also the Director of the research for the firm where your son in law works!"

"Yes. Why?" said Trevor.

"Jack Lucas knows all. He knows that it is located in Switzerland, and it is a private enterprise."

"What...Jack is *involved?*"

"Yes. But perhaps for not the reasons you think..."

"So. We have three separate launching missiles" said Trevor. "There is ours. That's my signature, that is the SubTeck 8 relating to the US Government. Then, there is private claim using the same technology propulsion system in Switzerland. Where is it launching from?"

"There is this!" said Jacques. "I show you!" He walked over to another wall and lit up the screen with another schematic.

"The French Satellite system that was launched a year ago. Its capabilities are these, and they are developing new operating capacities..."

"How is that?" asked Amanda.

"Well. It was the Americans that launched it for them. Well, for NATO, ostensibly. But it was chiefly funded by the French following their Paris attack by terrorists" said Jacques. "It can be re-tasked in orbit..."

"You discovered all this?"

Jacques face glowed.

"Good man!" smiled Trevor. "I'll work on that on my end..."

"So. All we have to do is to survive the next few days..." said Amanda.

"OK" beamed Jacques. "So, we plan like a team!" he moved to the massive doors " ...Et why not over a glass of cognac upstairs?"

Jacques remained behind to lock up.

"I'm not sure about the sound of that..." muttered Trevor as they climbed the steps from the great foyer to reach the upper level of the apartments.

"He's having fun" said Amanda.

"Yes. That's what worries me!"

* * *

"That's a lot to absorb" said Amanda, falling back into the cushions of a damask white sofa. "And to think that Jack is implicated... What about Sandra? Is she safe?"

"There is no question that he has targeted your family" said Jacques, passing around a drink to each. "So, let's just work like a family team..."

"You know that you're also being watched by him? Your every move is under surveillance. Your phones. Your images. Your staff, chauffeur."

Trevor put down his drink "He must certainly know I'm here by now" said Trevor

"Not necessarily!" said Jacques gleefully. "He cannot eavesdrop in this room, nor the lab downstairs..."

"Nor the condo in Brussels, I'm sure?"

Jacques grinned.

"But you forget that you have Jacques, your friend. And I am good, too! I am monitoring his communications: He is asked to be kept informed by the police about your whereabouts. That means they are in his pay. But you are still at large, they are saying. So, no. I don't think so."

"Thank you Jacques..." began Trevor.

"I have thought ahead. So, here I have a new telephone for your Trevor - since he confiscated yours and will expect you to have a new one. And he will doubtless listen in, eventually. So, we act like a group of friends and acquaintances all of us communicating and sending messages, just like the French would do!" he grinned. "But we will give ourselves a sort of code as we talk...."

A big bang sound came through the room like a sharp explosion. They jumped.

A metal clanking followed, and then a loud crash brought Jacques abruptly to his feet, his face full of horror.

They froze. Jacques immediately shielded them and put his finger to his mouth for silence.

Then without a sound, a small creature wafted into the room. A black cat. It entered, paused, then sat on its haunches, washing its paws.

Jacques' face went red. "That damned cat..." he spluttered, chasing it from the room and exhaling "*Mon Dieu! Allez!*"

The cat, which had entered the front door in pursuit of a mouse, had darted through the open door in pursuit of its prey. The vase it had broken was in the foyer. And clearly, by the protestations of Jacques, it was priceless.

It took a while of explaining and frantic apology at the alarm, but they calmed their nerves with another drink.

Finally Amanda brought them back to the present.

"I will be the "Cat" by handle-name" said Amanda.

"I will be referred to as the ...the...err 'Broken vase'" finished Jacques, forlorn.

"And I will be the "Housekeeping"...That way we make references to this event as we talk."

The long day was drawing to a conclusion when Jacques said "I leave you two to rest..." and he rose to his feet.

Amanda's phone rang. It was Sandra she intonated, waving at them. Then her face went pale.

"Sandra!" said Amanda "Hello?"

 "Mom..."said Sandra. "I'm in the States.."

"Sandra.."

"I have been taken hostage! Jack needs to talk with Dad. He will call you in the next two days!"

"Sandra? Oh My God...*Sandra!* Are you alright?"

"So far" she said "I am alive!"

The phone went dead.

Amanda stood rooted to the spot.

Trevor stepped closer.

Jacques spoke. "He traced Sandra's location from her telephone number. It was registered as a Contact to my cell phone...Yes. He will be eavesdropping!"

 He paused.

"So now we know. We go forward with our plan!" announced Jacques, his jaw resolved.

Trevor turned to Amanda.

"You'll have to go back to the States and work with Arguetta. She's there! I'll stay and contact the French Space Directorate..."

Amanda looked up at him, her mind a muddle.

"Oh God Trevor...*Sandra?*" she buried her head into his shoulder. "Will we make it?"

"We shall!" he announced. "We will stop this man! Look, we are launching a missile within a week. Our firm is supporting the effort. You can continue where you left off in Washington...Amanda, I need you to do this! You are quite capable to lead our staff in their support efforts for the government."

Trevor turned to her gently, and holding her by the shoulders he purposed "This is *precisely* what he's after! Stay with the countdown Amanda. You're strong. You can do this... Stand firm! I'll keep you informed...We will be working from this end in Europe. He has a plan. We'll keep him off balance from here. Trust me, please?"

She nodded, her mind in disarray.

"We will get this guy...*By God!*" he muttered.

* * *

Jacques opened the door to greet his guests. He looked colorful in dapper clothing with a bow tie and plaid shirt, smiling.

"Good morning Gentlemen!" he beamed. "Please come in. I have a surprise for you!"

They following him into his study, and he had a service of coffee ready.

Two of his visitors were members on the Board from the National Museum of Art in Paris; a third man was an Appraiser from a significant Insurance institution. The woman in the party was a specialist in conservation; and the last man, who remained standing, was a police officer from the Department of stolen Art property.

The meeting lasted an hour, and Jacques succeeded in utterly wowing them with what he presented.

Before them, resting on an easel, was the coveted painting that Amanda had taken to Auction a month earlier.

They all knew about the bidding war that it had elicited. They knew of the reported vandalism that followed, and its theft. They had questions.

How did he get possession of the original painting? What had happened to it? Then came the inspection.

Carefully they inspected it for signs of vandalism – including the frame. The paint. The canvas. Artistic composition... They viewed comparisons to picture in the catalogue, and they consulted their notes.

Jacques waited. He had not opened his lab to them. But his front office was equipped with shrouded desks for table lights, magnification lamps, and the room sufficiently illuminated with tall fenestration for daylight to give them the gallery space to function. Outside, two police cars watched the premises for added protection.

Jacques gave them an explanation together with a compete dossiers that would doubtless inform its provenance. That is, once they found it authentic.

They hesitated, he thought. Perhaps for the benefit of the police officer, they had lingered.

Jacques made his next decision.

"Come with me, Gentlemen..." he said, opening the rear doors of his study.

They entered his conservatory Lab.

The wall he had prepared for them was to the left side - far across the room from where Amanda and Trevor had stood the day before, now dark and obscured.

The police officer cast about, carefully observing the scope of the lab.

Jacques lit up the screens prepared for them and showed images of the painting and its evidence, including X-ray renditions tracing the tear in the canvas...

"The height of the damaged area suggests a plunging force with a sharp instrument of the right hand, from someone approximately 6ft'2". See here, the gash is shown cross-ways in a return-motion from left to right..."

They observed, attentive. Mostly satisfied.

Except for the Police officer, his face closed other than the eyes, which opened avariciously at the array of supporting equipment, if resting slightly on some valuables in paraphernalia. In that instant, Jacques knew that he should accelerate his plans to relocate. His repository here had been compromised. Just as soon the travel bans were lifted due to infectious contagion amongst populations, he would move all to Brussels.

Jacques repositioned himself between them and the legacy shelves he kept, obscuring them from view by switching off recessed lighting.

He turned to the party and directed their attention to questions about the milieu of the painting in its journey. He put up large projected images of a crowded street in London.

"What I would like to discover, if you will, is this: In your estimation, is *this* the man who vandalized it?" he said, pointing to the figure of Victor Alexandrovich standing with his cohorts outside the Auction House in London.

"Any light that you can shed..." said Jacques "with your forensic analysis and technological metrics, would go a long ways to solving this puzzle, Non pas?"

On their faces there was no recognition, clearly.

Jacques did not even glance at the policeman.

He knew the answer.

Two days later, he got a call from the Museum.

* * *

Amanda returned to Washington.

She felt as if she was stepping onto a platform that, for a few days at least, seemed never to have noticed her absence.

Still, the Cherry blossom festival was now in full swing as tourists braved the cold wind of the nation's capital city.

The cab that drove her to her apartment on Capital Hill showed a city clean, adorned by architecture of white granite buildings, and everywhere bound by a sea-blue ribbon of the Potomac River.

Here, Federal employees churned out paperwork for the management of governance with policy decisions, taxes, risk assessments, treasure, intelligence, planning, judicial findings and legislative bodies.

Yet the city functioned quietly. Efficient, clean and without much notice, this workforce remained underground as a bureaucracy with interests across the globe upon which the sun never set.

Today, Amanda was pleased to go unnoticed. Her anxiety could be well camouflaged.

She could find answers. She could find Sandra...

Her thoughts threatened to surge with panic.

Doubts filled her mind as she unpacked.

What could she possibly be doing here, she wondered.

Sandra was a hostage...

Jack was on the verge of God-knows-what and employed by a manic soon to make his demands known to Trevor...

And Jacques was waltzing around in his rarified world of antiquities and acquisition in Paris...

Jesus! What was she thinking?

She looked at the clock. Her office was unchanged.

She'd been on Washington for three days. And still Aguetta would not speak to her.

The front staff reported no returned calls.

Already, she'd spent long days upstairs with the technical staff...Others had popped their head at the door to say hello. Amanda was clearly liked.

But the hours ticked by without word from Europe.

Trevor had better be right!

Sandra had better be safe...

Please God?

Tonight she would call Arguetta. If necessary, she'd drive to his home.

* * *

"What exactly is your mission?" asked Trevor, miles of white sand stretching along the open beach at Ostend, Belgium.

"Our mission is directed at the future!" said Jack, walking at his side.

Trevor adjusted his collar against the wind from the sea, and seagulls followed.

Both knew they were being watched through binoculars. Surveillance could listen to all...

It was tense meeting between Trevor and his son in law Jack Lucas, each knowing the measure of madness that gripped Alexandrovich.

And Jack worked for him.

Trevor decided to lower the tension level.

"Do you remember the black diamond slopes in Switzerland? You were the fastest skier in the family!"

Jack looked at him, his face distraught with anxiety. "Yes. I know"

"Especially at night..." continued Trevor. "The sky was full of stars, air crisp and a snowy mountain alight with party-going skiers" He paused. "Amanda and I enjoyed that trip very much!"

"Yes" said Jack. "So did we, Sandra and I..."

Trevor turned and looked into his face.

Jack was clearly frustrated, and Sandra's name brought fresh anxiety into his eyes. His lips were dry, dehydrated, his eyes dark and his skin grey.

Alexandrovich had not made it easy for him. Jack had been in his lab. He had lost weight and he shivered uncontrollably in the wind.

"This man is a killer, Jack. Make no mistake about it..."

Jack glanced at Trevor, his expression said it all.

Jack was trapped, just as Trevor thought. Sandra's life was in the balance, and he was taking no chances.

"So what is the payload of your launch?" asked Trevor.

"Well. We're invincible, of course. And it would seem that we have the exclusive right to space propulsion technology designed for any lunar or solid landing on any terra firma..."

"You mean meteor sites?"

Jack looked at him, nodded, but said nothing.

"You know, there are those of us in the West that would consider a rogue missile perched on a meteor an enemy threat."

"Yes. We would guard against such an eventuality..."

"You mean retaliation?"

"If you put it that way..." said Jack

"I *do* put it that way" said Trevor, adding "So again, what exactly is the payload purpose of your launch?"

"Scientific discovery" insisted Jack.

Trevor said nothing.

The tide was coming in, inching its way up the shallow slopes of the beach at a steady rate.

Trevor stayed with him, close. Then he asked "Is that *all* he's interested in?"

"Yes!"

"No it isn't. That's crap! He wants to disrupt our stability and free market economies with ideas of socialism!"

Jack stopped walking, taking in shallow breaths, as if pleading for Trevor to stop.

Trevor was relentless. "Jack. You're Canadian. You did duty as a Ranger on the North Pole. It's where you met Sandra for God's sake... You're interests were in auroral winds. So, frankly, for this mission, your engineering background would be useful to see colorful clouds formed by the release of vapors from the two AZURE rockets, which will allow you – ostensibly, to measure auroral winds. Choosing *your* work was no accident! "

Jack nodded.

"Our SubTEC-8 sounding rocket mission is coming...You are aware. He does not just want to shut it down, he wants to destroy our position of listening in space...That would give your megalomaniac supremacy in space intelligence-gathering...If not downright control over social and sovereign networks..."

"Sandra is...my wife!" blurted Jack

"And she is my daughter!"

Jack looked up the beach, pointing to a boardwalk kiosk that sold *pommes frittes*. "Hmm. Ahum.. " he grunted.

They walked.

"So, let me understand you clearly. You plan to launch from the pole and you're threatening to take out our launch sequence at about the same time, is that it?"

"Yes." said Jack, affirmatively.

They reached the kiosk. "Either you give me your secured launch code, or we take it down!" Jack reaffirmed.

He reached into his pocked for change and ordered two cones of beach fries and relish pepper spice.

He paid.

The wind picked up as the tide continued to reclaimed most of the beach. Now the seagulls clustered above them and became raucous, almost deafening.

Jack looked at Trevor and as he handed over the wrapping of fries, he held his gaze.

In a motion too subtle to detect, Jack tilted his hand and let his fingers reveal a small computer stick that lodged itself into the wrapping between the fries.

Trevor accepted the wrapping, and picked out a large French fry to chew on...

Their eyes met with understanding.

"...You have 24 hours to respond" said Jack. "Or we loose Sandra!"

***

Amanda took her position at the rear of the conference room where everyone had gathered for the day's briefing led by George Myers, project manager.

"As you know, our overall mission is to deploy our rockets on schedule."

"Our payload? Well they're no bigger than soda pop cans, sub-payloads, released at varying altitudes as onboard miniaturized instruments that instantly gather multi-point measurements."

He paused. No questions.

"A distributed payload communications radio receiver located on the main payload then gathers the sub-payloads' data and a multiplex data stream gathers here, transmitting them to ground stations below..."

He turned to Amanda.

"Please, Ms Wells, I invite you to present the overall framework for our task for this mission? Kirt, would you assist with the details please.."

They were all smiles as Amanda moved forward.

"Thanks Gentlemen! You're all amazing...What you do, it's very much appreciated. So, as Kirt and I have discussed, this capability will simplify data gathering and payload-tracking, and allow scientists to study multiple regions in space simultaneously, which they can't do with current sounding rocket technology."

They nodded in awe and approval like a family collecting tokens of affirmation. Amanda was no hardship to have at the head of their helm, clearly.

Kirt took over the presentation when she finished.

"The concept is not unlike the launch from Norway's Andøya Space Center. During that mission, called AZURE, the Auroral Zone Upwelling Rocket Experiment had two Black Brant XI-A sounding rockets deploying gas tracers containing ingredients, like carbon powder found in fireworks..." said Kirt, adding "They created colorful clouds that allowed researchers to track the flow of neutral and charged particles in the auroral wind via ground-based photography and triangulation. They read the clouds' moment-by-moment position in three dimensions." He paused.

No questions, and he continued.

"So, our SubTEC is conducting - with our launch - technology - the next level" said Kirt. "Are we ready?"

"Oh yeah!" they chortled. "We're ready!"

Amanda had to smile at their comradery.

Later that night, she made several calls outside channels.

She discovered that Arguetta had been out of the country.

She sent a message on her Paris phone to her Jacques-"group." She sould report her progress:

 "My cat is now chasing mice over here. Miss you guys!"

A flurry came back suddenly. The first was from Jacques.

"My housekeeper has found another mouse to capture in my house!"

Jacques was following another lead, obviously.

The next came from Trevor. "I have glue to fix the Broken vase. "

Trevor was closing in.

If pleased, Amanda noted that no indication of Sandra's whereabouts was mentioned.

Her heart sank.

* * *

Chapter 12

Amanda felt like a dog on a leash.

The next few days would be long, and she had trained herself to rise early; exercise, eat regularly and sleep within appropriate measures of a routine.

Tomorrow, she was taking a flight down to Wallops Island, Virginia. And it seemed totally incongruous.

She had nothing but early memories of driving down there for a beach vacation with a car full of kids and gear! What had happened since..? Where had the years flow by so quickly? Sandra...in her sun hat with sticky fingers, and Tray with his fishing rod...both of them arguing in the back seat over floats and toys!

Still, she held some good thoughts. For one thing, she had managed to get in touch with both Arguetta and Trevor, even using their strange channels of communication. Not that there were any surprises, nor cause for alarm. But hearing their voice helped her...if what she heard was nothing less than military-grade concern.

It was the media had made no secret about launching a rocket from the East Coast of the United States. Wallops Island was ideally positioned for such launches, and NASA kept a minor coastal launch station there. It was on the way to the beach of Chincoteague Bay.

Information about launches and Press events were mainly designed for educational purposes and science classes. But this particular mission was supported with technical assistance by her husband's company Advanced Technologies.

Behind the usual fanfare of a rocket launch, Amanda felt the nuance of a darker side. Evidently, so did the media!

Sandra was a hostage taken by Victor Alexandrovich for "insurance," as he put it. She was after all, daughter of the man who had the contract from the US government to support the launch into space using the very latest research technologies...

Yet still no word from him.

Amanda thought of Trevor, Jacques, Arguetta. They all knew the man's intentions. They knew his political disposition. And they knew his lethal goals...

But how? When?

Amanda must play her role with a steady hand.

On the face of it, the task was mostly academic. All the heavy lifting had been done. But she represented the leadership of the firm. Trevor had asked her to step into his shoes in Washington. His corporate obligation was to the government. Those were his specific instructions.

And she must not flinch.

That was the prize, she knew.

The propulsion for space travel was technology experimenting with new developments. What began as a bidding war for space research was now a high stakes game of technology warfare...

This rocket launching into space from US soil was being watched by a competitor about to deploy his own operation and make his demands. He had found the agent whose Achilles' heel would bring down his enemy from within... *It was she!*

Amanda was not a member of the technical staff. But her presence as a Member of the Board of the company was necessary to promote a world-class brand. She needed to attend as a show of executive presence, never mind that she had bowled them over with her natural charm and elegant manner. They all loved her at the company.

She cared. And the staff responded.

Moreover, from a technical point of view, they had the most advantaged position. Trevor's firm was a defense contractor researching innovative payload subsystems and development propulsion systems...That was the prize, she knew. The propulsion for space travel was technology examining new advances. But it could be used for a new social order...

She must be careful. Amanda faced multiple questions on a number of fronts. She could hardly keep her thoughts straight, let alone her tasking and duties.

Had Trevor talked to Arguetta? And, there was more.

What about Sandra's husband, Jack Lucas? What roles added up for him? He was one of the foremost engineering specialists in polar research. He was married to Sandra, Trevor's daughter. He had travelled frequently to Norway. The Svalbard's location at the 79th parallel north was ideally suited for launching rockets to investigate Earth's magnetic field. That was Jack's specialty.

Amanda wondered what Alexandrovich, Jack's employer held over Jack's head? Already, one of his colleagues had been killed, Sophia.

She controlled her thoughts. If there was one thing the world understood, it was that unless you were a global enemy, "space" was a just a new and experimental frontier for science and for wonder. All launches were considered benign. And if there was one man who knew the artic parameters of the earth's orbit, it was Jack Lucas.

***

Bill Arguetta got back from the White House and met with his staff at the Pentagon. Their research had progressed nicely, he told them, and they had identified the anomalies that sank both ships.

NATO was apprised.

Further, the decision had been made to apply strategic responses suitable to avert future assaults of this nature in Europe. But the event was closed, even as forensic management of the events at sea drew fresh concerns. Diplomatic liaisons would continue on both continents to prevent disasters as a matter of routine.

Arguetta made no mention of space technology. Nor of deliberate and premeditated terrorism.

In all, Washington authorities could pause from alarm, he told them. The priority had been downgraded.

But Arguetta had also met with Trevor in Europe. There was clearly more intelligence at play. There was the motives of a competitor launching a rocket. A terrorist. For the moment it must stay between them.

Sandra's life was on the line. It was a dangerous threat at any level of business. But Arguetta had to keep the two incidents mutually exclusive. He must sub-vent the strike at sea in order to truncate the end game.

On one thing, they agreed.

Amanda could stand in for Trevor in Washington and proceed with the launch regardless. The answer was yes. The enemy here had to be stopped. She must play a steady hand.

As they parted company, both knowing the odds against Alexandrovich were not good, Trevor handed him computer electronic device not much bigger than a fried potato stick.

"Here, take this and analyze it. It's a full schematic of his launch sequence and telemetric projection."

"How did you.." began Arguetta.

"He gave it me as we spoke. The transfer was not detected I'm pretty sure..."

In the general way of things, Arguetta made arrangements. Known only to those who had the knowledge of secret missions with a security clearance of priority level, a plan was devised.

Two Royal Navy vessels were deployed from Scotland to the North Atlantic, and one artic attack submarine had just received a message to change orders.

Their coordinated destination was 79th parallel north, the *Svalbard Rocket Range* in Svalbard Norway. The destination puzzled both captains.

The place had been in use since 1997 and was owned by the Norwegian Space Centre. Mostly used by American, Japanese and Norwegian researchers for space-exploration, it was the world's northernmost launch site for routine rocket launches.

Arguetta closed himself in his office as he dialed the number of Air Defense. It would relay his signal to a hangar at a location on US soil, undisclosed.

"Operation Blackbird. How would you like a test trial? Get a scramble over Norway. Hot Live. I'll give you the co-ordinates."

He knew what the stealth task order meant. It meant that nobody would know what happened. Neither the Russians, nor their Allies.

One rocket launch would be destroyed as it passed into orbit. Taken down by a ghost. And total deniability.

He descrambled his call and left his office. Done.

Amanda had gone to Philadelphia. She got a message from Alexandrovich to meet him there.

She drove back to DC that night, even as it thundered and flooded the highways all the way back. She got back around 3 AM.

Time on the road gave her chance to get over the shock.

His demands were unreasonable. Dangerous. For Sandra is was a no option. She opened her laptop again. She was on a critical timetable.

Their sequenced launch countdown clock had their launch scheduled in 27 hours.

Twice she tried to call Trevor. Once he answered, but failed to follow through.

Jacques was only taking messages. She felt ridiculous sending messages in code.

Jacques was the Housekeeping service, and she left a few choice words about that.

Trevor's vase was being mended with the glue that he found – *whatever that meant*, and she the "Cat" had nothing intelligent to say in her state of panic.

She sent another message.

Nothing. She waited.

Then a message lit up. It was clear who sent it.

"...And I am the Dog!" he wrote. "Keeping count. So play it safe. Or you will know my bite!"

Alexandrovich was savvy to their code of communications, silly as it was between them all. Had he even copied the others into his message?

No. Of course not: He was focused on Amanda.

Tired, drenched and frustrated, she wanted to throw her laptop across the room.

Oh... Sandra!

Instead, she walked away.

In the morning she would call Kirt. Could they possibly put the Countdown on a Hold?

What public meaning would that suggest?

No!

By morning clock, they'd been clearing the launch site and preparing the pad for a firing. By noon, they'd be pulling back all non-essential personnel and management platforms.

By afternoon, they'd be loading cryogenic propellants into the power reactant storage and distribution system.

How to explain her situation to Kirt?

How to jeopardize the entire project because a madman had a strangle-hold? Surely, they'd insisted on calling the Police... *Then what?*

She'd have to explain what Trevor was doing...his absence...No. The media was have a field day. She knew what she was told to do. She had to proceed as if nothing had happened. That was the steel she was supposed to show.

Again, she called Trevor.

Nothing.

In Philadelphia, she had argued with Alexandrovich. "How did I know you'll keep Sandra safe?"

He was calm, malevolent and self-assured. "Oh, don't panic! She's fine. Actually she's in full view at an Auction in Paris where I have my valuables and collections up for Auction! Just...she can't make contact. But she is in plain view. See?"

"Ok then."

"Actually, it is simultaneous with your own launch..."

"*My* launch?"

"Oh yes. Of course you know! You are standing in for your firm in Washington as you launch from Wallops Island in....err...is it T-minus 30 hours?

"So. Here are my demands. Sandra will be returned, back to normal, as if nothing happened at the end of the Auction – where, by the way, I intend to make a big packet of money, you know..."

"And?" said Amanda brusquely

"And... you cancel your launch!"

"*What*?"

"Yes. You can scrub a launch in your countdown. Period."

"You're crazy. I can't stand down from a launch and you know that..."

"I do."

"So, why do you ask?"

"Because if the government has to cancel your company's launch, it will be damaged as an aviation technology expert. Your brand will be tarnished forever. You will loose your investors, your aviation contracts, your bonds and underwriters, your security credentials and your reputation. And that leaves the field open for me and my research. Simple!"

"I don't have that kind of means – to stop anything, if that's what you're thinking..."

"Ah, but you do! Admiral Arguetta has already spoken with the White House and consulted with the Chief of Staff. You would be authorized only if they thought you could not find the preparedness to complete a launch..."

Amanda absorbed his meaning.

They would have to impugn themselves, to show a failed launch prep, in order warrant a cancellation of launch by the government."

"So. You see. It's simple!"

"You are asking me to sabotage the procedure and falsify our capabilities in order to induce a *cancellation?*"

"Yes"

"With all our technology and expertise under the tightest security. I'd say you're misguided."

"Yes. Well. That's another thing. All that security clearance that your company enjoys...It's too hard to penetrate. So, a simple declaration by *your* hand is simpler. Now you understand?"

"That's sabotage"

T-27 hours and counting...

T-19 hours and holding

He was right. There was a built-in Hold in the Countdown. And while it was the US Standard to treat all rockets with the same precision and countdown as any Shuttle launch, much of the procedures and safety mechanisms in the launching sequence of an unmanned cargo rocket were simplified and augmented only for its mission. But for four hours, everything would halt.

Amanda picked up the phone to Kirt who was already on station.

'Hi Kirt, how are you doing?"

He liked hearing from her.

"Excited?" she asked.

He was brimming with enthusiasm. He and the team were ready, with everything working well and according to schedule. He filled her in on the details. Morale was high, all of them imbued with a sense of wonder going out into space. "We can't wait to get you down here!" he added.

She paused. "I'm on your live feed Kirt, I'm watching every step and keeping track of the Countdown on my phone"

They laughed, with everyone the background listening in.

"Yes Houson!"

She smiled, waited. Then she said "Err...Look Kirt, I'm tied up in Washington and I'm sorry to say I can't be down there with you. But umm..."

"Everything ok?" asked Kirt.

"Oh Yes. Thanks for asking. Hey, it's great that I'm part of your team!"

"Absolutely, you are!"

"So... You're an excellent Flight Director and Manager. I'm just one electronic device away, if we need to talk. But please proceed with your management as planned?"

"You sure that err...everything is ok?"

"Yes" she said firmly. "I'm feeding the Washington Brass public relations media as they are spectators to your launch. You know how that goes?"

"I do. Glad to know you're watching! All the guys are waving at me. They say Hi!" He added, "want me to pause longer?"

The built-in "Hold" protocol typically lasted four hours. But it could be extended, she knew. And it could also proceed.

She hesitated for just a moment. "Only if you have to Kirt. It's your call now. Good Luck!"

"Right then. Talk to you later. We've got it!"

That was the correct response, she knew.

For now.

* * *

Chapter 13

Trevor was with Jacques.

Jacques explained all that Interpol had on Victor Alexandrovich, concluding with "he's a piece of work, that one!"

At his side was an old friend, now retired. He had been contracted to the local police force with access to intelligence, a Detective whom Jacques had commissioned for many investigations. Sam, was his name.

For now, there was much to discuss. For one thing, they had the real-time live feed image of Sandra at Christies Auction. She was across town.

Jacques already had a tail on her, and the police were informed, but nowhere visible.

Trevor had just returned from a meeting at the NATO Headquarters of Brussels. The threat to security by an industrialist launching a missile from Norway was taken seriously. And though Trevor had much information, he was nevertheless restricted in his capacity as a retired minister. One thing, he assured them. The NATO defense of the Atlantic was unwavering in its commitment to deploy whatever counter-measure necessary if there was a threat.

Trevor had given them all the intelligence and data he had.

Their concern, as they told him, was beyond the personal loss of life - or kidnapping of any individual, or even a criminal in an act of terrorism: This was a case for defense forces, or the domestic police. Not even if economic and social warfare were threatened. It was outside the scope of their jurisdiction. It belonged, they insisted, in the realm of sovereign managements.

Space conventions were different, they knew.

Trevor's company, they also knew, was collaborating with the Americans. It had its own brand interests to protect...

Trevor felt despondent. It had been a long and fruitless effort.

Jacques served tea and coffee.

Now, as they sat around a big round table filled with files, photographs, papers, electronic devises, printers and digital images. On the walls just feet away were more maps, routes, notes, pages, profiles and schematics. It was a full investigative procedure.

The profile of Victor Alexandrovich was searched for evidence of links, connections, associated reasons that could be identified and devolved.

Sandra was hostage. No question.

For hours they conferred. Here, Trevor, Jacques and Amanda had sat. And it was in this very room where the cat had walked in...Like everything else, the assailant had been one step ahead of them, rendering every anticipated consequence futile. No, this man was a spectacular mastermind with a lot of money. Ostensibly a techno-industrialist, he had a global agenda of his own.

Interpol called periodically, as did the police. The gentlemen to whom Jacques referred as Sam spun away frequently to field other calls coming in.

"So. What do we have, so far as a profile? And where is this man going with his scheme?" proceeded Jacques.

Sam returned to them at the table.

"I don't think he's working alone..."

They stared at him.

"His company can afford it...?" interjected Jacques.

"No. Not his company. His *Movement*"

Trevor and Jacques were surprised.

"Movement?" queried Trevor.

"Yes. His is well capitalized. But he'd need a network that is *sans pareilles* with underground investors, in the way of Activism and terrorism..."

"Why?"

"Because of the access he has to advance aviation technology..." said Sam "it has global implications for a change of commerce and opportunity, in a world less regulated by sovereign constraints?"

"What ...makes you say that? There are others interested?"

"For him, this is *personal*. But yes. There are others seeking to change the world order of wealth and redistribution. He likes that..."

Sam turned to Trevor. "This man...He is competing with your company for the Americans. He knows NASA also has its eye on atomic technology to power human colonies once they get to Mars. NASA has employed radioisotope thermoelectric generators — batteries that run off the heat from radioactive materials — on previous space missions, including the Mars Curiosity rover.

"What kind of a man is this?" asked Jacques.

"Far from it" responded Trevor, who proceeded to fill in for Sam. He got up and faced them, alarmed.

"NASA had associations in the race to Mars from industrialists like Elon Musk – allegedly promising to get people to the red planet. *Space Exploration Technologies*

Corp founded by Musk, is developing a liquid oxygen and methane fueled engine."

He paused. "Then there's Jeff Bezos' *Blue Origin* testing an engine that uses liquid oxygen and liquefied natural gas."

He walked over to a map of geo-special-spectrums.

"NASA's human exploration plan for Mars, developed in 2009, includes nuclear thermal propulsion as the preferred option. Two other technologies being considered are solar-electric and chemical propulsion. Nuclear thermal rockets were first researched and tested by NASA between 1955 and 1972, before the program was canceled by Congress over cost concerns..." Trevor turned, glad at last to tell all.

"NASA has revisited nuclear thermal propulsion a few times over the years, but it didn't go beyond feasibility studies..." He stopped.

 "He's coming in from this angle, with a launch of his own! Russia's Rosatom Corp. has said it plans this year to test a prototype nuclear engine for a spacecraft that can go to Mars. Russia so far has led research in the field and has deployed more than 30 fission reactors in space according to the World Nuclear Association. .."

Trevor sat down. "Even China aims to use atomic-powered shuttles as part of its space exploration plans through 2045 according to state Xinhua News Agency."

Trevor paused, his face red. "NATO thinks that a private interest with a missile launch based on a potential meteor is a threat. This man is defying us to stop him...Of course he wants us to stop our launch!" finished Trevor.

"... Sandra's life is what he plans to gamble on" added Sam.

"My God" said Jacques. "We underestimate him!"

* * *

From their position, Flight Direct Kirt Sandringham was seen on the monitor. He stood in a room of subdued lighting and surrounded a bank of computers, workstations and plasma screens. To talk, he could walk about and look up at a central monitor for direct communications. Or he could be connected by an ear phone that could be switched on as a speaker, if needed. Around him were several technicians. He was the project manager of the launch. He could work directly, or remotely. Located with his team at the launch site, he was also connected directly to Amanda as the executive manager of the firm he represented.

Amanda had her own facility in which to monitor all systems in Washington DC. Normally, it was the privilege of the company to invite their executives and senior government liaison officers to be spectators to the launch in a small theater lounge on company premises.

But Amanda chose differently..She would keep it to minimal viewing. She would add nothing, but simply hold the line.

As it happens, the launch of their rocket had been the object of some publicity. And many within the company were smitten by the attention.

There was an inherent interest in witnessing the launch of a rocket into space. And she accommodated with an open monitor in various offices. But it was restricted. Only air-flight feeds. No internal communication feeds. She was careful.

A list of guests invited for the event would be limited to a short viewing session, for sure.. That much she had arranged.

The moment came none too soon. From Washington, she gave Kirt the "Go Ahead."

Finally, the ascent switch list was ignited for all systems check. And for this, the viewers witnessing the launch were thrilled.

At this point, the rocket was no longer a vessel. It was a live entity to be played by her guardians and technicians. The Flight Director, satisfied with the system check that was underway, gave an indication to activate the fuel cells.

Amanda, seated alone in her display room, watched. She had a feed relaying from Kirt directly at the control center.

One by one, they lit up for their consumption in space flight after launch. Critical to each mission's success was monitoring its sustainable supply of fuel for orbital flight and functions.

Ignition, Amanda knew, would deliver a burn rate of disproportionate thresholds and exhaust fuel at a rate of consumption critical for the Flight Director to monitor. From now, every decision, every alternative deviation from the protocol would be defined by the parameters of burn-rate and fuel consumption.

Amanda got her call. She knew who it was. "How's the launch going?" asked Victor Alexandrovich.

"As scheduled!" she answered sharply.

The Countdown would now pause for a mandatory 2 hour break.

* * *

Amanda greeted her guests at the offices of her Washington DC corporate headquarters. They were here to witness the launch, and to engage in the event a significant event in the defense industry.

If all went well, they would celebrate the company's success. From the launch site at Wallops Island, where engineers were pushing new avionics technology like distributed payload communications, they would get new capability in sounding rocket-based research. It helped to keep the peace on earth, as they put it.

That was what Bill Arguetta had expected from Trevor's company as a government contractor. And that was what she must do!

Amanda looked down at her phone. There was still no message about Sandra.

* * *

If there was an indication or a flaw, the mission could here be scrubbed. Barring that event, the countdown would resume for 6 hours minus-launch, then Lift Off.

But the call did came in.

"Just thought I'd check in for any last minute delays, as scheduled!" said Victor Alexandrovich.

Amanda listened carefully.

"I understand that your husband is making some local inquiries about our launch from Norway, scheduled in....err...precisely 28.7 hours and counting! Hello...?"

"I'm listening" said Amanda.

"That's good. That way Sandra remains unharmed. You see, my dear, I don't know what catastrophic event should scrub your flight, but there can only be one launch from planet earth this week. You know that, right?"

"I heard you."

"Good. So far, Sandra is in open view and under no threat..."

"You mean under guard and in danger of her life?"

"Well. I'm glad you grasp the situation in full" he said. He hung up.

Amanda could see that Mission management was receiving its final weather update. Clearly, the launch director was satisfied as he turned to his technicians and huddled over some last minute charts and sequences.

They would await word now from the legal verification consulting agents. All that remained was clearance that verified no violations of launch steps, nor air traffic interference, no omissions of safety precautions or criteria. The external tanks could begin loading propellants...

By now, essential ground personnel were clearing from the site, and with only the chill-down propellant transfer lines visible, the site looked ready and rich for ignition. Gradually, the lines juggled with internal fluidity.

Next stage was liquid propellants.

With all platforms fully abandoned by personnel, they were now fully accelerated to load external tanks with 500,000 gallons of cryogenic propellants.

Trevor was nowhere near any resolution. His meeting in Brussels at NATO headquarters was disappointing. His petition to disable the functionality of the Norwegian launch site for any scheduled space flight was met with little more than ridicule.

Who would want to stop a research test rocket designed for the advancement of European aviation technologies, they told him. This was a legitimate commercial venture.

He made notes as to how to proceed, knowing the dangers ahead. He was met with resistance. And he understood why.

Europe had been devastated by WWII. In the years that followed, it needed rebuilding and redevelopment. From broken infrastructure to democratic governance; from social devastation to freedom of market capitalism; from horrific militaristic warfare to charitable social welfare. As Churchill aptly put it, Europe was to enter a new golden age of opportunity. And it did so brilliantly, today flourishing as a free Western civilization.

But he was getting desperate. The stakes were high. The timing critical...His company. Sandra. Amanda...

There was no negotiating with a terrorist, he knew.

But he was surprised. Europe was gripped by indifference, immune to alerts against social manipulation...

It was not that they could not understand his petition. They did. But for different reasons. The High North gap was a sea with potential danger.

Not to be confused with the iconic Greenland, Iceland, United Kingdom (GIUK) gap, the "High North" gap was further north: It comprised of Greenland, Svalbard, North Cape line at the northern limit of the Norwegian and Greenland Seas.

As far as NATO was concerned, the potential for naval warfare in the in the "High North" was a major concern.

Trevor's issue of a space flight that needed to be scrubbed for geo-political reasons was marginal.

They entertained his presentation with one of their own.

NATO faced challenges with a renewed Russian threat, or so they said.

The Norwegian and Greenland Seas are considered NATO leaks with receding sea-ice. Norwegian naval force structures, they told him, was facing domestic political demands for reduction, planning for qualitative improvements, as they put it, under their socialist leadership.

Today's Russian Navy could remain within its Barents bastion and still launch accurate attacks against ships in the Norwegian Sea, they asserted.

Best not to interfere...

As they saw it, organizing for maritime war in the High North against a revanchist Russia, which was able to strike from within in lattoral boundaries, was not their only concern.

Trevor left feeling disappointed.

He did have the opportunity to share some of the sensitive content on a stick given him by Jack with all the launch codes, he was glad after all, that he had not exposed the rest of those schematics also contained within the data-set related to the launch mission.

Jack had passed them on.

He was glad he gave them to Arguetta.

* * *

Jacques called Trevor from Paris.

 "I'd like you to stop by. I have someone who wants to talk with you. My place. Dinner?"

Trevor agreed.

The person who wanted to speak to him was a surprise. He was a Russian government official.

"You see Mr. MacDonnell, we too have spies and saboteurs in our midst! If neither NATO nor the European Union can concern itself with this technocratic terrorists...then...we can!" he said.

Trevor looked at Jacques, both of them impressed.

"Remember, we are no longer a socialist regime although that reputation seems to linger with the West. We are now a quasi-independent nation with a free market economy. We are on our way to absolute democracy as a people. And still we are a super power. There is the United States. China. And us... Russia!"

"What are you saying?" asked Trevor..

The Russian softened.

Jacques passed Trevor a plate of candies and, in a display of relaxation, he rested back into his chair.

Trevor was uncomfortable, edgy. Jacques eyed him repeatedly.

The Russian continued. "We have no intention of returning to the dark ages of a socialist regime. But we do have our own priorities. Sovereignty for one, of course."

Trevor looked at him, wondering where this was turning.

"I understand your daughter is being held by this man, Victor Alexandrovich."

"A Russian" blurted Trevor, his face contorted with anxiety. He would have said more, but Jacques held him back.

"Yes a Russian. A man who wants to turn back the clocks to an era where his socialist roots once held sway. And power! That too, is amongst our threats, today.

He paused..

"This man Victor Alexandrovich, he has caused us considerable damage. He has targeted some of our vital resources. We have had him in our sights for a long time" he glanced at Jacques. "But... no more. Mr. deToulaine has explained things. Can you trust me?"

"How do you mean?"

"I mean, that you did the right thing with proceeding with your own company's obligations to the government. And...if this man thinks that two launches will result in the scrubbing of one, then he is not mistaken. One will be scrubbed. *But not yours!*"

"I don't follow..."

"NATO cannot effect the reactionary interception of a launch from the Norwegian site. It is a legitimate commercial venture..." He leaned forward and put down his coffee cup.

 "If a man crazed and bent on reshaping the world can now operate from our own littoral seas without breaking any rules of war. Well...err..." he paused to look at Jacques who assured him to proceed, "Well we can exercise our military war games, as it were. So, if there is a rocket on its way to orbit... Well then, let's just say, we have... what is that phrase you use 'justifiable deniability' to intercept its trajectory?"

"You would do that?"

"You will never know what happened... Only *he* will see that his test flight failed, Mr. MacDonnell"

Later that night, Jacques and Trevor were able to talk. Jacques was pleased.

Trevor was elated. He could speak freely.

"Trevor, I heard from Interpol: They have legal grounds to issue a warrant against this man for multiple crimes. One, amongst them is vandalism of a precious painting from a certain Auction in London!"

Trevor looked at him in utter disbelief.

"Sandra?" he asked

"Don't worry we have her under the eyes of police. She is already safe. We will get her out in a very short time..."

Jacques leaned down and showed Trevor his iphone.

There was an image of Sandra in protection of the local French police, Jack was standing at her side. "I have sent it to your phone" he said.

Sandra came out first. She looked fatigued and unkempt, if relieved.

"No cat?" asked Trevor, to Jacques.

"No cat!" said Jacques, sinking into the sofa, relieved.

"Thank you..." said Trevor.

Jacques and Trevor discussed the current situation. How it happened that the Russian government agent had found him was through Jacques' contact, Sam, within the police department.

And how the case for vandalism against Alexandrovich was a preliminary accusation with more indictments to follow, the priority was to get him into police custody.

Above all, what was surprising was how the NATO information had been monitored by the Russians.

They moved down into Jacques' laboratory and switched on secure viewing monitors. He entered his codes for an encryption.

Trevor added his own secure codes for access to a feed.

They looked down at his Countdown. "The test flight at Wallops Island on the East coast has launched into orbit. It is a success!"

Trevor forwarded an image of Sandra to Amanda.

Sandra could be seen standing, smiling. The police were there. Jack was at her side.

They went to the police station where Sandra was with her attorney.

At the debriefing, Trevor spotted Jack through the crowd.

Jack looked up. Trevor said nothing, but with a slight nod, he acknowledged the risk taken by Jack. It aided greatly to solving the problem.

Jack got a salutary thanks.

Trevor sent a message to his offices in Washington. "Congratulations on a successful launch... Thank you!"

"You're welcome" came the immediate answer.

Trevor answered. "I love you"

* * *

End